MEDIUM

WONDERFALL BOOK TWO

BIX BARROW

eBook ISBN: 978-1-964616-04-9

Print ISBN: 978-1-964616-05-6

❀ Formatted with Vellum

AUTHOR MISCELLANY

AUTHOR'S NOTE

If you find any typos or continuity errors in this book, please email me at bixbarrow@gmail.com. Reporting errors through Amazon does not trigger an alert to the author.

ACKNOWLEDGEMENTS

Thank you to Lewis for the car recommendation!

Thank you to Beck Grey, Riley Long, and Lee Blair for brainstorming help!

Thank you to Beck Grey, Lee Blair, and Dani Gainer for beta reading.

Professional beta reading by the amazing Amy Pittel.

Thank you, Alexandria Corza, for the beautiful cover!

Love, as always, to the Sparrows!

CONTENT WARNINGS

- Side characters are ghosts
- A minor is held captive, threatened, and held at gunpoint
- Off-page death of parents and grandparents of a main character
- A main character is kidnapped
- A side character (not a ghost) uses a Ouija board as their primary means of communication
- Mention of a side character dying from starvation and thirst
- A character vomits on page
- A side character sustains severe injury from claws
- Combat with bladed weapons and claws
- Discussion of memory-wiping and dubiously consensual vampire feeding
- On-page death of side characters by decapitation, gunshot, heart attack, and sudden expansion of an internal object

BOOK DESCRIPTION

Battling evil is a huge time suck when all you want to do is romance a couple of cute cinnamon rolls...

Most people consider mediums to be con artists. Heck, even my grandfather was pretty embarrassed when he had to admit my abilities were real—after he passed away of course.

So it's a nice—very nice—change when I meet Shane and Ellis, who not only believe I can see ghosts, they have interesting abilities of their own. Bonus, they know how to help the dryad I rescued from an evil billionaire. It doesn't hurt that they're both sweethearts and easy on the eyes. Did I mention I'm polyamorous?

But I've barely had a chance to hint at how good the three of us could be together before our world gets turned upside-down. My non-magical best friend is all up in our magical business, I find out some guy has messed with my memories, we're attacked by fanged fog creatures, Ellis gets kidnapped, and the three of us have to bond permanently *right now* or lose one of us forever.

We only met a few days ago, and no one would blame me if I ran.

But I'm staying right where I am.

Medium is a low-angst contemporary paranormal MMM romance with ghosts, magic, suspense, humor, friends-to-lovers, day job issues, found family, Ms. Jackson, and Yo-Yos. HEA guaranteed!

The author recommends reading Seer *before reading* Medium *for maximum enjoyment.*

MEDIUM

CAL'S CAMPAIGN COMPENDIUM

INTRODUCTION

Greetings, Adventurers new and old! This compendium is intended to be a reference resource for you as you navigate the campaign. I wish I'd had something like this when I joined, so I wanted to make sure no one else went without.

If you've gotten this far, you've registered and been approved to access this document with three-factor authentication. This compendium cannot be downloaded or copied. Do not share any information contained here with anyone who does not also have the same security credentials. Remember, the safety of Wonders and magic-carriers is in your hands.

This compendium contains:

- *Definition of terms commonly used in the campaign*
- *Overviews of different types of Wonders, magic-carriers, and magic use*
- *Links to the most up-to-date list of District Monitors and Wonder rescue organizations worldwide*

Thank you so much to all the Adventurers who provided information for the entries, particularly Greg Shaw, Edgar Ketcham,

Bettina Ketcham, Aileen Erskine, Reno Torres, Ziana Bhat, Bloom Alarie, and Oluska Vesely. Any errors are mine alone.

This compendium is a work in progress, so some entries may be unfinished or lack significant data. If you have information to add or a correction to be made, please email or message me.

Right now this compendium is only available in English, but ultimately the plan is to have it translated into multiple languages. If you have the time and ability to help with translations, please contact me.

Thanks,

Cal Steadham

CHAPTER 1
SHANE

NOTHING TO SEE HERE, JUST TWO GUYS ROAD-TRIPPING FROM Houston to Bent Oak to pick up a sentient Elven artifact.

"But what are we supposed to *do* with them?" Ellis had driven down to Houston from Dallas last night so we could ride to Bent Oak together. I didn't have the cash to fly, and Ellis' car was much larger—and nicer—than mine. We could've driven to Bent Oak separately, but neither of us wanted to be alone in the car with Ms. Jackson—that was the Elven artifact's chosen name—on the way home. Not because they were dangerous, but because we were nervous about how to interact with them.

Two weeks ago, they'd announced they wanted to visit Ellis and me. At the same time. He and I lived in two different cities, but they'd insisted we both be present for the entire visit. It didn't help that they couldn't explain *why* they wanted to visit us. And did I mention they could turn into a panther, a tiger, and a freaking *dragon*?

"I have no idea. I hope they'll tell us when we meet them. Worst case, we can take them back to my house and order pizza. Greg said they liked pizza."

We were taking Ms. Jackson to Houston first. Ellis and I both owned free-standing homes, so sneaking an enormous predator inside wouldn't be a problem at either place. But Ellis' neighbors were nosy, and he'd told me they'd reported him to the homeowner's association several times for minor shit. We'd decided it was safer to start out at my house. We could always go to Dallas later on.

This was only the second time I'd met Ellis in person. We were both District Monitors—magic carriers who acted as sort of a sheriff-slash-social worker for the Wonders in our area. We'd chatted on Discord for years, ever since I'd taken over my District. Ellis had already been a DM, and he'd been super helpful as I got my feet under me.

But we'd met face-to-face for the first time three weeks ago, when we'd both gone to Bent Oak to introduce ourselves to Cal, a Seer who'd been brand new to magic and the campaign.

The less said about that interaction the better, but at least it'd given Ellis and me the chance to spend the weekend hanging out together. We'd gotten along really well, and even after we'd returned to our respective Districts and homes, we'd continued texting and occasionally talking on the phone.

I might have developed a tiny crush on Ellis, but DMs didn't bond with DMs. I could ignore my attraction until it went away.

He glanced over at me. "I forgot to tell you. I painted my living room last weekend."

"Yeah? What color?"

He grimaced. "Off white."

"That's... nice? What color did it used to be?"

"Blue. I really liked the blue, much better than the off white. But I couldn't *not* paint it off white, you know?"

I got it. He and I were both nesting, which is what happens when magic carriers were about to meet their mates. We were compelled to make our homes more appealing to whoever would show up. Greg, the DM of the Central District, had gone so far as to buy a new house.

Luckily, to date the only things I'd had to buy were new sheets, a comforter, and a hammock for the back yard. Those purchases had stretched my budget further than I liked, so I was hoping they were the last of it.

Ellis, on the other hand, had traded in his MINI Cooper for this much bigger SUV, and he'd put flowers in planters around his back deck. And now the paint.

"That sucks. So you're thinking, what, your mate will be someone who doesn't like color?" I frowned. Ellis was wearing a bright orange polo with royal blue shorts. Surely the magic wouldn't give him a mate who only liked neutrals.

"I don't know." But he sounded worried. "I have a strong urge to paint the bedrooms the same color."

"Maybe... maybe your mate is an artist, and they need a plain wall to display their work."

He flashed me a startled grin. "Yeah? That would be cool."

I smiled back, my crush making my face go hot. Ellis was really attractive. Not in a model gorgeous way like Greg was, but in a friendlier, guy-next-door way. I especially liked how his dark brown eyes always found mine when we were in the same room. And the way his cheeks puffed up under his glasses when he smiled. He was a few years younger than me, and his umber skin was smooth except for the laugh lines next to his eyes. My magic was always reaching out to his when we were near each other, and it was hard to tell it to back down. And I really, really wanted to dig my fingers into his mane of coils.

I wished badly that DMs mated other DMs. I could only dream of getting someone as amazing as Ellis. The walls in my house were already white. Well, they'd been white when my grandfather had painted them twenty years ago at least.

But Ellis and I were each destined for somebody who was either a different type of magic carrier or a Wonder, a paranormal creature who'd originated in the Elven dimension. They were the source of most myths and folk tales, like shifters, trolls, or pixies.

The Elves had gone back to their own dimension after World War II. I couldn't say I blamed them. Humans as a species were fucked up. But they'd bestowed a certain amount of their magic on a bunch of trusted humans before they'd left, and Ellis and I were descendants of those original magic carriers. Sometimes random people showed up with magic, like Cal, the Seer who was now bonded to Greg. Ellis or I might end up with someone who was also new to our world.

My phone rang. I sighed when I saw the screen. "Hi, Jed. I'm off today, remember? Ricky approved it last week."

Jed grunted. "Right, and I'm sorry, but Ricky's not answering his phone."

I groaned. Ricky was the boss' son, and he did as little actual work as possible. "I get it. What's up?"

What was up was that Ricky had bungled an order to our supplier, asking for azaleas when the client wanted rhododendrons. We were supposed to do the installation next week. Luckily Jed had noticed when he was reviewing the paperwork to see how many people we'd need on the crew. I told him to call the supplier and find out if it was too late to correct the error.

I hung up and rubbed my face. I doubted that would be the last call I'd get today.

"Everything okay?"

"They can't survive without me at work," I joked. Or maybe I only wished it was a joke.

Ellis chuckled. "I know what that's like."

Unlike me, Ellis' career was going places. He was in sales for a mobile phone company, and his clients were corporations who wanted their employees to have dedicated work phones. He made good money, and he liked his job.

Two things I didn't have with my job.

When we were getting close to Bent Oak, I googled a bakery for us to stop at. Greg had told us he and Cal were making lunch, so Ellis and I picked up some lemon bars for dessert. We weren't sure if Ms. Jackson would eat them, but at least we'd have something in our hands when we arrived.

When we got back in the car, I texted Greg to let him know we'd be at his place soon.

But then I read his response. I glanced at Ellis. "Um."

"What?"

"We're meeting them at Cal's apartment, not Greg's place." Of course I'd known Cal would be with Greg. But I'd pretty much avoided acknowledging that we'd actually have to *talk* with Cal.

"Shit. I'd been kind of hoping Cal would be at work or something." Good, it wasn't just me.

"Yep."

Ellis rubbed his mouth. "We apologized on Discord. He'll be nice to us. Right?"

"Fuck, I hope so."

Ellis and I had been a little... overenthusiastic when we'd tried to meet Cal to see if he was our future mate. In our defense, there wasn't exactly a guidebook for that sort of thing. But Cal had reacted poorly to having two strangers try to force him to hold our hands.

Which, in hindsight, was completely understandable.

Ellis walked me through entering our new destination in the car's maps app. We were twenty minutes away.

My phone rang, and this time it was Ricky. I closed my eyes for a second, then I answered. "Yes, Ricky?"

"Where are you?"

I suppressed a hiss of outrage. "You approved me to take two days off, remember?"

"Yeah, yeah, I know. But I mean, where are you right now?"

"I'm out of town." No good would come of giving him my exact location.

"Well, I need you to come back." He said this as if it were a perfectly reasonable demand.

I clenched my fist and struggled to keep my voice calm and even. "I'm sorry, I can't. What's going on?"

"We have a new client. They need a plan drawn up by tomorrow."

I pulled the phone away from my face and stared at the screen for a few seconds. "Ricky, even if I were in town, I wouldn't be able to do a full landscape design by tomorrow.

I'd have to walk the site, get measurements, look at the soil, and everything before I could even start."

Ricky made a dismissive noise. "You can use one of your other ones as a starting point."

"I'm sorry, Ricky, but I can't come back before Wednesday." Ellis was throwing me concerned glances from the driver's seat.

"Well, Shane, that decision could have long-term repercussions on your tenure with this company. My father took you in and gave you a job when you were a teenager, and this is how you repay us?"

I cringed. It was true. Mr. Fredericks had given me my first job almost twenty years ago now.

Ellis patted my fist where it lay on my thigh. I looked up into his commiserating eyes and found the balls to stay firm. "I'm sorry, Ricky, but it's my time off and I have things I need to do."

"What am I supposed to tell the client? If we lose this account, it'll be your fault!" He hung up.

I sighed. It was just like Ricky to promise an unrealistic turnaround time. I'd spent more than one night at the office trying to meet his deadlines.

"That sounded rough," Ellis said.

I shook my head. "It's nothing I'm not used to."

I stared out the window in silence, stewing over my job. I knew I needed to find a new one, but change was hard, and it wasn't like I was a licensed landscape architect or anything where I could make big bucks. I hadn't even been to college. I supervised yard crews and drew up landscape designs when they were needed. As Ricky constantly told me, anyone could do it.

We reached Bent Oak, and after about ten minutes Ellis slowed the SUV and turned into the parking lot of an apartment building.

He parked and turned off the car.

We looked at each other, and I held out my fist. "Cal will be nice, and Ms. Jackson won't be scary."

"Cal will be nice, and Ms. Jackson won't be scary." He bumped his fist to mine.

We got out and headed for the elevator. All too soon we were knocking on Cal's apartment door.

Greg opened it and ushered us inside. I managed to nod a greeting at Cal before my eyes were glued to the freaking *four-foot-tall hedgehog* sitting on the floor.

"Uh, Ms. Jackson?" I squeaked out.

"That's them," Cal said. "They were trying to find out how small they could get, but as you can see...." He gestured at them. "Not very."

The huge black eyes examined us as the long nose quivered in our direction. The spines—or were they quills?—that appeared cute on a regular-sized hedgehog had to be lethal at this length. Ms. Jackson stretched out one oddly naked-looking paw before their form morphed into the tiger we'd seen on Zoom a couple of times. The tiger form was disconcerting for a whole lot of new reasons.

They stalked toward us, and Ellis and I inched closer to each other. He was as tense as I was, but he grinned widely and said, "Wow, Ms. Jackson, I'm so happy to meet you!"

"Me too," I managed.

Ms. Jackson sniffed our hands, then they circled us, rubbing against us like a ginormous housecat. Except a housecat couldn't make you almost stumble off your feet. They had to weigh two hundred pounds or more.

Cal said, "Lunch is almost ready. Do y'all need some water or anything after your trip?"

Maybe it was cowardly, but I needed a minute to get used to Ms. Jackson. "Uh, the restroom?"

Cal pointed down the hall, and I edged carefully past the tiger. At least Cal didn't seem so intimidating anymore. I threw Ellis an apologetic glance, but he was stroking the top of Ms. Jackson's head. I didn't know why they were triggering my flight reflexes. I'd met a lion shifter and a grizzly shifter in their fur forms before. They hadn't bothered me at all.

Was it because Ms. Jackson didn't have a human form? Did my brain think that made them more alien?

By the time I'd washed my hands and headed back to the living room, I felt more centered. I'd just treat Ms. Jackson like a shifted Wonder, and it'd be fine.

Except they'd manifested the Ouija board they used to communicate. On their chest.

I'd seen it on Zoom of course. But in person, the hard wooden board seeming to grow out of Ms. Jackson's warm fur was much more disturbing.

My steps slowed until I stood next to Ellis again. I wanted to do my usual thing of shutting down and being quiet while I absorbed whatever was bothering me, but it wasn't Ms. Jackson's fault the way they were made. I didn't want to offend them.

I forced myself to talk. "Uh, hey, Ms. Jackson. Um, did Ellis tell you we're going to my house tonight? I hope that's okay. It's not nice like this or anything." I swept my hand in an arc to take in Cal's living room. He had eight—eight!—bookcases and a gigantic TV. The apartment was in good repair, with new-ish carpet and no obvious dents or scratches in the walls or fixtures.

Unlike my place.

Ellis scoffed. "I like your place. It's nice and homey."

I shook my head. "He means homely." Ellis thwacked me on the arm with the back of his hand.

Ms. Jackson spelled out, *I-S-P-E-N-T-D-E-C-A-D-E-S-I-N-A-R-O-O-M-F-U-L-L-O-F-D-U-S-T-Y-B-O-O-K-S-I-A-M-N-O-T-P-I-C-K-Y*.

"Oh. Um, I get it. Just, you know, tell me if you need anything to make you more comfortable, okay?"

T-H-A-N-K-Y-O-U.

I felt better.

Cal called us to the table. I hadn't noticed before, but the tether of Cal and Greg's bond glowed super strong between them. I hoped I ended up with a mate bond like that.

He and Greg had bought a cowboy casserole from Central Market. Chicken, pasta, poblano peppers, and cheese—all good stuff. They'd also heated up a take and bake pizza, which had only cheese on one half and mushrooms and artichokes added to the other.

Greg sliced the pizza into smallish pieces and put the entire thing in front of Ms. Jackson. "We've been testing out different vegetables for them to try."

They sniffed at the artichokes and mushrooms but chose to start with a piece of the cheese-only half.

Ellis eyed Ms. Jackson's plate. "You don't eat meat?"

No flashed on the Ouija board.

I nodded. "Good to know. We'll make sure you have options."

Greg said, "They tend to eat about as much as an average adult human, but if they've shifted into something really big, like the dragon a couple of weeks ago, then they need more."

Fuck, I kind of wanted to see them as a dragon, but I kind of really, really *didn't* want to.

Ms. Jackson ultimately decided the artichokes and mushrooms were acceptable, and they finished their meal much faster than the rest of us. Without warning, they got up from the table and wandered over to the couch, stretching out on it.

I snorted to myself. It wasn't like they'd grown up with a grandmother giving them the evil eye every time they didn't use good manners.

Ellis took a sip of his iced tea. "Cal, I love the compendium you put together. Once I started reading it, I was shocked we didn't have anything like it before."

I nodded emphatically, my mouth too full to politely comment. Good for Ellis, thinking of a way to compliment Cal. Anything to help us stay on his good side.

"Thanks." Cal shook his head as he poked his fork at his plate. "My learning curve would've been much easier if I'd had it to reference in the beginning. Let me know if you think of anything to add."

I finally cleared my mouth enough to speak. "Any info on the vampires?" Because there'd been no news on Discord, and every Wonder and magic carrier in Texas was waiting for the next attack.

"No. Nothing. I haven't had any visions, and neither have Edgar, Delphia, or Reno."

Four Seers. That's all we had in the entire state of Texas. And their range was limited. They couldn't see visions of events more than a hundred miles or so from themselves. Slightly farther if they were bonded, but Texas was huge.

With Edgar and Delphia near San Antonio, Cal here in Bent Oak, and Reno down by the coast in Corpus Christi, if the vampires were planning an attack in my District or Ellis', we'd better hope it'd be near the borders of the other Districts. The far north and east parts of Texas would be too far away.

Greg stood up to clear the plates. "Before y'all drive home, I've arranged for us to test whether Wonders can connect to more than one DM."

Ellis' eyes lit up, and I was excited too. A few weeks ago, Cal had asked Greg why Wonders could only connect to one DM at a time, when it'd be safer for them to connect to every DM whose Districts they were traveling through. Ellis and I had volunteered to test the theory out by connecting to a couple of Greg's Wonders.

"I forgot we were going to do that. I hope it works." And it would give me a little more time to spend with Ms. Jackson before they were locked in a car with me and Ellis for three hours.

"Great. If you don't mind driving over to my new house, a couple of Wonders will meet us there. One of them is my general contractor, so he's already on site, and the other is his daughter."

We cleared the dishes, and I opened the box of lemon bars Ellis and I had brought. Ms. Jackson heaved themself off the couch to come try them. After one lick they swallowed two of them whole. I was glad we'd bought a dozen.

It was still broad daylight out when we left, but Cal and Greg didn't seem worried about walking downstairs with a giant tiger.

"They can still turn into inanimate objects like the cat statue we first met them as," Cal told us. "But when they absorbed all the magic I gave them, they gained a larger mass as a result. It's not easy to carry them down to the car." He waved his hand to indicate the empty hallway outside his apartment. "It must be their magic, but no one seems to cross our paths when they're out with us in public."

So we walked out of the apartment with a huge tiger by our sides. No one was in the hallway. No one was in the elevator, and it didn't stop for anyone else on the way to the ground floor. Then we walked to Ellis' SUV and not a single other person was in the parking lot with us.

But after Ms. Jackson got in the back seat and Cal shut the door? People drove up and parked. Others walked out of the building. It was the weirdest fucking thing.

None of the human magic carriers could affect their environment like that. Our magic was more receptive than proactive. We were magical bottoms, if you will.

And Wonders were made of magic. Some of them had magical skills, like undines could become invisible in water, and shifters could change into their animal selves. But they couldn't do the equivalent of casting a spell.

Like Ms. Jackson just had.

I was a fuckton more comfortable with Ms. Jackson now than when we'd walked into Cal's apartment, but at the same time, I thought they might be the scariest creature I'd ever met.

CAL'S CAMPAIGN COMPENDIUM

DISTRICT MONITOR

Type: District Monitor

Class: Magic Carrier

Overview: District Monitors resonate with a geographical area called a District, where they set up as sort of a point of contact for all the Wonders within that District. They form magical connections with the Wonders and assist them with navigating the mundane world and dealing with any accidental sightings by NPCs. (See also the entry for *Non-Player Character*.) When a District Monitor retires or is no longer able to carry out their duties, magic carriers with District Monitor traits are encouraged to visit the area. If the District resonates with their magic, the new District Monitor has been found.

Skills:

- *Heightened senses (smell, sight, hearing)*
- *Ability to create non-permanent connections to Wonders or other magic carriers*
- *Ability to resonate with a geographical area and sense when the boundaries of that area need to change due to population growth/decline*

- *Ability to go into "combat mode", also sometimes called "hunter mode", (hyperfocus, ultra-enhanced senses, improved reflexes) when under threat or periods of stress.*

<u>Enhanced Skills When Bonded</u>: *Can use the connections to sense where a Wonder or magic carrier is geographically and what their current overall emotional state is.*

<u>Childhood Aptitudes</u>: *You may have a budding District Monitor on your hands if your kid exhibits one or more of these talents:*

- *Extroversion*
- *Mediation*
- *Negotiation*
- *Patience*
- *Goal orientation*
- *Helpfulness*
- *Problem-solving*
- *Interest in criminal justice or social work*

CHAPTER 2
ELLIS

HOLY FUCKING FUCK.

Next to me, Shane glanced back at Ms. Jackson, who was lying flat on the rear seat, their tail twitching in time to the 80s song on the radio. He widened his eyes at me, and I bugged out mine back at him. Ms. Jackson's demonstration of their abilities had been unreal.

I didn't know of any beings on Earth who could use magic like that. I mean, we'd all heard stories about the Elves, and how they'd been able to use magic to manipulate objects and their environment, but I didn't think Elves started out their lives as magical artifacts.

It wasn't a mystery I could solve right then, so I shoved it aside to worry about later.

I followed Greg and Cal out of the parking lot to go over to their new house. Okay, I was pretty sure Greg was technically the sole owner, but given the bond between them, Cal would be moving in too. Their bond was only two weeks old; they wouldn't be able to be apart from each other much yet.

I checked on Shane again, but he'd relaxed into his seat, tapping his fingers on his leg to the music. Ms. Jackson had intimidated him when we'd gotten to Cal's place, but he seemed to have adjusted to their presence, even with the freaky display of magic.

He noticed me looking at him, and he gave me a shy smile. Damn, I could not get enough of that smile, with his wide, pink lips and white teeth against his tanned skin and coarse black stubble. I couldn't help but imagine those lips around my dick, and it made me hard and slightly embarrassed at the same time.

DMs didn't bond with DMs. We were both nesting, so our mates would be arriving in our lives at any moment. Having sex with Shane—even *thinking* about having sex with Shane—would be a disservice and an insult to our future mates.

Dammit.

Greg wound through a residential neighborhood before parking in front of a house currently being remodeled. The roof looked new, but the green paint was peeling and a few shutters were missing. A dumpster took up half the driveway, and two cars were lined up in the other half, so I pulled in behind Greg at the curb.

Ms. Jackson bumped their forehead against the door, waiting to be let out. Probably more fun to join us than stay in the car. Shane stepped out and, after scanning the completely empty street, opened the door for them.

Greg and Cal walked across the yard to meet us, and we followed them up to the front door. Greg knocked as he opened it, calling out, "Hello? Ruben? Kayla?"

"Hey, Greg and Cal, good to see you." An enormous man, a porcupine shifter with their typical brown-blond hair, came out of the stripped-down kitchen. A much smaller young woman, also a porcupine shifter, walked out behind him.

Greg and Cal shook their hands, then Greg gestured at me and Shane. "Ruben and Kayla Tooley, this is Ellis, the DM of the Northeast District, and Shane, the DM of the Southeast District. And this is Ms. Jackson." He put his hand on their back. "Everyone, Kayla is Ruben's daughter. They both travel frequently. Kayla visits Houston, and Ruben goes back and forth to Dallas and Ft. Worth."

Shane and I shook hands with Ruben and Kayla, and they both waved awkwardly at Ms. Jackson. Once the pleasantries were over, Greg offered us a tour before we got down to the connecting.

The house was old. Probably not as old as Shane's place, but old enough to have been in pretty bad shape before Ruben started working on it. As it stood now, almost all of the fixtures, cabinets, and flooring had been ripped out. The kitchen walls were still covered in some godawful wallpaper, but there weren't any countertops or appliances. The only intact rooms were a huge game room upstairs and an office in what had once been the attic. I could absolutely picture Cal working up there at the top of the house.

When we returned to the ground floor, Ruben said, "I've got some folding chairs on the back deck, if you'd like to do the connections out there."

We were all agreeable and trooped outside. Ms. Jackson, who'd followed us silently through the house, perked up. They bounded off the deck and onto the grass before running in a circle. Suburban neighborhood yard sizes were not meant for exercising tigers.

"Crap. This is their first time on grass. We should've taken them to a park or something before now. Fuck." Cal rubbed his face.

Well, that was just sad. But Ms. Jackson was making up for lost time, rolling on their back and stretching in the sun.

"Hey, Ms. Jackson," Shane called. They stopped twisting their back into the grass and lifted their enormous head to look at him. "I have a hammock in my back yard. Uh, it's like a swinging bed made of knotted rope. Don't let me forget to have you try it out."

Ms. Jackson rolled over and bounded to their feet. Then without even a running start they leapt onto the deck, landing next to Shane. He took a couple of steps back but otherwise held his ground. I put a hand on his shoulder in case he needed support. Ms. Jackson walked forward and rubbed their head against Shane's hip. They didn't leave any fur behind like a housecat would, though I wasn't sure if that was a tiger thing or a Ms. Jackson thing.

"Uh, you're welcome?" Shane chuckled uneasily.

Ms. Jackson turned around and jumped back to the grass. They proceeded to walk along the fence, inspecting the overgrown shrubbery.

Shane turned to Greg and Cal. "When you get around to it, let me know if you want some help with your landscaping." He looked around the yard. "I can put together a few designs. Or at the very least I could help you pick out some native plants that'd be more drought-tolerant than what you have here already."

Cal's eyebrows hit his hairline. "I didn't know you were a plant expert, Shane. It's really nice of you to offer."

Shane turned ruddy under his tan. "Oh, well, I don't know if I could be called an expert. But I do work with plants all day."

I shook my head at him. "He's being modest. While we were on the way up here his boss called him because no one else can do landscape designs like he can."

Ruben said, "Shane, I frequently need a landscape designer—mostly for single-family homes, nothing too difficult. Would you be willing to show me a couple of your designs?"

Shane's face turned even redder, and he shoved his hands into his pockets. "Oh, I don't know if I'm good enough for something like that. I'm not a licensed landscape architect or anything."

I could tell Ruben was about to argue, but Shane had his mouth pressed into a thin line and his shoulders were hunched over.

"Tell you what, Ruben," I interrupted. "Why don't you give me your contact info. I mean, we're going to be connected anyway, right? And Shane, when we get back to Houston, I'll convince you to show me some of the things you've done." I flashed him a winning grin, and I was relieved at his tentative smile back. "Would you trust me to tell you if I think they're good enough to send Ruben some photos?"

"Um, okay." Shane clasped his hands together and looked down at his shoes, but he didn't seem upset.

I had trouble continuing the conversation because my eye caught on Shane's fingers where they interlaced. They were thick and strong. They probably wouldn't have the dexterity required to do a Boingy Boing, but they'd feel damn good in my ass.

Fuck. Objectifying Shane was inappropriate. I should've been paying attention to the conversation. I dragged my eyes away. "Um, that okay with you, Ruben?"

"Sure. Didn't mean to pressure you, Shane. I just really prefer to give my business to other members of the campaign, you know?"

Shane nodded but didn't speak.

"Why don't we sit down and do the connections?" Kayla said. She pointed at the folding chairs arranged in a circle on one side of the deck.

I sat next to Ruben, and Kayla sat by Shane. She told him, "My best friend Fantine is in your District."

Shane brightened. "Fantine Walker? She's great."

Kayla beamed. "She is. She's the reason I go to Houston so often."

"Well, I'm glad we'll be connected." He didn't say anything else.

I stepped in. "Okay, well, Ruben, are you ready to try a connection?"

"Sure." The big man turned in his chair so he was mostly facing me. He held out his hand.

I clasped his wrist, and Ruben wrapped his fingers around my forearm. I closed my eyes and looked for our magic. Ruben's wheel was bright and spun swiftly, like most shifters' magic did. He had about thirty or so connections already, and I could easily see which one led to Greg. I used my magic to tease out a tendril of his, then I wrapped mine around it. I pushed my intent to connect through the spot where our magics joined, and I felt Ruben doing the same.

And it was done. It felt just like every other connection I'd ever made with a Wonder. I opened my eyes and released Ruben's hand. I chuckled. "That was way too easy for all the buildup."

Ruben laughed, clapping me on the shoulder with his big palm. "No kidding." He made a sweeping gesture toward Shane and Kayla. "Your turn, but I daresay you won't have any more trouble with it than we did." No doubt. The experiment was a success, and hopefully more Wonders who traveled outside their Districts would connect with multiple DMs going forward.

I glanced over at Greg and Cal, and they were beaming at us. Greg was holding Cal's hand in both of his, and I felt a pang of envy. I wanted that.

I looked back to Shane, who was smiling his shy smile at Kayla as they celebrated completing their connection. My heart went pitter-pat in my chest.

My mate had better get here before I did something stupid.

CAL'S CAMPAIGN COMPENDIUM

MEDIUM

Type: Medium

Class: Magic Carrier

Skills:

- _Can talk to ghosts???_

Enhanced Skills When Bonded: Unknown.

Childhood Aptitudes: Unknown

Note from Cal: _At this time there are no known Mediums in the campaign. I have only found validated records of three Mediums worldwide so far and all have passed away. As with other psychic talents exhibited by magic carriers, there are unsubstantiated reports of Mediums existing long before the Elves granted magic to humans in the 1940s. It is unclear whether these talents merely manifest more strongly/accurately in magic carriers than regular humans, or if the Elves based the abilities they were granting on human legends._

CHAPTER 3
RORY

"Rory, wake up! Wake up, dammit!"

I jerked upright and gasped, my heart pounding. "Fuck, Grandfather." I pressed a palm against my chest. "Did you have to yell so loud?" At least the neighbors couldn't hear him.

"Yes, I did! You need to come with me right now!" His incorporeal form brightened and faded as he punctuated his words by jabbing a translucent pointer finger into my knee.

"Stop that! What's the emergency?" Jerking my leg away, I rubbed my eyes and ran my hands through my hair.

Grandfather scowled. "I followed your uncle to another party. This one was at some billionaire's house in River Oaks. Randolph Chamberlain," he spat.

"Okay. Sounds like somewhere he'd want to go." Uncle Hugo wasn't a billionaire, but after he'd inherited all of Grandfather's millions, he'd received plenty of invites to the homes of those who were.

Grandfather put his hands on his hips. "Those wastrels

weren't even talking business. I wanted to give you more stock tips."

I rolled my eyes. "I told you, you don't have to keep doing that." Though I did appreciate the information he passed on to me. I used each and every tip, keeping my investments small enough so no one noticed when I kept making trades at exactly the right times.

I felt around on the floor for my shoes. I'd pretty much passed out on the couch as soon as I'd gotten home, and I was still wearing my dress shirt and suit pants. At least I'd taken off my tie.

"I'm mostly keeping tabs on your idiot uncle. And if I happen to learn something to benefit you, well, all the better. But that's not why I'm here."

Hoping he'd get to the point soon, I stood up and carried the shoes into my bedroom.

Grandfather followed. "Like I said, Hugo and his cronies were talking about some stupid nonsense, so I wandered around to see if there were any other more interesting conversations. That's when I saw her."

He paused, and I knew he was dying for me to ask. Better to just get it over with. "Saw who?" I tossed my shoes into the closet and started unbuttoning my shirt.

"The ghost!"

I didn't roll my eyes, but it was close. "Grandfather, you see other ghosts all the time, and so do I." Much to my ever-lasting irritation.

"Not like this ghost!" He zipped around to hover in front of me, startling me into backing up a step.

Fuck, he wasn't going to leave until he told me his story. I sighed. "Okay, I'll bite. What was so special about this ghost?" I looked around, but thankfully he didn't seem to have brought her with him. Once a ghost meets you, it can show up anytime, anywhere. Those tales of salt keeping ghosts out are crap. Do you know how much salt is in the human body?

"She looked like a tree." He crossed his arms and waited for my response.

I blinked. "Trees have ghosts?" I'd never run into one of those.

"No, no. In life she was a tree spirit. A dryad."

"A dryad." I dredged my brain for any related information. "Like, Greek myths?" I wasn't sure I believed him, but on the other hand he'd never lied to me, even when he was alive.

He shrugged. "Not sure. When I first saw her, she had the form of a tree with a face, and she was standing behind that asshole Randolph Chamberlain, whacking him with her branches and yelling at him. But of course he couldn't hear or feel her," he added bitterly. Even after two years, Grandfather still hadn't resigned himself to the limitations his new existence placed on him.

"Anyway, I went up and asked her what the hell she was."

I winced. Grandfather had no tact.

"She changed so she looked like a human, and then she told me she was a dryad and Randolph Chamberlain was holding her daughter captive."

"*What?* Captive?" Now he had my full attention. I palmed my phone. This wouldn't be the first anonymous tip I'd called in to the cops.

"Yes, and the little girl's dying. The fucker doesn't know exactly what she is, so he didn't put a tree in her cage with her." He began to pace. "Lorraine, the dryad, was killed trying to keep Chamberlain's goons from getting her daughter. She showed me the room where he's keeping her. That jackwaffle's got the child in a glass enclosure on wheels. Like he rolls her out for his parties or some shit."

"Fuck." I got ready to dial 911. "How do I tell the cops where to find her?"

Grandfather put a chilly hand on my forearm. "You don't. Didn't you get the part where the kid's a dryad? She's not human. The cops can't get hold of her; she'll only end up in a different kind of cage."

Well, shit. It was a valid point.

"You have to go in and get her."

My mouth fell open. "Me?"

"Yes, you. Do you know any other Mediums I can ask? There's still time to go to the party. Put on your monkey suit and I'll talk you through how to get in. Lorraine says there are a couple more ghosts who'll help."

"Fuck." I stared at the floor, trying to think of any other way to get the girl out. Any way not involving me. "How old is she?"

"Thirteen."

My head shot up. Grandfather nodded, grim-faced. "Whatever you're thinking, Lorraine's worried about it too. Assuming the girl doesn't die. I don't know how long she has."

"Fuck me." I sighed again and reached for the tuxedo Grandfather had badgered me into buying. I'd never worn it before, but last year he'd gone on a rant saying I might need to go to a fancy party for work. One of his tips regarding a company on the verge of imploding had made me over five thousand dollars, so I'd thought it was little enough to do for him in return.

I hadn't considered I'd need it for a jailbreak, though.

I got dressed, and on the way out the door I grabbed a granola bar, since I hadn't had dinner. The girl and I would have to stop for food after I got her out of there.

Assuming dryads could eat fast food, that is.

Oh, and assuming I didn't get caught.

I took the stairs instead of waiting for the elevator. Luckily my parking spot was on the ground floor, so I didn't have to wind through the parking garage to exit the building.

Grandfather popped into the passenger seat as I started my Range Rover. It was new, and I still didn't know what'd possessed me to buy such a huge SUV. I only had one real friend to drive around.

"Grandfather, this car is nice, but it's not on a level with the ones the other party guests will be driving. Plus, they'll have a valet. I can't make a quick getaway waiting on a valet to get my car."

"Pfft. You'll park around the corner. We're going in through the servants' entrance. Just head for River Oaks and I'll show you where to go."

I glared at him before focusing on the rear camera to make sure I could back out safely. "If we're going in through the servants' entrance, then why am I in a tuxedo?"

"Use your brain, Rory. It's in case Chamberlain or one of his staff sees you."

Personally, I thought I'd stand out more in the servants' area in my tux vs. in more casual clothes, but it was too late now, so I kept my mouth shut.

At ten o'clock at night, it took less than fifteen minutes to get to River Oaks from Midtown.

Grandfather directed me through a series of residential streets lined with grand homes. His house, where I'd lived for most of my teenage years, had been several miles to the west and about half the size of these. Still, he'd had enough River Oaks friends to know this area well.

He directed me to park against the curb where several other cars lined the street. This must be where the valets were stashing the guests' vehicles. My Range Rover didn't stand out as badly as I'd feared, but the huge lawns I'd have to cross would make it difficult to get back to the car unobserved.

I got out and shut the door quietly, wishing I had a weapon of some kind. The sounds of the party floated on the muggy air from the next street over. I swallowed, my throat dry. I was a finance guy, for fuck's sake. I wasn't Keanu Reeves.

But the girl. Fuck.

Grandfather pointed me up a nearby driveway. My dress shoes clacked on the concrete, and I hissed at him when a motion sensor triggered a spotlight.

"Bah, nobody's home. Don't worry about it."

"What about security cameras?" I wished I'd worn a ski mask or something, except it would probably have just gotten me shot.

"I disabled them," a deep voice said from somewhere in front of us.

I stifled a shriek and dropped to a crouch. "Who's there?"

A ghost came toward us. A big ghost. A big *wolf* ghost.

Animals—land-based ones at least—didn't generally end up as ghosts. The simpler the brain, the less likely to result in a ghost. And if you did see one, they didn't talk.

"Uh, hi?"

The wolf shimmered and became human-shaped. I'd never seen a ghost do that before. He was still big, with bushy hair all over. *All* over. He wasn't wearing any clothes in the afterlife.

Okay then. I kept my eyes firmly on his face.

He nodded at me and Grandfather. "Name's Garfield. Lorraine sent me." He tilted his head as he examined me skeptically. "I floated near all the cameras along this route and fried 'em."

"Oh, uh, thanks. I'm Rory."

He nodded again, his eyes now scanning the darkness around us. "This way." He led us through a gate into an empty back yard. We skirted the pool, and Garfield pointed me to a magnetic key box on the underside of a chaise lounge.

I used the key to unlock a gate on the back wall, and we were immediately faced with another gate, which was fortunately unlocked. The second one opened into the yard belonging to the party house. Chamberlain's house. His pool was off to one side, and a putting green took up most of the rest of the space. Some shrubs were planted along the perimeter wall, but otherwise there wasn't any cover. I'd be completely exposed getting to the house.

"Ready?"

I locked the first gate and shut the second. "Um, how do you suggest I get to the house without being seen?"

Garfield scoffed. "This party's full of rich assholes who act like they own the place. Just pretend you're one of them. They won't look at you twice."

Good point. I dropped the gate key in my pocket and pulled out my phone. Straightening my spine and lifting my chin, I held my phone to my ear and strode confidently across the putting green toward the door Garfield indicated.

"How did you get here, Garfield?"

He spat toward the ground, though of course nothing landed. "I'm from Wyoming. Some asswipe sent a team of what looked like mercenaries in to capture my pack. Ten of us died, and five of us lived. Got me with a tranquilizer dart." He spat again. "We were auctioned off. They put us on camera and shot us with lasers until we shifted. I ended up here, in the tender care of Randolph Chamberlain." He snorted. "He didn't dare have anyone else look after me, feed me, give me water, all that. But he also liked to go on long trips." Garfield shrugged. "Coulda been a worse death." He pressed his lips together. "I hope my packmates didn't suffer."

I couldn't help my horrified gasp at Garfield's terse recounting of his awful death, but I quickly schooled my expression into one more appropriate for my pretend billionaire persona.

We crossed the back patio, which was dotted with ceramic urns and planters of various sizes holding shrubs pruned into unlikely shapes.

I cleared my throat. "I wish I could just call their names to see if they've passed on, but my gift doesn't work like that. I have to run into a ghost or have a ghost I know bring them to me before I can communicate with them."

Garfield gave me a stiff nod. "Understood."

But there had to be a way to find his pack members. Or at least take down the people putting on these auctions. Surely if rich fuckwads were trafficking paranormal creatures, someone was tracking the rich fuckwads.

The door to the house was unlocked. I kept my phone to my ear and spoke loudly about KPIs, portfolios, currency adjustments, and yield fluctuations as I walked through the mudroom and the laundry room as if I did it all the time. I passed a few house staff in black and white uniforms. After giving me a double-take, they ignored me. Garfield floated ahead of me, and I resolutely kept my eyes trained at his shoulders. One glance at his hairy ass was enough.

We turned down a couple of corridors, and the sounds of the party grew fainter. We didn't run into any other staff. The doors along the hallways were all shut, and these walls weren't decorated with artwork.

We were almost at a T-junction when a ghost whipped around the corner straight into Garfield. "Chamberlain!" she shouted. "Go back! He's coming!"

Fuck. I whirled, plowing right through Grandfather. I power-walked back the way I'd come, trying not to make any noise. "Are any of these doors unlocked?" I whispered.

"Don't know," Garfield said from behind me.

I didn't dare try the handles for fear of the sound they might make.

The ghost woman—she didn't look like a tree, more like a Valkyrie with her height and long blond hair—appeared ten feet ahead of me at the junction of another hallway. I was grateful she was wearing clothes—leather pants and a jean jacket over a t-shirt. She pointed to my right. I followed her around two more corners, then I was in a dead-end with three doors. I spun around, but she was looking back the way we'd come.

"They shouldn't turn this way if they're going back to the party," she said.

Shouldn't. Fuck.

Carefully I tried the door handles. Locked.

We heard voices and the clinking of ice in glasses. The woman and Garfield vanished, but Grandfather stayed by my side.

A man's voice said, "I contacted my source, but they said they weren't responsible for the health of the specimens after the sale was final."

"What terrible customer service. They're the only source, you said? I would love to get my hands on a specimen for myself." He sighed. "Maybe next year after some investments come through."

The men passed the hallway leading to my hiding spot.

The first man said, "Perhaps we can come to some sort of agreement. I find I require assistance keeping the specimens alive." The voices trailed away.

My mouth fell open. I met Grandfather's eyes, and his snarling face told me I was right.

Uncle Hugo.

Randolph Chamberlain had taken him to see the captive dryad girl, and Uncle Hugo wanted one for himself.

CAL'S CAMPAIGN COMPENDIUM

BONDING, PART ONE: INTRODUCTION

A bond is a permanent uber-connection between mates. It creates what is effectively a mind-meld between the partners, with the following attributes:

- *Speaking mind-to-mind*
- *Rapid healing*
- *Sharing of magic resources*
- *Sharing of connections*
- *Sensing the other partner(s)'s emotional state(s) and geo-location(s)*

In order to be created, bonds require five elements from each partner:

1. *A strong enough connection*
2. *Consent*
3. *Skin-to-skin contact*
4. *Intent*
5. *Exchange of pheromones*

The next sections will go through how a connection grows strong enough to be able to become a bond, how the bond is created, and the bonding aftereffects you should prepare for.

CHAPTER 4
SHANE

I CLEARED AWAY THE TAKEOUT CONTAINERS WHILE ELLIS PEERED out my back window at Ms. Jackson, who was lying in the hammock again. They'd had a big day today, with their first car ride to Houston. Ellis had had the brilliant idea to have them transform into a large stuffed tiger, which allowed them to sit up and look out the window the entire journey without anyone calling the police. It'd been fun to see little kids waving at them.

When we'd arrived at my house, they'd wasted no time in heading for the back yard. After a cursory inspection of the tiny patio, the dozens of potted plants I'd rescued from the dumpster at work, and the shrubbery lining the privacy fence, they'd made a beeline for the hammock, which was in the shade of my live oak tree.

After a couple of hilarious false starts, Ms. Jackson managed to successfully climb into the hammock and lie down. I was glad I'd bought the stand to go with it, because Ms. Jackson's weight as a tiger could've damaged any trees I might've tied it to.

"I guess I'll have to wait my turn," Ellis had said, his eyes twinkling at me. I'd forgotten he'd told me how much he loved hammocks.

I'd chuckled. "I'm sorry it didn't occur to me to buy two." As if I'd had the budget to do so.

He'd waved this away. "Ms. Jackson will have to get up sometime."

Then we'd gotten a couple of beers out of my fridge and sat on my patio, enjoying the humid but for once not too hot evening air while watching a tiger swing gently in the breeze. I'd ordered Indian food for dinner, and I'd swear Ms. Jackson had pouted as they'd dragged themself inside to eat. As soon as they'd gulped down their vegetable korma, they'd promptly gone back outside to the hammock.

I dropped the takeout containers in the trash, and Ellis followed me into the kitchen with the plates and cutlery. "I kinda thought Ms. Jackson wanted to spend time with us so they could impart some wisdom about the vampires or something. I didn't expect them to just sleep."

I pursed my lips as I glanced out the window. "If I'd spent decades trapped in one room with only piles of dusty books for company, I'd want to spend as much time outside as I could too."

"Good point. But if they're still out there this time tomorrow, I might have to flip the hammock over and dump them out so they'll talk to us."

I eyed him dubiously. "*Hmmm.* They look pretty heavy in their tiger form."

He flexed a bicep. "I'm motivated."

I laughed and shook my head. "You want another beer?" We'd already had three apiece, but they'd been spread out over a couple of hours, so we'd be fine. We were both staying here tonight anyway.

"Please." He loaded the dishwasher, and I got two more bottles of Dos Equis out of the fridge. I usually drank whatever was cheapest, but since Ellis was visiting, I'd splurged a little. He was probably used to more expensive craft beers, but he hadn't complained so far.

I took the beers into the living room and sat on one end of the sofa. Ellis washed his hands, then he came and sat down next to me on the middle cushion. Which was a lot closer than I'd expected him to sit. When we were near enough to each other like this, our magic reached out, humming a little as it intermingled. If DMs could bond with other DMs, I'd say we were resonating.

But I didn't say anything as I handed him his beer. He thanked me, then took a long sip. His throat was so sexy when he tilted his head back and swallowed. I wanted to lick it. I wanted to see it bulging with the head of my dick.

I looked down at my beer. "Um, it was cool how we were able to connect with Ruben and Kayla today. Do you want to connect with some of my Wonders while you're here?" I could think of a few who regularly traveled to Dallas and would feel safer having a connection to the DM there.

Ellis made a face. "How many Wonders do you have? Because I've got almost a hundred, and tracking down even half of them to connect with you will take forever."

"Crap. Same here." I picked at the label on my bottle. Ellis' magic flared a little, and it felt nice brushing against mine. I looked up. Was his face closer than it'd been a moment ago? I shifted in my seat. "Um, what if, like, you and I connected? Wouldn't we automatically get connected to each other's Wonders in one go?"

Ellis stilled. Then he smiled, his cheeks pooching up under the rim of his glasses. "I'd love to be connected to you."

My face went hot. "Um, same." I'd guard a connection to Ellis with my life, even after I was bonded to someone else. Some future mate I hadn't met yet didn't mean as much to me as Ellis did. But at least when I was eventually bonded, my magic would be stronger. Every so often—not too often of course—I could check my connection with Ellis and see where he was and what emotions he was feeling. I'd just have to be careful not to let my own feelings about how much I missed Ellis bleed through to him.

Or to my mate.

He plucked the beer from my hand and reached around me to set it, along with his own, on the side table next to the sofa. I inhaled as silently as I could, because who knew when I'd get this close to him again? He smelled of some spicy cologne or body wash. I couldn't identify the scent completely, but it had sandalwood undertones. His hair was soft when it briefly brushed against my jaw.

All too soon he straightened. With a shy smile, he held out his hand, palm up. I smiled back, glad to have an excuse to touch him. I put my hand in his. He was warm, and his hand was firm and sure in mine. Our magic buzzed together, giving the impression it'd been waiting for this all day.

Ellis looked down at our joined hands. "I don't think we'll have any trouble connecting."

I chuckled. "Nope." I closed my eyes and focused on visualizing my magic where it spun in a big sparkling wheel inside me. I was startled to also be able to see Ellis' wheel, spinning next to mine. All of our connections to our Wonders stretched outward. As I watched, the wheels adjusted their speed to turn in tandem.

I urged my magic to extend a tendril out toward Ellis', pushing my intent to connect with him along with it. I wanted to be connected to Ellis. Hell, I wanted to be as close to Ellis as I could get.

To my surprise, both of our wheels extended multiple shoots outward, twining around each other and pulling the wheels together into one giant sparkling, spinning mass.

I sucked in a breath and opened my eyes. I was... in Ellis' lap. Straddling his lap. His dick was thick and hard beneath my ass cheek. Mine was grinding into his belly. Our arms were wrapped around each other, and our faces were mere inches apart.

"Oh," I breathed. "I, um, is this okay?" I couldn't stop a tiny thrust. Fuck. My eyes almost rolled back in my head. But what was weird was I could vividly imagine what it had felt like from Ellis' perspective, how most of his dick was constricted by his shorts but the head had managed to peek out of the leg opening. My jeans-covered ass was giving it the most delicious friction.

Ellis' eyes blazed, the rich brown brightening to a molten copper. I could smell the many individual scents that made up his body wash or whatever it was. I could also smell his precum, which was soaking into the fabric of my jeans.

He dropped his gaze to my lips, then back to my eyes. Accepting the invitation, I leaned in and touched my mouth to his. Ellis made a strangled sound, and his hands slid down my back to my ass. He opened his mouth, and I welcomed the sensual slide of his tongue on mine. When he pulled me against him, I arched my spine to keep the kiss going while we were plastered together from groin to chest.

Ellis speared his hand down the back of my jeans. I cried out when his fingers found my hole, and I dropped my mouth to the side of his neck. His scent was stronger here, and I mouthed his skin. He licked a stripe across my neck behind my ear. Fuck, why was that so sexy?

"Clothes. Off," he muttered. "I want you naked."

"Yes, fuck." I could've come like this, dry humping fully dressed. But Ellis was right. Naked skin would be so much better.

Neither of us made a move to separate. My fingers wouldn't let go of the fabric of Ellis' shirt, and his fingers were still massaging my crack.

"On three?" I suggested in between panting breaths.

He nodded, the arm of his glasses scraping through my hair. "On three."

"One," I gasped out, unable to stop myself from adding a thrust.

Ellis grunted, then he whispered, "Two." He caught my lips in his and slowly slid his hands out of my pants. But he kept pushing down on my back so our dicks didn't lose contact.

"Fuck. Um, three." I groaned as I pushed away from him, dropping my feet to the floor and standing on wavering legs. I kept one hand on his arm as I moved back, then I caught his fingers in mine. I wasn't ready to be separated from him.

He stood, adjusting himself and breathing heavily. His eyes were brighter than I'd ever seen them. I wondered if mine were the same. I could see every tiny glistening bead of sweat on Ellis' skin. Greg had mentioned going into what we called "combat mode", a state of hyperfocus and enhanced senses usually reserved for fighting, when he'd first been with Cal. Maybe the same thing was happening to us.

A thrill went through me. We'd speculated that going into combat mode when you were aroused happened when you were with your mate. Could Ellis be my mate, even if he was a DM? Was he the one I'd been waiting for?

I smiled. "Come on." I gave him a quick kiss before leading him by the hand to my bedroom. The bed itself was ancient, but at least it was a king size. My grandfather had been a large man. He'd passed when I was a toddler, and when I hit puberty Granny had switched bedrooms with me, saying I needed the en suite bathroom more than she did.

I urged Ellis to sit down on the edge of the bed. I couldn't bring myself to let go of him, so I trailed my hand down his belly, skirting his dick, and then down his leg. Crouching down, I leaned my head against his knee and removed his shoes and socks. He shivered when I ran my hands up his lightly furred calves.

Ellis undid the buttons of his shirt, pulling it off and tossing it to the side. I kept my cheek on his leg but looked up at his large, sexy pecs and soft pooch of a stomach. He stroked a hand through my hair and I licked my lips.

"I wasn't expecting this," he said, cupping my jaw. "But I'm so glad it's you. I've been wanting you all day."

I popped back up to my feet, surging to meet him with a kiss. He fell back onto the bed, and I crawled over him, straddling his lap like I'd done on the couch. But this position was much better, giving me more access to his body.

His fingers tugged at my t-shirt, so I released his mouth long enough to pull it over my head. Then I went back to kissing him while I fumbled between us for the buttons to his shorts and my jeans. It didn't matter which came off first; I'd get to them both eventually.

Ellis, however, was using his hands to drive me crazy. He teased my nipples over and over, until I was trembling, only able to focus on bracing myself above him, giving him the most access to my chest. Getting rid of our pants could wait. They were unbuttoned and unzipped at least, and the heads of both of our cocks poked above the waistbands of our underwear, catching on each other as we ground together.

But ultimately our zippers were hella uncomfortable, so finally I had to lean on one arm long enough to push our pants and underwear down to our thighs.

After that, all I could do was writhe against Ellis, thrusting my cock into his while we devoured each other with our mouths and tongues. I still kept myself propped up to give him access to my chest, but luckily this pressed our cocks together even harder. We were leaking enough precum to create a nice slide, which I also got to experience from Ellis' perspective. Fuck, this echo thing was amazing.

I loved being able to tell what turned him on, and not just relying on how hard his cock was. No, I was talking about experiencing the actual sensations *he* was experiencing. Live and in person. Directly from his mind to mine.

Which was fucking hot.

I couldn't remember being more turned on than I was right then. My balls were ready to explode.

I tore my mouth away from Ellis'. "Gonna come."

He curled his body up so we were kissing again. Then he twisted my nipples, hard. I jolted at the sensation and moaned as I came. His hot cum mixed with mine, and I felt what he felt as his orgasm pulsed through him. It was so arousing I got an unexpected extra jet myself, and I cried out into his mouth.

I collapsed on top of him, sweaty and panting, but happy. So happy.

I'm happy too.

I froze, staring at Ellis.

His lips, shiny from our kisses, curled up. "What?" His eyes twinkled behind his smudged and off-kilter glasses.

Holy fuck.

Did we bond?

His eyes, back to their normal brown, got serious. "I'm pretty sure."

Holy fuck.

A bunch of different emotions ran through me. Excitement, nervousness, unworthiness, happiness, among many others. It took me a minute to realize not all of those emotions were mine, but they were so jumbled up I didn't know how to start separating them out.

I cleared my throat and ran my finger through the sparse hair on his chest. "Um, are you okay with being bonded to me?"

Worry came through loud and clear, so I rushed to assure him, "I'm good with it. I mean, it's a little fast. I wasn't expecting.... But I'm glad. Really." I pecked him on the lips.

Ellis's face cleared. "Me too. Um, I'm glad too."

I tucked my face into his neck and hugged him to me. Closing my eyes, I breathed in the scent of him. My mate.

I woke up after what had to have been a couple of hours at least, based on how stiff I was and the crusted cum trapped between our bodies. At least I'd slid off Ellis to the side, so while we were still holding each other, I wasn't squashing him or cutting off his air.

I knew I needed to get up and get us clean, but first I just wanted to bask in the feeling. We were bonded. Ellis and me. I smiled and focused inward to check out our magic, the one wheel shared between the two of us, big and sparkling.

I could see and feel all of the connections to our Wonders, twice as many as I'd had before, and my sense of my District had expanded, doubling in size. That was all good.

But the wheel.

Something was wrong with the wheel.

Belly clenching, I sat up. My jeans were still caught around my ankles, so I tossed them over the side of the bed before shaking Ellis' shoulder. "Hey, Ellis, wake up."

"Huh?" He was still wearing his glasses, which were adorably crooked.

I reached out and straightened them on his face. "Hi. Sorry to wake you."

His forehead scrunched. "What's wrong? You feel... worried." He sat up, then irritably kicked off his shorts, which had been tangled around his knees.

"Um, can you look at our magic? Is it supposed to be... doing that?"

Yes, the wheel was big and sparkling. But it was also lopsided. And it didn't spin smoothly. It sort of... limped.

Ellis gasped, "Shit, did we screw up our magic with the bond?"

"How? We weren't even trying to bond. Unless... is there a certain way it has to be done?"

He rubbed his face. "I didn't think so? I mean Cal and Greg bonded without having sex. And it wouldn't have taken if we hadn't both wanted it, right?" His expression was tentative, and I felt his uncertainty through the bond. At least the sharing of emotions was working the way I'd heard it was supposed to.

I nodded, sending him my determination and reassurance. "Right. We both wanted this, and we're not trying to undo it." His expression eased, and I leaned over and kissed him. "Um, who knows the most about bonds?"

He shrugged as he stared down at his torso. His concern came through to me loud and clear. "I'm not sure, maybe Cal? He had to research them for the compendium, right?"

I reached for his hand. "Good idea. And it'll be alright. We'll figure it out and fix it." I tried to project all the tenderness and affection I had for him. He smiled, so I must've done it correctly.

Ellis took a deep breath. "Yeah, okay."

Our phones were in the living room, so I slid to my feet. Then I looked down at myself and grimaced. "I'm gonna clean up." I gestured at the cum. "You wanna come with?"

Smiling, he scooted toward me to the side of the bed. "Yeah. I don't want to talk to people while I'm still covered in spooge."

My shower wasn't huge, but we made it work. There was just enough room for both of us to get some of the water no matter where we stood. I took my time covering Ellis in body wash. I wanted to learn his body, every inch of him. I could've spent hours tracing my fingers over his pecs, his back, his thighs.

But he was doing the same to me, and our bodies were reacting. The feedback loop of feeling every sensation from both sides was like pouring an accelerant on our arousal. We were close to coming within minutes. Ellis let his head fall forward onto my shoulder and groaned, "Shane."

I pressed myself flush with his body and snaked my soapy hand between us. We both gasped when I took our cocks in my grip and slowly twisted. Our breaths were harsh, echoing off the tile.

Ellis was so close, and I was going to be right behind him. Just one more—

BANG!

BANG!

Ellis and I jumped. I let go of our cocks and turned the water off.

The banging came again, from the front of the house. Fuck, was someone at the door? At this hour?

"Hey!" a male voice shouted. "I need some help out here!"

"Fuck," I muttered. We grabbed towels and swiped off the worst of the soap and water.

"One of your Wonders?" Ellis asked. He shook his head. "No, I'd be able to feel it too."

Then the man screamed.

CAL'S CAMPAIGN COMPENDIUM
DRYAD

**Type**: Dryad

**Class**: Wonder

**Overview**: Tree- and plant-affiliated being who can assume three forms: a human form, a humanoid form with plant characteristics, and an ethereal "tree spirit" form which allows them to enter into a tree or plant itself. Their humanoid form can have brown, green, or mottled skin, and their hair can resemble vines and leaves. In this form they are able at will to produce sharp teeth and defensive thorns across their entire body.

Contrary to popular mythology, dryads are not tied to one tree for life, though some do have preferences for certain trees or tree species.

**Skills**:

- _Through the exchange of magic between a dryad and a tree or plant, both receive significant health benefits._
- _Enable plants to propagate faster and produce higher yields of crops._
- _Can identify the cause of a plant or tree's illness at a glance._

Requirements: Dryads must have regular contact with tree or plant life in order to renew and maintain their magic and therefore their lives. Dryads are omnivores, though when eating fruits and vegetables they prefer those that have fallen naturally from the plant/tree and are not harvested.

Enhanced Skills When Bonded: Broader range of magical interaction with plants. The distance varies by individual, but after bonding the dryad no longer has to touch a plant to use it to renew their magic, and they can heal plants from a distance as well.

CHAPTER 5
RORY

GARFIELD AND THE BLONDE GHOST REAPPEARED. "THIS IS Mercy." Garfield gestured at his companion. "She was in the box before me." I was still digesting that when he went on. "The way's clear. I fried the cameras while Chamberlain and the other guy were in the room. It'll freak 'em out when they look at the footage later. Let's go."

I'd deal with Uncle Hugo after the girl was safe.

I hurried to follow Garfield and Mercy, Grandfather muttering to himself behind me. "Later," I hissed at him.

He huffed but fell silent.

At the end of yet another hallway, Garfield pointed at a closed door. It had a keypad lock.

"4321," Mercy supplied helpfully.

I rolled my eyes at the idiocy of middle-aged rich guys and punched in the numbers.

The door swung open, and my heart broke.

Other than a floor drain and a rubber hose on a reel in the corner, the room was empty except for a clear Plexiglass box, about five feet wide and three feet deep. It was taller than I was, and it sat on four wheels. The young girl inside stood facing me. She was emaciated, her bones prominent. Her skin reminded me of a dying leaf, all brown with yellow spots, and her hair looked like withered vines. She was wearing what was probably a sleep outfit, blue tie-dye shorts and a matching tank top with a drawing of a shark on it.

The only other items in the box with her were a covered bucket, a bowl of water, and a plate containing an uneaten peanut butter and jelly sandwich.

A ghost, a stunning woman with long greenish-brown hair and bark-like patches here and there on her skin, stood outside the box. When I stepped inside the room, she bared her teeth at me, and the girl inside did the same. Their teeth were noticeably sharp.

Garfield held up a hand. "Lorraine, this is the Medium. He's here to help."

I waved a hand awkwardly. "I'm Rory. I'm here to get you out. Um." I spun around. "Where's the key?"

Lorraine said, "It's not locked from the outside. Just flip the latch. There's no way to open it from the inside." She clenched her fists and floated to my side. "I can't manifest enough to flip the latch myself."

I nodded, stripping my jacket off. "I understand." The girl must've thought I was talking to myself. I was used to it. "I'm a friend of your mom's."

Her eyes narrowed, but she didn't speak.

Oh, shit. "Um, what's your name?" I could've slapped myself. Way to destroy my credibility. The girl glared harder, so I looked pleadingly at Lorraine.

"Her name's Pia."

"Pia. Right." Pia held her hands up, and fucking thorns popped out of her skin all up and down her arms and legs and across her forehead. Shit, I was doing the best I could. "Okay, I'm going to open this door and let you out, but I'd really appreciate it if you didn't attack me."

She didn't move.

I twisted the latch, and two-thirds of the front panel swung open. She moved then, scrabbling back into the farthest corner of the box. She pulled her lips back, and her teeth seemed even longer and sharper.

I crouched down and held out my jacket. "I'm a Medium. It means I talk to ghosts. Your mom, uh, she's a ghost now." Pia's eyes went wide. "Uh, she's fine. She's just worried about you. She sent some of her ghost friends to find me so I could get you out of here."

She stayed right where she was.

I looked at Lorraine. "What's something only you and Pia would know?"

Lorraine closed her eyes for a moment, then opened them. "When Pia was six years old the cherry tree in the park was hit by lightning. She and I were in the tree for days helping it heal."

"Got it." I turned to Pia. "Your mom told me how when you were six, the cherry tree in the park got hit by lighting and the two of you spent days helping it get better."

"Mama?" Pia clapped her hands over her mouth, and her eyes filled with tears.

"She's here." I held my coat out to her again. "I hate to hurry you, but we really need to leave before that jerk who put you in here comes back."

Slowly she reached out and took the jacket, and the thorns subsided back into her skin. She put the jacket on, but she looked unsteady on her feet.

"Can you walk?"

Pia took a step toward the door of the cage, but she crumpled. Lorraine cried out as I caught her, barely in time.

"Okay, I'm going to carry you, and we're going to go fast." I swept her up in a bridal carry. She hardly weighed anything. I'd have preferred her to hang onto my back or my front so I could have my arms free, but I didn't think she had the strength. Up close her skin was dried and puckered.

I turned, but Garfield was between me and the door, holding up a hand. "One sec." He spun around and poked his head through the door—I never got used to that—then pulled it back inside. "Hallway's clear."

I shifted my grip on Pia until my right hand was freed up to turn the doorknob. I eased the door open. No sense making more noise than I had to. As promised, the hallway was empty.

I exited the room and shut the door quietly behind me. I shifted Pia more securely in my arms and walked as fast as I could the way I'd come in. Garfield and Mercy took turns scouting ahead and reporting back. Once I had to dodge into what turned out to be a bathroom for about sixty seconds, but then we were on our way again.

I slowed when I heard the sound of the service staff. "Put your face to my chest," I told Pia. She did it without question.

The first staff member we encountered, an older Latino man carrying a tray of dirty glasses, stopped in his tracks when he saw us. He blinked at Pia, whose mottled-leaf legs and feet were on full display, but he didn't speak. I didn't say anything either, just continued on my way out. I heard him follow me, but I decided to ignore him unless he did something.

The other people we ran into behaved similarly. Their eyes would widen, they'd look closely at Pia, and they'd either go on about their business, or they'd follow us. My back was stiff with tension, waiting for one of them to try to stop me.

I walked through the laundry room, then into the mud room. Mercy came through the back door and said, "Patio and yard is clear. Security guards are on the side of the house."

My skin crawled at the thought of crossing the back yard, exposed under those lights. But needs must.

"Hang on, Pia, we're going to run for a minute, okay?" She nodded her face into my shirt.

"Wait," one of the people behind us said.

I spun around. It was the first man, the older guy, who had spoken. Five more people ranged behind him, all with worried expressions.

"Yes?"

He pointed to the wall next to the door. "Those three switches control the lights to the backyard."

I frowned. "But won't turning them off draw the attention of the people inside?" I jerked my head downward. "The lights from the house will still be on. My shirt's going to be visible."

A young woman in the back said, "One second." She opened the clothes dryer and pulled out a black rectangular table-cloth. She approached me with it. "May I?"

"Um, sure."

She snapped the fabric out to its full length and draped it over my head and body. Then she tied it in front, covering Pia.

"Why are y'all helping me?"

The woman scowled as she stepped back. "We all know when he brings in a new one. But we don't know the code for the door, and there are cameras." She shrugged. "Most of us are not in the country legally, and jobs are hard to find."

"Understood. The code to the room is 4321." That brought out even more scowls. "If I give you my phone number, will you contact me if he brings in someone else?"

They nodded, and I rattled off my number. Three of them, including the first guy and the young woman, put it in their phones. One of them, I wasn't sure which, texted me. I felt my phone vibrate in my pocket.

The older guy asked, "Is the camera in that room dead?"

"Yes. And the hallways."

He smiled. "We will make it look like the little miss escaped."

I frowned. "He'll know she didn't have the energy for that." Then I grinned. "She's a dryad. They live in trees. Can you get your hands on some dead branches, or even just a pile of dead leaves?"

His eyes lit up. "We'll put it in the cage in her place. Chamberlain is stupid enough to believe it." The others smiled.

"Okay, now I really need to go."

"I'll turn the lights on as soon as you're at the gate." The older man put his hand over the switch plate.

I took a deep breath before opening the back door. The lights went out, and I ran. The ghosts zipped ahead of me, and their faint translucence provided a small bit of light for me to see by. I crossed the putting green in three strides, then I ran through the grass.

Pia, who'd seemed so light when I'd picked her up, was getting heavier.

"The key!" Grandfather cried out.

Fuck. The key was in my pocket. My left pocket. I'd have to put Pia down. Unless.

"Pia, when we stop at the gate, the first one's unlocked, but I have a key to the second one. Can you reach into my pants pocket with your right hand? I don't want to have to put you down."

She nodded.

I skidded to a stop next to the gate, and I loosened my hold on Pia and slid her to my left so she could reach into my pocket more easily. Then she turned in my arms and reached through the knotted tablecloth to turn the handle on the first gate. That done, she held the key out toward the lock on the second one.

"Good idea," I praised. I held her so she could reach the lock, and she had no trouble turning the key. We were through in an instant, and Pia pulled it shut and locked it behind us.

"Garfield, should I put the key back where I got it or take it?" I was too tired and stressed to decide for myself.

"Take it. You'll lose too much time putting it back, and these rich assholes can get another made easily enough."

Nodding, I ran around the pool. Pia opened the side gate for us, and I bolted as fast as I could down the driveway.

Grandfather shouted, "No one's on the street. The car's clear!"

I ran to the SUV. Thanking the manufacturer for keyless entry, I still winced at the beeping sound as the doors unlocked. I put Pia on the floor behind the driver's seat. "Hang tight. We'll get out of here then figure out where we're going next."

I sure as fuck couldn't take her back to my apartment building with its dozens of security cameras.

I whipped off the tablecloth and threw it on the passenger seat as I got in. I had the car in gear and moving before I'd put on my seat belt. Mindful of the security guards who roamed River Oaks, I made sure my headlights were on and I was traveling just above the speed limit. Grandfather commandeered the front passenger seat, with the other three ghosts in the back with Pia.

"Okay, Lorraine, what does Pia need? Where can I take her?"

"She needs trees, plants, but not a park or anywhere random people will go. Even a potted plant will help right now."

Mercy said, "Is there a Wonder rescue here? Or who's the District Monitor?"

I shook my head. "I don't know what any of those words mean." Then I saw something. I turned off my headlights and pulled over to the curb. "Hang on." I flipped off the interior lights and got out of the car, leaving my door open for a quick getaway.

I ran around the rear of the SUV to the curb. There, flanking the white brick mailbox, were two topiaries pruned into weird spirals about four feet high. Muttering, "Sorry," I grabbed the nearest one and opened the rear passenger door to shove it into the footwell. It was heavier than I'd expected since the pot turned out to have been made of concrete. After shutting the door as quietly as I could, I ran back to the driver's side and jumped in. I peeled away from the curb with a squeal of my tires, only turning my headlights back on when I'd turned the corner.

I heard rustling leaves. "Did that help?" I glanced over my shoulder, but I couldn't see down onto the floor.

Pia didn't reply, but Lorraine said, "Yes. The plant is helping renew her magic. Thank you."

"Good. Um, Mercy, can you explain what you were saying a few minutes ago? Something about a District? Can we go there?" It was past 1am, but I'd wake up the entire city to get Pia the help she needed.

Mercy appeared next to me, sitting in Grandfather's lap.

"I say!" he harumphed.

She ignored him. "You're not part of the campaign?"

I stopped at a light and turned to stare at her. "What campaign?"

"Crap. I'm from Canada, but I'm sure the campaign exists down here too."

Garfield asked, "Did you have a District Monitor up there? Maybe Rory can call them for help."

She shook her head. "No, my pack preferred to be unaffiliated."

"Same with my pack," Garfield said.

I turned west on San Felipe, relieved to be among more traffic. "What is a District Monitor, please?" I tried not to sound aggravated, but it was fucking late, and I was stressed beyond belief.

"Sorry," Mercy said. "They're a magic carrier who basically looks after the magical beings who live near them. The area is their District."

I let off the gas. "I'm sorry, did you say *magic*?"

Grandfather pointed at the green light ahead, so I started driving again.

Garfield patted me on the shoulder. "Yes. Didn't you see my wolf? And Pia's a dryad, remember? Not to mention you can talk to ghosts. Magic, Rory. It's all magic."

I did not give in to the impulse to pull over and have a lengthy argument. "I.... Okay. I grant you all have magic. But me? I thought I was psychic. Wouldn't I know if I had magical abilities?"

Grandfather pointed at me. "Is that what that swirly thing is? I've been wondering about it since I died. Pia's got one too." He hiked a thumb toward the back seat.

The ghosts all nodded. Fucking hell. I could not deal with this right now.

"You can't cast any spells or anything, Rory," Garfield told me. "You just get to talk to ghosts."

"And this District Monitor?"

Mercy said, "They connect with Wonders, keep them safe." I opened my mouth, but she anticipated my question. "A Wonder is one of us." Her gesture included herself and the back seat. "Non-humans."

I wanted to ask what the hell she'd been in life, but I figured it was rude. And who were all these magic people who had nicknames for supernatural creatures?

I stopped at another light. "I'll ask more questions tomorrow. Right now, we need to figure out where we're going."

There was a Target up ahead on the left, so I turned on my blinker. Once we were in the parking lot, I stopped and pulled out my phone. "Okay. How do we find a District Monitor?"

The ghosts all looked at each other but didn't have any suggestions. I tried googling it, but didn't get any results.

Mercy said, "We need to find some Wonders. They'll know."

I looked at her, then at Garfield. Lorraine was only paying attention to Pia. "Where do you hang out when you're not in Randolph Chamberlain's house?"

Mercy gave me a scathing look. "We're not from here." She left the *idiot* unsaid.

"What about a cemetery?" asked Grandfather. "I mean, you die, obviously. At least some of you need to be buried, right? Maybe there're ghosts."

Mercy and Garfield agreed it was worth a shot, so I started googling again. The only cemetery I was familiar with was Glenwood, which was where the rich people got buried. Not the most likely spot to find any dead non-humans. But the internet told me Glenwood had annexed a smaller cemetery which was home to many working immigrants and other less well-off dead folk. It was worth a shot.

I plugged Glenwood Cemetery into the GPS and got back on the road. Twenty minutes later we were there. Except when I turned off the road, the entrance was gated. Because it was fucking closed at night.

I slammed my hand on the steering wheel. "Fuck!" Then I cringed. "Sorry, Pia. I don't know why it didn't occur to me the cemetery would be closed."

Grandfather patted my knee. "We can take it from here. You play on your phone or something."

He, Mercy, and Garfield vanished. I peered through the gates, but I couldn't see them anywhere. I couldn't see any ghosts in fact. I rubbed my eyes. If this was a bust, I could always find a motel with rooms that opened onto the parking lot so I could sneak Pia and her plant in. I needed sleep.

Oh, shit. I was supposed to be at work in the morning. But Pia was more important. I fired off an email telling my boss I'd be out sick, most likely for more than one day. If he was mad, he could fire me. Pia was worth more than any job.

I twisted around and looked in the back seat. She'd twined herself around the plant. Her eyes were closed, and her breathing was regular. It was hard to see in the darkness, but her skin didn't appear as mottled as it had been before.

"She needs rest and food, but she'll be okay."

I grimaced at Lorraine. "Physically, you mean." No doubt the poor kid could use some serious therapy.

Lorraine sighed and stroked her hand through Pia's hair. Not that Pia could feel it.

Suddenly the car was full of ghosts.

"Fuck!" I jumped in my seat.

Grandfather chuckled. "That never gets old. Rory, this is Dimitra. She goes by Dimi."

Dimi, who was squeezed in the back seat between Garfield and Mercy, looked to have been about Grandfather's age when she'd passed. She was tiny, maybe five feet tall at most, with bright black eyes, a strong nose, and a round face. Her white hair was pulled back in a bun.

Dimi completed her inspection of Pia, then finally gave me her attention.

"Hi, I'm Rory."

She made a show of looking me up and down before making a dismissive *hmmph* sound. Okay then.

Grandfather chuckled. "We lucked out. Dimi heard us asking around about Wonders and District Monitors. Her grandson is the current District Monitor for this area. She can take us to him."

I blew out a breath. Thank fuck. "Fantastic. Thank you, Dimi." I started the car then twisted around to look at her. "Which way should I go?"

She gave me a stink eye. "You think I don't know my own grandson's address? Especially when it was my house first?" Dimi's accent sounded Greek, possibly? She waggled a pointer finger at my phone in the cupholder. "You put it in your phone so I don't have to tell you where to turn like you're a baby."

My head started to pound. "Great idea." I made a show of picking up my phone and unlocking it. "Okay. What's the address?" She told me, and I typed it into the maps app. I connected the phone to the car, and our route was displayed on the dashboard.

I got the car turned around, and we were on our way. Dimi's grandson—I could not make myself care about his name right then—lived in Houston's Second Ward. It wasn't a great neighborhood, so being a District Monitor must not pay very well.

It only took fifteen minutes to get to our destination, which was fortunate, since it was pushing past 2am.

The house was original to the neighborhood, probably less than 1500 square feet, with white wooden siding, and a covered front porch. The carport on one side contained an older sedan with a brand-new SUV right behind it. Someone in the house had money.

I parked at the curb. "Hey, Pia, I'll come around and get you, then we'll go meet the District Monitor and see if he can help us."

"Of course he'll help you," Dimi sniffed. "He's a lunkhead, but he's a good person."

I got out of the car, wondering if I'd have the energy to drive home after this. Maybe Dimi's grandson would let me nap on his couch. Maybe he'd also offer us snacks, since I'd forgotten to stop at a drive-thru.

I went around to the rear passenger door, where Pia was attempting to become one with the plant. Didn't dryads live inside trees or something? Hopefully the District Monitor would know.

I opened the door and considered my options. Pia was essentially sitting in the pot, with her arms and legs wrapped around the plant like a koala. Her face was tucked into one elbow. My jacket was still covering most of her.

"Okay, Pia, I'm going to try picking up the pot with you staying where you are. But if you feel off-balance, you grab onto me, okay?"

She didn't look up, but she nodded.

I crouched down and got my hands around the cement pot. I couldn't lift it straight up without slamming both of our heads into the roof of the car, so I tilted the pot toward me and backed up, dragging the pot and Pia out of the footwell. When I had the pot resting on the doorframe, I lifted the pot, Pia and all. Which made Pia's right knee jab me in the stomach, so I shifted the pot around until we were both more comfortable. After shutting the car door with my butt, I headed up the walkway. Slowly.

Pia wasn't at her full weight, but I'd carried her a good distance earlier. My gym routine didn't include cradling heavy items in my arms, and I was straining with the combined weight of Pia, the pot, and the plant.

"You should spend more time working out," Dimi advised. She drifted along on my right, with Lorraine on my left. The other ghosts brought up the rear.

"I'll keep it in mind," I wheezed. There were two steps up to the wooden porch. I dreaded them more and more the closer I got, but ultimately I had no choice. I took a deep breath, gritted my teeth, and went up one step at a time. I let out a big whoosh of air when I got to the porch, leaning over to better fill my lungs again.

I hobbled to the front door, which had a screen door covering it. There wasn't a doorbell. Shit. I really didn't want to put Pia down.

"Pia, could you reach the door handle for me, please?"

Without looking, she shook her head and squeezed herself tighter around the plant.

Got it.

Big breath again. Then I heaved the pot and Pia up so the bottom of the pot could rest on my hip. My hand shook as I reached for the handle on the screen door. I pulled it open and stepped forward so my body prevented it from closing.

Not wanting to wake the neighbors, I knocked at what I thought was a considerate volume. Then I waited. Nothing.

"They're in there," Garfield said. "Two people. But I can hear the shower running."

"Two!" Dimi scowled and put her hands on her hips. "Shane better not have one of those app hookups over."

Fuck. I did not have time for this. I banged my knuckles as loud as I could against the door. It made a satisfying echo. They had to have heard it.

For good measure, I did it again.

"Shower's off."

I nodded my thanks at Garfield, then I shouted, "Hey! I need some help out here!"

The air suddenly became warmer on my right side. The ghosts shrieked, and I whipped my head around to look.

A giant green reptilian head was peering at me under the roof of the porch.

"Aaaaaaaah!" I clutched Pia to me and ducked, moving back against the railing on the other side of the porch. The screen door slammed closed.

Keeping my body between the creature and Pia, I stared at it over my shoulder. What the fuck was it? It looked like a fucking dragon from a movie or something. But I could smell the smoke coming out of its nostrils, so this was real. Pia had lifted her head from the plant and was trying to peek around my arm. Her teeth were long and sharp again, but I was grateful she didn't have any thorns.

Lorraine materialized between me and the dragon. "Get away from her, you, whatever you are!" She shook her fist at it.

Dimi joined her, shouting, "Shoo! You're not welcome in my house!"

The dragon pulled its head back slightly. Its eyes darted around the porch. Could it see the ghosts?

The other ghosts moved to stand with Lorraine and Dimi, exclaiming about not knowing what that thing was, though it wasn't a shifter.

I couldn't run down the porch steps without getting too close to the dragon's mouth for comfort. I shot a quick glance over the porch railing to gauge the distance to the ground. There were some bushes to break my fall, but I wasn't confident I could keep Pia safe if I jumped. Maybe I could lower her and the pot first?

The front door swung open, and two men wearing only towels around their waists rushed out.

Too bad I had to keep my eyes on the dragon.

CAL'S CAMPAIGN COMPENDIUM

HUNTER

<u>Type</u>: Hunter

<u>Class</u>: Magic Carrier

<u>Overview</u>: Taking their name designation from Dungeons & Dragons, Hunters are the Navy SEALs of the magic carriers. They are generally responsible for rescuing Wonders in difficult situations, such as kidnapping or from areas where humans are encroaching or fighting.

<u>Skills</u>:

- *Extremely heightened senses (smell, sight, hearing)*
- *Ability to go into an extreme version of "combat mode" (hyperfocus, ultra-enhanced senses, improved reflexes, night vision, ultra-fast running speed, super-strength) when under threat or periods of stress.*
- *Can stay still and silent for extended periods of time*
- *Can slow down their bodily functions to enable them to survive underwater or in environments lacking oxygen*
- *Self-healing even without being bonded*

Enhanced Skills When Bonded: Heat-sensing (like thermal imaging), echolocation, telescopic vision, skin becomes more resistant to injury.

Childhood Aptitudes: You may have a budding Hunter in the family if your kid exhibits one or more of these talents:

- *Physical feats of agility, strength, speed, etc.*
- *Tracking or locating lost pets, people, or objects*
- *Needs a lot of calories to maintain their body weight*
- *Excels at games of strategy*

CHAPTER 6
ELLIS

I REMEMBERED TO GRAB MY GLASSES OFF THE COUNTER BY THE sink before I ran after Shane to the front door. I was actually a little relieved to have a potential emergency to deal with, because then I could stop freaking out about my bond with Shane for a while.

Not that I wasn't happy to have it—I was fucking ecstatic— but ever since we'd woken up, I'd been low-key stressing, thinking of all the issues we'd have to deal with. We didn't know each other well; what if all my little habits irritated Shane? What if his irritated me? What if he thought my hobby was too dorky and made fun of me? Where would we live? What about our jobs? What would our families and friends think? Not to mention, what was wrong with our magic?

So, yeah, right now I was glad to focus on who or what was on the other side of the door Shane was pulling open.

Which was nothing.

No one was standing in the doorway. Shane opened the screen door and stepped outside. I followed closely.

To our right, a tall blond guy stood by the railing on the side of the porch. He was a magic carrier of some kind, wearing a white button-down and black pants, and he was holding what appeared to be a potted plant wrapped in black fabric. I couldn't see it clearly since he had his back turned. The guy looked over his shoulder and blinked at us, but then he went back to staring at something else. I turned to see what had his attention.

"Fuck!" I stumbled backward into Shane. There was a fucking *dragon* looking at us from the side of the house!

Shane grabbed my arm, and through our bond he sent calming thoughts. "It's okay, it's okay. Ms. Jackson, is that you?"

The dragon bobbed its head.

I put my hand on my chest. Right. Ms. Jackson had been in dragon form before, and I'd seen the picture someone had posted on Discord.

"Hey, what's up?" Shane was talking to the guy with the plant. "Don't be scared. That's just Ms. Jackson. They're, uh, not going to hurt you."

I looked at the guy's pasty-white face, then I looked at Ms. Jackson's sharp teeth and the smoke curling out of their nostrils. Yeah, I wouldn't believe Shane either. And I fucking hoped none of the neighbors were looking out their windows right now.

I stepped between the blond guy and the scary dragon. "Ms. Jackson, you're frightening our visitor. I don't think they mean any harm. Can you maybe change to something a little more... friendly-looking?"

Ms. Jackson tilted their head, considering the guy. Then the vertical slits in their reptilian eyes widened. I spun around. He was now facing us, and I could see the potted plant he was holding also contained a young girl. A dryad, based on her yellow and green-mottled skin and hair. She bared her fangs at us.

Ms. Jackson made a crooning noise. When I glanced back at them, they pushed their head further under the roof of the porch. Shane and I backed up, but before I could say anything, they shimmered, and the creepy four-foot-high hedgehog from this morning was sitting on their ass on the porch.

The blond guy made a choking sound. He had a horrified expression on his face.

Ms. Jackson twitched their very large snout, and their extremely long and sharp spines moved threateningly.

Shane held up a hand. "Ms. Jackson, this form is, uh...." Through the bond I felt his frustration at not being able to find the right words.

"Scarier than the dragon," I supplied. "Hedgehogs aren't supposed to be that large, so when you turn into one it makes our human brains freak out."

"Exactly," Shane said.

Ms. Jackson snuffled discontentedly but nodded. They shimmered again and became a... fluffy donkey. They were a little taller than the hedgehog, but the fluffy gray hair didn't look like it would stab you if you got too close.

It would have to do.

"Um, thanks. That's cute and not frightening." I threw a glance over at the guy and the dryad. "I promise, they won't harm you. They're, uh, very protective of their friends and you were a stranger. But now they've, uh, met you, you'll be their friends too." Or something. At least the color was coming back to the guy's face. The little girl blinked at Ms.

Jackson with bright green eyes. She smiled briefly then hid her face in the potted plant.

Behind me, Shane chuckled. I turned to see Ms. Jackson had manifested a crown of flowers around their ears.

Shane came to stand beside me. Our visitor—the guy—was in his mid-twenties, good-looking in a rich white boy way. The rich part was reinforced by the late model hybrid Range Rover parked by the curb, his expensive haircut, and the tuxedo he was wearing. Or had been wearing. The jacket was wrapped around the little girl as she clung to the potted plant, and his bow tie hung loose from his open collar.

"I'm Ellis," I said. "This is Shane. Uh, sorry we aren't dressed for visitors." I gestured at our towels and naked chests.

The guy shook his head. "It's not like I had an appointment. I'm Rory, and this is Pia. She was being held captive by an asshole with too much money on his hands."

Holy fuck. I tamped down the rage I instantly felt, which was echoed across the bond with Shane.

"We'll get his info from you later."

Rory, who must've been a Hunter, nodded. "Absolutely. Pia here didn't have any plants in the cage with her. Uh, I was told the District Monitor lived here, and you could help?"

Shane moved closer to them. "We're both District Monitors, but I think I'm the one you're looking for." Keeping a firm hand on his towel, he bent down so his head and Pia's were on the same level. She didn't look at him. "Hi, Pia. I'm Shane. I like plants a lot too. What's your favorite kind of tree?"

She tucked her head down even further. Rory cleared his throat and said, "I was told she likes fruit trees the best."

Shane made an exaggerated delighted expression. "Really? I have an apple tree right here in my backyard! Let's go see if it suits you better than that juniper you've got there."

I held the screen door open. Ms. Jackson clopped inside, then Rory and Pia. Shane followed them into the house, chattering like it wasn't the middle of the night and he wasn't wearing next to nothing. I smiled. He was so good at putting people at their ease.

He told Pia, "It's a Granny Smith apple tree. My granny lived here, and she used to tell me wild stories about this other granny the tree was named after."

I followed them in, pausing to close and lock the front door.

Pia didn't respond, but Rory said, "She, uh, must have loved you a lot."

Shane was probably going to reply, but I was distracted by something inside my chest suddenly yanking me toward him. I grunted and stumbled forward, one hand outstretched to catch myself, and one hand clapped over my junk as my towel slipped.

Rory stopped walking and looked between me and Shane, who was bent over clutching his chest. "What's the matter? Are you okay?"

Ms. Jackson snorted and rolled their eyes.

I grimaced. "Um, sorry. Just bonded. Forgot we need to stay close to each other for right now. Let's get Pia settled." I hurriedly refastened my towel and went over to stand next to Shane.

Most people would've congratulated us on our bonding, but Rory's expression said he had other things on his mind. He shifted the pot in his hands, and I noticed it was made out of concrete, like the kind people had in their front yards. It must be heavy as fuck, plus Pia's weight on top of it. Damn.

Ms. Jackson nosed the thumb latch on the back door, then they used their chin to press down on the handle. Nudging the door open, they flicked their tail as they went outside. Shane and I could see in the dark pretty well, and as a Hunter, Rory could see even better than we did. Nevertheless, I flicked on the outside light as I passed through the doorway. A little light might make Pia more comfortable.

Shane put his hand on my back, and we followed them onto the concrete patio. He pointed to the far right corner of the yard, where a tree was covered in white and pink blossoms. "How does that look, Pia?"

Ms. Jackson trotted over to the tree, and Rory walked swiftly after them. I found myself admiring how his ass filled out his tuxedo pants. Shane jerked his head around to look at me, and I was swamped with guilt. Fuck, I hadn't even been bonded for half a day, and I was looking at other guys? It wasn't supposed to be possible, so did this mean our bond was even more screwed up than we'd thought? I hated that Shane had felt my attraction to Rory.

"Sorry," I muttered, continuing to follow Rory to the tree.

He set the pot and Pia down next to the base of the trunk. Then he patted her on the shoulder and stepped back, shaking out his hands and arms. "What do we do now?"

His hands were beautiful, with long graceful fingers. He wouldn't have any trouble doing the Boingy Boing.

Crap. I yanked my gaze back to Shane, who was kneeling in the grass near the tree. He said, "Pia, do you want to hang out with the apple tree for a while?"

She lifted her head and looked at the tree, then she turned to Rory and reached out a hand. His jacket was so big on her that the extra fabric of the sleeve hung limply where her hand didn't reach. She was wearing some sort of t-shirt with a shark on it under the jacket.

He took her sleeve-covered hand. "I won't leave you, kiddo, but you need the tree's magic. Your mom says so."

I blinked at his words. Her mom? Pia didn't have any active connections other than what appeared to be a brand-new tenuous one with Rory, so she couldn't have any living relatives or close friends. What an asshole move to pretend like her mom was still alive and communicating with him, especially when Pia would know he was lying.

For his part, Rory didn't have any connections either, other than Pia. Which was weird, because Hunters had connections to their teams. But that wasn't important right now. Maybe he just didn't know how to talk to kids. It was the middle of the night, and he'd rescued her from a bad situation. I should give him the benefit of the doubt.

For now.

Shane cocked his head, and I felt his discomfort with Rory's comment about Pia's mom, but he didn't say anything. He asked Pia, "What if we bring some chairs over here and sit with you while you make friends with the tree?"

She seemed to tug on Rory's hand, and he crouched down next to her. She leaned away from the plant enough to whisper in his ear.

Rory's expression turned sympathetic. "I'm so sorry, Pia. I didn't think of that." He looked at us. "She wants clean clothes. The... jerk who held her kept her in a glass box with no running water. Is there a 24-hour Walmart around here or something?"

Ms. Jackson's ears went back, and they kicked out their hind legs. Same, Ms. Jackson. I felt the exact same.

Shane said, "Well, if you don't mind old lady clothes, Pia, I still have some of my granny's things. If those would do for tonight, we could get you something a little more fashionable tomorrow."

She nodded and gave Shane a small smile. I felt his heart-break-slash-pride through the bond.

"Okay I'll be back in five minutes." He stood up. "Uh, make it ten minutes, because I'd like to put some clothes on myself. Pia, do you need water or food or anything? Do you want to wash up?"

Pia shook her head. She hadn't let go of Rory's hand, and he eased himself to the ground, sitting cross-legged next to her.

"Rory, you want some water?"

"God, yes, please."

"Got it." He touched my arm as he passed me, and I fell into step beside him. He opened his mouth to protest, and I could feel through the bond that he didn't want to leave Rory alone until we knew him better, but then he said, "Oh, right."

I snorted. "We need to figure out how long our leash is." I winced when I stepped on a twig. I hadn't noticed my bare feet on the way to the tree, but now I was ready to put some shoes on.

When we went inside, Ms. Jackson had walked over to Pia and lowered their head to be scratched.

CAL'S CAMPAIGN COMPENDIUM

BONDING, PART TWO:
STRENGTHENING
THE CONNECTION

In order to bond with a partner or partners, your connection has to have grown strong enough to support it. This follows a few steps:

1. <u>*Resonance and Compatibility:*</u> *On first meeting a potential romantic interest, if your magics are compatible enough to eventually bond, you will notice what is called resonance. Resonance is displayed when your respective magics can be seen reaching out to each other when you are in close proximity. If you and your potential partner wish to see if you are compatible, touch each other in a non-sexual way (e.g. holding hands) for a few seconds. Compatible magics will intermingle with each other.*

2. <u>*Connection:*</u> *A connection for bonding purposes is a voluntary* non-permanent** link that over time, as the partners grow to care for each other, becomes permanent. As the connection grows, some of the abilities enjoyed by bonded partners will manifest when the connected partners are touching skin-to-skin. These abilities might include mind-speaking and sensing each other's emotions.*

<u>Note</u>: See the <u>Connections</u> compendium entry for more information on the different types of connections and how to create them.

* Highly compatible partners may find their connection is created without their consent or intent simply by touching each other.

** Highly compatible partners may find their connection to be so strong initially that it is immediately permanent. In these cases, if the individuals do not wish to move forward with bonding, it is recommended they do not spend any further time together, and they absolutely should not continue to touch each other skin-to-skin.

CHAPTER 7
SHANE

I WOULD'VE PREFERRED ELLIS TO STAY BEHIND WITH RORY. NOT that I had any specific suspicions about the man, but we didn't know him, where he came from, or what his intentions were.

On the other hand, I was glad Ellis couldn't stay behind, because I'd been getting flashes through our bond of the attraction Ellis felt for Rory. Our bond which was only a few fucking hours old.

I'd been working hard to hide my hurt and anger from him, but the bond kept fighting me. Which was understandable. It was still trying to set itself in place, and not only was it wonky, but one of the parties involved was already looking elsewhere.

I couldn't blame him. Rory seemed like a fucking catch. Gorgeous, rich based on the car he drove, and he had to be a ton smarter than me. Ellis was probably regretting our bond now that he saw what he could've had.

But I wasn't about to be a doormat. If he wanted out, I deserved to know.

It was hard to stomp into the house in bare feet, but I was giving it a go. As soon as the door shut behind us, I whirled and rounded on Ellis. "Are we done? You want someone else already?" I hated the wobble in my voice. I stopped talking and dropped the hold I'd been keeping on my emotions.

Ellis took a step back, his eyes widening. "I didn't mean to! I'm not—I'm happy we're bonded! I don't know why I keep looking at him!" He held out his hands pleadingly.

"You don't know? Ellis, your fucking magic was reaching for him when he walked past you!"

His face looked shocked. *Really?* He had to have noticed it.

I was furious, but we didn't have time to deal with this right now. "Come on. We've got to get dressed and find some clothes for Pia."

"Shane, please. It's you I want."

Blinking back tears, I shrugged off the hand he put on my arm and strode into my bedroom. The same bedroom where we'd created our bond only hours before.

I didn't look at the bed or at Ellis as I pulled on underwear, sweatpants, and a t-shirt. He didn't say anything, just stood in the doorway looking down the hall to the living room the whole time.

"Your turn," I told him as I stuck my feet in flip-flops. We went into the guest room where he'd put his stuff the night he'd arrived from Dallas. While he pulled clothes out of his suitcase, I opened the dresser drawers I still hadn't cleaned out after Granny's passing.

Her favorite turquoise velour track suit would work, I decided. I added a pink long-sleeved t-shirt with a cat sitting on a rainbow on the front. I pulled out a camisole but wavered over the underwear, deciding to bring some just in case. If Pia was squeamish about wearing someone else's underwear, she could skip it. I threw in pink socks and some slip-on shoes in the remote chance they'd fit. I wished I had some baby wipes or something, but clean clothes would have to do.

When I turned back around, Ellis had finished getting dressed. He looked edible in black shorts and a royal purple short-sleeved button up. I cursed myself for wanting him right then.

I led the way back to the living room. When I got to the back door, Ellis said, "Wait."

I spun around, ready to tell him that we didn't have time to discuss our relationship, but he was headed toward the sofa. He got to the end of the distance the bond would allow us to separate, and he looked at me until I followed him. "What?"

When he could reach it, he grabbed the throw blanket off the back of the sofa. He held it up. "So she doesn't have to get changed in front of us."

Well, fuck. It wasn't fair of him to be so thoughtful.

Shoving thoughts of Ellis out of my mind—as much as I could with him on my heels—I marched to the back door.

Then I had to detour us again, this time to the kitchen. We'd promised Rory some water. Ellis picked up five bottles, and it took me a minute to realize the fifth one was for Ms. Jackson.

That reminded me. "Don't Hunters usually work in pairs so they have backup?"

Ellis nodded. "Yeah, in my experience, but this might've been an emergency or something."

We could ask Rory after Pia went into the tree. I sighed. He'd be here until she came out, and that could be a good ten or twelve hours from now if her magic was severely depleted. This was going to suck.

When we finally made it to the back yard, Ms. Jackson had manifested their Ouija board on their side, and Rory was in the process of dragging the hammock frame over from under the oak tree to under the apple tree. Pia was still sitting in the plant pot, but she was watching. She'd lifted her head and everything.

She noticed us approaching, and I saw her head bob as if she wanted to hide her face again, but she firmed her jaw and looked at us directly.

I smiled and held up the clothes. "Okay, none of this is stylish, but it'll be warm and comfortable until we can get you to a store in the morning."

Rory came over to stand on Pia's other side as I set the clothes down. His magic and Ellis' reached for each other, but Ellis moved to my other side, out of range. I ignored it.

I showed Pia the underwear. "These are clean, but they're used, so it won't offend me if you don't wear them. And the shoes might not fit, but I figured I'd try."

She nodded and whispered, "Thank you." She extended one jacketed hand toward the pink t-shirt.

Ellis held out a corner of the throw blanket to Rory. "Here. This'll give you some privacy, Pia." He and Rory each took a corner of the blanket and held it so it fell to the ground, creating a curtain between us and Pia. Then they faced away from her, and I did the same.

I opened a water bottle and handed it to Rory. He thanked me.

Desperate for a conversation-starter, I asked, "Where are you from?" Hunters—and there weren't that many of them—were based all around the state so they could move quickly as needed.

"Houston, all of my life."

I cocked my head. "Really? I thought I knew all the magic carriers in the area." We'd never had a Hunter here. Well, up until now I guessed. "Are you new to being a Hunter?" Maybe he'd finished college before going through training.

He frowned, then glanced toward the house briefly. His face cleared. "This is actually my first rescue."

Ellis said, "And you did it all by yourself? Damn, that's impressive."

And my jealousy was back. Fuck.

CAL'S CAMPAIGN COMPENDIUM

BONDING, PART THREE: CREATING THE BOND

As mentioned in the Introduction to this entry, creating a bond requires five elements from each partner:

1. *A strong enough connection: Once your connection is strong enough that new bond-related abilities are manifesting between the partners, you should be able to complete the bonding process at any mutually agreed upon time.*

2. *Consent: Discuss the desire for bonding between all partners. Your magic will know if each of you has consented or not.*

3. *Skin-to-skin contact: Make sure you are touching each other's bare skin. Even a minor contact will do.*

4. *Intent: Each of you should visualize your connection and push your intent to bond with your partner(s) through.*

5. *Exchange of pheromones: Many people use sexual intimacy to facilitate the exchange of pheromones, but alternatively*

you merely have to breathe in your partner(s)'s pheromones from a location on their body such as armpit or groin.

Once these steps are completed, you will be able to see your magics combine and become a singular source between all partners, and then the bond is in place.

CHAPTER 8
RORY

THEY THOUGHT I WAS A HUNTER. SOME SORT OF MAGICAL GREEN Beret, based on what Mercy and Garfield told me. A Hunter would've definitely been helpful in rescuing Pia. And someone like that would've been easier to wrap my brain around than the freaky dragon-slash-giant hedgehog-slash-donkey who a few minutes ago had casually popped a Ouija board out of their side and ordered me to move the hammock around.

Could I just go back to my boring life from yesterday?

But when I glanced over to check on Pia, who had dressed in Dimi's clothing and was tentatively smiling up at me, I dismissed my wistfulness. Rescuing her was the most important thing I'd done in my entire life.

I didn't bother correcting Shane's assumption that I was a Hunter, or Ellis' that I'd performed the rescue on my own. I handed Ellis my end of the throw blanket, and when our fingers touched, I felt a zap of static electricity.

Shaking my hand, I asked Pia, "Do the clothes help?"

She nodded. She'd put on everything except the shoes and socks. I could only imagine how clothes might feel like armor to her now. I hoped dryads had therapists. She'd need to talk to someone.

"How about some water?" Ellis handed her one of the bottles he'd brought out.

"You know," Grandfather said. "You're going to have to tell them about us at some point. Some point soon."

I made a face at him but covered it up by rubbing my sleeve across my forehead like I'd felt an insect or something.

He waved toward Shane and Ellis. "They're magic people. Do you think a man who can see ghosts is any stranger to them than... that creature?" He jutted his chin at Ms. Jackson.

Okay, he made a good point.

Lorraine looked up from where she'd been stroking Pia's hair. "We need their help to get Pia to the local dryads. She needs people like herself."

Well, fuck. I hated, fucking hated, explaining my ability to people. Especially after what'd happened the last time.

Dimi appeared next to Shane, pointing at something midway between him and Ellis. "And look at this piece of crap bond they made without you. Better get started by spilling the beans about being a Medium so you can get to the fun part."

She'd been complaining about the state of Shane and Ellis' "bond" since we'd walked into the house. All I knew was that their "bond" was why they couldn't be more than a few feet apart from each other. It didn't seem fun, but I didn't want to know why Dimi thought I was responsible for fixing it. I wasn't getting involved. I'd just make sure Pia would be okay, then I'd go back to my regular little life.

Except I did need to do something about Uncle Hugo and that asshole Randolph Chamberlain. Maybe I could borrow one of those Hunters. No need to involve Shane or Ellis, or their "bond".

Pia handed the empty water bottle to Ellis. I asked her, "Are you ready to, uh, try out the apple tree?" It wasn't like I knew exactly what she'd be *doing* with the tree, but I wanted to be supportive.

She reached for my hand. I walked with her over to the tree trunk, and she threw her arms around my waist. "I'll be right here if you need me," I told her.

"Me too, baby," Lorraine whispered, though of course Pia couldn't hear her.

She released me and turned to the tree. Then she just... walked into it. And she was gone.

I sucked in a breath. "Where did she go? Is she alright?" I gazed wildly around at the ghosts, Shane, Ellis, and Ms. Jackson.

"She's fine," Shane said, echoing what I was hearing from the ghosts. "She's in the tree. She'll come out when she's ready."

I sagged. "Okay. Thanks." I went over to the hammock. "Can I sit here?" I asked Ms. Jackson. They nodded, and I sank down into the rope netting. I leaned back and closed my eyes. Shit, what a fucking night it'd been. My arms ached, and I didn't want to move.

"Why don't you put your feet up and take a nap?" Ellis suggested.

Okay, I'd move for a nap. I scooted around until my whole body was on the hammock. It swayed gently, and I sighed. I might never get up.

Ellis draped the throw over my legs.

"Thanks. Talk later," I slurred as I let sleep take me.

―――――

The smell of bacon frying woke me. The sun was up, but the light filtering through the apple tree leaves was still weak.

"He wakes!" Grandfather announced.

I groaned and rubbed my eyes. The muscles in my arms were fucking sore. Sitting up, I examined the apple tree. No sign of Pia. Hopefully she was healing.

I put a foot on the ground to stop the hammock from swinging, then I stood up. Crap. I hated sleeping in shoes and socks, and these dress shoes were pinching my toes. Maybe one of my hosts had large enough feet that I could borrow a more comfortable pair.

Grandfather, who was pretending to sit on the end of the hammock, smirked. "Shane and Ellis were arguing about you last night."

I frowned. "Why?"

He chuckled delightedly. "Apparently that Ellis likes you. You know, *likes* you. And since Shane and Ellis are bonded, which Mercy says means they're permanently married with magic, Shane's a little miffed. But I told Mercy you're polyamorous, so if you can win over Shane, there won't be a problem." He winked at me.

I groaned. "Is that what Dimi meant when she said I needed to fix Shane and Ellis' bond? She wants me to, what, sleep with them? I don't have a magic dick." Though it wouldn't have been a hardship to have sex with them. Ellis was attractive, and so was Shane, but I'd been focused on Pia last night, so it hadn't seemed important.

He cackled some more. "That's a good one. I'll have to tell Dimi."

"Grandfather!" Fucking hell. "Tell her I'm not doing it." Especially if only one of the pair was interested in me.

Shit, was I *disappointed* Shane wasn't attracted to me?

Shaking my head, I turned to the apple tree. The potted plant was still next to the trunk, and it had grown at least a foot during the time I'd been asleep. The new leaves were blurring the twisty shape it'd had the night before.

"Hey, Pia, if you can hear me, I'm just going inside to clean up and get some breakfast. I'll be back as soon as I can." At least it was only April, so the weather was bearable.

I walked to the house, grimacing at my uncomfortable shoes. The back door was cracked open, and I could hear dishes clinking.

When I reached the patio, I took my shoes off. I pushed the door wide, and the first thing I saw was a huge tiger sitting next to the kitchen table. I gasped, clutching my shoes to my chest.

The tiger turned, showing me the Ouija board on their chest. Fucking hell.

"Oh, Ms. Jackson. Hey." Did I sound as casual as I was trying for? Hopefully I'd get used to their different forms before they gave me a heart attack.

"Good morning," Shane called out. He and Ellis were in the kitchen emptying the dishwasher. At least none of the ghosts were in here. Grandfather had stayed in the back yard.

"Good morning. Um, is there a bathroom I could use to clean up?"

"Sure. Down that hall on the left." Shane eyed me up and down. "You want to borrow some sweatpants?"

"Thank you, but what I really need are some different shoes."
I rubbed my hand through my hair. "I promised Pia I'd stay.
Would it be okay if I asked a friend of mine to bring some
clothes from my apartment?"

He shrugged. "Of course. Are they your partner?"

I shook my head. "I'm not in a relationship."

Shane frowned. He opened his mouth to say something, but I
held up my phone. "What's your address? No, wait. I have it
from last night."

I opened my texting app. The phone still had a decent charge,
but I had a cable in my car in case it got low.

> Hey, are you at home?

I headed for the bathroom while I waited for a reply. I'd hold
off on the shower until I had clothes to change into, but I
needed to piss and wash my face.

I'd barely shut the door behind me when he replied.

MANNY
> Just got off shift. Whatchu need?

> Can you please run by my place and pick up
> some clothes for me? I'm in the Second
> Ward. Long story, but I only have my tuxedo
> and I can't leave. These shoes are fucking
> torture.

MANNY
> You can't leave? Is last night's hookup
> holding you hostage? Or is this a BDSM
> thing? Do you have a safe word?

> Fuck off. No, I promised this little girl. Again,
> long story.

MANNY

I gotchu.

Thanks. I owe you. Here's the address.

MANNY

Cool. I used to have a client on that street
back when I did in-home caregiving. I can be
there in 30. I'll text you when I get there

You're the best

When I returned to the kitchen Shane asked, "You want coffee? I was about to make eggs and toast."

"Sounds great, thank you. Black is fine."

"Sure. Have a seat."

There were four place settings at the table, one of which was in front of Ms. Jackson. I could either sit next to or across from them. Fuck it. I pulled out the chair to Ms. Jackson's left. I didn't know what real tiger fur looked like up close, but Ms. Jackson's seemed to have squiggly lines running through theirs. Weird.

Shane and Ellis came out of the kitchen. Ellis handed me a cup of coffee, and Shane put a bowl of it in front of Ms. Jackson. The two of them went back to the kitchen, and I watched Ms. Jackson lap from the bowl. Only a little splashed onto the table.

I sipped my coffee, hoping the caffeine would help me make sense of everything around me.

Shane's phone rang, and he groaned.

Ellis said, "Tell me that isn't your fucking boss again."

Shane shook his head and set the carton of eggs on the

counter before answering the phone. "Ricky, it's my day off, remember? I'll be back tomorrow."

I couldn't hear exactly what the man on the other end of the call was saying, but it had a real *my-way-or-the-highway* tone to it.

Shane put his hand over his eyes. "Fine, fine. I'll call him. Text me the number."

He hung up as his phone pinged with a text.

"What's the matter now?" Ellis' expression was grim.

"Ricky tried to do a landscape design on his own, and the client threatened to hire another company."

"Can you at least eat before you call them? You didn't get much sleep."

Shane sighed. "No. I won't be able to relax until I deal with this."

Ellis shook his head. "I can't believe they won't pay you for working on your day off."

We listened as Shane placated the client and promised them a new design as soon as he returned to work on Thursday. He must be some hotshot landscape architect or something.

Ellis put plates of biscuits in front of me and Ms. Jackson. "This'll help tide you over while we wait for Shane to finish his call. Rory, would you mind putting butter and jelly on Ms. Jackson's biscuit? I'll bring it over in a second."

"Sure, no problem."

He brought out a stick of butter on a plate with a butter knife, then jars of jelly and marmalade with individual serving spoons for each.

He went back to the kitchen, and I turned to Ms. Jackson. "What would you like on your biscuit?"

The letters sparkled on the Ouija board. *I-L-I-K-E-B-U-T-T-E-R-A-N-D-I-W-A-N-T-T-O-T-R-Y-B-L-U-E-B-E-R-R-Y-J-A-M*

"Got it." My stomach growled. I hoped there were more biscuits.

I got Ms. Jackson's biscuit ready. As soon as I put their plate back in front of them, they ate the whole thing in one bite.

A moment later I decided I couldn't throw stones at their table manners since I ate my biscuit in only a couple of bites myself.

My phone chimed.

MANNY

You dog, you hooked up with Shane Costa? He's my old client's grandson! I haven't seen him since then, but he was hot as fuck. BTW I'm outside

I hadn't even finished reading the text when the doorbell rang.

"Sorry, that's for me," I said, pushing my chair back.

Before I could stand, Ms. Jackson got up and loped toward the front door.

"Shit!" I raced after them, but I wasn't very fast in my socked feet. Ellis and Shane came out of the kitchen and followed, but none of us would make it in time.

Like a slow-motion nightmare, Ms. Jackson put their huge paw on the door handle and somehow opened it.

"No! Manny, they're friendly!"

Manny's face changed from a grin to a shocked "O" in an instant. He threw the Trader Joe's bag he was carrying at Ms. Jackson's head and darted to the side. Ms. Jackson ducked to avoid the bag then leaped forward.

I finally made it to the door. Ms. Jackson was standing in the middle of the walkway between the house and the street, in plain view of the entire neighborhood. I didn't see Manny. Or anyone else for that matter, which was lucky.

"Manny?"

"Shhh!" came from my right. "It'll hear you!"

I went to the side of the porch and looked over the railing. Manny, still in his cartoon character scrubs from work, was huddled in the low bushes that lined the side of the house.

"It's okay. The tiger won't hurt you."

He peered over the edge of the porch. Ms. Jackson was walking toward us. "Fuck!" He stood up and I helped him climb back over the railing. Luckily his slight stature meant he wasn't too hard to lift, but my sore arms protested the entire time. "Get inside, hurry!" He pushed past me, but Shane and Ellis blocked his path to the door.

"Manny?" Shane asked, his eyebrows popped high. "You know Rory?" He turned to Ellis. "Manny was Granny's main caregiver before she died. Manny, this is Ellis."

Manny fidgeted, fists clenched and shifting back and forth on his feet. Ms. Jackson was almost to the porch steps. "Yeah. Hey. Nice to meet you. Uh, can we please go inside?"

I positioned myself between him and Ms. Jackson. "They won't hurt you. I promise. I've been here for hours, and they've been perfectly nice."

He blinked at me, then craned his head around me to watch Ms. Jackson approach. "Um, it's a pet? Like, who keeps a tiger as a pet in Houston?"

"Um. Not a pet. It's complicated."

Ms. Jackson walked up the steps. Ellis walked over and reached out his hand to stroke their fur. "See? They're friendly."

Ms. Jackson slowly approached Manny. He backed up until he ran into Shane, but he didn't try to move further. Ms. Jackson sniffed at him, then butted the top of their head right into Manny's stomach, hard enough that Shane had to steady him with his hands on his shoulders.

"Uh, what's complicated about them being a pet or not?" Manny didn't take his eyes off Ms. Jackson. They nudged their head in between Shane and Manny, and then shoved Manny toward the front door.

"What's happening?" he whisper-shrieked.

Shane opened the door. "Just go with it. They have their own agenda, we're finding out."

Ms. Jackson herded Manny through the door. The rest of us crowded after them, though I remembered to snag the Trader Joe's bag, which had my clothes in it. Ms. Jackson didn't stop until Manny was at the dining table. They pushed out the chair to the right of where they'd been sitting earlier. If I sat down in the same place I'd been sitting before, Ms. Jackson would be between me and Manny.

"I'll, uh, set another place. Rory, could you get the desk chair from the guest bedroom? It's down that hall." Shane pointed. "Manny, you want some coffee?"

Manny responded with a faint affirmative. I went into the guest bedroom. A small desk with a rolling chair and a desktop computer filled one corner, and the other side of the room had a double bed with an old-fashioned lace coverlet and a nightstand. A duffel bag sat unzipped on the bed with an orange shirt half inside, but the bed was made so I couldn't tell if anyone was sleeping there. I left the Trader Joe's bag on the bed so I could change later.

I rolled the chair to the table. Shane and Ellis had arranged the other chairs and placemats so there was room for all of us.

I peeked out the back window, but I only saw the ghosts hanging out by the hammock. When I took my seat at the table, someone had refreshed my coffee. Manny was staring at Ms. Jackson.

"You can pet them," I told him.

He looked at them doubtfully. "Why does their fur look like it has writing on it?" He tentatively brushed the back of his fingers along Ms. Jackson's shoulder.

"They're magical," Shane said from the kitchen. "Like we're pretty sure literally created with magic."

Manny raised his eyebrows at Shane then looked at me. I shrugged. "Wait til they decide to talk to you. You'll see."

Ms. Jackson slurped their coffee and ignored us. Manny picked up his mug but just stared around wide-eyed and didn't speak.

Shane brought out plates of eggs, bacon and biscuits for me and Manny. Ellis followed with one for Ms. Jackson, though they didn't get bacon. I would've thought a tiger would want meat, but maybe magical dragon-hedgehog-donkey-tigers were different.

Shane and Ellis sat down with their own plates, and Manny finally perked up. He gestured between me, Shane, and Ellis.

"I like this for you, *guapo*. Much better than that last couple you were with."

My mouth was full, so I bugged my eyes out and shook my head, taking a sip of coffee so I'd be able to speak. But before I could, Ellis said, "With as in, in a relationship with?"

I cleared my throat, but Manny powered on. "Oh, yeah. They were jerks. Decided he wasn't good enough for them or some shit. It really messed with his head."

"Manny!"

He didn't look at me, but pointed his fork at Ellis. "Can you believe it? Kicking him to the curb because of the gifts God gave him."

"Manny, that's enough."

He turned to look around the room, his face lighting up. "Oh, I forgot. Is your grandpa here? Hi, Grandpa! How's it hangin'?" He set his fork down and waved his hand furiously while turning in a half-circle.

Shane and Ellis stopped eating.

"Manny, no. He's not here."

"You know, I liked it better when he called me Mr. Blackbourne." Grandfather said from beside me. I started, then covered my eyes with my hand.

"Oh, I know that look!" Manny crowed. "Hi, Grandpa! How's the stick up your ass? Are you clenching tighter since Rory's found new partners?" He casually flipped the bird in the general direction of the living room. "Rory's grandfather is a homophobic, polyphobic ass," he informed Shane and Ellis as he scooped up some eggs.

I rubbed my forehead. "He *was*. I keep telling you, he's changed since he died."

"And I keep telling *you*, it doesn't make up for the shit he did when he was alive."

I held up a hand toward Manny. Why did we have to keep having this argument? "He apologized and I accepted his apology. Plus, he helped me rescue a little girl last night, so I think even you can agree he's making an effort not to be a jerk anymore."

Grandfather chuckled. "You don't need to defend me, Rory. He's not wrong about how I used to be."

"What little girl?" Manny demanded.

"Wait," Ellis said. "Are you talking about a ghost?"

Shane chimed in. "You're a Medium? I thought you were a Hunter." He shook his head. "There aren't any Mediums in the campaign. We discussed it on a Zoom call."

Manny said, "Dead people can wait. Where's this little girl?"

I groaned. Time to spill the beans, as Dimi had put it. I held up both hands. "I will answer all of your questions if you'll let me talk."

They all shut up. Ms. Jackson slurped at their coffee.

I held up one finger. "I can see ghosts. I'm not a Hunter, but I didn't correct you because I was hoping to be gone from here before we had to have this conversation."

Manny opened his mouth, probably to ask what a Hunter was, but I pointed the finger I'd raised at him. "All of your questions will be answered eventually."

He rolled his eyes but didn't speak.

"My grandfather is a ghost. Last night he was following my Uncle Hugo around, and Hugo went to a party at Randolph Chamberlain's house."

Shane and Manny sucked in breaths in unison.

"Right. The billionaire. Uncle Hugo moves in expensive circles."

"Thanks to your grandfather's money," Manny muttered.

I ignored him. "When Uncle Hugo was talking to Randolph Chamberlain, Grandfather noticed another ghost, who turned out to be a dryad." I looked at Manny. "Like the tree spirits, but they can look like humans too, apparently."

"Um, okay?" His eyebrows were trying to merge with his hair.

I told them how Lorraine had shown Pia to Grandfather, and he'd come to get me. Then I described sneaking into the mansion and hearing that Uncle Hugo wanted a captive of his own. "The ghosts helped me get Pia to the car, and then they figured out we should come here for help."

Next to Grandfather, Dimi snorted. "Don't tell my grandson I'm here until you have to. He won't be able to handle it."

Ellis frowned. "I think we're going to need the long version of that story soon, but are you saying you don't know about the campaign?"

I cocked my head at him. "Like a political campaign?" I dimly remembered Mercy mentioning a campaign last night.

"Not important right now!" Manny shouted. He gripped the edge of the table so hard his fingers were white. "Where. Is. The. Little. *Girl?*"

Shane took that one. "She's in the apple tree out back. Um, like inside it, not climbing it. She needs to hang out with it until her magic heals up. She'll come out when she's ready."

Manny frowned but relaxed a little. "Okay?"

I nodded. "I promised her I wouldn't leave, which is why I asked you to bring my clothes."

He chewed on his lower lip while he stared around the table at us. "And Ms. Jackson? Where does she—sorry, they—fit in?"

Ms. Jackson turned their head toward Manny, then they leaned over and licked the side of his face.

"Ewww!" He rubbed his cheek with his napkin.

The rest of us laughed. Ellis said, "We're not really sure. They were... inanimate originally. It's a long story. But they asked to come visit me and Shane. I live in Dallas, so we came here first."

Ms. Jackson stood up before bumping Manny with their head until he stood as well. They shoved him until he started walking, herding him out to the backyard.

I stood up to follow. "Manny's a pediatric nurse, in case you couldn't tell by the scrubs."

Ellis *hmmmed*. "Interesting how Ms. Jackson seemed to know that even before they met him."

CAL'S CAMPAIGN COMPENDIUM

CASSANDRA

**Type**: _Cassandra_

**Class**: _Magic Carrier_

**Overview**: _Cassandras are magic carriers born into NPC families, or whose families have hidden their gifts for generations. They are usually not aware of the campaign. The name derives from the Greek myth about the prophetess Cassandra, who was cursed to have accurate visions but no one would believe her when she warned them._

So far Cassandras have only come to light every few decades or so, depending on the geographical area.

CHAPTER 9
ELLIS

I FOLLOWED RORY AND SHANE TO THE BACKYARD, BUT AS SLOWLY as I could without getting too far from Shane. I unlocked my phone and brought up my text messages. No doubt Delphia would prefer I contacted her, but she tended to take over anything she was involved in. I wasn't ready to just hand Pia over to her, not to mention Rory.

I was tempted to text Greg by himself, since I didn't know Cal that well and to be honest he still kind of intimidated the hell out of me. But Cal was the only other Cassandra we'd found in recent memory. Rory would need his advice. So I texted both of them.

> Can you please have Dominic call me or Shane? We have a billionaire who's been holding Wonders captive. He doesn't have any right now but is planning to get more.

> And I need somewhere to bring a 13 year old dryad. Her mom is dead, no other connections. She was being held captive. Is TWIST the best place? There's a grove of dryads in my District, but they don't have any kids

> Oh, and we found a Medium. Or he found us.
> He's a Cassandra

By the time I finished typing, we were all gathered around the apple tree. I stopped next to Shane, who turned his back slightly toward me.

I sighed and unlocked my phone again.

> And Shane and I bonded, but there's
> something wrong

I silenced my phone, not wanting their responses to interrupt Pia leaving the tree. I felt the vibration of a new text, but I ignored it.

Pia stepped out, blinking in the morning sunlight. Her magic was bright. Maybe not as bright as it could be, but so much better than last night. She also looked more human, only a little bit of green showing at the ends of her brown hair.

She gasped at Ms. Jackson, who was still in their tiger form but was also now sporting a crown of flowers on their head.

Rory said quietly, "Hey, how do you feel?"

Pia didn't respond but walked over and threw her arms around him. He hugged her close. Manny watched them, his hands over his mouth.

Pia finally let go, and Ms. Jackson was there next to her, waiting for their own hug. Pia didn't hesitate, just leaned into their huge body.

When she stood up again, Rory said, "Hey, Pia, I want you to meet my friend Manny. I've known him since I was a teenager, and he used to take care of Shane's grandmother before she passed away. He's never met a dryad before."

Manny waved. "Hey, Pia. I like your outfit. Shane's granny would get a kick out of you wearing it."

She gave him a small smile and a little wave.

Shane asked, "Are you hungry or thirsty? I'm sorry I'm not up on dryad nutrition."

Pia shrugged, but Rory said, "She needs water, and she likes eggs and bacon if there are any left."

My scalp prickled. Rory would only know that if someone had told him. And Pia's mother was dead.

Shane smiled. "Sure. Come on into the house and we'll get you set up. You want to take a shower?"

Pia's eyes went wide. "No!" She glanced toward the apple tree like she was going to jump back inside.

Oh, fuck. I did not want to know what the poor kid had gone through. Shane and I simultaneously held our hands up and stepped back from her.

Rory did the same, but Ms. Jackson rubbed their head against Pia's shoulder and made a weird grumbling sound. Pia gripped their fur with one hand.

Manny said cheerfully, "Showers are overrated. But, gurrl, you need a hairbrush bad. And Rory needs to change his clothes. It looks like he slept in them."

Pia stared at Manny, wide-eyed, but allowed him to catch her free hand in his. He said, "Shane, you got a spare hairbrush?"

"Sure. Granny's stuff is in the dresser in the guest bedroom. Top drawer."

"Sweet. Pia, Shane's granny had a hairbrush made out of silver. It's really cool. Ms. Jackson, do you like to be brushed?"

Ms. Jackson made an inquiring noise, and Manny gave an exaggerated gasp. "You've never been brushed? Pia, come on, we've got to show Ms. Jackson how it's done." He marched off toward the house, Pia walking next to him with Ms. Jackson on her other side.

Rory and Shane and I exchanged glances. I pulled out my phone. "I texted Greg and Cal about Pia. They want to talk to us." I told Rory. "Greg is the District Monitor for Central Texas, and Cal is his partner and also a Seer."

Shane started walking to the house, so Rory and I followed him.

Rory said, "A Seer? Like a psychic?"

I nodded. "He only found out about all this a month or so ago, so I thought he'd be a good person for you to know." For some reason I felt compelled to add, "He and Greg are bonded."

Shane said in a biting tone, "You already told him they were partners." He didn't turn around, just kept walking.

I shrugged at Rory, though I wasn't sure exactly what I was trying to convey.

When we got inside, Rory helped me and Shane clear the dishes from the table. There was some bacon left over, but Shane decided to hold off on making the eggs until Pia was ready to eat. We refreshed our coffee and sat at the table to wait.

I wanted to ask Rory about the ghosts, but as soon as we sat down, I realized we could clearly hear Manny talking to Pia in the guest bedroom.

He was saying, "I guess twigs in your hair are a hazard of being a dryad, but tigers don't have the same excuse." Pia gave a little giggle.

I looked, but the bedroom door was pulled almost shut.

Shane frowned. "The acoustics in here don't usually work like that," he whispered.

Manny said calmly, "Hey, Pia. I get what you're saying on the shower thing, but eventually you'll need to get clean. What's your stance on baths? Maybe with bubbles?"

"Bubbles are good," she said. It was the longest sentence I'd heard from her since she arrived. But she followed with, "Then no one could see me."

I covered my mouth with my hands. Fuck.

Manny, however, calmly said, "Did Randolph Chamberlain watch you take a shower? That's creepy."

"No. I mean, he turned the hose on me every few days, but I still had my pajamas on. I just didn't like being stared at all the time."

"Bastard," Manny snarled. Then he said, "Look, Ms. Jackson really likes being brushed under their chin."

Was it wrong to be thankful that the fucker who kidnapped Pia hadn't gotten off on it?

Pia said in a lower voice, "He and his friends would come look at me. He didn't let me have a blanket or a tree. I was so cold. And I missed my mom." This last was said with a hiccup, and then we heard crying.

I got up and walked over to the window. Dominic and the other Hunters had better make sure Randolph Chamberlain didn't get his hands on any other Wonders.

Rory said, "Pia's mom says Chamberlain treated her like an animal at the zoo. Some of his friends made comments, but Chamberlain didn't let them touch her or anything."

"Thank fuck," Shane said.

We heard movement from the guest room, and Shane got up to go into the kitchen. I felt the bond tugging, so I went with him, busying myself getting a glass of water for Pia.

We heard Rory say, "Wow, Pia, I like the braid thing with the rhinestones. And, uh, Ms. Jackson, that's a mighty fine tiara you've got there. I'm sure Shane's Granny would be thrilled to see you wearing those."

Shane and I stuck our heads around the corner. Pia's face was blotchy, but she smiled at Rory. Her hair was braided into a crown around her head, and Manny had woven what was probably a sparkly necklace into it.

Shane said, "Wow is right. You both look amazing."

I made toast and warmed up the bacon in the microwave while Shane fixed scrambled eggs for Pia and Ms. Jackson, who'd decided they were hungry again.

When we sat back down, I said, "Uh, so, Rory, can you tell us a little about your Medium abilities?" I didn't want to bring up Pia's mother, so I stayed away from anything to do with the ghosts themselves.

He shrugged, turning his coffee cup in his hands. "I've been able to see and speak with ghosts from when I was a little kid. I get it from my mom; she could do it too."

Manny opened his mouth, but Rory pointed at him and said, "Not the time."

Shane leaned back in his chair. "Not the time for what?" His tone was borderline hostile.

Rory slid his eyes to Pia, then he sighed. "Fine. My mom was a professional Medium. My dad came from money, and my grandparents decided my mom was a con artist. So when

Mom and Dad got married, Grandfather disowned my dad and never spoke to him again."

Shane grimaced. "I'm sorry. It must've been tough."

Rory held up his hand in a *stop* gesture aimed toward the living room. "My parents died in a car accident when I was sixteen, and I went to live with my grandparents. I'd never met them before, but I knew better than to let on that I had my mom's gifts." He made a face. "That lasted until my grandmother passed away." He gave a wry smile. "Grandfather found out about my gifts at the same time he realized I was in a polyamorous relationship. He disowned me."

He glanced over his shoulder toward the living room. "Grandfather would like me to tell you how once he passed away, he realized not only were my Medium gifts real, but he finally understood that people are all the same on the inside, so it doesn't matter who anyone loves."

I suppressed a shiver at the thought of ghosts in the room with us. Through the bond I felt Shane's discomfort as well.

Manny snorted. "A little too late to change the will though."

Rory toasted him with his coffee cup. "True, but he's been giving me stock tips ever since, and that's benefited you as well, *chico*."

Manny stuck his tongue out at Rory, and Pia giggled.

I asked, "Um, how did the ghosts help you rescue Pia last night?"

He frowned. "Pia, do you want to hear this?"

"Yes, please." Then she bit into her toast.

Rory nodded gravely. "Okay. I was very brave, as you will see. Truly a hero." His blond hair fell over his forehead. He was adorable. "It all started after I got home from work last night. I sat down on the couch to, uh, do some internet research, but I fell asleep. The next thing I knew...."

Rory's story was enthralling, even if some of it was obviously exaggerated or made humorous for Pia's benefit. I couldn't take my eyes off him.

"And so Grandfather, Mercy, and Garfield found a ghost who knew Shane here was the District Monitor, and she told us how to find his house." He smiled at Shane, and I thrilled to see the warmth in his gaze. Rory was polyamorous. Could he possibly be attracted to both of us? Or was it only Shane?

I glanced at Shane, but he was looking at Pia. I wasn't getting anything through the bond. Had he learned how to block it?

Fuck.

CAL'S CAMPAIGN COMPENDIUM

THE CAMPAIGN

"The campaign" is obviously one of the D&D-derived terms we've adopted over the years, and it has evolved to have two main meanings.

First, it is a generic term for the world of magic beings that exists alongside the mundane human world. The campaign is made up of Wonders and magic carriers, as well as a very small number of humans who are aware of their existence

But "the campaign" also refers to the efforts to maintain secrecy around Wonders and magic, for if humans learned of their existence, the results would be catastrophic.

(See also the entry for <u>Non-Player Character</u>.)

CHAPTER 10
SHANE

I noticed the way Rory was smiling at me. How could I not? And, being a Cassandra, he probably didn't realize the way his magic was reaching for mine.

That's right. It wasn't just Ellis he was attracted to. And how many times did he have to mention he was polyamorous? Too bad. I'd never had polyamorous inclinations, so nothing would be happening.

Except Ellis kept flirting with Rory, even though last night I'd told him it upset me.

Yeah, I was jealous. Pissed. Butthurt. All of the above.

But dealing with that would have to wait.

I turned to Ellis. "You said you texted Greg and Cal? Why don't we call them?"

He glanced at Pia and Manny. "Right now?"

I shrugged. "This concerns Pia, and Manny's involved already." I looked at the man in question. "Unless you'd rather go home?"

Manny's grin took over his thin, almost elfin face. Though I'd always imagined Elves to be blond and Nordic-looking rather than dark-haired and Latino. "Oh, no. No way. I have no idea what's going on, but I'm here for it!"

I shrugged. My give-a-shitter was broken. I'd get Pia taken care of and that fucker Randolph Chamberlain put out of business. Everything else could go fuck itself.

I pulled out my phone and dialed Greg. He answered on the second ring.

"Hi. Sounds like a lot's been going on down there in Houston."

"Yeah. Is Cal with you?" Why was I even asking? They'd only been bonded a couple of weeks. Of course Cal was with him.

"He is."

Cal said, "Hi, Shane."

I put the call on speaker. "Hi. Everybody, this is Greg Shaw, who's the District Monitor for Central Texas, and Cal Steadham, who's a Seer and Greg's partner. Guys, let me tell you who we have on this end. It's me and Ellis, plus Ms. Jackson. Then we have Pia, who's a lovely young dryad lady."

"Hi, Pia," they said together.

"And Rory, the Medium I think Ellis told you about."

They greeted Rory.

"Then we have Manny, who is Rory's best friend, and it turns out was also my grandmother's caretaker a few years ago. He's a pediatric nurse and Ms. Jackson has taken a liking to him."

Cal laughed. "I guess you've had quite the introduction to the campaign, Manny. Welcome."

I saw Rory open his mouth to ask what the campaign was, but Ellis could explain it to him later. "Rory, can you please run through how you came to rescue Pia last night for Greg and Cal?"

He launched into the tale again, this time leaving out the funny bits he'd tried to distract Pia with earlier.

When he wound down, Greg said, "Pia, I'm so sorry to hear about your mother's death. And we heard you don't have any other family left, but are there any dryad friends you'd be comfortable staying with?"

She reached out and clutched Ms. Jackson's fur in one hand as she shook her head. "No. Mama moved us to Vancouver to get away from her family. We hadn't made any friends yet when, uh, it happened."

Greg's voice gentled. "I understand. That must've been awful. I'm so sorry it happened to you. Um, we'd like to introduce you to some dryads in the area. Do you think you'd want to meet them?"

Pia's eyes went wide, and she looked at Rory with a pleading expression. He said, "I'll go with you. If you don't like them, you don't have to stay. I promise."

She still looked on the verge of tears, so I said, "We'll all go with you, okay? Including Ms. Jackson here. They'd never let you live with a bunch of mean people." I was supposed to go back to work tomorrow, but Ricky would just have to deal with me being gone a few more days.

Then I mentally smacked myself. I couldn't be more than a few feet from Ellis. Neither of us were going back to work tomorrow, maybe not even next week. Fuck. Well, something else to deal with later.

Ellis nodded at my suggestion, and Ms. Jackson butted their head into Pia's shoulder. She finally smiled. "Okay."

"Great," Greg said. "I talked to my mom—she helps out Wonders who've lost their homes or whatever, for those of you who don't know her. She recommended the dryads you mentioned, Ellis. She said they might not have any kids now, but they had some who went off to college ten or so years ago."

I frowned. That didn't seem the best environment for a traumatized thirteen-year-old. I wanted to ask about therapy services for Wonders in their area, but I'd wait until Pia was somewhere else.

Manny was making faces at Rory across the table, and Rory shrugged. He mouthed, *Later*. I wondered if Manny was having similar thoughts to mine.

Cal cleared his throat. "Shane and Ellis, have you by any chance briefed Rory on the situation with the vampires?"

Rory and Manny stopped their silent bickering and gaped at us. "Vampires?" Rory sputtered. "I mean...." He looked over his shoulder. "None of the ghosts know about any vampires."

How the fuck many ghosts were in my house?

"Yeah." Cal's voice was wry. "You know the legend about vampires getting in your head and making you do their bidding or forget stuff?"

Rory scrunched up his forehead. "Kind of?"

"Well, turns out that legend has some basis in truth. We recently discovered vampires are real. They've been, uh, attacking Wonders—those are what we call paranormal people like dryads. We think the vampires have been messing with people's minds for centuries and making us all completely certain they're not real."

On either side of Pia, Manny put his arm around her shoulders and Ms. Jackson leaned into her.

"Shit." Rory's eyes widened. "Sorry, Pia. Um, that's scary."

"Yeah." Cal sighed. "We need information about the vampires. Badly. Rory, we were hoping you could speak to the ghost of the most recent Wonder who was attacked. His name was Thomas Baird, and he died three weeks ago."

Rory shrugged. "Sure. Where is he?"

No one spoke for a moment. Eventually Greg said, "What do you mean? His body?"

Rory rolled his eyes. "No, his ghost. Is he haunting the place he died or something?"

"Uh. We don't know?"

Rory rubbed his face. "Okay, here's how it works. I can talk to ghosts if they're in front of me, but I can't call them to me if I can't see them. It's not like I have a ghost dog whistle or something. And if they've moved on to the other side, then forget it. They're not coming back. But if they're around, or if we can find the ghosts of friends of theirs who might know where they are, then it's doable."

There was another pause on the other end of the call. "Thomas Baird lived and died in Pflugerville. Would you be willing to stop there on your way to take Pia to meet the dryads?"

"If it's on the way, sure."

Ellis nodded. "Those dryads are in Mineral Wells, which is a little west of Ft. Worth. We'll just take the long way to get there."

Pia looked relieved.

Manny interjected, "Wait, is it safe for Pia to go there? Are you sure the vampires are gone?"

"Yes," Greg said. "They never stay in the same place. We're hoping Thomas Baird's ghost has information on where they went after they, uh, attacked him."

I made sure Pia was looking the other way and I mouthed, *They took his body*, at Rory.

He grimaced. "Okay, that makes sense. Sure, if everyone else is on board, we can make a road trip out of it."

CAL'S CAMPAIGN COMPENDIUM

VAMPIRE

**Type**: _Vampire_

**Class**: _Wonder (assumed)_

**Overview**: _We have very little information about actual vampires, as they were believed worldwide to be a myth up until very recently. Only four vampires have been verified to exist, and one of those is most likely deceased. The vampires can pass for human, but they can also exhibit glowing eyes and produce fangs._

Skills:

- _Can move at a faster-than-human speed_
- _Can generate or turn into fog (more data is needed to determine which)_
- _Can manipulate another person's memories and possibly compel behavior or thoughts_
- _Difficult to kill. The one friendly vampire told us that cutting off a vampire's head is the only way to make sure they "stay dead"._

**Requirements**: _Due to the attacks that have happened over the past few decades, we are assuming vampires feed on the blood of_

Wonders, but we don't have enough data to be certain. The attacks have occurred in clusters every ten or so years, so it's possible vampires don't need to feed all the time, or they go into some sort of hibernation between kills.

CHAPTER 11
RORY

Manny decided he wanted to come with us to Pflugerville and Mineral Wells, which was a relief. Pia had really clicked with him, and I could use his feedback on whether leaving her with the dryads was the right choice. It probably was, because what did I know about the needs of teenagers in general, much less teen dryads?

Except my gut kept telling me to let her stay in Houston.

Manny and I drove to our respective homes to pack for an overnight trip, and I was picking him up on my way back to Shane's house. Luckily the Range Rover SE Hybrid with the long wheelbase I'd bought on impulse last month was plenty big enough for four adult men, one small girl, and a tiger. Ellis had assured me that Ms. Jackson could make themself look like a stuffed tiger for the car ride, which the highway patrol would no doubt appreciate.

I never did change into the clothes Manny had picked up for me. It was easier to take a shower at my apartment and get dressed there. I threw another set of clothes, some boxers to sleep in, and my toiletry kit into a backpack, and I was set.

Oh, except I had to deal with the little matter of my job. My boss had been less than pleased at my last-minute call-out for today, and no doubt another call-out would piss him off further, but he'd live. I sent a quick email that I was feeling worse, and it must be some sort of stomach bug. I'd be out tomorrow for sure, but I'd try to make it in Thursday or Friday.

Or maybe I just wouldn't go back. The thought lingered seductively in my brain as I tossed my backpack over my shoulder and left the apartment. I didn't love the job, but I was good at it, and it was certainly lucrative. But Grandfather's illicit help with investments was starting to mean I wouldn't need a regular job anymore.

But that was a problem for another day. Today I had to survive being trapped in a vehicle with Ellis and Shane. Ellis had flirted with me a little. It was good for my ego, but I could tell Shane wasn't on board, and I didn't want to come between them. My version of polyamory required full consent from all parties involved.

Too bad. Those two tripped every one of my wires.

I was so busy imagining scenarios where Shane had a change of heart about me, I didn't notice the stranger leaning against my SUV until I was only ten or so feet away. "Oh. Can I help you?"

Any other day I'd have been less abrupt in my tone. He was stunning. Thin—a little too thin, honestly—and taller than I was. He had gleaming amber eyes and auburn hair falling almost to his shoulders.

He didn't respond, just walked over to me. It was hard to tell in the dim light of the parking garage, but I thought I caught a glimpse of a sort of sparkle around him. Was he involved in Shane and Ellis' world?

I opened my mouth to ask, but nothing came out.

He stopped with only about a foot between us. I wanted to look away from his laser stare, but I couldn't make myself.

"Hey, there, Rory. I'm Simon. Can I touch your hand?"

I almost held out my hand in reflex, but I managed to get out, "Why?" just in time.

His eyes lit up. Like, literally they glowed. I wanted to step back. I wanted to look away.

I couldn't.

"You have great willpower. Color me impressed. I need to hold your hand to find out if we're compatible to be mates."

"I'm sorry, mates?"

"Oh, yeah. A bonded couple. Once I'm mated, I'll get the acceleration of my abilities I need to help complete my mission. A Seer told me my mate will be a human with psychic skills, so when I found out about you, I came right over." He gave a self-deprecating chuckle. "Sorry. You have places to be. I don't get to talk to as many people as I'd like, so I tend to go on and on."

His eyes seemed bigger, like whirlpools I was spinning around in. I felt him take my hand. I was pretty sure I should be scared, but I couldn't seem to feel anything.

Simon made a disappointed sound. "Turns out you've already got a couple of romantic connections started. Congratulations."

His phone beeped. He pulled it out of his pocket, and he *tsked*. "They're on the move. Time for me to go." His eyes drilled into mine again. "Tell Cal he needs to call a vision about the next victim. You'll remember to do this."

I blinked. "Okay."

"Good." He smiled. Damn, he was pretty. Too bad it was a cold and scary beauty. "Have fun on your road trip, even though your new friends won't find what they're looking for. Still, if those are your future mates, you need to spend time with them anyway." He looked down at our joined hands, then back up at me. "Hey, can I ask a little favor?"

I snapped out of my reverie. Dammit, I didn't have time to stand around daydreaming about... whatever.

Rubbing my wrist, I resumed my walk to the car. I was lucky I'd only gotten the one bug bite after spending the night outdoors.

———

After filling the SUV with gas, I picked up Manny and drove back to Shane's house, pulling up to the curb right out front. The potted plant from last night was on the front porch along with another potted plant of a different variety. I thought I remembered seeing it in Shane's back yard.

The front door was unlocked, so I just knocked as I opened it. Ellis was standing in the living room with his hands on his hips. He gave us a wave, but then he went back to staring at Shane, who was slumped on the couch with his phone pressed to his ear.

"I'm sorry, but I can't. I told you, I have a family emergency."

I couldn't make out the words on the other end of the call, but I could hear the shouting. Damn. His boss might be more of an asshole than mine. I walked over to Ellis, with Manny trailing behind me. "Where's Pia?" I whispered.

He pointed toward the guest room. "Taking a bath. Ms. Jackson is guarding the door for her."

I glanced at Manny. "Do we need to stop and get her some new clothes?"

He shrugged. "She says no. Shane found her a couple more of his granny's outfits, and she seemed to get a kick out of them."

"Smart girl," observed Dimi from near my left elbow. I stifled the impulse to jump and curse. "Unlike my grandson," she sniffed. "He should've quit that job years ago. Do you know he barely makes more than people who work in fast food?"

What? I'd thought Shane was a landscape architect. I shot him a worried look. The amount of grief his manager was giving him was more than he should've had to deal with, especially for that little money.

Dimi crossed her arms and pursed her lips as she regarded her grandson. I wanted to go over and... help him somehow. Provide comfort, maybe? I looked at Ellis. Why wasn't he sitting on the couch next to his partner?

Shane clenched his fist. "I don't know what to tell you, Ricky. If you have to fire me, you have to fire me. I gotta go."

He hung up and tossed his phone onto the coffee table. He leaned forward, putting his elbows on his knees and his head in his hands.

Ellis took a hesitant step forward, his arms going up and out, but he stopped as if unsure of his welcome.

Pia and Ms. Jackson came into the living room. Pia had left her hair in the sparkly braid crown Manny had fixed for her earlier, but she'd changed into calf-length pants my own grandmother used to call "pedal pushers". They were lime green and she'd topped them with a bright orange t-shirt that had a sequined cat on the front. On her feet were white sneakers, and she was holding a gold metallic tote bag dotted with fake jewels and with "Las Vegas" stenciled across it.

Manny said, "Pia, that is one fab outfit. Did you pick it out yourself?"

She grinned and nodded, petting Ms. Jackson, who still sported the tiara.

Shane put on a fake smile and said, "I guess we're ready to get on the road."

———

The potted plants on the front porch came with us. We set Pia up in the third row of seats with Ms. Jackson next to her in their stuffed tiger form and the potted plants on the floorboards by her feet. Ellis produced an iPad and offered it to Pia with the comment, "Just don't open the Kindle app, please."

Pia had wrinkled her nose and fervently agreed.

We'd loaded everyone's overnight bags in the back, and then I'd gotten in the driver's seat. But Ellis and Shane had performed an awkward shuffle next to the car, neither willing to commit to where they wanted to sit. After watching this for almost a full minute, Manny had thrown up his hands and pushed Shane at the front passenger seat and Ellis at the second row of seats. Manny got in next to Ellis and informed me we were ready to go.

Manny, Pia, and I were the only ones who spoke the first hour of the trip. Eventually Ellis started participating, telling me and Manny all about Elves and magic carriers, but Shane stared out the window and didn't look at the rest of us. He also didn't look at his phone, which kept beeping every so often with text messages.

Pflugerville, where we were meeting Greg and Cal, was near Austin, about two and a half hours from Houston. We stopped for lunch in Brenham, which was roughly halfway. Manny tried to get Pia to join him in checking out the Blue Bell Ice Cream factory, but Ms. Jackson was the only one interested, and none of us wanted to deal with *that*, so Manny didn't go on his excursion. Shane perked up a little after he ate, and he even engaged Ellis in a little conversation.

Seeing them interact with each other, even such a small amount, made me warm inside. I didn't want to be the cause of tension between the two of them. And, to be completely honest, if Shane had seemed open to having me join them, I'd have done it in a heartbeat, even if it was only for a night.

Because I *was* attracted to them. To both of them. I hadn't spent any time with either man one-on-one, but just being near Ellis made me smile. He was so calm and positive, never demanding anything for himself, but there to help everyone else. But who helped Ellis other than Shane? Who took care of him?

Shane, he was a tougher nut to crack. He was gorgeous, no doubt about it. And at first, when he'd been so focused on helping Pia, he'd come across as this take-charge guy—the kind who usually made my dick stand up. But when he was dealing with his boss, he seemed smaller, less confident. It made me want to hug him and tell him everything would be okay.

But that wasn't in the cards today. Or any other day, apparently.

Ms. Jackson had had to stay in the car when the rest of us had gone into the restaurant. We'd gotten their lunch to go, and they scarfed down the grilled cheese sandwich and fries before we'd even left the parking lot. Then they decided they were tired of being a stuffed tiger and had become a live tiger again, lying down across the seats with their head in Pia's lap and watching her play a game on the iPad.

It was about 1:30pm when the signs told us we were almost to Pflugerville. Everyone had been quiet for the past several minutes, so I tapped Shane on the leg. "Where am I going from here?"

He jumped in his seat. "Uh, sorry. It's a cemetery. Let me check." He opened his phone and winced. Then he schooled his expression and scrolled. "Here we go. Forest Rest Memorial Park. I'll pull up the directions."

The guy had died in a cemetery? Ouch.

In a moment the navigation app announced we should take the next exit, and our destination was twelve minutes away.

Ellis called from the back seat, "I texted Greg and Cal to let them know we're almost there."

"Thanks." There was something I'd wanted to ask Cal, or maybe tell him, but it was escaping me. Oh, well. I'd remember eventually.

"Greg says they're waiting for us."

Manny twisted around in his seat to look at Pia. "*Chica*, if you don't want to get out of the car when we get to the cemetery, I can hang in here with you."

I glanced in the rearview mirror. She was frowning down at Ms. Jackson's head. Finally she said, "I've never been to a cemetery. Can Ms. Jackson get out with us?"

Ellis said, "I don't think the cemetery allows tigers. But this would be a good time for them to practice another form. Like a big dog or something?"

Shane cocked his head. "Irish Wolfhound?"

I offered, "Mastiff?"

Manny said, "Saint Bernard!"

Pia ducked down so I couldn't see her in the mirror for a moment. Then she popped up. "Ms. Jackson says it'll be a surprise!"

"Oh, god," Shane muttered beside me. "As long as it's not a six-foot tall Chihuahua."

I laughed, and he gave me a wry smile. I said in a low voice, "Yeah, the hedgehog was... unsettling."

He gave an exaggerated shudder. "I hope they never do that again."

"You said Ms. Jackson started out as an inanimate object? How...?" I waved my hand toward the back seat.

Shane blew out a breath. Then he turned so everyone else could hear him too. "Ms. Jackson, I'm going to tell the short version of your story if it's okay with you."

They made a weird soft yowl, which Shane seemed to take as assent. "They aren't sure what they were originally, but they're definitely from the Elven dimension. Somehow they came to Earth and ended up in the book room at TWIST, which is the Wonder rescue organization Greg's mom runs."

"Okay."

"Greg and Cal were searching the book room for information on vampires, and they came across a statue of a cat. When Cal dusted the statue off, they changed into something else; I can't remember what."

Ellis leaned forward. "I think it was a typewriter. Then a toilet seat."

Manny and I laughed.

"Eventually someone suggested they become a Ouija board so they could communicate, and they said they were called Ms. Jackson. This, uh, larger and more animated version came about when Cal was experimenting with his magic, and he accidentally gave it all to Ms. Jackson. It was, what, three weeks ago?"

I shot him a startled glance. They'd only been able to walk around for three weeks? Before I could ask for more information, the navigation app directed us down a side street, and then we were cutting though a subdivision. The houses ended and the cemetery appeared on our right. I drove through the huge wrought iron gates, and for the second time in less than twenty-four hours I was in a cemetery.

This one was wide open, with trees and tall grave markers here and there, but mostly grass and gentle little hills. There was a wall around most of the cemetery, with the subdivision bordering it on one side and some trees on the other. I didn't see any other visitors.

Shane directed me to follow the drive until we got to the far end near the trees. A silver SUV was parked along the curb, and two men, who I assumed were Greg and Cal, were standing next to it.

Ms. Jackson's head rose up behind Ellis's seat, and they made a weird growling-yowling sound. Ellis turned to look at them and chuckled. "You miss Greg and Cal already? You just saw them yesterday."

Both men turned to watch as I pulled in behind their vehicle. Shane hopped out and started to walk over to them, but then he stopped mid-step. Ellis, who hadn't left the car yet, grabbed his chest and made a coughing sound.

Manny had opened his door to exit, but he whirled around

and said, "What's the matter? Are you choking? Chest pain? What is it?"

Ellis waved him off. "I'm okay," he gasped out. "Shane and I can't get very far from each other."

Shane walked back toward the car, and Ellis sighed in relief. "That's better." He looked at Manny. "I'm fine, I promise."

Manny frowned. Shane opened Ellis' door. "Sorry."

I got out of the car and helped Manny slide his seat forward so Pia and Ms. Jackson could get out.

"What the fuck was that?" Manny whispered.

I shrugged. "They just got bonded? Which sounds like magically married, I guess? They can't be very far apart from each other right now."

Pia hopped out, landing on both feet at once. "Bonding is more permanent than marriage. Can't you see the bond between them?" She tapped right below her sternum.

I scrunched up my face. "No? Should I be able to?"

Then Ms. Jackson exited the car. They were a tiger as they emerged, but on the way to the ground they shimmered and a very, very large pig landed gracefully on the pavement. They had a black head and shoulders, and their rear half was white with black spots. They still wore the rhinestone tiara they'd sported as a tiger, and over their back was a red blanket which read "Service Animal".

I suppressed a laugh. "Um, Ms. Jackson, that's a, uh, great choice." What the hell else was I supposed to say?

Pia clapped her hands before petting Ms. Jackson's neck. The pig's back was higher than her waist.

"Okay," Manny said. "Let's go meet these people and then we can walk around."

We started toward the front of the SUV. Grandfather appeared beside me. "The girl looks better today."

"Thanks to you." I glanced around. "Where are your friends?"

"Not sure about Dimi. She was here a minute ago. Garfield and Mercy decided to watch Randolph and Hugo. They're supposed to check in with me every few days."

I raised my eyebrows. "You're in charge of the investigation?"

He scoffed. "I didn't run a company for decades for nothing, boy."

I was grinning when I walked up to stand next to Ellis. One of the men, the slimmer, model-quality gorgeous one, was saying, "I've never seen a bond do that, but I'm no expert."

The heavyset guy, who was wearing a t-shirt saying, "Shh... No one cares", glanced at me, then he smiled at Ms. Jackson. He turned back to Shane and Ellis and scowled at the couple of feet of air between them. "I just started being able to see bonds, so I don't have a lot to compare it to, but that doesn't look comfortable. How does it feel?"

Ellis crossed his arms. "Like any minute the wheel will stop spinning."

Shane nodded. "Or like the magic threw its back out and needs someone to crack it and get everything aligned."

"Uh huh. And what's with the way you're standing?" He waved a hand between them. "You're acting like you're acquaintances at best. A bond requires consent and intent to form. Are you regretting it? Is that why it's... unbalanced?"

Shane rubbed the back of his neck. "We... it was kind of the heat of the moment. And we've been arguing some."

I saw Ellis' eyebrows pop up, but he didn't comment.

The big guy pointed at them. "Maybe figure out your relationship and then let's see what happens to the bond?"

Shane and Ellis both sagged in defeat. Whatever fix they were looking for, they weren't going to get it here.

The handsome guy turned to the rest of us. "Hi, I'm Greg and this is Cal."

We all introduced ourselves, and Pia said, "And this is Ms. Jackson. They learned a new form today!"

Cal grinned. "Much better than the hedgehog, Ms. Jackson. Good job."

They trotted forward and butted their head between Cal and Greg, who automatically started petting them. Those two, who'd bonded a few weeks ago, stood so they were always touching or almost touching. Shane and Ellis rarely got that close.

Shane's grandmother popped up beside me, and I flinched. "Shit! Please don't do that."

She waved this away. "You need to toughen up. We're ghosts. Scaring people is what we do."

I rolled my eyes and said to my corporeal companions, "Sorry. Ghost."

Dimi pointed back toward the main part of the cemetery. "The other ghosts here, they saw the imp get taken away."

"Imp?" I looked at Cal and Greg. "We're here about an imp?"

Both of them smiled in what appeared to be relief. Greg said, "Yes. Thomas Baird, is his ghost here?"

Dimi scoffed. "Wasn't dead when they took him, so how could his ghost be here?"

I blinked and turned to Greg. "He wasn't dead when they took him."

Greg and Cal gaped at me. Greg said, "But his connection to me was severed. Death is the only way that can happen." He looked at Cal. "Right?"

Cal threw up his hands. "Why are you asking me?"

"Right. Sorry." He pulled out his phone. "Excuse me, I'm going to see if anyone else knows."

I turned back to Dimi. Several ghosts ranged behind her. Some were in modern dress, and some looked like they were from much earlier time periods. Most of them were staring at Ms. Jackson, who was nosing at some flowers with Manny and Pia a few yards away. Shane was heading over to join them, and Ellis wandered in the same direction, looking glum.

I addressed the group of ghosts. "Did any of you follow the, uh, vampires?" I had trouble even saying the word. How did I get to be here, talking about vampires, driving around with a dryad and a... whatever Ms. Jackson was?

The ghosts all shook their heads. One guy in the back shouted, "If they done that to an imp, they mighta been able to do it to us!" He looked like a cowboy, complete with hat and a shirt with silver snaps on it.

I held my hands out, palms up. "What exactly happened?" Cal came to stand beside me.

A woman in a power suit with large shoulder pads glided forward. "We didn't know anything was wrong until the imp came over the wall." She pointed at the stone wall separating the cemetery from the forest. "Three of those... well, I guess they were vampires as you say, but we didn't know what they were at the time. None of us had ever seen magic like they had. Anyway, they came over the wall after him. One of them jumped from the top of the wall and *landed* on him." Several of the ghosts winced and nodded. "He didn't move after that. The vampires lifted him up, and all his connections...." She looked around at the other ghosts. Then she shrugged. "Disappeared."

"Like they drained his magic?" Could that happen? They were vampires after all.

The ghosts all shook their heads. The cowboy who'd spoken before came forward. He said, "The magic didn't go nowhere. It was like they chopped off anything going outside him." He made a slashing motion with his hand. "Cut him off from anyone else."

I wasn't sure how connections worked, but that sounded awful. "Okay. Then what happened?"

The first woman said, "They carried him back over the wall. We didn't follow, in case they could see us."

A young guy, probably about sixteen years old, said, "I wish we'd gone after them, though. They didn't notice us standing around. It would've been fine." He threw a frustrated glare at the others.

A new man zipped up. He hadn't been with the group up until now. He was dressed like he ran a saloon in an old Western movie, with a white shirt, string tie, and a vest. His hair was slicked back, and he even had big sideburns and a mustache waxed into curls at the ends. He positioned himself between me and the teenager. "You're new here, Ethan. You'll learn it's safer not to meddle with magical beings. Look at this one. A Medium." He pointed at me. "Sure, he's being all nice now, but he could suck out our energy or rip us into shreds with just a thought if he wanted to."

My mouth dropped open. "What? No. I can't do that."

The man sneered at me. "Seen your kind afore this. All, *Tell me what I want to know or no more afterlife for you!*" He spat on the ground—or appeared to. "Or drain us of what life we have left so we're only a remnant, doomed to nothing more than walking through the same room over and over for eternity!"

He ballooned in size, looming over me like an old timey Incredible Hulk. "We're done here! Get out!"

CAL'S CAMPAIGN COMPENDIUM

COMBAT MODE, ALSO KNOWN AS HUNTER MODE

Overview: _Certain magic carriers, such as District Monitors and Hunters themselves, can, when needed, go into a state called Combat Mode or Hunter Mode. This gives them heightened senses and faster reflexes than the baseline for their type of magic carrier._

While the specific attributes of Combat Mode can vary slightly by individual and type of magic carrier, overall they include:

- _Hyperfocus_
- _Even greater enhancement to the senses_
- _Improved reflexes, speed, and strength_
- _Night vision_

CHAPTER 12
ELLIS

Rory held up his hands and took a step back. "It's not something I know how to do or want to know how to do. You're safe from me." What the hell were the ghosts saying to him? I looked around again, wishing I could see them too. I wanted to intervene and tell them Rory was a good person.

Once it had been obvious the ghosts were telling Rory about Thomas Baird's death—or rather his capture—the rest of us had gathered around to wait for him to finish. I was leery about Pia hearing what had happened, particularly now since it seemed to involve kidnapping, but Ms. Jackson would alert us if she got too upset.

"I promise I'm just here to ask some questions, but you don't have to answer." After a few seconds Rory said, "Right. I swear. You can ask these ghosts here." Finally he relaxed and let his hands drop. "Can you think of anything else you noticed about the vampires or what they did to the imp?"

Apparently the answer was *no*.

"Got it. Thank you very much. My name is Rory Blackbourne. If you think of anything else we might need to know, or if someone gives you trouble like this gentleman said—" He gestured off to his left. "—come find me."

Then he cocked his head like he was listening again. He turned. "Ms. Jackson, the ghosts here want to know what you are. Do you mind if I tell them what Shane told us?"

Ms. Jackson made a shrugging movement and trotted over to stand next to Rory, who turned back to face in exactly the same direction Ms. Jackson was looking. Could they see ghosts?

Rory patted Ms. Jackson's back. "They were originally an artifact from the Elven dimension, but they were given some extra magic, and now they can change their shape."

Probably as good a summary as any.

Rory nodded some more, then thanked the ghosts before joining those of us who were still alive. "It sounds like the vampires didn't kill the imp." He relayed what the ghosts had told him about Thomas Baird's magic getting "cut off".

We all looked at each other uneasily. Pia piped up, "So the guy might still be alive?"

Greg ran his hand through his luxurious hair. "Good question." He turned to Rory. "If Thomas died later, would his ghost return to his house, do you think? Or would it stay where he was killed or buried?"

Rory spread out his hands. "There's no way to know. It varies by the individual. He might also have crossed over, in which case we'll never be able to talk to him."

I asked, "How far away did he live?"

"Only a couple of miles from here." Greg appeared to be hesitating to ask, but I could tell he wanted to.

I raised my eyebrows at the rest of the crew who'd driven from Houston. "Want to go check it out just to make sure he's not there? We have time. We don't have to meet the dryads until later."

Pia scowled, but everyone else nodded.

After checking with Rory to make sure nothing else could be learned here, we all headed back to the cars. Greg and Cal would lead us to Thomas Baird's house.

A short drive later we pulled up in front of a small bungalow in an older subdivision. The house was neatly kept except the grass was overgrown. When we got out, Greg muttered something about a lawn service and made a note in his phone. Was he managing the missing guy's estate?

Rory stood next to the car staring at the house. He said, "Thanks," and turned to Greg and Cal. "No ghosts here."

They both looked startled. Greg asked, "You can tell so quickly?"

Rory chuckled. "Me? No. My grandfather did a pass through the house looking for ghosts, and he says there aren't any. But the house next door has one, and that ghost hasn't seen Thomas Baird's ghost."

Cal made a face. "Well, shit."

Greg rubbed the back of his neck. "Yeah, I'm not really sure what to do from here. We have no idea where the vampires are or who they'll go after next."

Rory sucked in a breath, snapped his fingers, and pointed at Cal. "That's what I wanted to tell you! You need to call a vision about the next victim."

We all went still. Cal said, "I do?"

Rory frowned. "Yes?"

"A ghost told you that?"

He shook his head. "I don't really know why, but you need to call a vision."

I asked, "Uh, do Mediums have psychic powers?"

Rory threw me a horrified look. "I hope not! The ghosts are plenty."

Cal walked toward him, looking concerned. "Rory, when did you first realize you needed to tell me that?"

Rory's forehead creased. "I don't know. Um, I remember thinking I needed to tell you something when we were driving to the cemetery, but I couldn't remember what it was." He crossed his arms. "That's weird though, right? Why would that even occur to me?"

I wanted to go put my arm around him, but Shane was too far away and I'd have to get him to come with me.

Cal and Greg exchanged a long look, then Cal said, "Rory, at any point recently have you found yourself sort of... standing around with no memory of why?"

Rory's face went gray, and his eyes looked huge as they stared at Cal. "Um, when I went home to pack a bag. I was in the parking garage, about to leave." His voice went higher. "*Why?*"

Fuck it, Shane would have to come with me. I walked over to Rory. Fortunately Shane started walking too, so we didn't have to play tug-of-war. I put one arm around Rory's shoulders and my other hand on his bicep. He was stiff with tension, so I felt like a jerk when I couldn't help noticing the woodsy scent of his body wash and the defined muscles under my hands. Shane must have been blocking the bond, because I couldn't tell what he was feeling. And I was a jerk again for being relieved about it.

Cal was kind enough to delay his explanation until I was in position. Maybe he wasn't such a hardass after all.

"Rory," Cal said gently. "Shane or Ellis may have told you. One of the vampires—the only one we've actually spoken to—appears to be trying to stop the vampires who've been attacking the Wonders."

"Okay?"

"We've only interacted with him once, um, that any of us remember." Rory sucked in a harsh breath, and Cal nodded. "He said something to me indicating he and I had met before, but I have no memory of it." He paused, and said carefully, "What I do remember is going for coffee one morning about a week earlier. I was walking from my car to the door of the bakery, and for some reason I stopped in the middle of the sidewalk. I snapped out of it when someone opened the door, and I felt the need to immediately go wash my hands, but I didn't know why. We think the vampires can manipulate memories."

Rory looked down at his hands. Then he tore out of my arms and rushed over to the shrubs lining the front of Thomas Baird's house, where he began vomiting up his lunch.

I started to follow, but Shane caught my arm. "Here." He handed me a water bottle that Greg had passed to him.

Ms. Jackson rushed over to Rory, and he patted their head in between heaves. When it seemed like he'd thrown up everything he could, he leaned against the corner of the house with his head on his arm. I cracked open the water bottle and passed it to him. "This should help." Shane's hand reached over my shoulder with a bunch of napkins.

Rory took them. "Thank you." His breath was coming in pants, and his face was a mess of tears and snot. I wanted to hug him again, but instead I just stood nearby as he wet the napkins and wiped his face. Then Shane passed over a doggie poop bag, of all things. I opened the bag and held it out so Rory could dispose of the used napkins, and I handed the bag back to Shane. Rory swished some of the water around in his mouth and spat it out.

After swallowing a few more sips of the water, he closed his eyes, pressed the bottle to his forehead and said, "I remember noticing I felt like I had a bug bite on my wrist."

He held out his free hand, fingers fisted and palm up. I took it in mine, and a chill went through my entire body. He had what appeared to be the healing remains of a small cut about an inch long, right on top of the vein that ran down to his hand.

"Fuck," Shane whispered from behind my shoulder.

I looked around for Cal and Greg, who'd been hanging back, probably trying to give Rory some privacy while he threw up. I jerked my head for them to get their asses over here.

Manny had taken Pia back to the SUV, thank goodness.

I showed Cal and Greg the cut on Rory's wrist. "He thought he had a bug bite."

Rory, his eyes still closed, nodded.

Cal put his hand on Rory's back. "Did you feel dizzy or anything afterward? Thirsty or hungry?"

Rory shook his head. "No." He opened his eyes. "What does that mean?"

Cal patted Rory's back and moved to stand next to Greg again. "Probably only that he didn't take very much blood."

I winced. Cal could've been a little more diplomatic. Rory looked like he was trying not to get sick again. I turned his hand in mine and interlaced our fingers. He shuddered, so I pulled him into a hug.

"Thanks," he said, his voice catching on a sob. "I don't know why I'm so upset. I just feel...."

"Violated?" Shane said softly from behind me. "Like someone else had more control over your body than you did?"

"Yeah." Rory tightened his arms around me. Then he lifted his head and said, "It's not your fault, Grandfather." He grimaced. "He's blaming himself because he didn't come with me to the apartment."

Shane put his hand on the small of my back, well below Rory's arms. It might've been the first time he'd voluntarily touched me all day. I was getting concern for Rory through the bond, but not much else. "I'm glad he wasn't there. We don't know what the vampires are capable of. If they can take away your memories, who's to say they can't see ghosts? Maybe harm them in some way?"

Rory nodded. "That's what the ghosts at the cemetery were afraid of." He breathed in and out, then patted my back and pulled out of the hug. "Thanks."

Shane dropped his hand too, and I felt alone. Cut off, like Thomas Baird.

"Anytime," I said.

I don't know how long we'd stood there, but when I turned around, Greg was standing outside the passenger door to their SUV, and I could just make out Cal inside with the seat tilted back. He must've been calling a vision.

Rory finished off his water then strode toward the garbage bin next to Thomas Baird's garage.

Shane gasped, and I whirled to face him. "What?"

He looked from Rory to me. To my stomach. I glanced down.

Oh, shit.

Rory and I had formed a connection. A strong one.

"Shane, I didn't mean to...." I waved helplessly at the shimmering band coming out of my body. Coming from the exact same place my only slightly brighter bond with Shane emerged.

"I know." He was blocking his emotions from the bond again. He turned away, blinking rapidly, his trembling lips pressed together. I reached for him, but he moved to the farthest point the bond would allow to avoid me.

Cal got out of the car, and Shane started down the driveway toward him. I trudged behind, worried and miserable.

Cal saw us and shook his head. "I couldn't get a vision to come. I'll give it another go when I get home."

"Okay, thanks for trying." I shoved my hands into my pockets. "Uh, I guess we're headed to Mineral Wells now to see if Pia likes the dryads there." I glanced over to where she was standing on the sidewalk, petting Ms. Jackson while Manny and Rory hung out next to them.

Shane cleared his throat. "I get the feeling she's not excited about going to live with strangers."

"Understandable." Greg put his hand around Cal's waist and leaned into him. Then he straightened. "What... when did this happen?" He pointed at my stomach, then at Rory.

Shit.

Cal looked back and forth. "Holy fuck. I may not be used to seeing connections yet, but I don't know how I missed that one. I guess y'all are in a triad?" He snapped his fingers.

"That's why your bond doesn't look right! You're missing your third!"

I twisted my hands together and glanced at Shane, who was staring at the ground. A muscle popped out along his jaw. "Uh, no. The connection wasn't intentional, and Shane isn't, uh, interested."

Cal shifted awkwardly. "Oh. Sorry."

Rory walked over. "Did you get anything from your vision?" His skin wasn't as pale as earlier, so hopefully he was feeling better.

Cal gave him a pained smile. "No. I'll try again in a while, once Greg and I get home."

"Crap, that sucks." Rory looked at me and Shane. "Ready to go to Mineral Wells?"

I pointed at Pia, who'd thrown her arms around Ms. Jackson and was shaking her head at Manny. "Will she get in the car?"

Shane finally stirred. "I'm with Pia. We can figure something else out. She's had too much upheaval in her life recently. Let's just keep her with us."

I smiled, happiness fluttering through my chest. "I love that idea."

Rory put a hand up. "Wait. Pia's mom really wants her to be with dryads. Something about otherwise she won't learn to properly heal plants?"

I crossed my arms. "There must be a dryad willing to tutor her. She doesn't have to live with them."

Rory made a face and kind of cringed away from something to his left. "Uh, what if we go and at least introduce Pia to them? We won't tell her about our backup plan, and we'll give her a chance to decide for herself."

"I can agree to that." Shane turned around and cupped his hands around his mouth. "Pia, Ms. Jackson, and Manny, get your butts in the car, please!"

Ms. Jackson nudged Pia, and she started walking very slowly toward the SUV. It would be a long afternoon.

———

It was a three-hour drive north to Mineral Wells. We crossed into my District—well, now it was Shane and my District—about an hour out from our destination. It was nice to feel the area resonating with me again.

When we were getting close, I texted Clementine, the leader of the dryad grove we'd be visiting.

She texted back several heart emojis and exclamation points. This grove hadn't had any children born in a couple of decades, and I felt guilty for hoping Pia wouldn't choose them.

Clementine's family owned a campground with cabins and hiking trails a little ways off 281. It was pretty, with lots of trees and rustic architecture. We parked in front of the main house, a huge three-story hotel-type building with a sign advertising an event hall and a restaurant.

Pia had been silent the entire drive, just staring out the window with one hand in Ms. Jackson's fur. But when we stopped, she burst out with, "I don't want to live here! I want to stay with you and Ms. Jackson!"

I didn't know how to respond, but fortunately Manny stepped in. "*Chica*, remember what we talked about. You're going to meet these people, and you're going to be polite to them. Ms. Jackson will know whether you belong here or not. If they don't like this place for you, we'll figure something else out."

Ms. Jackson, who'd stayed in their pig form for the car ride, transformed into their tiger form. They opened their mouth and gave a kind of rusty mini-roar.

I grinned. "Good job, Ms. Jackson! You've been working on your vocal cords!" I opened my door and got out of the car. I pushed my seat forward, and Ms. Jackson oozed out with feline grace. The "Service Animal" vest had disappeared, but they were still wearing the tiara. Where did the tiara go when they weren't wearing it? It'd belonged to Shane's granny, so it wasn't magical like the vest had been.

I shook myself. I could worry about it later. Now I had to see if these people were a good fit for Pia.

Pia dragged herself out of the car, pouting the whole way. By the time everyone else got out, Clementine appeared on the porch of the main house.

"Ellis! Hi! It's good to see you!" She hesitated on catching sight of Ms. Jackson, but then she rushed down the steps.

She appeared to be around fifty years old, but I knew she was more like ninety. She was dressed in jeans and a brightly colored blouse.

I gave her a little hug, then I turned to introduce her to everyone. Ms. Jackson got a wide-eyed, "Hi," but Clementine didn't ask any questions. I was sure she could tell they weren't a shifter.

When I got to Pia, Clementine didn't reach for her. She knelt down on the ground and said, "Hi, Pia. I'm so sorry to hear about your mom. She sounds like she was a brave lady."

Pia stared at her with an angry look on her face. "She was."

"I'd like to introduce you to my family, but there are a lot of us, so we thought it'd be less stressful if we were outdoors. There's a lovely picnic area down that path, and we've set up some food and drinks for all of you. It's a little early for dinner right now, but we can hang out as long as you want to. We have rooms ready for all of you to spend the night."

Pia didn't say a word, but the rest of us feigned enthusiasm. I put a hand on Pia's shoulder, and she and Ms. Jackson walked on my right as we followed Clementine down a manicured gravel path across the parking lot from the main building. The trees had been cut back to provide space on either side, and it gave the path a lovely airy feel.

"We have fifty acres here with forty-four campsites and twenty cabins. Our busiest time is the summer, of course, because everyone loves the lake for fishing, boating, and swimming. Do you like to swim, Pia?"

She didn't answer, and Ms. Jackson bumped her with their shoulder. "Yes," she admitted grudgingly.

Up ahead, another path—this one slightly less manicured—crossed the one we were on. An older man, who I recognized as Clementine's father, waited for us.

"Hello! Welcome to our home!" He didn't bat an eye at Ms. Jackson, and he completely ignored the rest of us, focusing only on Pia. "Hey, there, little miss. I'm Levi. You must be Pia! We're very happy to have you here."

He walked next to Clementine, talking loudly about the drinks and food laid out at the picnic area. "It's just around this bend. Here we are!"

We emerged from the trees into a clearing almost the size of a football field. Around twenty-five dryads waited for us, everyone positioned in small groups of two to four people standing near picnic tables scattered throughout the clearing.

I appreciated how they were taking care not to overwhelm Pia, but she stiffened at the murmuring that started as we stepped into the space.

Some people waved and called out, but no one approached, either by design or because Ms. Jackson was suddenly a much larger tiger than they'd been a minute ago.

Even Clementine took a step back when she noticed. "Uh, Pia, I'd like to introduce you to my family, if that's all right."

Rory smiled, and it only looked a little fake. "Of course. Why don't you and Ms. Jackson go with Clementine, Pia, and the rest of us will make our way around at our own pace?"

After sweeping a glare over the four of us, Pia turned her back. She kept one hand firmly in the fur between Ms. Jackson's shoulders as Clementine took her over to the first group of dryads. They offered her some apple juice, and she wrinkled her nose and asked for a soda.

"She'll be okay. Let's get something to eat. I'm starving." Manny headed for the nearest table, which had platters of fruit and cheese laid out.

I waved Rory forward. "You go with Manny. I need to say hi to everyone here." I made an apologetic face at Shane. "Sorry." I was connected to them after all. It'd be rude for their District Monitor to ignore them.

Shane just nodded and walked with me toward a group of dryads. I started on the opposite side of the clearing from where Clementine had moved Pia and Ms. Jackson to the second group of her relatives. I shook hands and offered hugs all the way around. Luckily, other than some questions about Pia and, more urgently, Ms. Jackson, no one wanted to chat much. They were keyed up waiting for their turn to be introduced to their potential new family member.

Eventually I paused at the far end of the clearing and grabbed a couple of bottles of water from the ice chest on the table. None of the dryads were hanging out here, and I needed a break before tackling the second half of the crowd. Shane, who was more introverted than me, no doubt needed a respite too. He took the bottle I handed him and sat down on the bench.

Clementine, Levi, and Pia hadn't made it this far yet, but we'd all cross paths in a few minutes. The sun was still a couple of hours from setting, so we had plenty of time to say hi to everyone. I waved at Rory and Manny, who were walking the same path Shane and I had taken, checking out the snacks on the picnic tables as they passed them.

My phone buzzed in my pocket. I was impressed they had cell service out here. Ugh, it was my boss.

My job was okay. I didn't love it, but I didn't mind it, which was more than a lot of people could say. Selling cell phone plans to corporations wasn't going to solve world hunger, but it certainly kept food on my table. Too bad being a District Monitor didn't come with a salary.

"Hey, Frank, what's up? You remember I'm on vacation this week, right?" I'd taken the whole week off in case Ms. Jackson wanted to hang out in Dallas with me after visiting Houston. But Frank wasn't an asshole, so if he was calling it was probably important.

"Yeah, Ellis, sorry to interrupt." He cleared his throat. "I wanted to let you know that, while your sales in particular have been consistently above goal, overall the corporate division hasn't been doing so well."

I sank down onto the bench next to Shane. "Okay?"

He cleared his throat again. "So the CEO has decided to fold corporate sales into the call center, and the entire sales team, including you and myself, are being laid off effective today."

"What? Laid off?" I jumped up and started pacing, barely remembering to turn around before I got to the limit of my bond with Shane. Rory and Manny had reached us and were looking at me with concern.

"I'm afraid so. You'll get six weeks' severance, so take some time to decide what you want to do next."

My phone buzzed. Greg was calling on the other line. I sent it to voicemail.

"I'm happy to be a reference for you, and I know you'll do great things."

"Um, wow. This is kind of a shock."

"Yeah, I understand completely."

Frank started to tell me how long I had until I needed to turn in my company laptop and cell phone, but Greg called back. Fuck.

"Look, Frank, can I call you later? I need to wrap my head around all this."

"Sure, sure."

He was still speaking when I accepted Greg's call. "Hey." Shane was now talking to Rory, Clementine, and Pia. Ms. Jackson was staring at me with their head tilted.

"Ellis." Greg's tone was urgent. "Are you in an open space with picnic tables surrounded by forest?"

I stopped pacing. A chill wriggled down my spine. "Yes."

"Don't go into the woods. The dryads will be safe if they merge with individual trees in their spirit forms, but don't let anyone walk into the woods in physical form."

"Vampires?" Holy shit. Everyone around me stopped talking. I spun in a circle, but I didn't see any fog.

"Vampires. Cal couldn't tell when, but he felt like it'll be soon." I was so thankful Cal's geographical range for his visions had extended when he bonded with Greg.

"Got it. Call you in a few."

Ms. Jackson was right next to me. "Keep Pia safe," I told them. They nodded and loped over to stand by her side.

I put two fingers in my mouth and gave the loudest whistle I could. Most of the dryads stopped what they were doing and looked at me. "Everybody! A Seer had a vision that the vampires are coming here! Right now!"

I heard Shane cursing, and Manny asking questions. The dryads started milling about, and some of them ran for the trail to the main house. Shit.

"Stop where you are!" I was relieved to see them follow my directions. "The vampires attack from the forest. You can merge with a tree, but don't walk through the woods in your humanoid form. That's what the vampires want. Either keep to the middle of the clearing, or merge with a tree. If we stay in a group, we'll be protected."

Probably.

Ms. Jackson nudged Pia into the middle of the clearing, stopping when they were almost in the exact center. I followed with Shane, Rory, and Manny on my heels. Clementine and Levi kept pace with us.

"Clementine, is everyone accounted for? Nobody's back in the camp or the main house?"

She shook her head. "They were all here."

Thank fuck. Most of the dryads chose trees to step into. Only Clementine and her father joined us in the middle of the clearing.

"I want to see these bastards for myself," Clementine hissed. She held a bread knife in her hand like a sword.

I wished I had a weapon, but at least I had my combat mode. I reached for my magic and felt the change come over me immediately. I hadn't had to use combat mode very often, but I felt more capable, more in control now. I listened, but all I could hear were the sounds our group was making, plus the leaves moving in the wind, and the birds and insects.

We arranged ourselves in a circle with Pia and Ms. Jackson in the center. Pia and the other dryads sprouted thorns from their skin.

"Wow," Manny said. "Seems like that'd be a pretty good defense against vampires. Why would they bother targeting you if you can do that?"

Levi grimaced. "Probably because they know the thorns disappear when we're unconscious."

Manny looked sorry he'd asked. "Oh. Got it."

We all faced outward, scanning the trees for fog. Shane and I both had our hands up in loose fists. District Monitors were required to take hand-to-hand fighting lessons, and our combat mode made our reflexes super fast.

Manny held his phone out, either recording or ready to. "What are we talking about here? Are they like Dracula? Can they turn into bats?"

Shane shook his head. "No one's seen them turn into bats. They can make fog somehow, and they have fangs."

"And they can cut your magic off from other people, it sounds like," Rory added. "Good thing I don't have any connections."

Shane snorted, and Ms. Jackson coughed. It sounded like a laugh.

I winced. "Sorry, Rory, but you do. You just can't see them."

The forest went silent. No bird sounds, nothing. Only the wind through the trees. I held my breath and scanned the edge of the clearing, searching for vampires.

Rory sucked in a breath. "The ghosts say there are eight of them."

Fuck. We were sitting ducks.

Ms. Jackson crouched down and nudged Pia until she got on their back. Were they going to make a run for it? If anyone could make it through a forest full of vampires, it'd be them.

Instead Ms. Jackson walked several feet away from our group and... *grew*. They turned into their dragon form, and they moved so their legs were bracketing the six of us on the ground. They spread their wings and opened their mouth. Smoke came out along with a disturbing groaning sound. A dragon's vocal cords must be harder to use than a tiger's.

Clementine and Levi looked ready to pass out.

"Do you want to step into a tree?" I asked.

Clementine eyed the open space between us and the tree line and shook her head. "I think I'm safer here." She moved closer to Ms. Jackson's leg.

Since Ms. Jackson's tail was pretty much blocking attack from behind, I made everyone but Shane and I stand under their belly. Manny was at my back next to Ms. Jackson's left front leg, panning his phone at the woods. Rory was behind Shane, and the two dryads were as far under Ms. Jackson as they could get.

Shane pointed to his right, and we all watched fog start to roll out of the trees. I twisted around, but it was only coming from the one area. Ms. Jackson leaned their head toward the fog and made a sound that was slightly closer to a roar. They lifted their wings threateningly.

A large body collided with mine, making me grunt and stumble forward. An arm circled my waist, lifting me off the ground. Manny shrieked in my ear as I started to struggle. A fucking vampire had grabbed both of us and was running for the trees. Pain filled my chest as my bond with Shane was pulled past its limits.

Ms. Jackson gave a full-on roar, and I heard the others shouting. I kicked my legs and flailed my arms, and Manny was doing the same, but the vampire didn't have any trouble keeping up his speed. I was facing outward, and the vampire was tall as fuck. The way he was holding me, almost horizontal to the ground, I couldn't grab onto anything except his arm or the outside of his leg. My efforts to dig in with my fingernails to hamper his movement didn't have any effect. I tried to tangle my legs in his, but I only succeeded in kicking Manny, who was doing the same thing.

We were still several yards from the trees when another vampire joined us, easily keeping pace. She took Manny out of the first vampire's arm. The vampire holding me changed his grip, wrapping my arms and body in both of his. Now I could only struggle like a fish on land, and he easily kept me still.

"Human!" the second vampire shouted angrily. Manny made an awful sound, and I smelled blood.

"No!" I bucked and struggled, but the vampire's grip was impossible to get out of. I caught a glimpse of Manny, crumpled on the ground, blood soaking the front of his t-shirt. "Manny!"

In the distance, Pia screamed.

The vampire slowed slightly as we got to the trees. If my arms had been free, I might've been able to grab for some branches.

Even more pain tore through my body as my magic slammed back in on itself. I cried out as my bond with Shane was ripped away. My connection to Rory, all my connections to the Wonders in my District and Shane's, severed.

Everything went black.

CAL'S CAMPAIGN COMPENDIUM

MS. JACKSON

Type: ????

Class: ????

Overview: Ms. Jackson (they/them) is a sentient Elven artifact whose origins are unknown. They are ambulatory, can shift form, and must eat food to replenish their energy.

History: Ms. Jackson began their existence as an Elven artifact of unknown purpose. We are not certain exactly when they became self-aware, but they say it was after they arrived on Earth. They were passed along to a series of Wonders, concluding with an armadillo shifter named Karsha Bennett, who brought them to Texas in the 1960s. The building she lived in was a boarding house for Wonders, and it eventually became the main house for TWIST (Texas Wonder Intervention and Support Team), the Texas-based Wonder rescue organization. Ms. Jackson was assumed to be nothing more than a stone statue and was put in the book room of TWIST and left there.

Ms. Jackson states they were able to hear conversations, radios, and TVs, and thus they educated themselves about Earth and its people.

They were discovered in late March of this year by Greg Shaw and Cal Steadham, who accidentally came across them. Ms. Jackson changed shape and made their sentience known. At that time, they were only able to take the form of inanimate objects, but they communicated by becoming a Ouija board.

In early April Cal Steadham accidentally gifted Ms. Jackson a significant portion of his magic, and as a result Ms. Jackson became ambulatory and able to shift into living beings. At the time this entry was written, Ms. Jackson still communicates mostly via manifesting a Ouija board.

<u>Skills</u>: *We—and Ms. Jackson—are not aware yet of their full capabilities, but this is what has been observed to date:*

- *Can change shape, fully or partially, becoming as small as a panther or as large as a dragon*
- *Has at least a small amount of precognition*
- *Can influence their surroundings so no one observes them or those they are with*

CHAPTER 13
SHANE

I'D BEEN WATCHING THE FOG INTENTLY WHEN FIVE VAMPIRES RAN out, heading toward us. But Ms. Jackson sent a stream of flame at them, and they veered toward the path to the main house.

Ellis hitting the limit of our bond had almost jerked me off my feet.

The vampire that grabbed him had to have come from the opposite side of the clearing from the others. When I looked up to see him carrying Ellis and Manny toward the trees, I yelled and sprinted after them, the combat mode making me almost as fast as the vampire.

Clementine shouted a warning, but I ignored her. Rory followed behind me. He kept up well, so maybe Mediums had a combat mode too.

But even though I'd started out close behind the vampire, the gap between us became wider and wider. No matter how I pushed my muscles, reminded my body that this was our mate, I still couldn't run at his speed.

And then there were two vampires, running side-by-side, still at the same insane speed. The second one took Manny from the first. She shouted something, and then just casually tossed him to the ground. I didn't see the blood until he rolled over, clutching his belly.

Ellis screamed Manny's name.

Fuck! I had to decide. Ellis, I knew, would want me to help Manny. But... *Ellis*.

Rory yelled, "Get Ellis!"

Thank fuck. I raised a hand in acknowledgement and continued running. When I passed Manny, he was losing the battle to keep his guts inside his body. *Fuck*. My breath sawed in and out of my lungs, the muscles in my legs burned, and I really had no chance of catching the vampires who had Ellis, particularly as they were entering the woods, but—

I yelled and tumbled face-first to the ground. My chest felt like it was on fire as the wheel of magic I shared with Ellis tore apart, and my half recoiled into me. I curled into a fetal position and tried to breathe through the agony.

"Shane!" Rory shouted.

"I'm... okay," I gasped out. Not in a million years would I be okay again. Regrets flitted through my head, and I stifled a sob. Crying was a waste of time right now.

Ellis was gone, at least taken, possibly dead. I wanted to believe he was still alive, like the ghosts had told Rory about Thomas Baird. But our bond was severed, so I couldn't tell. My body jittered with the need to run after him, but there was no point. They were too far ahead. I could only try to help Manny now.

Rory was muttering to him to hang in there, so I dragged myself upright and staggered over to them. I fell to my knees next to Rory at Manny's side.

Rory had his shirt pressed to Manny's stomach. It was solid red with blood. More blood covered Manny and the grass around him. His eyes were closed, and he wasn't moving.

Tears dripped down Rory's face. "Please, please, please live."

I yanked my t-shirt over my head and handed it to him, but I didn't think it would be much help. Rory nodded and added my shirt on top of his own.

A vampire skidded to a stop next to us. I jumped to my feet, getting between him and the two on the ground. The vampire raised his hands, one of which was holding a bloody sword.

"Hold up there, *compadre*. I'm Simon. I'm here to help. I killed four of those assholes. The *dèideag dìon* can vouch for me." He pointed toward the center of the clearing, and I saw Ms. Jackson, Pia still sitting on their back, galloping toward us. Clementine and Levi jogged after them on foot. "So can Cal and Greg. Cal gave me this beauty a few weeks ago." He held up the sword, which I realized was a replica Klingon weapon, like the one Cal said he'd let the "friendly vampire", as we'd been calling him, have after the first vampire fight.

Cautiously I stepped aside. The vampire—Simon—shoved the sword into the ground. He was tall and thin, and he sparkled like a Wonder.

He knelt beside Rory at Manny's side. "How bad is it?"

Rory swallowed. "I can see his intestines."

Simon grimaced.

A shadow covered us. "Let me down!" Pia shouted.

Ms. Jackson shrank from her dragon form into the tiger. Pia slid off her back and ran over to Manny. She knelt next to me, across from Simon. "Can you help him, mister?"

Simon's expression was regretful. "Not my skillset." He turned to Ms. Jackson. "This one doesn't have a mate to bond with. Using your mojo wouldn't be against the rules."

My breath caught. Ms. Jackson could heal Manny?

The Ouija board appeared on Ms. Jackson's chest. *I-D-O-N-T-K-N-O-W-H-A-T-Y-O-U-R-E-T-A-L-K-I-N-G-A-B-O-U-T* flashed. My heart sank.

Simon reared back, blinking. "Oh. You don't remember? You don't remember me?"

What? Simon knew Ms. Jackson before they were stuck in a room at TWIST? He was a lot older than he looked.

The *No* on the board flashed.

"Huh. Well, uh, in your original, uh, state of being, you were allowed to heal as a last resort if everything else had been tried, so the child in your care—" he pointed at Pia. "—wouldn't be traumatized."

"I'm traumatized!" Pia shouted.

I glanced at Rory. He gazed at Ms. Jackson with desperate hope in his expression. I reached across Manny to put my hand on Rory's shoulder. I tried not to notice how our magic fizzed together as I touched his warm, bare skin. I missed Ellis with a ferocity I could barely tolerate.

Ms. Jackson cocked their head. *D-O-Y-O-U-K-N-O-W-H-O-W*

"Nope, sorry. Go with your instincts?"

Ms. Jackson looked down at Manny. Then they walked up his body until they were close to his wound, straddling his legs with two paws on either side. All of us except Rory, who was still holding our shirts to Manny's gut, moved back.

They closed their eyes for a moment, then they raised one paw to their opposite shoulder and dug their claws into their... flesh? It created a pretty gross squelching sound as Ms. Jackson gouged out a big glob of sparkling light. Their shoulder reformed instantly. They held the sparkling clump above Manny's belly. The Ouija board flashed, *R-E-M-O-V-E-T-H-E-C-L-O-T-H.*

Rory pressed his lips together but nodded. He carefully lifted the bloodied shirts. I caught a brief glimpse of Manny's wound gaping open, bloody and torn. I wanted to look away, but I needed to see what Ms. Jackson would do so I could tell Ellis later.

Swiftly they pressed the chunk of sparkling whatever—themself? Magic?—into Manny's wound. The sparkles appeared to get absorbed into Manny until only Ms. Jackson's paw— claws thankfully retracted—was visible, splayed across the intact skin of his belly.

They lifted their paw, and every one of us sucked in a breath. Manny's wound was healed. He had a nasty-looking scar, red, raised, and angry, but the cut was closed. He was still unconscious, but hopefully he'd wake soon.

"Thank you," Rory gasped. He reached out and grabbed Ms. Jackson's paw. "Thank you."

They made an odd bowing nod, then they backed up until they were sitting on the grass near Manny's feet. Pia jumped up and hugged them.

Rory wiped his face with his forearm, but he just ended up smearing blood across his forehead.

I let myself sink down and sit. I was grateful Manny would be okay. So grateful. But Ellis was still in the vampires' hands. I rubbed my chest. My magic had been torn in half, but all of Ellis' Wonders were still connected to me. District Monitors didn't usually have over two hundred connections, and I could tell why. I wanted Ms. Jackson to claw my chest open and let them out.

But I needed to keep them so I could give them to Ellis when we got him back.

Simon yanked his sword out of the ground. He removed a kind of oblong leather backpack I hadn't noticed him wearing and put the blade inside. Shit, was he about to leave?

I pushed to my feet, which took more effort than I'd anticipated. I faced Simon. "The vampires have Ellis. Is he alive? Do you know where they would've taken him?"

He hesitated. "Maybe." He looked tired. No wonder, since he'd taken out several vampires by himself. He pulled out his phone. I couldn't help noticing that his wrist bones were strangely prominent. His jeans hung off his hips, and he didn't seem to have an ounce of fat on him. He was as tall as the other vampires, but they'd been more muscular and seemed to have a normal amount of body fat.

He said, "Four of them got away. They came in two vehicles, but I only have a tracker on one." He glanced around at us. "That's how I knew they were here." He punched at his phone. "Unfortunately, they take different routes with each van. I could follow the one with the tracker, but I can't be sure Ellis will be in it."

I took half a second to process this, and then I saw red. Rory started to speak, but I got up in Simon's face. "You have a tracker on one of their vans, and you let them go around attacking people? What the fuck? Why didn't you kill them when they stopped for the night or something?"

Simon let his friendly demeanor drop. He looked exhausted, but also like no one I really wanted to fuck with. "Because I didn't get the tracker on the van until Wimberly a few weeks ago, and I've been waiting for them to return to their home base, where they *keep their captives*." He snarled that last bit, letting his fangs show.

Well, fuck. "Oh, um, sorry." I moved back a couple of steps. "Sorry. I'm a little on edge about Ellis." I rubbed my chest again.

He blew out an exasperated breath. "I tried to prevent this attack, but I'm only one guy. If I go after their van now to get your friend, there's a fifty percent chance he won't be in it. And either way I'll have to kill the vampires, so I won't be able to follow the van to the other captives, and I don't know when I'll get the chance to put a tracker on the other one."

I opened my mouth, but no sound came out. Multiple captives were objectively more important than Ellis, but he was my mate, and I needed Simon to save him.

"Is the van with your tracker on it heading south on 281?"

We all turned to look at Rory, who had propped Manny's head on his thigh.

Simon held up his phone and tapped a few times. "No, it's on Interstate 20." He raised his eyebrows and waited.

"I have three ghosts playing relay to update me on where they're taking Ellis." He looked at me. "He's still alive."

I felt so dizzy with relief, I had to sit back down on the ground.

Rory said, "They just got on 281 going south. We can stop that van, and hopefully the other one with the tracker will go to where the other captives are."

"Thanks, Rory." My voice was raspy with unshed tears. "Please thank the ghosts as well."

Simon smiled. "That's excellent information. Those vans have a range of four hundred and fifty or so miles on the highway before they have to stop for gas. They've already got about twenty minutes' head start. If they have a full tank of gas, we have five or six hours to catch up with them."

He glanced around. Several of the dryads had left their trees to come see what was happening. Simon fiddled with his backpack strap, seeming uncomfortable for the first time since I'd met him. Though I hadn't actually met him, had I?

"I'm sorry," I said. "I didn't introduce myself. I'm Shane. That's Manny, who you helped to save. And Rory...."

"Apparently we've already met." Rory's voice was clipped.

Simon's eyes lit up. "Gave my message to Cal, did you? I was wondering if he'd figure out it was me. Too bad he couldn't warn y'all in time."

"And you *fed* from me?" Rory, I could tell, was trying hard not to explode. I hoped he could keep it together. We needed Simon's goodwill to help us get Ellis back.

Simon made a regretful face. "Technically you consented, but I admit I may have influenced you." He spread out his hands. "I need blood with magic in it to survive, and magic carriers or Wonders aren't easy to find. I didn't take more than a sip. If you want, I can put your memory back."

Rory paused. "I'm not sure."

"No worries. Let me know when you decide." He glanced around at everyone. Even more dryads had gathered. Simon tugged on his backpack strap again. "But, uh, if I'm going to go after the vampires who have your friend, my energy's pretty depleted. I'm afraid I need to feed again. Uh—"

"I'll do it." Clementine stepped forward. "You saved us. I'm glad to be able to offer you something as a thank-you."

"Same here. How much blood do you need, son?" Clementine's dad asked.

The other dryads murmured amongst themselves, and a few of them moved to stand behind Clementine and Levi, apparently lining up to have their blood sucked. I tried not to think about those other vampires feeding from Ellis.

"I, uh, really?" Simon's eyes were wide. "Um, I can get by with very little, I promise."

I scowled, rubbing my chest. "Is that why you're so skinny? You're not drinking enough blood?"

He put his hands on his hips. "No one believes in vampires, so no one volunteers of their own free will. I have to put the whammy on people so they don't remember me, and I don't enjoy taking blood from those who aren't completely consenting." He gestured at Rory. "I only take the bare minimum I need."

"What about goth clubs and those people who like to pretend to be vampires?" Rory suggested.

Simon shook his head. "Humans." He gestured at Manny. "His blood didn't even smell good to me before he was healed. My people are from the Elven dimension. We can only survive on blood with magic in it."

"Can we bag it for you?" Levi asked.

Simon goggled at him. "What?"

"Well, obviously not tonight." He waved a hand at the clearing. "No supplies. But we could set up a sort of blood bank for you. Are there any others of your kind who are, um, friendly?"

Simon covered his mouth with both hands, looking like he was tearing up. I heaved myself to my feet, wishing Ellis was here. He was much better at the people part of being a DM.

Before I could do something like give Simon a hug, he blinked rapidly then cleared his throat. "Um, thank you so much. I appreciate the offer more than I can tell you. There aren't any other vampires on Earth, at least not that I'm aware of. Just me and the other six. The four in the vans and the two who weren't here today. But as much as I'd like to take you up on your idea, I have to follow where the others go, so I wouldn't be able to come back here to, uh, partake."

Levi walked over to Simon and hugged him. Simon's eyes went so wide they were about to fall out of his head. He gingerly patted him on the back.

Levi didn't release him. "First, I'm sorry you're all alone, and I don't reckon it's easy killin' the last few others of your kind, no matter how evil they are. But even though we're not vampires, we're signin' up to be your family now. And don't worry about havin' to return here to feed, son." He stepped back but kept a hand on Simon's shoulder. "We've got that Discord thingy. Won't take nothin' to set up a network. And if folks are squeamish about you drinking from 'em directly, we'll sort out a supply of bags and donation setups. The magic will stay in the blood when it's in a bag, right?"

"Yeah. Uh, yes, it will. I once had a friend...." He looked away. "Never mind. I'm sorry. I don't—people aren't generally nice to me."

"Well, those days are behind you, son. Now, let's get you fed up good so you can go after Ellis. He's our DM, you know. You'll be doing us a right favor. Let's see, we've got...." He pointed at the dryads who were raising their hands. I considered volunteering, but holding Ellis' connections along with my gut-clenching worry for him was making me nauseous. I didn't think I could handle Simon feeding from me on top of that.

"Twelve," Levi announced with satisfaction. "We've got twelve people ready to give you some blood. Think it'll be enough?"

"More than, thank you. Thank you all." The dryads all smiled back at him.

"Okay. Why don'tcha go over to that table so you can sit down while we feed you?"

Simon hesitated. "I need to cut the heads off the vampires I killed."

Levi waved this away. "We got the trees to do it. Used their roots to pull the bodies apart right quick. The nutrients'll do 'em good." The dryads looked grim as they all nodded.

Simon seemed taken aback. "Oh, um, thanks. That's... I appreciate it." Did no one ever help him?

Levi moved his hand from Simon's shoulder to his back and gestured in the direction of the nearest picnic table. "Do you eat regular food as well? We can pack some up to take with you. Shane? I'm guessing you're going along. Who else?"

"Me," Rory said. He gently laid Manny down on the ground. "If you'll look after Manny. I need to be there to talk to the ghosts." I felt a surge of emotion toward Rory—gratefulness, admiration, and maybe even affection.

We were going to get Ellis back. I wouldn't stop until we did.

And then I'd apologize to him.

I gazed at the barely-there connection between me and Rory. He'd be well within his rights to stay here with Manny, but he was putting Ellis first. I was doing the same.

Things would be different once we got Ellis back. If he wanted both me and Rory, I'd do whatever it took to make it happen for him.

CAL'S CAMPAIGN COMPENDIUM
GHOST

Type: Ghost

Class: ????

Overview: Ghosts are Earth-based entities, so they are not technically Wonders. They are the incorporeal spirits of people—human, Wonder, or magic carrier—who have died. The existence of ghosts was confirmed several decades ago by the three documented Mediums. However, none of the Mediums wrote down any information about ghosts (such as who becomes one, what they can and can't do, etc.), so this entry remains incomplete.

CHAPTER 14
RORY

I NEEDED FOR THIS DAY TO STOP. JUST FIVE MINUTES WHERE I could regroup and get my head and my emotions under control.

Instead I was spending those five minutes watching Ms. Jackson—in their dragon form—carry Manny back to Clementine's house. Seeing him get taken by the vampire, watching him be thrown to the ground with a life-threatening injury, and not being able to do anything to save him? Yeah, the nightmares would be coming for years. He was still unconscious, and Ms. Jackson didn't know how long he'd need to recover.

But we couldn't wait because we had to go rescue Ellis.

Ellis, who was another reason my head and my heart were hurting. He was adorable, so caring, and so unintentionally flirty. With the ghosts' help, I would get him back.

So he could be with Shane.

My eyes drifted to the man in question, who walked silently next to Pia, right behind Clementine. He was rubbing his chest again. Was that his bond? Or what was left of his bond? I was pretty sure that was why he'd fallen earlier. I'd been surprised at how fast he'd been able to run. But if the vamps had cut his bond with Ellis, like the ghosts had told me they'd done to the imp in Pflugerville, no wonder he'd collapsed.

He had to be out of his mind worrying about Ellis, but he'd been kind and supportive to me when Manny'd been injured, and I hadn't missed how he'd jumped up to protect us when Simon had appeared. And when he'd put his hand on my bare shoulder, it'd felt like he was trying to send comfort through the contact.

So, now I was dealing an inconvenient romantic attraction—okay, it was a crush—on Shane too. Manny would have a field day with this when he woke up.

Shane's phone rang. He looked at the screen, and his shoulders sagged. "Cal." His voice sounded clogged with unshed tears as he answered. "They took Ellis. They almost killed Manny. Ms. Jackson saved him, but he's still unconscious." He listened for a moment. "No, the rest of us are fine. There were eight vampires, but Simon showed up, and he took out four of them." He ran his hand through his hair. He looked around and met my eyes, so I gave him what I hoped was an encouraging nod. He closed his eyes and nodded back. "Yeah, the friendly vampire. He's going with us to get Ellis back."

Shane pulled the phone away from his ear with a wince. Then he said, "Rory's ghost friends are tracking them, so we know exactly where they are. Ellis is still alive." He threw his free hand in the air. "I appreciate it, but there's not enough time for you to get here. What you can do is call Ellis' brother Arch. You know he's a Hunter on Dominic's team, right? Yeah. Okay, thanks. I'll keep you posted."

He hung up as we reached the house. After Clementine directed Ms. Jackson to put Manny in a bedroom, she said, "The bathroom's down the hall. I'd recommend you two get cleaned up if you're going to be out in public."

Well, fuck. I looked down at myself. My chest and jeans were covered in Manny's blood. At least the leather of my hiking sandals was dark enough that I could probably just wash them and they wouldn't be too bad.

Shane had escaped being covered in blood, but he was drenched in sweat. Shirtless was a good look for him, I noted numbly. He obviously did a lot of his landscaping work himself.

"Come on," he said. "I'm guessing it'll take Simon a few minutes to feed. Let's get some clothes out of the car so we can clean up."

He let me shower first, and as I was getting dressed, Grandfather appeared to update me on Ellis.

"You aren't even in the car yet? They're getting farther and farther away!"

I silently glared at him, then I left the bathroom so Shane could clean up. "Thanks," he said as he passed me.

Grandfather stuck his head through the bathroom door after Shane closed it. "Grandfather!" I hissed. "Stop that!"

He *tsked* as he joined me again. I led the way into the guest bedroom so I could spend a few minutes with Manny before we left.

"Too bad their bond got whacked. Shane's magic is like a jumble of badly cooked spaghetti. One man can't keep that many connections."

"I don't know what you're talking about, and I can only handle one problem at a time right now. What's going on with Ellis? Any change?"

"He's still out cold. They haven't snacked on him any more at least." He grimaced. "I'd give a lot not to have witnessed that.

Anyway, they're still heading south. Just went through Stephenville."

I heard the front door open, so I squeezed Manny's hand and smoothed back his hair. "I'll be back in a few hours, Manny. I expect to see you and Pia eating junk food and watching trash TV, okay?" My voice was quavering a little, but I managed not to cry.

I went into the living room, where Levi and Simon were waiting. Simon could've used a shower as well, but I didn't think we had time. He looked worlds healthier though. His eyes were bright gold, his skin was flushed, and I'd swear even his auburn hair looked thicker and shinier.

I still needed to wrap my head around Simon feeding from me and then wiping my memory. But I kind of understood his rationale, and fuck if I didn't have bigger problems. I'd set it aside and see if it still bothered me next week or something.

I said, "Shane's getting cleaned up. He'll be out in a minute. The van just passed Stephenville."

Simon looked blank. "How far away is that?"

"Oh, sorry. Forty or so miles."

He nodded then looked toward the hallway to the bedrooms.

Shane walked out carrying his duffel bag. "I'm ready, let's go."

"Wait!" Pia shouted from the kitchen. She ran into the room and wrapped her arms around my waist. "You'll come back, right? With Ellis?"

I met Shane's worried gaze. "We're going to try our best. And we have Simon to help us."

"And Ms. Jackson," she announced. She let go of me and bounced over to hug Shane, then Simon, who appeared stunned but quickly gave her a grave smile when she released him. "I'll take care of Manny so you don't have to worry!" She gave us an officious nod and trotted off to the guest bedroom.

I remembered to get Clementine's phone number before we left so we could keep her updated on what was happening. She handed me a cooler she said was filled with drinks and snacks.

Ms. Jackson, it turned out, was waiting in the back seat of the SUV. They were in a black panther form. A better choice for nighttime, I guessed.

Levi charged out of the front door, waving his arms. "Wait! Wait right there! One minute!" Then he trotted down the front steps and went around the side of the house.

I tossed Shane and my bags into the back of the SUV and set Pia's tote bag on the front porch for Levi to grab when he went inside.

He came back carrying two axes and a shotgun. "I thought these would help."

"They will, thanks." I couldn't believe we'd been about to go after two vampires with only Simon and his Klingon sword for weapons. Cal and Greg had made it clear that Ms. Jackson would only fight in defense, but at least their dragon form was scary.

The sun was setting as we left the property. Shane sat up front with me, and Simon was in the back with Ms. Jackson. I was merging onto the highway when he said something unintelligible in a sing-song voice that kind of hurt my ears.

"What the hell?" I shook my head to get the sound out of my brain. Next to me, Shane had hands clapped to his head.

"I was seeing if Ms. Jackson remembered the Elvish language. They don't."

"Thank fuck, because I don't think I could listen to much more of it, especially while I'm driving. It's painful."

"Oh, right. My bad. I forgot humans, even magic carriers, can't tolerate it. The intonations are done with magic."

"Huh." I set the cruise control to eighty miles per hour, twenty miles over the speed limit, and hoped for the best. This being Texas, we weren't the only vehicle traveling that fast, but the highway was only two lanes on each side, so I had to do some weaving in and out of traffic.

Lorraine had reported the van was traveling right at the speed limit, and, because the vampires had stopped to feed on Ellis, they had a head start of only about thirty minutes. So unless we got pulled over by the cops, we should catch up to them in an hour or so.

Simon opened the cooler, and he passed out snacks, along with water and sodas. Not wanting to come across as nosy, I'd been hesitant to ask if he ate human food, but it turned out he did.

Shane accepted a box of crackers and a container of cubed cheese. "Simon, can you please make sure Ms. Jackson eats as much as they want? Turning into a dragon uses up a lot of energy, and I'm guessing healing Manny wasn't easy either."

"Can do."

Luckily Clementine had supplied us with multiple containers of cheese, which apparently Ms. Jackson adored. But after Simon handed them an Oreo to try, they took possession of the package and growled when he tried to get it back.

"Leave some for Ellis," Shane scolded. "He'll need the sugar if they've taken a lot of his blood."

Ms. Jackson made a grumbling sound, and I turned my head to hide my grin at the crinkling of the cellophane wrapper as they passed the cookies back to Simon.

"I can't believe Cal and Greg never gave them any chocolate," Shane muttered.

I forced a chuckle. "Why don't we stop for milkshakes on the way back?"

I caught the wistful smile he sent my way. "Ellis likes strawberry."

Oddly, I was certain Shane was feeling worry, fear, and almost despair at the thought of Ellis in the kidnappers' hands. But at the same time, I could see and understand his hope and determination. I'd never been quite that empathetic before, and it was a strange awareness to be having in the middle of our conversation.

I made myself smile back at him. "It's a plan."

He nodded and looked down at his phone. "I'm going to message Reno so he knows the vampires are heading in his direction." He glanced at me. "Reno's a Seer in Corpus Christi, and he's also the acting District Monitor for the South Texas District."

Simon leaned forward. "The van with the tracker on it hasn't gone this far south yet. It's possible they're heading for their home base." I heard the longing in his voice. Then he shook his head. "But it's just as likely they're trying to make sure they're not followed before they change their route."

I asked, "If this Reno is a Seer like Cal, can he have a vision to find out where they're going?"

Shane shook his head as his thumbs flew over his phone's screen. "He's not bonded. Calling a vision is an ability that only manifests once a Seer has bonded. Until then he has to wait for visions to appear on their own."

Simon stuck his head further through the gap between the seats. "I remember his name from your Discord chats. He's in Corpus Christi, you said?"

Shane's head came up, and he twisted in his seat to stare at Simon. "You're on our Discord server?"

"Uh, not officially? But, yeah, that's how I knew to show up in Wimberley."

I raised my eyebrows, and Shane seemed about to ask more questions, but his phone rang. He groaned. "It's my boss. Let me get rid of him." He answered the call. "Ricky, I can't talk right now."

The voice on the other end was at a reasonable volume, which was a nice change from the last time Shane had spoken to his boss.

"No. I can't. I'm off work."

His boss' voice increased in volume. In the rear-view mirror, I could see Simon's eyebrows go up. And over his shoulder, I noticed Dimi was sitting between Pia's potted plants in the last row of seats, her arms crossed and lips pinched tight.

"I'm sorry you promised them that, but you didn't ask me first, and I haven't even seen the site. I can't do it. You'll have to figure something else out." Shane's tone was firm, which was also a change from the last phone call I'd heard him have with this Ricky guy.

But I clearly heard his boss' response. "...or you won't have a job to come back to!"

Shane dug his fingers into his knee. "Maybe that's for the best. I've got more important things to worry about than you promising designs to clients in an unrealistic timeframe and then passing my work off as yours." Sputtering noises came through, loud and clear. "Consider this my resignation notice." He hung up the phone.

I glanced over at him and patted his thigh, only realizing too late the gesture was probably overly familiar. "Good for you, Shane. Nobody should talk to their employees like that."

He dropped his phone in the cupholder and rubbed his chest. "Yeah, well, I think I just got used to it over the years. But I'm done. I'll find something else. And at least I don't have a mortgage."

I wanted to offer to help him find a job, but it wasn't like I knew anyone who was in landscaping. But I could help him with his resume. I had an overpowering urge to fix things for him, which was odd. We weren't that good of friends yet.

I jumped in my seat when Dimi popped up, sitting on the center console. "It's about damn time. The idiot needs a job where people won't take advantage of him." Ms. Jackson nodded in the back seat.

I cleared my throat. "Any update on Ellis?" Shane and Simon snapped their attention to me.

Dimi crossed her arms and huffed. "Fucking vampires. Sorry that this one—" she indicated Simon. "—has to share a species with those assholes."

"Agreed, but what's happening?" I changed lanes to get around a slow-moving Honda.

She scowled. "They're looking for a rest stop so they can pull over and *have dinner*." She unfolded her arms to make air quotes.

"Shit. Grandfather said they already fed from him earlier. Simon, how often do they need to feed?"

He pressed his lips together in an expression eerily reminiscent of Dimi's. "They expended a lot of energy today, so it wouldn't be unusual for them to feed twice, especially if they didn't take a lot the first time."

"Shit."

Shane shifted restlessly in his seat, his foot tapping on the floorboard. I glanced over, and his eyes were glowing.

"Shane? What's up with your eyes?"

He turned his head to stare out the window, but I could still see the reflection of the glow.

Dimi patted her grandson's leg, but not nearly as high up as I'd done earlier. "It's his combat mode. It's a magic thing. He's worried about Ellis, and he's frustrated he can't do anything."

"Combat mode? Wait is that how you were able to run so fast earlier?"

Shane nodded but didn't turn around.

Simon sat forward, leaning between the seats, which put his head between Dimi's shoulder blades. She made another huffing noise and moved to sit on Shane's knees. He didn't notice.

Simon said, "We need a way to stop the van on the highway. We can't ambush them at a rest stop or a gas station because there'll be too many people around."

I glanced over at him. "Even if we had some way to stop the van, wouldn't the other cars notice us fighting with the vampires?"

"Um, not if Ms. Jackson here doesn't want them to." He cocked his head. "How do you think we haven't been stopped by the highway patrol before now?" He looked over at Ms. Jackson, and I could see the light of flashes from their Ouija board reflected in the passenger-side windows.

"That explains so much," Shane muttered. His eyes weren't glowing anymore, and he was slumped dejectedly in his seat.

Simon leaned forward again. "They say they'll help."

"Great." I tapped on the steering wheel. "Now all we need is a way to stop the van without injuring Ellis."

Dimi reached out and slapped my head. I flinched away. "Stop it!"

"Apparently my grandson's not the only idiot in this car."

I rubbed the side of my head. Her hand didn't hurt, but the cold went right through my body. "What do you mean?"

Shane was staring at me with narrowed eyes. "Rory," he said slowly. "My grandmother used to do that to me when she thought I was being an idiot. Who's the ghost in the car?"

I held up a finger. "Just a sec. Why am I an idiot?"

Shane covered his face with his hands and said, "Oh, fuck me."

Dimi rolled her eyes at him. "You remember Garfield killing the security cameras at that billionaire's house, right?" She waved a hand at the dashboard of the car. "Didn't it occur to you that's the same reason us ghosts never get too close to your car's electrical stuff?"

My breath caught.

"That's right. A few seconds hovering over the ignition system, and they'll be left with a brick on wheels."

"What? What's she saying?"

I grinned. "Dimi, you're the best."

She scoffed. "It's not like your grandfather and Lorraine don't know this too."

I told the others. "The ghosts can short out the electrical system in the van."

Shane sat up, animated again. "How far away are we?"

Dimi disappeared.

"She went to find out."

Almost instantly Grandfather popped into the third row seats. "You're only five or six minutes behind them."

Yes! After discussing it with Shane and Simon, we decided, based on how little traffic there was, that the ghosts should disable the van as soon as it was on a section of the highway without guard rails along the side. Most of 281 was at ground level and open to fields or trees, but there were some overpasses. We'd pull over like we were trying to see if they needed help. Ms. Jackson agreed they would keep the vampires from running away if they attempted to.

After Grandfather vanished, Shane posted an update on a Discord server that Cal and Greg, among others in the know, used to communicate. It'd kept everyone from calling and texting him, so I wasn't complaining.

Lorraine appeared next. "It's done. They've stopped ahead on the right."

My heart pounding, I relayed this to the others as I slowed down to the speed limit. Shane's eyes were glowing again.

Simon handed Shane the two axes. I assumed one was for me. "No guns," he said. "Vampires are too fast to aim at accurately, and it's too risky with the cars going by."

"Got it." Shane pointed ahead. "There it is!" The van didn't have any lights on, but they'd managed to pull onto the shoulder. The hood was up, I saw as we got closer. I put my turn signal on and pulled over, stopping about twenty feet behind them.

"I'll go first and draw them out," I said. "They're least likely to recognize me."

"Don't look them directly in the eyes," Simon cautioned.

Shit, I hadn't thought of that. "Thanks." I released my seat belt and took one of the axes from Shane. Opening my door, I slid to the ground. I held the axe just under the head, with the handle pointing upward behind my arm. My heart was beating as if I'd run a marathon. I wished I'd asked Simon if vampires could hear heartbeats from a distance.

"Hello? Do you need help?" I walked over to the passenger side of the van so I'd be away from traffic and would have room to move. I kept my eyes on the top of the van. Simon, Shane, and Ms. Jackson got out of the SUV.

Grandfather zipped over. "They called their friends to come pick them up."

The female vampire, the one who'd almost killed Manny, stuck her head out the passenger window. "We're fine, thanks. We've got a tow truck coming."

"Is it your battery? I can give you a jump."

"No, thanks. Don't worry about us. You can go on your way. We're fine."

I kept my eyes just above her head as a swirl of fog whipped past me to the back of the van. It coalesced into Simon, sword in hand. He smashed the hilt into the safety glass in one of the rear windows. The vampire spun around in her seat, then jumped up to rush to the back of the van. Simon planted his feet, then reached through the broken window with his free hand and pulled the door off its hinges. It was still locked to the other door, so, holy fuck, he bent both doors to the side so he could enter the van.

The female vampire leaped out at him. Simon had the sword at ready, so she dodged to the side. The male vampire was right behind her.

I brought my axe up in case they ran at me, but they were focused on Simon. I tried to be stealthy, moving closer in case I could figure out a way to help. Shane skirted around me, heading for the van with his axe also held high. Ms. Jackson slunk up in their panther form on the other side of the fight.

The female vampire was only using her claws, but the male had a long knife. Still, Simon held his own due to the longer reach of his sword.

I moved to keep myself between Shane and the combatants. He climbed into the van, and Ms. Jackson jumped in behind him. A moment later Shane stepped down to the ground, then turned back to pick up an unconscious Ellis.

"Rory," Grandfather called. "Simon's hurt. He's limping!"

Shit. I'd taken my eyes off the fight. I spun around and ran forward, trying to get behind one of the other vampires. The male rushed Simon with his knife held high, and Simon caught it on his blade. The female vampire circled, trying to get at Simon's back.

I didn't think I could flank her, but the male vampire was occupied grappling with Simon. I ran forward and swung my axe, burying the head into the back of the vampire's knee. He screamed, and I yanked the axe out as he fell to the ground.

Simon darted away, intercepting the female vampire. He wasn't limping now, so I let him handle her. It was up to me to finish off this guy. The male vamp flipped over to face me and sat up, waving his knife to keep me back.

I shifted my grip on the axe. The thing was, I didn't know how to use an axe to chop things, not really. It wasn't anything my parents had taught me, and I'd certainly never even laid eyes on an axe once I'd moved in with my grandparents. But what Grandfather *had* taught me—or rather had made me take lessons for—was golf. Golf was a rich man's sport, and he'd told me I needed to be able to play with the movers and shakers in my future career. I'd dropped the sport after he'd cut me off, but I still remembered how to put my hip and shoulder into the swing, to get under the ball and send it flying.

I waited until the vampire on the ground flicked a quick glance at his companion, who was being soundly trounced by Simon. Then I swung with a form my grandfather would've been proud of, and the flat of the axe head hit his hand with a revolting *thwack*, sending the knife flying into the darkness toward the trees. The vampire cried out, clutching his hand to his chest. His eyes turned red, and he bared his fangs.

He pulled his good leg in, preparing to launch himself at me, but Simon walked up behind him and casually sliced off his head with the sword. The vampire's head and body separated, both dropping to the ground, blood pouring out. I spun away, swallowing against the nausea.

Shane trotted up with the other axe resting on his shoulder. He winced and grimaced when he saw the decapitated body. Make that *bodies*, because Simon had also beheaded the female vampire.

"Ms. Jackson is putting Ellis in the SUV. I got the zip ties off him."

Simon leaned over to stick his sword in the ground and pull it out again. Was that his way of cleaning it? "Why don't you two go see if you can get some water in him? I imagine the other vampires mesmerized him into unconsciousness, so he could be out for a few more hours. I want to look through the van, but then I'll need your help moving it over here so the blood gets burned up in the fire."

"Would they have anything with their home address on it? Driver's license?"

He shook his head. "They use fake addresses for everything. But there might be other clues." He winced as he lifted the strap for the sword's carrying case over his head.

I examined him. He was bracing his left leg oddly. "Grandfather said you were injured. Your leg?"

He shrugged. "It'll heal on its own."

I gave him a flat stare. "Fine, but you're feeding again before you leave the dyrads' place tomorrow." I looked at the van, suddenly aware of the cars whizzing by on the highway. "Wait, what did you mean fire? We're burning it? And the bodies?"

He shrugged. "A little gas tank explosion. The skeletons will appear their actual age, which is well over a century old, during a postmortem, so they won't seem to have died recently. It'll be all over the news for a day or two, then no one will care."

He went off to search the van. I tested hacking the axe blade into the dirt to clean it off, but it just seemed messier. I ended up finding a towel in the back of the vampires' van to wrap the head in. Hopefully Levi had some bleach to get rid of the blood when we got back to the dryad's compound.

CAL'S CAMPAIGN COMPENDIUM

NESTING

The magic gives most Wonders and magic carriers a kind of advance signal when they are about to meet or recognize their mate(s). This signal takes the form of what is called nesting.

During a nesting period, the individual will feel an unexpected compulsion to improve or change their home or surroundings. They might spruce up their house with new paint, new furniture, etc. Or they might feel compelled to get a different job or move to a larger apartment.

Usually, once the mate(s) reveal themself or themselves, the changes are identified as being beneficial to the relationship(s) or to the new mate(s).

CHAPTER 15
SHANE

Ellis looked like shit.

I know, I know, he looked pretty good for someone who'd been kidnapped and had his blood sucked. Before we'd gotten in the car, Simon had spit into his palm and rubbed his saliva all over Ellis' neck wounds. Which was gross, but he said it would promote healing.

My emotions were seesawing back and forth between relief that we'd found him, rage at what had been done to him, and worry about how he would react to the trauma when he woke up.

My hands shook as I carded my fingers through his hair, which had been in beautiful coils this morning but was now a dirty, disheveled mess. We were in the third row of seats, and his head was in my lap. His glasses were missing, and his normally pristine clothes were covered in dirt and blood. He had a few scratches on his arms and legs, probably from being carried through the forest, but his neck was a mess of half-healed bites.

Apparently, unlike in the movies, vampires didn't make two neat puncture wounds and suck the blood out through those.

No, the wounds on Ellis looked like they'd used their fangs to bite through his skin, leaving ragged cuts about an inch and a half long. There were four cuts, so the two vampires had each fed twice.

Simon had told us that the person's magic was what sustained vampires, and drinking blood was how they accessed it. Which explained why Ellis' magic was almost completely gone. He'd need a lot of time to build it back up.

All I wanted right then was to take Ellis, Manny, and Pia back home to Houston where Rory, me, and Ms. Jackson could keep them safe, feed them, and let them heal. I shook my head when I realized I'd automatically included Rory in our odd little family unit. My jealousy over Ellis' attraction to him seemed petty now.

Rory had reported that Pia's mom's ghost had gone to check on her, and Manny was awake. Rory's relief had come through our connection loud and clear, which had startled me so much I'd automatically focused on it. Unlike when I'd looked at it earlier, Rory and my connection was solid now. Strong. Not as strong as a bond, but it wouldn't wither away if we were apart from each other.

That was a good thing, especially if Rory and Ellis ended up bonding. I wanted to bond with Ellis as well, and Rory and I would need open communication and a firm friendship to make a relationship like that work.

Rory was still driving. He must be exhausted, but he'd turned down Simon's offer to replace him at the wheel.

I hadn't had time to wrap my head around the fact that my granny was one of the ghosts he'd been talking to. Knowing her, she'd stuck around on Earth to make sure I'd be okay. Trying to tell her I'd be fine and she'd earned her rest would be pointless.

Simon, who was sitting in the front passenger seat, was quizzing Ms. Jackson on their food preferences. They'd already turned their nose up at hamburgers, because of course those were meat-based. "Um, how about Sonic? They have mozzarella sticks, and you can get tater tots with cheese on top."

Rory perked up. "Get them one of those soft serve ice cream things with the chocolate pieces mixed in."

I asked for some chicken tenders for me and Ellis, who would hopefully wake up soon. Rory added a strawberry milkshake, and I teared up at his thoughtfulness. Fuck, I was a mess.

In the end Simon ordered enough food that we'd have some left over for Pia and Manny, plus any of the dryads who were still awake when we got back. We put the milkshakes in the cooler for later, except Simon held Ms. Jackson's out to them right away. "See? It's got the Oreos you liked earlier, plus soft serve ice cream. It's like, um, frozen milk." He placed the cup, lid and straw removed, in the cupholder between the second-row seats.

Ms. Jackson, who had decided to make the journey home in their panther form, sniffed the cup, then tentatively stuck their tongue into it. Their eyes widened and they made a sort of grunting *Mmmm* sound. Then they opened their mouth and dug their tongue down into the milkshake.

"Slowly!" I called out. "The cold can cause a nasty headache if you eat it too fast."

They licked their whiskers and gave me a disappointed look, complete with milk mustache. I grinned for the first time in what felt like hours.

"One day soon you'll have to learn table manners. That'll be the worst."

They snorted and went back to their ice cream treat.

Ellis' hand landed on mine where it rested on his chest. I gasped as his eyes opened. "Hey. How, uh, how are you feeling?" I tried for an upbeat tone, but I wasn't terribly successful.

He blinked, then squinted. "Shane? What happened? Where are we?" He struggled to sit up.

"Okay, here, take it easy. You've been through a lot today. We're in Rory's car."

I helped him sit upright in the middle seat. He rubbed his eyes, and I pulled a water bottle out of the cooler for him and uncapped it. "Here."

"Thanks." He took a swig. "Uh, Ms. Jackson?" They nodded at him. "Right, and, Rory, is that you driving? I can't see much in the dark, especially without my glasses. Does somebody have them?"

"Glad you're awake, Ellis," Rory replied.

"And this is Simon." I pointed over the back of the seat.

Simon twisted around and waved at Ellis. "Good to see you're feeling better."

"Uh, thanks?" Ellis turned to me and frowned. "What happened? Do you know where my glasses are?" He patted the seat around him.

Fuck. "Um, remember the picnic with the dryads?"

He took another sip of water. Ms. Jackson handed me one of the bags of food, and I pulled out a container of chicken tenders.

Ellis didn't take the one I held out to him. "I remember we left the cemetery. Did I hit my head or something?" Without his glasses, he seemed young and vulnerable.

I met Rory's gaze in the rear-view mirror. "Uh, something like that. Look, you're probably starving. Why don't you eat and then we'll tell you what happened?"

Ellis rubbed his chest with his free hand. "Shane... what— where's our bond? Where are my connections to the Wonders? I can't feel my District! I can't feel you!" His breath started coming faster, and he was stiff with tension.

Shit. I wrapped him in my arms. "I've still got all your connections. The vampires grabbed you. Remember what the ghosts told Rory about the vampires cutting Thomas Baird's connections when they took him?"

He sucked in a breath, then he slapped his free hand to his neck. He shoved his water bottle at me, putting his other hand on his throat as well. A sob tore from him. "They took me? They fed from me?"

"Yeah, but we got you back, baby. It's okay. You're okay."

He shuddered. "How long did they have me?"

"Only a few hours. Rory's ghost friends kept track of you, and we followed. Simon over there, he's the friendly vampire who helped Cal and Greg a few weeks ago. He killed the ones who took you, and four more of the ones this afternoon as well."

"I don't remember any of it." His voice was high and thready. I hoped he wasn't going into shock.

Shit, what was I supposed to say? *It's probably for the best* was the truth, but that wouldn't make Ellis feel any better.

Simon turned around in his seat again. "I'd guess you were out cold the entire time they had you, Ellis. All they would've had to do was look you in the eyes, and you would've gone unconscious. The loss of your memory right before it happened is just a side effect. If you like, I can see if I can help you get it back."

Ellis thought this over. "Thanks. I'll think about it." He leaned into me and put his head on my shoulder. "I miss our bond so much, Shane. Even though it was kind of broken, it was ours."

"I know, baby." I kissed his head. This close, I could smell the blood that had dried on his neck. "Me too."

"Where are we going? Can we go home? I want to go home."

I hugged him tighter. "We have to go back to the dryads' compound. Pia and Manny are there, and we all need to sleep. We'll go home tomorrow, okay?"

"Okay."

———

We got back to the dryad's compound around midnight. I'd texted Clementine when we'd started on our way back, so I'd expected her or Levi to be waiting up for us. Instead everyone was awake.

Seven dryads milled about on the front porch of the main house. When Rory parked the SUV, they came over and helped us unload. Somebody took the unused shotgun and the axes off to be cleaned. Two people grabbed the cooler and Sonic bags to take to the kitchen. Multiple people checked with Simon to see if he needed to feed. He asked them to come back in the morning, and they said they would.

Pia ran outside and first hugged Ms. Jackson then Rory. She looked through the rear passenger door at me and Ellis and gave me a big smile. "Clementine said Ellis will be okay, so tomorrow before we leave, we can make new connections with him, right?"

I smiled back. "Right." I didn't comment on her assumption she wouldn't be staying here. She belonged with Rory, Ellis, and me.

Plenty of time to figure out all the logistics later.

Ellis, who'd fallen asleep after eating some chicken and tater tots, didn't stir during all the commotion.

Rory nudged Pia out of the way. "Need help getting Ellis out?"

"Please." I imagined Rory and me in the future, working together to take care of Ellis and make him happy. It could work.

He pulled the lever to tilt the seat in front of me forward, then he took hold of Ellis' shoulders and pulled him through the door. Levi was there to help hold Ellis' feet until I got out of the car, but I quickly took him back. I wasn't ready to let him out of my sight, much less out of touching range.

Rory and I got him up the steps and into the house. Manny waited in the living room, paler than usual but with his grin undimmed. He didn't glow with magic quite as brightly as he'd done right after Ms. Jackson had healed him earlier. Maybe it would just fade completely with time. After giving Rory a quick side hug, Manny patted him on the back. "We're putting you three in the room next to mine. It has the biggest bed." Then he turned to Pia. "I heard there're tater tots in the kitchen. Wanna go get some?"

Pia cheered and grabbed his hand.

I stared after them, then I looked at Rory. "Um...."

He jerked his head in the direction of the bedrooms. "It's up to you, but I'm good with it if you are. Let's get him settled and then we can talk about it."

Internally I shrugged. Might as well start out as we meant to go on.

Levi brought Ellis' overnight bag in from the SUV. God, it seemed like a lifetime ago when we'd packed up this morning. He led Rory and me into the bedroom we'd been assigned and set the bag down on a chair near the door. He pulled the comforter and top sheet off the king-sized bed so we could lay Ellis down. "Y'all let me know what you need. I'll be in the living room for a while."

We thanked him, and Rory set to untying Ellis' shoes. I pulled his shirt over his head. Rory put Ellis' shoes, socks tucked inside, on the floor of the closet. He helped me pull Ellis' shorts off, leaving him in just his boxers.

"I wish we could get him into the shower," I said as I pulled the top sheet over him.

Rory neatly folded the comforter at the foot of the bed. He picked up Ellis' dirty clothes, folded them, and placed them on top of his shoes on the floor of the closet.

I got a washcloth from the bathroom and dampened it, then I ran it over as much of Ellis' skin as I could, paying careful attention to his neck. He didn't rouse.

Rory pulled Ellis' other clothes out of his bag. "I don't see any spare glasses." He began to put the clothes on hangers in the closet.

"That's okay. We're going to his place tomorrow." I paused with Ellis' hand in mine and the washcloth against the inside of his elbow. "I mean, are you good to go with us? Do you need to get back for work or anything?"

He looked down at Ellis' shirt. "Nah. I called in sick for the rest of the week." He carefully hung the shirt on a hanger.

"Um, we'll probably be leaving in the morning. You don't need to hang stuff up." I dried Ellis' skin with another cloth.

He shrugged. "It's something to do." When Ellis' bag was empty, Rory placed it next to his dirty clothes on the floor of the closet. Then he walked over to the bedside table and turned on the small lamp before flicking off the overhead light. "That's better. He'll still be able to see if he wakes up, but it's not so bright. *Hmmm*."

He went over to his backpack and rummaged through it before pulling out a light blue button-down. He went back over to the bedside table and draped the shirt over the lamp. The light dimmed even more, and the blue material gave everything a soft, almost romantic vibe. Rory nodded to himself. "Better."

He walked around the room, moving the armchairs slightly so they were equally spaced below the window. Then he straightened the pictures on the walls—bland landscapes I doubted Ellis would've looked twice at.

Was Rory... *nesting*? The thought speared my heart with an unexpected pain. Of course he and Ellis were mates. Otherwise Ellis wouldn't have been attracted to him right after he and I had bonded. I knew this. I wanted this for Ellis. I wanted Rory for Ellis.

But, even if they were mates, Ellis and I could be mates too. We'd proved one Wonder could connect with more than one District Monitor, so there was no reason Ellis couldn't bond separately with both Rory and me. I'd thought myself not capable of polyamory, but it'd been a knee-jerk reaction when I'd been jealous of Ellis wanting Rory. I'd never really consid-ered the possibility before, but now... I couldn't think of an objection to trying it. Ellis would have Rory, and I would have Ellis.

That's what I wanted.

But I looked at Rory, that gorgeous man trying to make the sterile guest room as comfortable for Ellis as he could, and jealousy slammed back into my gut. Only this time I was jealous that *Rory* didn't want *me*.

It was stupid to be so emotional about this. I was just exhausted. I barely knew Rory, and it was Ellis I should be focusing on.

But my throat was tight with tears as I took the washcloths back to the bathroom. I shut the door and ran the water so Rory wouldn't hear me crying.

I washed my face and got my breathing under control. My chest felt too small, and the connections were making it a little hard to breathe, but I'd be fine. Ellis and Rory were good men, smart, and going places. They'd be amazing together, and I'd be grateful to have Rory's friendship along with Ellis' bond.

"Hey, Shane?" Rory knocked softly on the bathroom door. "Do you want me to ask Levi or Clementine for an iron? Your shorts for tomorrow are a little... wrinkled."

My shorts? *Mine?*

I yanked open the door. Rory stood there holding the cargo shorts I'd wadded up in the bottom of my duffel bag.

"For me? I mean, I don't usually bother...."

He looked down at the shorts and his face flushed. "Yeah, it's probably stupid. We'll be in the car. I just thought it'd be nice for you—never mind. I'll hang them up and maybe some of the wrinkles will fall out."

He started to turn away, but I grabbed his arm. "Wait." My magic sparked out, touching his, resonating. I could feel our connection getting stronger by the second.

He glanced down at my hand, then at my face. His eyebrows scrunched up. "Have you been crying? Ellis is okay. He'll be fine." He put his hand on my shoulder.

"I know. It's not that. Don't worry about it."

Our connection flared, blew wide open, and I felt all of Rory's attraction and concern. His eyes were huge, and I hoped he wasn't scared by the jumbled emotions I was sure he was getting from me.

I stepped forward and put my hand on his cheek. Damn, he was pretty. My stomach felt all fluttery, like I was in high school and the boy I liked had said he liked me back. Rory was nesting for me. For Ellis *and* me. Instead of the Ellis-centric triangle I'd been imagining, Rory wanted both of us. I went up on my toes and pressed a kiss to his lips.

I'd meant it to be a quick *I-like-you* peck, but he pulled me in, one hand holding the cargo shorts against my back, and his other hand sliding down to my hip and pressing me against him. He opened his mouth on mine, and before I knew it, we were plastered together from mouths to groins. His hand landed on my ass.

The sheets on the bed rustled. "Wait."

Rory and I broke apart and whipped our heads toward Ellis, who was sitting up. He waved us to come closer. Oh, shit. Still, Rory kept one hand around my waist as we walked over.

But instead of being upset, Ellis gave us a smug little grin. "I didn't mean for you to stop. I just couldn't see you very well at that angle, especially without my glasses." He wiggled his eyebrows.

I huffed. "How are you feeling?"

"Tired." His smirk dropped. He pushed some of the pillows behind himself. "Come sit on the bed with me."

I patted Rory's stomach and pushed him lightly away. Then I toed off my shoes and crawled onto the bed.

Rory picked up my shoes and put them in the closet before draping my cargo shorts neatly on a hanger.

I leaned over to put my mouth next to Ellis' ear. "He's nesting."

Ellis sucked in a breath, and he turned his head to look in my eyes. "Yeah? For both of us?"

I nodded and kissed the edge of his mouth gently. "I'm sorry I didn't understand before."

He leaned his head on my shoulder and watched Rory take his own shoes off. "There was a lot going on. I didn't understand it myself." He picked up my hand. "Do you... would you be willing to try again with the bond? One day?"

I smiled against his hair, even though he really needed a shower. "I want to. Rory, come over here."

He shut the closet door and walked over to the other side of the bed. His expression was tentative, and his eyes flicked back and forth between me and Ellis.

"Come cuddle. The room looks great. You did a good job for us."

Ellis nodded. "Yes, Rory. It's perfect. I feel so relaxed and at home. But you should be on the bed with us. And I'll be able to see you better over here."

He hesitated at the side of the bed. "You two are going to bond again?"

Ellis opened his mouth, but I shushed him. "Get over here. Right there, on Ellis' other side. He needs you."

Rory looked wary but climbed onto the bed, arranging himself so he was plastered against Ellis.

I threw my arm across Ellis' stomach, and Rory did the same, so the three of us were cuddled close. I silently thanked Clementine and Levi for the excellent air conditioning.

"That's the stuff." Ellis sighed dreamily. "I can't wait until we do this naked."

Rory choked with laughter, and I grinned. "Rory. When you look right here...." I lifted my arm and pointed at Ellis' torso. Ellis gasped and grabbed my and Rory's forearms. "What do you see?"

Because what I saw was solid, strong connections between the three of us. Between me and Ellis, between Rory and Ellis, and between Rory and me. Equal in all ways.

CAL'S CAMPAIGN COMPENDIUM

CONNECTIONS

Connections are magical tethers between magic carriers and other magic carriers, Wonders and other Wonders, or between magic carriers and Wonders. Most Wonders can perceive connections between people starting from birth, but magic carriers do not develop that ability until their late twenties to early thirties.

Types:

- *Friend and family connections: Occur spontaneously without conscious intent by the parties involved. Non-permanent. If the relationship fades, the connection will too.*
- *District Monitor connections: Intentional, non-permanent connections between DMs and Wonders. Only active within the DM's District, but Wonders can connect to multiple DMs if they travel.*
- *Hunter Team connections: Intentional, non-permanent connections between team members. Allow real-time communication and geo-location to maximize strategic advantage.*
- *Romantic connections: Can occur spontaneously without conscious intent by the partners involved, particularly if*

they touch each other skin-to-skin. Once the connection reaches a certain strength, it's permanent.

- *<u>Bonds</u>: Permanent connection between partner(s). See the entries for <u>Bonding, Parts One through Four</u>*

CHAPTER 16
ELLIS

I ADMIRED OUR CONNECTIONS, ALL GOLDEN AND SPARKLY EVEN without my glasses, but Rory's face scrunched up. "Uh, Ellis? His stomach? I'm not sure what you want me to say."

Shane smiled at him and grabbed his hand where it rested on my belly. I still had hold of their wrists, so we were solidly joined.

"How old are you?"

Rory looked even more confused. "Twenty-five. Why?"

"Some magical abilities manifest early, like your being able to see ghosts. But other abilities come later in life. What Ellis and I can do, that you'll be able to do one day yourself, is see connections."

Rory stared at my stomach for an uncomfortably long time. My dick considered being interested, but ultimately decided it needed more sleep before anything fun would happen.

I felt Shane squeeze Rory's hand. I loved Rory's long fingers. I had so much to teach him if he was willing to learn. Shane's fingers I loved for other reasons. Reasons I couldn't take advantage of right now.

"You're saying you see connections? Between me and Ellis? And you?" Rory raised his eyebrows at Shane.

I couldn't stop smiling.

Shane smiled too. "Between the three of us. Strong connections. Really strong." He focused his gaze on where his hands joined with Rory's. I let go of their wrists and put my hands over theirs. Shane smiled. He glanced almost shyly at me, then at Rory. "If Ellis and I bond again in the future, it looks like you'll be bonding with us too."

A smile bloomed over Rory's face, and through the connection I felt his happiness. Tension eased from his body.

I cleared my throat. "One of us hasn't been kissed yet tonight. Just pointing that out."

Rory's smile turned naughty. He leaned toward me, but before he got close enough for our lips to touch, he turned his head toward Shane. "Well? Get in here. We can't have him complaining later how he didn't get the full experience."

Shane's eyes almost bugged out of his head. Then I felt a rush of lust through our connection. It was strange, feeling him at a distance like this after being bonded. But at the same time it felt right. Because the connection to Rory balanced out the connection to Shane. And when we bonded—because that was absolutely happening—it would be beautiful.

Shane bent down, and his and Rory's heads approached mine. I didn't know where to look, so I closed my eyes and waited.

The kiss was glorious. A little awkward, but it was worth it to feel both sets of lips, both tongues, touching mine. I moaned, letting go of their hands to lift mine to rest on their necks.

Rory was the first to break away.

"Nooo!" I gripped his neck harder to keep him in place. Shane gave me one last peck on the side of my mouth, then he sat up as well.

Rory chuckled. "You're in no shape to do anything more."

I opened my mouth to protest, but then I stopped. He was actually right. I was ready to sleep some more. "Well, fuck."

They laughed, but Rory froze. He turned toward the door and held one hand up in a *Stop* gesture. "No. You get out. Especially *you*." He pointed in the direction of the dresser. "I won't have you making them uncomfortable and worry that you're spying on us."

Shane sat forward. "Is that Granny? Listen, you old bat. I didn't put up with your nosiness when you were alive, and it goes double now. I'll be happy to visit with you in the morning, but right now, Ellis needs to rest, and Rory and I aren't planning on wearing any pajamas. So get out or get an eyeful. It's up to you."

He jerked his t-shirt over his head and tossed it in the general direction of the closet.

Rory relaxed and turned around. He got out of bed and picked up Shane's shirt. "They're gone."

"Hold up." I glanced between Shane and Rory. "Are you saying Shane's grandmother is one of the ghosts who's been helping you?"

Rory winced. "Yeah. She didn't want me to tell Shane."

I fell back against the pillows, my hands over my face. "This is too much for my brain right now."

Shane kissed my cheek. "Sleep. Rory and I will get ready for bed, and we'll be right back, okay?"

"Okay." I closed my eyes, smiling to myself as I listened to them moving about the room and speaking softly to each other.

I managed to avoid dwelling on the giant gap in my memory, and especially the reason for it, before I fell asleep.

———

I woke up when Rory got out of bed. He patted my arm. "I'll be right back." He headed for the bathroom.

Now that I thought about it, I really needed to go as well. I sat up and looked around. I'd been pretty out of it last night, but we—the three of us! Fuck, yeah!—were in a guest bedroom, probably in the dryad's compound. I automatically checked my magic to see if everything was right with my District and my connections, but all I could feel was Rory and Shane.

Shane was still asleep next to me. I resisted the urge to run my fingers over his stubble. I missed our bond, but—at least based on what we'd discussed last night—we were heading in that direction again. This time with Rory.

I smiled as I looked around for my phone. My smile dropped. The vampires must've tossed it. I shivered uneasily and moved my hand so it rested against Shane. Our connection was strong enough that the skin-to-skin contact gave the illusion of a bond.

I wanted to speak to him mind-to-mind, but he was having a pleasant dream. A sexy one, if I wasn't mistaken. I looked down at my dick. It wasn't reacting.

I probably needed more rest and recovery from losing all that blood. I shivered again.

Rory came out of the bathroom, so I slid to the edge of the bed and stood up.

He rushed to my side. "You feeling okay?"

"A little tired. But I need to piss, and I desperately need a shower."

Shane stirred and opened his eyes. "No showering without help. At least until you get breakfast."

I tapped my finger on my chin. "I am hungry, but if I take the shower now, you just promised to help me." I wiggled my eyebrows.

They laughed, as I'd intended, but I regretted the innuendo. I didn't want them to think I planned on having sex; my body was not up for any shenanigans this morning.

I went into the bathroom by myself and shut the door in Rory's face. "I can pee alone. I'll open the door right after."

Without looking at the huge mirror over the sinks, I rushed over to the toilet and pulled down my boxers, closing my eyes in relief. When I was done, pulled my boxers back up. Normally I didn't have any issues about the size or shape of my body, but right now I wasn't ready to bare it all for Rory. Shane had seen me before, but still.

I took a big breath. Okay, I could do this. I walked over to the sink and looked at myself in the mirror. I tilted my head back and squinted so I could examine the marks on my neck. There were four of them. They didn't look fresh, so—like the mark on Rory's wrist—the bites were healing more rapidly than normal wounds.

Vampires had fed from me four times. Clutching the lip of the sink, I closed my eyes and breathed through the nausea. I completely understood why Rory had thrown up yesterday.

I needed a shower, and I needed it now.

I washed my hands and finally looked around. The bathroom was fairly large for a guest room. There was a cream-colored granite counter with a double sink, the toilet, a cupboard for towels, and a shower stall.

I walked over to turn on the shower so the water could warm up. Our hosts had provided sample-size bottles of shampoo, conditioner, and body wash, which I appreciated. I hadn't brought any shampoo with me since I usually only used it once or twice a week. But after whatever the vampires had done to me, I needed to wash my hair as well as my body.

I pulled open the shower door and leaned inside to turn the faucet handle. I grabbed the lever but froze without turning it.

The shower stall felt like it was closing in on me. I was dizzy, and the nausea was back. I forced myself to step away. I made it over to the sink, and I grabbed the edge of the counter as I sank down on my knees.

Still hanging on to the granite, I hung my head and gulped in air. I must've made some sort of noise, because Rory opened the door. "Ellis!" He rushed over and squatted down next to me. "What happened?"

"I—the shower—" I jerked my head toward it.

Rory looked over his shoulder at Shane, who leaned over Rory's back and stared down at me in concern. "The shower scared you? Made you remember something?"

"I—sort of? Not really. It felt like... a trap." My voice went down to a whisper on the last part.

Shane's eyes shot to the shower, and he made a hissing noise. "The vampires—in their van—they had you in a metal box with a lock on it. Ms. Jackson had to rip the lock off so we could get you out."

I shuddered. "I thought I was unconscious."

Rory rubbed my back. "Um, maybe you were in and out. Okay, well, I'm sure Clementine will let us use another bathroom that has a tub."

Shane nodded. "I'll go check." He started to straighten up.

"No! Wait. Please. Can you just... go in there with me? I want to try that first." I had a shower stall at my house in Dallas. I didn't want to live there anymore, but I might have to stay there while I got it ready to sell.

Rory and Shane eyed the shower stall, which, okay, wasn't big enough for the three of us.

Shane walked over and reached inside to flip on the water. "How about one of us is in there with you and the other stands outside. We'll pull you out if it gets too stressful."

"Okay." Rory seeing me naked suddenly wasn't much of a concern in light of my issues with the shower stall. I let him help me stand up again.

Without ceremony, Shane pulled his t-shirt over his head and tugged off his boxer-briefs.

Rory muttered, "Fuck."

Relieved to have something to smile about, I elbowed him. "Right? It's all the landscaping he does."

"Your turn." Shane walked over and tugged on my boxers. I couldn't decide if I was glad he wasn't hard or embarrassed.

Once I was naked, he grabbed my hand and led me over to the shower stall. He checked the water temperature and got inside. Rory stood at my back and rubbed my shoulders. "You can do this."

I glanced back at him. "How did I miss you getting undressed?" I gave him a thorough once-over, but even if I'd had my glasses I wasn't in the right mindspace to appreciate his lean muscles, golden treasure trail, and sizeable dick. He was at least half-hard, which I decided was a compliment, though it might've been for Shane, who could turn anyone on all by himself.

"I'm sneaky that way." He nudged me toward the shower stall.

I sucked in a deep breath and got in next to Shane. Rory held the door open. I didn't enjoy the cool drafts of air, but it was better than being shut inside.

Shane and I couldn't avoid touching each other, and I focused on where my skin brushed against his, which helped me not think about how small the box we were in really was.

Once we were both completely wet, I reached for the shampoo.

"Let me?" Shane intercepted my hand.

"Okay."

He turned me so my back was toward him. I heard him set the bottle back on the little shelf, and then his hands were in my hair, massaging the shampoo into my scalp. I lifted my gaze to Rory's. He gripped the frame of the shower door with one hand, and the edge of the glass wall with the other. His eyes burned into mine, and his cock was rock-hard.

"Ooooh, look," Shane said into my ear. I felt his erection brush my ass cheek. "Rory likes what he sees."

He tipped my head back to rinse out the shampoo. When he released me, I said, "Guys, I don't think I'm...."

"Shh." Shane wrapped his arms around my front. "A little blue balls won't hurt us." His reassurance came through our connection, but I still felt guilty.

"Y'all can—"

"No." Rory reached in and ran his hand over my cheek. "We'll wait until you're ready. All of us or none of us, at least until we figure out our relationship. Okay?"

Shane nodded, the stubble on his cheek rasping against my ear. "Okay." He nudged me. "Conditioner?"

"Um, no, thanks." I couldn't look away from Rory's smiling eyes. He wasn't trying to send his emotions through our connection—I was pretty sure we'd explained connections to him—but I could feel his want when he looked at me and Shane. And it wasn't just lust. He wanted us. Our time, our emotions, and our futures.

Shane lathered me up with the body wash, cleaning everything, including my ass and junk, tenderly but efficiently. When I was rinsed off, he kissed me before handing me over to Rory, who dried me with the same care. Then I was wrapped in a towel and seated on the closed toilet.

"Now you get to watch." Rory winked at me and swung his hips as he got into the shower with Shane, who was almost done shampooing his hair. Rory grabbed the body wash and, after dumping some in his hand, began to lather Shane up. Based on the way Shane's cock jumped, and the bolt of lust that came through our connection, Shane enjoyed the touch.

I really wished my libido was interested, but I was fighting fatigue. Shane shot me a worried look and took over washing himself. He muttered something to Rory, who hastily snatched the shampoo off the shelf and began on his hair.

Well, fuck. I was a killjoy today.

A very few minutes later, Shane and Rory got out of the shower and dried off. I decided to let my hair do whatever it wanted. I didn't have any product here, and nobody was going to judge.

We all went into the bedroom where it turned out Rory had hung up all of our clothes. After I got dressed, I was told to sit in one of the armchairs, and Rory packed my dirty clothes into my bag and his into his backpack. Shane packed up his own bag. We stripped the bed and left the sheets in a pile on top of the comforter.

We got to the living room in time to hear Levi yell at Simon. "Don't be a damn fool, son!"

Simon put his hands on his hips. "I'm not your son!"

Levi waved this away, but before he could open his mouth again, Shane said, "What's going on?"

Levi pointed at Simon. "This one won't wait for the others to get here to feed him. Plus, Roberta went to the medical supply store to get some bags and tubing so we can send a cooler along for the road. But that'll take even more time, and he—" He jabbed his finger in Simon's direction again. "Says he needs to get going."

I felt slightly ill thinking about Simon feeding from someone, even if it was consensual. But on the other hand, he'd risked his life to rescue me yesterday, and Shane and Rory had said he'd saved the dryads from the vampires.

Rory walked up to Simon and poked him in the chest. "You promised. Last night, you injured your leg. You promised you'd feed before you left today."

Simon's expression said he'd hoped Rory wouldn't remember that. His shoulders slumped. "Fine."

Shane walked over. "Give me your phone."

Simon gave him a wary look but pulled it out of his pocket and handed it over.

"I'm putting all of our numbers in here, and the number for Dominic Shaw, who heads up the Hunters out of TWIST." Oh, good call.

Simon scowled. "I can handle the vampires on my own. There are only four of them left on the planet besides me."

"Maybe. But it'll be easier and less risky for you to have backup. Plus, didn't you say they had hostages? The Hunters know all about handling trafficking victims."

Simon huffed and rolled his eyes. "Fine."

Clementine stuck her head around the corner. "If the shouting is over, y'all can come get some human-style breakfast."

As I turned to follow Rory into the kitchen, a flash of gold between Simon and Levi caught my eye. Oh ho! All of that shouting covered up some real affection. Even without my glasses I could see they had a tentative family connection between them. No wonder Levi was calling Simon "son". Simon was going to get help whether he wanted it or not.

Smiling, I walked over to the table, where Ms. Jackson was in their tiger form along with Pia and Manny. Pia cheered when she saw me, jumping up from her chair and running over to hug me.

"I'm glad you're okay!" She stepped back, pointing at the newly reformed connection between us. "That's better!"

I smiled at her as she skipped back to her seat, but Rory said, "Hey! Is she talking about a connection? How come she can see them, and I can't?"

I shook my head. "She's a Wonder. They have more magic than we do." But speaking of things we could see.... I stopped in my tracks. "Why's Manny sparkling?" I squinted, but it didn't go away.

Manny looked down at himself and frowned.

Shane put his hand on my lower back. "He got injured and Ms. Jackson healed him. It's fading."

"Wait." Manny put his hands up and turned them this way and that. "What do you mean I'm sparkling? Why can't I see it? I want to see it!"

Pia giggled. "Only magic carriers and Wonders can see the magic sparkle, silly."

He gave her an exaggerated pout. "Huh. I'll just have to find some extra sequins or rhinestones to make up for it."

Had Ms. Jackson given him some of their magic as part of the healing? Just how badly injured had he been?

Shane pushed me toward one of the empty chairs. I smelled bacon and toast, and my stomach growled. I'd get Manny's story out of Shane and Rory later when Pia wasn't around.

Clementine reappeared. "Ellis, is this your phone?" She held it up.

My mouth dropped open. "Oh my god, yes, it is! Where did you find it?"

She handed it over then gestured vaguely toward the front door. "One of the others found it in the woods when it rang."

I pressed it against my chest. "Thank you so much, and please tell whoever it was that found it thanks as well. Now I don't have to deal with getting a new phone on top of everything else."

I clicked on the screen. Without my glasses I couldn't make out the percentage of battery left, but it looked small. I'd only received one phone call, and although I couldn't read the town name, it was from somewhere in Arizona, so most likely spam. Well, at least it'd helped me get my phone back.

Simon joined us at the table and scarfed down a large plate of food, same as the rest of us. He had nice hands, large and long-fingered. He'd be easily able to do a Double Iron Whip if he wanted to. When he was done eating, he put his fork on his plate and drained his glass of orange juice. "I'll be leaving soon. Rory and Ellis, if you want your memories back, now is the time to tell me."

I didn't have to think about it. I shook my head almost violently. "No. Not me. Thanks for offering, but no."

Rory rubbed my back, but said, "I want them back. Please."

"Sure. Shane, can you switch seats with me?"

Shane got up, and he and Simon moved around each other to exchange places. Simon caught Shane's arm. "You guys should bond soon. That's a shit-ton of connections you're holding. If your magic decides they're too many, it'll either start cutting some of the connections or just kind of...." He clapped his hands together. "Implode."

"Wait, what? You mean because he's holding both of our Districts? Can't I take mine back now?" Fuck, I didn't want Shane hurt.

Simon shrugged. "If you're resonating with your District, sure. Have you felt it since yesterday?"

My shoulders sagged. "No." And I was smack dab in the middle of it too.

Shane hadn't sat down again yet. He shifted nervously, gripping the back of the chair Simon had been sitting in. "I bet that's because I'm resonating with your District as well as my own. Or they're combined now. But, Simon, what did you mean by *implode*? That sounds... violent?"

Simon lowered himself into the chair next to Rory. "I've never seen it myself, but it would mean your magic would essentially collapse in on itself from the strain and you'd pretty much burn out. Some of your magic might come back, but most of it probably wouldn't."

Shane plopped into the chair, rubbing his chest. His face was pale. Ms. Jackson nudged him with the side of their head.

I raised my hand. "I'm all for bonding ASAP."

Rory's eyes darted between me and Shane. "I'm on board if you'll have me."

I put my hand around his back.

Shane emanated worry through the bond. "It's a big step. Are you sure—"

Simon held up a hand. "You can discuss it later. I need to get going. Ellis, let go of Rory for a minute." I pulled my hand back. "Okay, Rory, give me your hand." He took Rory's hand in his and then stared into his eyes for a moment. "Okay, done." He let go. Simon scooted his chair back as if he were about to stand up.

Rory grabbed his wrist. "Wait."

Simon froze.

Rory said, "I forgive you for taking my blood with, um, minimal consent. I can see you didn't like doing it."

Simon ducked his head. "Thanks."

Rory patted Simon's wrist. "I hope you find the one you're looking for."

Simon smirked. "Which one?" He shoved the chair back and picked up his and Shane's plates to take to the kitchen.

Just as he returned, Levi came in through the front door. "Where's Simon? Oh, there you are. A bunch of people are here ready to donate blood. And we have bags so you can take some with you."

We all said goodbye to Simon and Levi so they could go off to deal with that. Then Shane helped Clementine clean up the dishes while Rory put our bags in the car. Manny and I were allowed to go to the front porch and watch Pia ride on Ms. Jackson's back as they trotted around in their donkey form. It looked hella uncomfortable to me, but I wasn't a teenager anymore.

I was looking forward to getting into the car, because I really needed another nap.

I turned to Manny. "Are you tired from being injured yesterday?"

He made a so-so gesture. "Not as much as I expected to be. Those sparkles must be the shit, right?" He grinned, but then dropped his smile. "But my head is pretty fucked up. I thought I was dead. I mean, I could tell I was on the way out. It's freaky, you know?"

I knocked my shoulder into his. "I know. Trust me, I know."

Finally everyone was ready to go. We thanked Clementine for her hospitality, and she hugged us goodbye. Pia and Ms. Jackson got in the third row of seats along with Pia's potted plants, and Manny and I commandeered the more comfortable seats in the second row. I had mine reclined as far back as it would go before we were off the dryads' property.

I yawned. "Wake me when we get there. I can't wait to be home."

———

I jerked awake when the car doors opened. Blinking, I looked around as I levered my seat upright. "What are we doing *here*?" Shit, they weren't planning on leaving me here, were they?

Shane pulled my door open. "What do you mean? You said you wanted to go home. This is the address you gave me a while back. Did you move or something?"

"I—I meant your home. I mean, I was hoping we'd live there." I eyed my zero-personality, cookie-cutter suburban home. "I guess I should've talked to you about it."

Shane seemed at a loss for words.

But Manny wasn't. "Great! We can pick up a bunch of your stuff to take back with us, then we can get on the road and be home in Houston tonight!" Pia cheered as he exited the car and tilted his seat forward for her to get out.

Shane extended a hand to help me out of the car. When I was on my feet, he kissed my cheek before tilting the seat for Ms. Jackson. "Sounds like a great plan to me."

"Yeah?"

"Um, Ellis?" Rory put his hand on my back. "Ms. Jackson seems to be letting your neighbor see them." He pointed toward the house next door. I squinted at the fuzzy figure of Gerald Rathbone, the biggest pain in my ass, who seemed to be tracking Ms. Jackson as they sauntered toward the front door.

"Oh, fuck. He's going to call the HOA. Or Animal Control."

Shane chuckled. "Ms. Jackson can handle it. Let's get inside and get your packing started. Pia could probably use a snack if you've got anything."

"You know what? You're right. Fuck him. I'll be moving out anyway." I waved cheerfully at Gerald as I walked to the house. Ms. Jackson had opened the front door, but I couldn't bring myself to care about how.

Selling the place would certainly help my finances now that I was unemployed. The severance check would only go so far.

Rory and Manny went to forage in the kitchen while Shane, Pia, and Ms. Jackson explored the back deck. I headed for the bedroom to get my spare pair of glasses.

Once I could see again—and that alone improved my mood a hundred percent—I dug a couple of suitcases and some duffel bags out of the closet in the office-slash-guest bedroom. I took those into my room and tossed them onto the bed.

The first thing I did was take my Yo-Yo collection off the shelf over my dresser and carefully wrap each one in a t-shirt and place them in a duffel. I only owned nine, but the Hornet and the Metal Drifter with the skull counterweight were my favorites. Hopefully Shane and Rory wouldn't think my hobby was too dorky.

After making sure Pia was still outside, I opened my night-stand and dumped my sex toys, lube, and condoms into the same duffel before zipping it up.

After that I shoved clothes into the suitcases without taking them off the hangers. I'd worry about wrinkles when I got to Shane's house. Our house.

I smiled.

Shane wandered in. "Those bougainvilleas you planted a few weeks ago look great." He opened a drawer and started rummaging through my shorts and t-shirts.

"Good. They'll help sell the house then."

He paused, a stack of my shorts in his hands. "You were nesting. I remember. You told me you bought a bigger car, you painted, and you planted the flowers." He dropped the shorts into the suitcase and walked over to me. "The bigger car was to carry me, Rory, and Pia. But the paint and the flowers were to help sell this house so you could move into mine." He kissed me, slow and sweet.

I reveled in the feel of his body, his lips on my mouth. I'd missed this. When he finally pulled back, I hugged him. "I can't wait to have our bond back, but I'm glad we know what was missing the first time." I glanced out the window to the backyard. Pia and Ms. Jackson must've come back inside. "Do you think we can get Rory to move in too?"

Shane snorted. "He's hooked. He'll come. Plus he lives in an apartment. It's not like Pia would want to move in there." His eyes went wide. "Do you mind.... We didn't talk about Pia living with us."

I gave him my most devious grin. "Hey, Pia?" I called.

"Yeah?" It sounded like she was in the kitchen.

"You wanna live in Shane's house with me and Shane and Rory?"

"Yeah!"

"Okay, good!" I winked at Shane. "See, took care of that. TWIST has someone who can help us get ID documents for her. We'll be all set."

Rory stuck his head around the doorframe. "I feel like I missed out on an important conversation."

I tilted my head up to squint at the ceiling. "*Hmmm*. No. No, I don't think so."

He came inside the room, allowing Shane and me to pull him into our hug. "Nothing you want to ask me?"

Shane kissed his cheek. "No, not particularly. Ellis and I got everything figured out."

He snorted. "Sounds like it. For the record, I'm with Pia. I wanna live with you two. And her."

We attempted another three-way kiss, but before we could work out whose head needed to tilt in which direction, someone pounded on my front door.

"I'll get it!" Manny shouted.

I groaned. "I bet Gerald called the homeowners association about Ms. Jackson."

Rory pulled back. "They'd show up that quickly? I thought HOAs just sent you nasty letters with fines for breaking the rules?"

"Ellis? Can you come here please?" Manny sounded amused.

I sighed. "They do that too." I squeezed them one more time then headed to the front door. Rory and Shane trailed after me.

Yep, there was Sharon White, the president of the HOA. She was dressed to impress in a navy power suit and heels. She had a clipboard in one hand and held up her phone in another.

"Hello, Sharon. What brings you by today?" As if I didn't know.

"Ellis. I received a very concerning complaint regarding a dangerous animal on your property. I'm afraid I can't allow such a creature to remain in the neighborhood."

I crossed my arms. "A dangerous animal? Is that really an HOA matter? Seems to me you should've called Animal Control if you or whoever made the complaint were that worried about it."

"Wait a sec." Rory held up his phone. "If she's recording this conversation, I feel like you should have a recording too. Okay, go ahead."

Sharon gave him a once-over. "And who might you be?"

He gave her a charming grin. "I'm Rory, one of Ellis' boyfriends."

Her mouth dropped open. "One of...."

Shane came up behind me and kissed me on the temple. "I'm Shane. The other boyfriend."

Sharon's eyes went wide. "Well, now, this is not acceptable. There's a morality clause in the HOA charter."

I raised my eyebrows at her. "Isn't that the clause where it says we can't do anything illegal? I don't remember a law against having two boyfriends."

Pia walked up with a peanut butter cracker in her hand. Sharon gasped. "You have a child in this home? Little girl, where are your parents?"

Pia wrinkled her nose. "Dead."

Sharon's jaw was getting a workout today.

Pia turned to us. "Ellis, is it lunchtime yet? I'm hungry." She stuck her bottom lip out and tipped her head forward slightly to make her eyes seem bigger and sadder.

I rubbed my hand over my mouth to hide my smile. "Sharon, I'm sure you have other things to do with your day. What exactly did you come over here for?"

She dragged her eyes away from Pia. "Right. The complaint about a dangerous animal. I need to see the animal to verify it and obtain your assurance you will get rid of it."

I scrunched up my face and tapped my finger against my chin. "I don't have a pet, and I don't recall seeing any animals today. What kind of animal? Like a coyote or something?"

"It was a tiger," she said flatly.

Pia gasped. "She wants to take Ms. Jackson away? Noooo! Ellis! Rory! Shane! You can't let her!" She threw her arms in the air—which I thought was a little overdone—and spun around before racing around the corner toward the small den I used for watching TV and gaming.

Manny, who was still holding the door open, coughed into his shoulder.

Sharon had a triumphant gleam in her eye. "So you *do* have a tiger."

I sighed. "Sure, Sharon. There's a tiger in the den if you want to look. Though really, aren't cats allowed under the HOA rules? I don't think the type of cat is specified." I waved her forward. I would not miss dealing with Gerald and Sharon after I moved.

With that heartening thought, I extended my arm to indicate Sharon should precede us through the living room and into the den.

She sniffed as she walked past me. "I feel certain that owning an exotic animal such as a tiger violates a city ordinance." She stopped in the doorway. "Is this some sort of joke?"

I folded my arms. "You tell me. You're the one who accused me of having a tiger. There's the tiger."

Manny stuck his head around my shoulder to chortle at Pia, who was hugging the tiara-wearing stuffed tiger form of Ms. Jackson and pretending to sob into their fur. "*Chica*, the tiger's not going anywhere. Stop crying and come help me and Shane figure out what we're going to order for lunch."

Pia looked around and wiped her dry eyes. "Lunch?" She leaned over and kissed Ms. Jackson on the cheek then bounced off the couch. "Ms. Jackson wants to try brownies!"

Sharon stepped aside to allow Pia to leave the room. She stared down at her clipboard. "I see I was provided with incorrect information."

"I guess so. Anything else I can help you with?"

"Um, no. Thank you." She held her head high as she walked past me.

I gave Ms. Jackson a thumbs up before I followed Sharon to the front door, running into Rory as he carried one of my suitcases out of my bedroom.

"You packed for me?"

He grinned and shrugged. "You're tired. And this way it'll be a surprise to see what you brought with you." He wiggled his eyebrows. "Or what you forgot."

Sharon ignored him but thawed enough to tell me, "If you're leaving town, I can have the citizen patrol drive by more frequently."

Well, shit. Now I felt bad. Maybe I should throw her a bone. "Thanks, Sharon, that would be great. Um, I'm actually going to be moving to Houston. Do you know a good realtor?"

She smiled, and as Rory went out the front door to put the suitcase in the car, Sharon pulled out her phone and texted me a number. "Gretchen is my sister. She knows the area well and will get you the best price."

Oh, fuck, her sister? I gritted my teeth and forced a smile. "Sounds great."

Sharon glanced behind her at Rory, then she eyed Shane and Manny, who were in the kitchen with Pia. "If you'll be tied up with... your boyfriends in Houston, she offers a remote closing option and she can contract out the packing." She looked around my living room. "If you can leave the furniture here, it's staged well enough now."

Shane had been right. My nesting instincts had helped me get my house ready to sell.

Manny edged past me carrying the tequila and Triple Sec I kept on top of the refrigerator. "Can't leave these behind!"

I cleared my throat. "Sounds great. I'll give her a call next week." Honestly, having someone else pack up my stuff might be for the best. Simon had said Rory, Shane, and I needed to bond sooner rather than later, and we wouldn't be able to be apart much for a while after that. I hoped Rory could work remotely. Shane's job would be a big issue though. I watched him in the kitchen, tossing peanuts at Pia, trying to aim for her open mouth.

We should probably sit down and talk about all this like adults.

CAL'S CAMPAIGN COMPENDIUM

CHILDREN OF WONDERS AND MAGIC CARRIERS

If a magic carrier or a Wonder has children, those children will, without fail, inherit magic. What type depends on the other parent.

Wonder + Wonder: *Obviously two Wonders of the same species will have children of their mutual species. Wonders of different species are not always able to cross-breed, but if they can, the children are genetically identical to one or the other parent.*

Magic Carrier + Magic Carrier: *When magic carriers have children with other magic carriers, their children can end up becoming any type of magic carrier. Even two magic carriers of the same type, such as a Hunter having children with another Hunter, can have children who are a different type of magic carrier.*

Wonder + Magic Carrier: *Children of a Wonder and a magic carrier are either born as the same type of Wonder as their parent, or as a magic carrier of any type.*

Wonder + Human: *The children of a Wonder and a human, if they are able to cross-breed, are always Wonders and are genetically indistinguishable from a Wonder born of two Wonder parents of the same species.*

Magic Carrier + Human: *Children of a magic carrier and a human will either end up as a magic carrier of any type, or as a magic carrier who displays no specific magical abilities other than those common to all magic carriers, such as being able to form connections and bond with Wonders or other magic carriers.*

CHAPTER 17
RORY

"DON'T SHUT IT YET!" MANNY CALLED AS HE JOGGED TOWARD me holding two bottles of alcohol. Rather, he left the house at a jog, dodging around the woman from Ellis' HOA on the front porch. But as he got closer to the car he slowed down considerably. His face was losing its color.

I rushed over and took the bottles from him. "Overdid it?"

He gave a jerky nod and grabbed my elbow as I walked back to the car. "I felt fine. Up until I didn't."

Grandfather snorted from where he hovered behind Manny. "His body's still absorbing the magic. Looks different than yours and the others'. Huh."

I ignored him, putting the bottles in the cargo area next to Ellis' suitcase before helping Manny sit on the bumper.

"You're still healing. Maybe after lunch you should lie down while the rest of us finish packing. Other than that, we only need to throw out the perishables in the fridge, so I'm hoping we can be on the road in a couple of hours." I rubbed my hand through my hair. "Um, I wanted to ask, but not in front of Pia. How does your belly look? Is the scar any better?"

"It's pretty gnarly." He looked around. The HOA woman was finally driving away. Manny stood, turned his back to the street, and hiked up the hem of his t-shirt. He was wearing two, one tucked inside his shorts and one outside. "The waist-band rubs against the scar." He pulled up the inner t-shirt as well and tucked them both under his chin while he yanked down the waistband of his pants with both of his thumbs.

The scar was indeed gnarly. It arced from the bottom of his left ribcage down and over to his right pelvic bone, cutting through his treasure trail. The skin had knitted back together unevenly, and the resulting ridge was as red and angry as it had been yesterday right after Ms. Jackson had healed it.

"Fuck, Manny, does it hurt?" I reached out but didn't dare touch.

Before he could answer, we heard wheels on the driveway. Manny dropped his shirts and took his hands out of his waistband as the big black Lincoln Navigator came to a stop a few feet behind us. I gently pushed him out of the way and shut the Range Rover's hatch.

The driver stepped out of the Lincoln. He was huge, easily six foot four and muscle-bound like he lived at the gym. He was wearing a tight black t-shirt whose sleeves could barely contain his biceps. His jeans looked painted on over his thick thighs. I didn't even look at his face until he whipped off his mirrored aviators.

Even though the man was bald and had a comically different body type than my boyfriend, this guy was obviously related to Ellis. He had to be Arch. Their faces were way too similar for them not to be brothers. But their eyes were vastly differ-ent. Even though the color was the same, Ellis' eyes were warm and friendly. Arch's were clinical and calculating.

"You must be Arch. I'm Rory. Ellis is inside. He'll be glad to see you."

Arch gave me an up-nod. "You're the Medium. Nice to meet you." His voice held zero emotional inflection. Okay then. I'd let Ellis tell him we were boyfriends.

"This is Manny. Manny, Arch is Ellis' brother."

Manny cocked a hip and crossed his arms. He raised an eyebrow and gave Arch a slow once-over. "You're the brother. Nice to meet you." His tone was exactly the same as Arch's had been, and I coughed to hide my laugh.

Arch gave Manny a once-over back. "And what is your... role here?"

Okay, that was enough of this shit. "He's my best friend," I snapped.

Arch raised an arrogant eyebrow at me. "Best friend must mean something different to you than it does to me, based on what I saw you two doing when I drove up."

"What an asshole!" Grandfather grumped. He reached out a translucent hand and swatted Arch on the back of his bald head. Except his hand didn't go through. It connected.

Arch ducked and whirled to the side, unerringly facing Grandfather even though he couldn't possibly see him. "Who's there?" His gaze bounced around the street. He had a knife and a gun in his hands that he'd pulled out of nowhere.

Manny backed up into the Range Rover. "The fuck?"

"It's okay," I said. "Sorry about that. My grandfather's ghost took exception to your comment. Um, usually you would only feel a cold spot, if anything."

Arch continued to stare around suspiciously for another moment before the knife vanished and he tucked the gun away at the small of his back. I caught a glimpse of a leather holster under his pants.

"Your grandfather's ghost packs a wallop." He rubbed the back of his head.

Grandfather was staring at his hand. "Rory, I felt it. I felt my hand touch his head!"

"That's... weird. I hope you're not turning into a poltergeist."

Grandfather scoffed. "Hardly. I still have my wits about me. I think it's all that magic you and the other two started sparking off."

Arch was eyeing me skeptically, so I waved Grandfather off. "Why don't you go check on Garfield and Mercy or something? We'll test your new abilities when we get back to Houston."

I turned to our visitor. "Come on. I'm sure you're anxious to see Ellis."

"Yeah. Is he okay?" We started walking across the lawn to the front door.

I weighed my response. I'd never had a brother, but I wasn't sure I'd want my boyfriend spilling all my secrets to one.

"He's doing a hell of a lot better than I think I would in his shoes." I opened the front door. "Ellis, you have a visitor!"

I was suddenly certain Ellis was tired and hungry and didn't want to delay lunch to deal with yet another person stopping by.

"In the den!"

I waved Arch forward. He knew the way.

"Hey, squirt!"

Ellis, who'd been watching from the couch as Shane and Pia chose their avatars for a video game, stood up. His face looked blank, but I could tell he was astonished. Absolutely shocked to see his brother.

"Arch? What are you doing here?"

"Are you kidding? My baby brother gets kidnapped by vampires, and you think I'm not gonna come check on you?"

Based on Ellis' expression, that was actually exactly what he'd thought.

"You're usually so busy saving people. I already got saved."

"Yeah? You wanna tell me about it? Shit, your neck!"

That's when I realized Ellis and Arch hadn't hugged. Hadn't even touched each other. Ellis was still standing in front of the couch, and Arch was just inside the door to the den. Manny and I hovered outside the room like spectators, and Pia and Shane weren't any better. Ms. Jackson was still in their stuffed tiger form at the other end of the couch, but their plastic-like eyes looked pretty judgy to me.

"Um, yeah. It's healing. Oh! Um, this is Shane, and this is Pia. And that's Ms. Jackson."

Arch barely glanced at the stuffed tiger, but he greeted Shane and Pia pleasantly enough. He was obviously curious about Pia's presence.

Manny cleared his throat. "Arch, would you like something to drink? We've got lunch coming, and there *should* be enough for you to join us."

I stifled a grin. Manny's tone made it clear that Arch had better not eat more than his share.

"Um, thanks. Some water would be great. Got to stay hydrated."

I put my hand on Manny's shoulder. "You need to sit down. I'll get waters for all of us."

"Fine." Manny squeezed past Arch to sit in the recliner at the end of the couch next to Ms. Jackson. He crossed his arms and stared stonily at Ellis' brother.

I made three trips to the kitchen to make sure everyone had glasses of water or iced tea. When I finally sat down in the chair at the opposite end of the couch from Manny, Ellis was telling his brother that he felt fine, just a little tired. I was glad I hadn't said anything when Arch had asked.

Arch was manspreading in the center of the couch between Ms. Jackson and Ellis. Shane and Pia were still on the floor, their backs to the couch and with controllers in their hands. They'd thoughtfully turned the volume off on *Super Mario Sunshine*.

Shane exchanged glances with me, and he grimaced. Arch was not winning any friends here.

"Glad to hear you're okay. Tell me what happened? How did you get taken?" His tone held a tinge of *That-never-would've-happened-to-me* that I didn't appreciate. At all.

I reached out and picked up Ellis' hand from where he'd been resting it on the arm of the couch. He smiled at me and threaded our fingers together.

Arch frowned at our hands. "What the hell is this? You're fucking this guy?"

Ellis tightened his grip. "You know I'm gay, Arch."

Arch waved his hand through the air. "Sure, sure. But him?" He pointed at me. "When I drove up he was on the driveway, and that one had his pants pulled down showing your boyfriend his dick." He hiked a thumb at Manny.

Manny sat up, his eyebrows low and his eyes hard. "What did you just say?"

I squeezed Ellis' hand. "That's not what happened."

He smiled. "I know." He looked at Arch. "Did you not notice this?" He pointed at his belly, then at mine, and then over at Shane.

Arch's mouth fell open. "The fuck? You're involved with two guys at once?"

"It's called polyamory. Look it up." I left the *dumbshit* unspoken.

With a quiet apology to Pia, Shane paused their game. He walked over and stood between my chair and the couch, putting his hands on my and Ellis' shoulders. "Is this a problem, Arch? Because our magic is pretty damn happy about it."

Arch blinked at us. "Sorry. I didn't notice your connections earlier. But, then why was this guy showing Rory his dick?"

"Arch!" Ellis pointed at Pia. "There's a child present."

Pia looked up from where she was flipping through Ellis' game collection and rolled her eyes.

Arch ignored his brother and turned to Manny. "You trying to break them up or some shit? Because that's my brother's boyfriend, and you can't have him."

What the fuck was this guy's deal? I could not keep up with the way his brain worked. Ellis started to speak, but I shook my head at him. Manny was more than capable of handling Arch.

Manny's lip curled, and he looked Arch up and down, obviously not impressed. "It's none of your business, but I'm going to answer your question so Ellis, Shane, and Pia have no doubts about me." He looked at Ellis. "When I took the tequila out to the car, Rory asked me if I had a scar from yesterday, so I was showing it to him." He sneered at Arch. "For your information, *Archibald*, the vampires grabbed me too, but since I was a pathetic human, they just disemboweled me and tossed me aside." He stood up. "Which reminds me. I owe Ms. Jackson a treat. Come on, Ms. Jackson. I saw some cookies in Ellis' pantry."

He picked up his ice water, walked calmly to the door, and didn't look back. Ms. Jackson morphed smoothly into their live tiger form and stepped regally off the couch.

Arch made a high-pitched shrieking noise and stumbled to his feet. He ran over to put himself between Ms. Jackson and Pia. The gun and knife were back in his hands.

"Arch! Put those away!" Ellis stood up and put his hands on his hips. "Ms. Jackson won't hurt you."

Pia slipped around Arch, neatly evading him when he side-stepped to block her. She skipped over to Ms. Jackson and ran her hands through Ms. Jackson's fur.

"See, Uncle Arch? Ms. Jackson is the best."

Arch pointed his gun at the floor, his face shocked.

Ms. Jackson sat down and manifested the Ouija board on their chest. *A-C-T-I-N-G-L-I-K-E-A-J-E-R-K-W-O-N-T-R-E-P-A-I-R-Y-O-U-R-R-E-L-A-T-I-O-N-S-H-I-P-W-I-T-H-E-L-L-I-S.* There was a pause, then they flashed, *B-E-S-I-D-E-S-Y-O-U-H-A-V-E-A-J-O-B-T-O-D-O-A-N-D-Y-O-U-L-L-N-E-E-D-O-U-R-H-E-L-P.*

They stared meaningfully at Arch for a moment, then they nudged Pia toward the door, sparkling out *W-O-R-K-T-O-G-E-T-H-E-R-R-H-Y-T-H-M-N-A-T-I-O-N* as they left the room.

Damn, Ms. Jackson hadn't been that wordy since I'd known them.

Ellis rounded on me and Shane. "Manny was *disemboweled*? You said he'd been injured, but what happened?"

I eyed Arch, who stared after Ms. Jackson and absently holstered his gun. I didn't notice what he'd done with the knife. "Um, we'll tell you later. I think you and Arch need to chat."

"What the hell is that thing?" Arch was not interested in Manny's injuries.

Ellis crossed his arms. "Their name is Ms. Jackson. They're an Elven artifact, and they're sentient. I thought you Hunters would've been briefed about them. They even have an entry in the Compendium Cal put online."

A Compendium? That sounded like something I needed access to.

Arch threw up his hands. "I've been in the field. I haven't had time to check my emails. I only heard you were kidnapped because Dominic called me." The *and you didn't* was heavily implied.

A sharp knock sounded. Pia shouted, "Lunch is here!" and we all heard her feet thundering to the front door.

Ellis and Arch were involved in some sort of stare-down I didn't want any part of, so I squeezed Ellis' shoulder, picked up my drink and his, and left the room. Shane followed me out carrying his iced tea.

Pia raced by with the bags of food. Manny was sitting at the small breakfast table with Ms. Jackson, who was for once seated in another chair. An open package of Fig Newtons sat on the table between them, and the chair added enough height that Ms. Jackson's head hung over it, as if they were about to scoop up the entire package as soon as Manny turned his head. When Pia dumped the food bags on the table, it was clear Ms. Jackson would be able to reach every inch of it.

Ellis' table was a smallish rectangle. It could probably seat six in a pinch, but he only had four chairs. We now had five adults, plus Ms. Jackson and Pia.

"Ms. Jackson, you'll have to sit on the floor."

They gave me a sour look but hopped down agreeably enough. While they weren't looking, Manny swiped the Fig Newtons from the table and held them out to Shane, who snagged them smoothly on his way into the kitchen.

I went into Ellis' office and rolled his desk chair out and over to the breakfast table.

Shane retrieved a small ottoman from the living room and placed it directly across from where Ms. Jackson had positioned themselves. "Arch is tall enough to sit on that and still see over the table."

Manny laughed and held up his hand for a high-five.

Pia wrinkled her nose. "Uncle Arch isn't as friendly as Ellis."

I patted her shoulder and guided her to the chair next to Ms. Jackson. "Let's give Uncle Arch a chance. He and Ellis seem like they might have had some issues getting along, but that doesn't make him a bad person. He did try to protect you when he thought Ms. Jackson was dangerous."

She made a *hmmm* noise and started opening the bags, so I guessed she wasn't buying what I was selling.

Shane helped me portion out food onto plates. Luckily we'd ordered a variety of Indian dishes, so there was plenty for everyone, Manny's comments to Arch notwithstanding.

When we all had our plates filled, I stood up to go get Ellis and Arch, because, dammit, Ellis needed to eat after yesterday. But they came out on their own. They weren't smiling exactly, but they didn't seem as hostile as before.

I wished I knew how to tap into these so-called connections, since apparently you could check on your partner's emotions. But Shane seemed relieved, so I'd just pretend everything was fine and move on.

I filled a plate for Ellis while Arch eyeballed the ottoman between me and Manny. "You're tallest," I pointed out.

Ellis, who I'd seated between me and Shane, shook his head. "Sorry. I don't entertain much."

Shane bumped shoulders with him. "We made do. Don't worry about it."

Arch sat down and scooted the ottoman up to the table, which was chest-high on him. He had to lift his elbows to fill his plate and eat. I grinned to myself.

We ate quietly for a few minutes, then Arch cleared his throat. "Um, Ms. Jackson, I apologize for freaking out earlier and pointing weapons at you. I was not aware of wha—who you were, and I promise it won't happen again."

The Ouija board appeared on their chest. *T-H-A-N-K-Y-O-U.*

"Um, I am curious, though. You mentioned a job? Is it maybe something to do with the billionaire Dominic told me to ask y'all about?" He looked from Ms. Jackson to me, Ellis, and Shane.

Yes sparkled on Ms. Jackson's board.

Shane put his hand on Pia's back. "But we're not going to discuss it at the table."

Pia made a face. "I don't mind, especially if you're discussing putting him in jail."

I looked around, but I didn't see Lorraine anywhere. Grandfather was in the kitchen trying to slap at things on the counter with his hands. I made a mental note to ask what Garfield and Mercy had found out.

Arch had frozen, staring at Pia. "You... were, um, being held by that... guy?"

I wanted to call Grandfather in here to whack Arch on the head again.

Ellis reached across me to slap Arch's forearm. Close enough. "Arch! We'll talk about this later."

Pia shivered, and Ms. Jackson morphed into a giant panda form. Arch dropped his fork, which made me super happy. Ms. Jackson reached out and hugged Pia, who leaned her head on their furry belly.

"Uh, sorry." Arch darted a glance at Ellis. He kept his eyes on his plate for the next few minutes.

Ellis took a sip of his water then set the glass down with a thump. "I told Arch I was moving to Houston to be with you two." He looked at Shane and me with a little smile.

I put my fork down and rubbed his back. "Can't wait."

"He'll help us pack and then caravan to Houston with us."

The rest of us nodded and continued eating, but Manny heaved a huge sigh. His eyes were closed, and his palms were pressed together in front of his face like he was praying. Then he dropped his hands and snapped his eyes open. "Pia, Ms. Jackson, and I will ride with Arch. You three haven't had much time alone together."

"Really?" Shane beamed. "That'd be fantastic!"

I smiled. "Thanks, Manny. You're right. We've got a lot to talk about."

Ellis smiled and put his hands on Shane and my knees.

Arch, however, had stiffened, his eyes darting between Manny, Ms. Jackson, and Ellis. But in the end he just nodded and didn't say anything. Sorry, dude. Partner time beat out estranged brother time. Ellis was riding in my car.

After dessert—Ms. Jackson had not been able to order any brownies, but they seemed content with more Fig Newtons and the leftover Oreos from yesterday—Arch helped us pack up the rest of what Ellis wanted to take. I took pictures of his furniture so we could decide what we wanted to keep after the house sold.

Since we had another vehicle, Pia and Ms. Jackson emptied the refrigerator and freezer into a couple of coolers Ellis had in his garage. Okay, Pia put food into the coolers. Ms. Jackson put food into their mouth. But, given that yesterday they not only turned into a dragon, but they also healed Manny, they could have whatever the hell they wanted.

I made sure Pia knew we were packing up all of Ellis' gaming systems and games. Shane didn't have any, and mine were at my condo.

Finally it was time to leave. I went outside and woke Manny, who'd been napping on a deck chair.

"You feel better?"

He groaned as he sat up. "Yeah, but I'm hoping I can sleep in the car on the way home. I don't think I'm up for four hours of Mr. Personality."

"Maybe Ms. Jackson will volunteer to sit next to him."

Manny scoffed. "Pia will make sure the snacks are in the back seat."

I laughed and gave him a hand to help him stand upright.

He walked a little slowly back inside, but as soon as his eyes fell on Arch, he straightened his back and added a swagger. "Did you miss me? You ready for some rockin' tunes in the Arch-mobile?" He waved his phone in Arch's direction. Then he looked at Pia and smirked. "Hey, Pia? Wanna listen to some Janet Jackson songs? They're Ms. Jackson's favorite."

Pia gasped. "Can we?"

Ms. Jackson, still in their giant panda form, stood upright on their hind legs, turned their head quickly to the left and back, then spread their arms and legs out in a big X. Manny cheered. "Go, Ms. Jackson! Pia, when we get to Houston, we'll teach you that entire dance sequence. It'll be fun!"

I shook my head, glad I was riding with Shane and Ellis.

I went out to the car to get the air conditioning going while Ellis did one last walk-through of the house. Arch got Pia and Ms. Jackson settled in his back seat, with Pia's potted plants in the third row.

Pia still had Ellis' iPad, and Manny had downloaded a few episodes of *Supernatural*, which Ms. Jackson was in the middle of watching. I would've recommended something lighter and more fun for Pia, but no one consulted me.

Ellis, Manny, and Shane finally left the house. They started across the lawn, and Manny pointed at me while saying something to my boyfriends. I narrowed my eyes and rolled down the window.

"...why his last polyamorous relationship went south, and you can remind him why that won't happen again." Then he shouted, "Right, Grandpa?"

"I should've paid his mother to give him away as a child," Grandfather grumped from the seat beside me.

I grimaced. "I do need to tell them. You don't have to stick around for that part though."

He didn't reply, just vanished as Ellis took the front passenger seat and Shane sat behind Ellis.

"Let's go home!"

CAL'S CAMPAIGN COMPENDIUM
FINANCIAL WIZARD

Type: Financial Wizard

Class: Magic Carrier

Overview: Financial Wizards are incredibly gifted at finding the best investments for creating any desired financial outcome, including short-term or long-term gains. In addition, these magic carriers tend to have altruistic personalities and prioritize making money to help Wonders instead of solely for their own personal benefit. Most areas with a Wonder rescue organization seem to end up with a Financial Wizard residing locally.

Skills:

- Extreme financial acuity; understanding financial data at a glance with no background information
- Financial "luck"

Enhanced Skills When Bonded: Financial "luck" will extend to partner(s)' financial decisions. Can work together with other Financial Wizards to affect local economies. _Note_: Knowledge of this skill is based on one incident in South America in the 1980's and must not be attempted again.

<u>Childhood Aptitudes</u>: Financial Wizards are identifiable from an early age, as their abilities are unique. <u>Note</u>: contrary to popular stereotypes, some Financial Wizards have been documented engaging in physical fitness, including team sports.

- *Begin reading at a young age*
- *Can solve complex math problems in their head*
- *Desire to save money rather than spend it on non-essentials*
- *Usually able to perform college-level mathematics by age ten, if not earlier*

CHAPTER 18
SHANE

ARCH HAD PARKED BEHIND RORY'S SUV, SO WE WERE following him heading to the highway. Not that I would've expected him to let someone else lead.

Ellis probably sensed my thoughts through our connection. "I'm sorry about Arch. He's always been like that."

Rory chuckled. "Half dickhead, half defender?"

Ellis relaxed. "More like three-quarters dickhead, one quarter defender. My dad was always holding Arch up as an example of the kind of man he wanted me to be. It didn't make for healthy sibling relations."

I reached over the seat and patted Ellis' shoulder. He put his hand on mine, and something inside me eased. "He seemed to want to be there for you. Or something. He didn't have to come."

He sighed. "Except when your boss tells you your brother's been attacked by vampires, you can't very well act like it's no big deal. Even if he hadn't wanted to come, he wouldn't want to look bad in front of Dominic." He turned his head toward Rory. "Dominic is exactly like Dad wished I'd turned out to be. Hell, he would've traded Arch in if he could've had Dominic for a son."

Rory reached over and put his hand on Ellis' knee. "What's so great about Dominic?"

I smiled. I was looking forward to being bonded to Rory. Hell, I was looking forward to the bonding itself.

I shifted in my seat. Ellis squeezed my hand, no doubt sensing my lust through the connection. "Sorry," I said.

Rory shot me a frown. "Sorry for what?"

I hesitated, but Ellis let go of my hand. "Show him."

Well, okay. But Ellis was going to fucking participate.

I looked around for any state troopers, but Ms. Jackson must have been keeping them away. I unlatched my seat belt then scooted over to sit on the middle seat so I could reach between Shane and Rory's backrests. I leaned forward and put one hand on Ellis' shoulder and one hand on Rory's. I made sure at least one of my fingers was touching their skin under the collar of their shirts.

"You know how we told you we're all connected?"

"Yeah?"

"The connection is stronger if we're touching. Especially skin-to-skin."

"And that means we can feel what the others are feeling?"

I tightened my grip on him. "Exactly. And a minute ago, I was thinking I was looking forward to being bonded with you."

He met my eyes in the rear-view mirror. "Yeah?"

"Definitely. But that got me thinking about the actual bonding part, and Ellis felt my reaction."

I remembered how Rory looked naked. Then I imagined Rory and Ellis naked together, kissing and writhing against each other, their hands and legs never still, touching and gliding together.

Rory gasped, stiffening in his seat. "Fuck!"

Ellis patted my hand. "Tone it down, Shane, he's driving, remember?"

I let go of both of them. "Sorry."

Rory squirmed in his seat and adjusted his grip on the steering wheel. "Um, no worries." His voice was a little higher than usual.

I caught Ellis checking out Rory's lap. I wanted to do the same, but I decided to behave myself, sliding back in the seat and buckling myself in.

Ellis cleared his throat. "Ah, speaking of bonding. Simon said we need to do it soon. Not to, I guess, kill the romance or anything, but what are we going to do about your jobs?"

Rory scrunched up his face. "What do jobs have to do with...? Oh, wait. You mean the thing where you and Shane were having to stay within a few feet of each other?"

"Yeah, it can take weeks before you can be apart for more than a couple of hours. Can you work remotely?"

He shook his head. "The boss likes to see us in the office. But honestly I've been making more money from the investments Grandfather's been helping me with. I wouldn't be sad to pull a Shane move." He raised his eyebrows at me in the rear-view mirror.

Ellis looked back at me questioningly, so I told him how Ricky had called me at the wrong time, and I'd let him have it.

Ellis laughed. "I'm so proud of you. I wish I'd been able to see it."

I didn't tell him that if he hadn't been kidnapped, I didn't know if I'd have ever found the courage to quit.

Ellis reached back and patted my leg. "We'll find you something better, something that'll make you happy."

"Thanks, Ellis."

I rubbed my chest where the two hundred connections clamored to be noticed. Ordinarily District Monitor connections were pretty quiet, only calling attention to themselves when the Wonder was stressed or afraid. But it was starting to feel like every one of them was on high alert, even though when I focused on an individual connection, nothing was wrong. It wasn't a problem with the connections, it was that I didn't have enough magic to maintain them all.

"Guys, would you have any issues if we did the bonding tonight?"

Ellis twisted in his seat to look at me again. "Simon was right, huh? No, let's do it. Your little experiment a minute ago woke my libido up like you wouldn't believe. Rory? This'll be the biggest change for you."

Once again, Rory met my eyes in the rear-view mirror. But this time they were full of heat. He swallowed, and I watched his Adam's apple bob up and down. A jolt of lust came through the connection.

Ellis swore.

"Yeah, tonight's good," Rory rasped out.

I was about to reply when my phone rang. I checked the screen, half-expecting it to be Ricky. "Oh, shit!" I couldn't help the panic in my voice.

"What is it?" Ellis turned around again. I had a stray thought that we should buy one of those ancient trucks with the bench seat in the front so the three of us could sit together.

I held my phone out so he could see the screen. "It's Mr. Yamamoto from Akagi Inc. He was one of our clients. I used to do all of his designs, but of course Ricky told him he'd done them. I only really dealt with him during installation. Shit, should I answer?"

"I've got it." Ellis took the phone from me and swiped to answer the call. "Shane Costa Landscaping, this is Ellis speaking. How may I help you."

I stared, my mouth hanging open. Did he really do that?

"Yes, sir, Mr. Yamamoto. I'm so sorry, but Shane is meeting with a client right now. However, I'm in charge of sales. Is there something I can help you with?" He tilted his head as he listened, then he smirked. His amusement came through our connection loud and clear. Rory kept glancing over at Ellis, so he must've felt it too.

Ellis did drop the smile as he replied. "Yes, sir, that's correct. All of the designs Ricky told you he drew up were in fact done by Shane." He gave us a thumbs up as he nodded at whatever Mr. Yamamoto was saying to him. "Of course. If you'll text the address of the new property to this number, we'll come see it tomorrow. Does 2pm work for you? Excellent. We can have an estimate to you by a week from today."

After a few more pleasantries, Ellis hung up the call. He grinned as he handed me my phone back. It buzzed with a text message. Mr. Yamamoto had sent the address.

"Ellis, you... I can't... I don't know how—"

"Breathe, Shane." Twisting around again, he reached through the gap in the seats to pat my knee. "You can do this."

I threw up my hands. "I mean, sure, I can do the design. But how much should I charge? Where am I going to get the plants? How will I pay for the plants before Mr. Yamamoto pays me? What if I don't charge enough? I don't even have a laptop to send an invoice!"

Ellis squeezed my knee. "Shh. It'll be fine. That's what I'm here for. I can solve all of those problems for you."

"And me." Rory waved a hand from the driver's seat. "If you need working capital, I'm your guy."

"But... but I can't ask you to do that!"

Rory glanced at Ellis, then back at me in the rear-view mirror. "I'm offering. But either way, you absolutely *can* ask me to do that. From what I've gathered, we're about to be effectively married. What's mine will be yours."

Ellis, still twisted through the gap in the front seats, nodded. "And it's not like we have much else to do with our time these days. Let's get you set up as a business. Hell, maybe landscape sales is my new calling. Who knows? Either way it'll be fun to help you out."

My head spun with how much work it'd be to set up my own company. I didn't even know where to start. I didn't know how to do any of it. My heart raced. "I just... I don't...." I rubbed my chest. The connections took up so much room, I didn't feel like I could take a good solid breath.

"Shane? Shane!"

Ellis' voice came from far away.

―――――

"...should bond right now. You said we could do it without sex." Rory's voice was tense and higher than usual.

"Let's give him a minute more. His pulse is steady, and Ms. Jackson said he'd wake up soon." Manny sounded like he was repeating himself. "You know, when I gave you alone time in the car together, I expected you to, like, get to know each other better, maybe flirt a little. Making Shane pass out was not part of the plan."

I wrinkled my nose. Making me pass out? Had I passed out? "There, see? He's coming around." I opened my eyes to see Manny smiling down at me. I was stretched out on the second-row seats of Rory's SUV and he was crouched in the footwell next to me.

"Shane! Are you okay?"

I looked upward, which meant toward the open passenger-side door, where Rory and Ellis were crammed into the opening. They both gave me bright, fake smiles.

"I'm sorry."

Their smiles fell.

Manny held up his hand to stop them from saying anything. "You have nothing to be sorry about. It was probably a panic attack, and Ms. Jackson said the extra strain on your magic made it worse."

I nodded and rubbed my chest. "It was hard to breathe."

"Understandable. You wanna sit up?"

"Yeah." With Manny's help I got upright in the seat.

"Psst! Shane!"

I looked over at Pia, who had crawled into the front passenger seat.

"Uncle Arch said I couldn't stress you out, but I wanted to make sure you weren't gonna die."

Yikes. I smiled as I rubbed my chest again. "I'm fine. I'm sorry I scared everyone. It's just all this extra magic. As soon as we get bonded it'll feel a lot better."

Rory opened his mouth, then looked at Pia and shut it. A wisp of amusement came through our connection. I shot him a glare, and he shrugged with a cheeky grin. At least he wasn't freaking out anymore.

Manny jerked his head at Pia. "Off with you. I need to talk to Shane for a minute, and then we'll get back on the road."

"Okay. Bye, Shane! Glad you're not dying!" She slid out of the seat and bounced over to Ms. Jackson, who escorted her to Arch's SUV, parked several yards ahead of us on the shoulder. Her connection to Ellis had been restored, and I was surprised to see she'd also formed one with Manny. Would it fade as Ms. Jackson's magic faded inside him?

But of course Manny couldn't see it. He grimaced. "Being overly focused on death is a common trauma response."

I smiled. "It's okay. I'm pretty glad I'm not dying too."

Ellis slapped my arm. "No talk of dying! We've all had enough stress this week!" A huge mass of worry and fear rolled through the connection.

I winced. "Sorry, y'all." I looked between Ellis and Rory. "I didn't mean to scare you."

Manny slid to the other end of the row of seats. "*Hombres*, you need to get bonded A-S-A-P. Emphasis on the ass." He pointed at his own to make sure we took his meaning. "I'm going to do you a solid and take another one for the team." He eyed us significantly. "That's *your* team, by the way. Arch, Pia, Ms. Jackson, and I will spend the night at Rory's apartment. No way is my place big enough for Arch's ego plus the rest of us. I won't be able to keep Pia away much later than 10am tomorrow morning, so do what you need to do before then." He stared each of us in the eye until we nodded and confirmed we'd agreed. Then he opened the door and jumped out of the car.

"I'm so sorry, Shane." Ellis wrung his hands before reaching out to pat my leg. "I didn't mean to stress you out. It just seemed perfect for you, since your old client reached out. But you don't have to do it. We can find you some other job."

"I don't know. I should probably look at all my options."

Rory hesitantly put his hand on my shoulder, so I reached up and grabbed it. Some of the tension coming through our connection eased. "I'll help. We can go over your finances to see what kind of salary you need. I'm guessing the stipend or whatever you get for being a District Monitor isn't enough to live on?"

I stared at him, and Ellis hooted. He slapped Rory on the back. "Hah! We don't get anything for that. It's a completely volunteer position. Even when we have socials or other celebrations for the Wonders, we have to do it potluck, because none of us can afford to foot the bill."

Now it was Rory's turn to stare. "Nothing? But you give up your free time, and your magic...." He gestured at me with his free hand.

I squeezed his fingers. "Cal found out some of the states have Financial Wizards—they're magic carriers whose gifts allow them to make really smart investments, but they're pretty rare. Anyway, those states have a fund for their District

Monitors, and their Hunters don't have to be paid out of the rescue groups' budgets."

"What'd I miss? Why are you stopped?"

Pia's shrieks had nothing on the one I let out as I ducked down and away from the elderly man who'd appeared in the front passenger seat.

"Holy shit, this one can see me!"

I cautiously examined the slightly transparent figure. "Fuck me, you're a ghost!" I turned to Rory, who was slack-jawed and glancing back and forth between me and the ghost. Next to him, Ellis was as wide-eyed as I probably was.

Rory leaned into the car. "You can see him?"

"I sure can." I patted my chest like it would slow my racing heart. "Um, hi. I'm Shane."

The ghost smirked. "I know. I've been standing right next to you since Monday night."

"Grandfather!"

The ghost turned to Ellis. "What about you? Cat got your tongue? Or was it my grandson?" He chortled.

"Uh...." Ellis rubbed his chin and gave Rory a side-eye. "I'm Ellis."

Rory sighed. "This is my grandfather, Carlyle Blackbourne."

"Hi, Carl!" I put on my perkiest Manny-esque voice. "It's so cool to meet a ghost!"

He wrinkled his see-through nose. "It's Carlyle."

Arch honked his horn, and we all jumped. Except for Carlyle, of course.

"We should get on the road." Rory backed up and herded Ellis away from the car as well. He shut the door and headed around to the driver's side.

Ellis pulled open the front passenger door. "Excuse me, Carlyle, but I'd like to sit here."

"I was here first, kid. There's plenty of room in the back next to your other boyfriend."

Rory rolled his eyes as he put his seat belt on. "Don't listen to him, Ellis. Just sit in the seat and if he doesn't like it, he'll move."

Personally I was more worried about whether Ellis wouldn't like it than Carlyle. I shivered as Ellis hesitantly climbed into the seat. Carlyle rolled his eyes—he was definitely related to Rory—and popped from the front seat to the seat on my left.

Fuck. This close, I could feel a chill.

"Grandfather, I thought you were going to meet us in Houston." Rory pulled out onto the highway behind Arch's SUV.

"*Hmmph.* That billionaire is going to buy another Wonder. The auction's Friday night."

As the rest of us gasped, Carlyle poked me in the shoulder.

"Hey!" I wasn't expecting his finger to feel solid.

"Hah! I can touch this one!"

I rubbed my shoulder and regretted choosing the middle seat. Ms. Jackson was probably keeping the cops away, so I could unbuckle my seat belt and move to the seat next to the window.

"Grandfather, stop that. Tell us about the auction."

He crossed his arms. "No. Not until one of you tells me why you were stopped on the highway."

I rubbed my forehead. "It was for me. I got stressed out and the connections made it hard to breathe."

Carlyle patted my leg. Again, it felt like a live person, though much colder. "I know just what you need. Be right back." He disappeared.

"Uh, is he always like that?"

Rory huffed out an exasperated sound. "Yes."

And then Carlyle was back. But he wasn't alone. He'd reappeared on my left, where he'd sat before. But now on my right was a woman I'd know anywhere. My mouth hung open, and I couldn't speak.

Granny patted my cheek. "Shane, my boy, it's so good to be able to touch you again." Then she slapped me not-so-gently on the same cheek. "What's this about you holding too many connections? When are you planning to bond to those hunka-hunkas of yours? You've got two of them now—plenty of magic to handle those connections."

"Granny?" I wrapped her in a hug—a very chilly hug—and blinked back tears. "I can't believe you're really here."

She made a scoffing noise. "Where else did you think I'd be? You think I'd leave you to live on your own? It's a miracle you haven't starved to death or burned down the house by now."

"Hey," Rory called from the front seat. "Sorry to interrupt, but we really need to know about the auction."

I sat back in my seat but kept an arm around Granny.

She patted my leg. "Blondie's right. We can catch up later.

Now we need to make a plan to take down that Randolph guy."

Carlyle harumphed. "And my fuckhead son."

Ellis turned around in his seat. "Maybe the planning part should wait until we can talk to my brother. He's trained in that sort of thing. But what do you know?"

Granny rolled her eyes. "What, they don't have speakerphones where you're from?"

"Granny! Pia's in that car. I'm not sure she should hear about this."

She blew a ghostly raspberry. "That kid's got more balls than you do. She'll be the better for helping take that asshole down."

Rory held up a hand. "Dimi might have a point. Why don't we ask Pia if it'll make her uncomfortable to listen to us talk about Randolph? I'm sure Ms. Jackson will keep an eye on her."

We all agreed. Since Rory's phone was paired with the car, Ellis picked it up, entered Arch's number, and dialed.

"Go for Arch."

Ellis glanced at Rory, who gestured for him to talk. "Hey, it's Ellis and... everyone. Um, we have news, but Pia? Are you okay hearing us talk about Randolph Chamberlain?"

"Yeah, I can handle it." Her voice was clear and firm.

"Great. Uh, Rory's grandfather is here, and he says Randolph Chamberlain and Hugo Blackbourne will be attending an auction on Friday night. A Wonder auction."

Ms. Jackson—or someone at least—made a growling noise.

"Fuck—er, fudge. That's... soon." Arch paused then said, "What exactly do we know?"

"Hey, it's Rory. I'm pretty sure you can talk to my grandfather directly now. So this is Carlyle Blackbourne."

Carlyle puffed up importantly. "Yes, this is he. You may call me Carlyle."

There was a shocked pause, then Arch sputtered, "I'm sorry, what? You're the ghost? We're talking to a *ghost*?"

Carlyle curled his lip. "I'm still a human being, you know. I've just moved on to the next level, or whatever the video game reference is, in case that makes it easier for your tiny brain to understand."

Granny sniffed. "This new generation has no respect for their elders."

"Wait, who's that speaking?"

"I'd like to introduce you to Shane's grandmother, Dimi Costa. She's joined us too." Ellis was losing his patience. "Something about our connection seems to have given Rory the ability to make ghosts visible and audible to others."

"Holy shit! Um, I mean, wow."

"I've heard swearing before, Uncle Arch. Don't worry about it." Pia's voice dripped with all the disdain of a teenager. Damn. And she was only thirteen.

Granny disappeared.

Carlyle cleared his throat. "Right. As I was saying—"

Granny popped back into the seat next to me. "I went over to their car, but they couldn't see or hear me."

"Good to know. Thanks, Dimi." Rory glanced back at her with a smile.

"Wait, one of the ghosts was over here? I—" Ahead of us, Arch's SUV slowed down, and I felt Rory take his foot off the gas so we didn't crowd them.

Manny intervened. "Arch, shut it. You can have your ghost crisis later. Let Grandpa talk so we can take down Randolph Chamberlain." I was a little worried about whether Manny would murder Arch if they had to spend the night in the same apartment. At least Ms. Jackson would be there.

"Ahem. Thank you, Manuel." Carlyle glared out the window at the other SUV. "As I was saying, my friends Garfield and Mercy, who were Wonders before their passing, have been following—"

"You mean haunting!" Manny called out.

Carlyle gritted his teeth for a second before continuing. "They have been following Randolph Chamberlain and my son, Hugo Blackbourne. Just before Pia's rescue, Chamberlain showed her to Hugo, and we overheard Hugo ask Chamberlain to help him acquire a Wonder of his own. Since Chamberlain has had trouble, ah, keeping his captives alive, we believe he will get Hugo to take over the care of his next Wonder."

"Wait. Sorry, excuse me for interrupting." Arch must've taken a manners pill while Carlyle was speaking. "How did Chamberlain react to Pia's disappearance? Did he search for her?"

Carlyle cackled. "Nope. Some of the staff helped Rory get Pia out, and they put some dead branches in the cage where she'd been held. Chamberlain didn't question it."

I chuckled along with everyone else.

"Anyway, today Chamberlain told Hugo he got a text from his contact for the auction. And, we can't touch his phone without killing it, but, Arch, if you can hack into it, Mercy knows when the text came in so you can trace it."

"Probably a burner phone, but it's worth looking into, thanks."

"He called Hugo right away, and they're going to the auction together. Chamberlain's already wired a deposit."

I felt sick thinking of the Wonders who were being held prisoner and sold.

"Where's it going to be?"

"He didn't say the address, but it's a warehouse on Chappell Street on the East side."

I snorted. "Yeah, that makes sense. The cops don't go down that way after dark."

"Okay, thanks, Carlyle. Anything else?" Arch was in full professional mode now.

"Just that they're supposed to get there at 10pm."

"Got it. I'll call my team. Thanks, and let me know if you find out anything else."

Rory ended the call. "Thanks, Grandfather. I'm glad you ghosts hung around Chamberlain and Uncle Hugo."

He grinned. "It's been fun. We've all enjoyed playing spies."

Granny patted my arm. "I'll see you at home. I think you three need some alone time."

"Uh." I looked out the window so I didn't have to see her expression. "It's good to see you, and I want to spend more time with you, but maybe don't show up until tomorrow. Um, like noon? We're going to bond tonight."

"Oh, of course!" She gave me a chilly hug. "Come on, Carlyle! Time for us to leave these lovebirds alone!" She vanished, and Rory's grandfather followed.

I slumped back into my seat. "Wow, that was a lot."

Rory exhaled loudly. "Yeah."

Ellis, however, turned in his seat so he could look back at me. "Now would be a great time to talk about our relationship histories."

CAL'S CAMPAIGN COMPENDIUM

NON-PLAYER
CHARACTER (A.K.A. NPC)

Type: NPC

Class: Human

Overview: "NPC", or "Non-Player Character" is used to refer to non-magical humans who are not aware of Wonders or the campaign.

Accidental Exposure: If NPCs are exposed to the campaign in any way, reach out to the nearest District Monitor or post in your local Discord server for assistance as soon as possible. Depending on the situation, the NPC(s) will be convinced they were mistaken in what they witnessed, or their story/photos/videos will be discredited.

Romantic or Other Close Relationships: Should you develop a close relationship with an NPC and decide you wish to tell them about the campaign and your role in it, please contact your District Monitor prior to doing so. Your DM may wish to meet the NPC and get a feel for how receptive they would be to the information. If the reveal goes badly, your DM can help to make sure the NPC does not tell anyone about what they now know.

CHAPTER 19
ELLIS

Rory and Shane didn't seem excited about my topic suggestion, but it needed to be discussed. "I guess I'll go first." I jabbed Rory in the upper arm with a finger. "But Manny's already referenced some sort of bad breakup you had, so don't think you're getting out of telling us."

He sighed. "Fine."

"Okay, so I wasn't out in high school." I pointed at myself. "I know it's hard to believe, but I had my dad convinced I was just a nerdy debate club kid and not a *gay* nerdy debate club kid."

Shane leaned forward. "He wasn't accepting?"

I snorted. "Hell, no. He always told me to be more like my brother, who was a man's man." I rolled my eyes. "He was super disappointed I didn't have Hunter abilities like him and Arch. Anyway, it was safer for me to not date in high school. When I went away to college, I pretty much slept with any guy with a pulse. I didn't have an exclusive relationship until my senior year, and that only lasted until graduation. I've had three long-term boyfriends since then, but none of them felt like forever, you know? I've only dated NPCs, but I've never even been tempted to tell any of them about the campaign. I told them all I did volunteer social work on the side."

"Yeah, I get it." Shane reached out and put his hand on my shoulder. "How did your dad react to you having boyfriends? And your mom? Is she still around?"

I shook my head. "No, she died of cancer when I was in elementary school." Shane and Rory made noises of sympathy. "I told my dad I was gay after college. He, well, I won't repeat what he said. But effectively, no son of his could be gay, so therefore I wasn't his son anymore."

Rory held up a hand. "Hang on. You said he was a Hunter, so he works with Wonders all the time. And I haven't met very many, but they don't seem like the types to be hung up on binary gender norms."

"They're not. And I'm pretty sure he never told anyone on the Hunter team what he thought. He retired a few years ago anyway."

"What about Arch?" Rory pointed at the SUV ahead of us. "He seems accepting."

I shrugged, the old pain flaring up again. "He never disowned me like Dad, but he didn't support me against Dad either. We don't talk much, as you could probably tell." I spread my hands out. "That's my sad history. Who wants to go next?"

Rory pressed his lips together. He might have been about to say something, but Shane spoke up instead.

"I'll go. Not much to tell, really. Granny knew I liked boys since elementary school, when I became obsessed with all the guys on *Dawson's Creek*."

Rory grinned, and I laughed. "I was more partial to Angel on *Buffy*."

"Yeah, but I started working at Fredericks & Son Landscaping after school my junior year. I didn't dare come out to them, so I stayed quiet and didn't talk about my personal life. They eventually figured out I was gay, but by that time Ricky had started passing my work off as his. Everyone pretended they didn't care since I was valuable, but...." He shook his head. "I can't believe I wasted twenty years of my life on that company."

I reached back and squeezed his knee. "It wasn't wasted. You had a steady job which allowed you to develop a valuable skill. You were just waiting for us to come along and help you to the next phase of your career, whatever that ends up being."

He sighed. "We'll see. Anyway, I've had three or four relationships, all with Wonders. But we were only passing the time with each other, since we could tell we'd never bond."

I turned my attention to Rory. "And you?"

He grimaced. "Okay. You asked for it. I knew I was bisexual by middle school, and my parents were very supportive. They died in a car crash right before my freshman year of high school, and that's when I went to live with Grandfather and Grandmother. They'd disowned my dad when he married my mom, because she made her living as a professional Medium, and they thought she just wanted his inheritance. I'd seen ghosts my whole life, but I knew better than to mention them to my grandparents."

Now it was my turn to put my hand on Rory's shoulder. "I'm so sorry for your loss. It's awful how you had to hide part of yourself when you were already grieving."

"Thanks. Um, my grandparents didn't have any issue with me being bisexual at least. I had a hard time academically my freshman and sophomore years in high school, mostly because I was dealing with the loss of my parents. I didn't have the grades I needed to get into Harvard or Yale or wherever, but Grandfather pulled some strings and got me into Rice University. And that's where I figured out I was polyamorous."

His tone was ominous, so I squeezed his leg again. "Go on."

"My grandmother passed away near the end of my sophomore year at Rice. She—her ghost, that is—came to check on me in the dorm before she crossed to the other side. I was in bed with my two boyfriends." He chuckled at the memory. "When she realized I could see her, she apologized for not believing my mother, and she was going to try to find my parents on the other side, as they'd chosen to cross over. She told me she was glad I had my boyfriends, and she hoped I'd be happy."

He put his hand over mine. "Then at her funeral, Grandfather heard me telling Manny about my conversation with Grandmother after she died, and he noticed I was holding hands with two guys at the time."

"Oh, shit."

"Exactly. He waited until the funeral was over, but then he told me he was cutting me off. No more tuition, no more inheritance. I got to finish the school year, but then I had to get a job and transfer to the University of Houston. I could only afford to go part-time, so I didn't finish my Finance degree until two years ago. Grandfather died about the same time, and he's been trying to make up for his assholery ever since." He gave us a wry smile. "But he'd left all his money to Uncle Hugo, and it's frustrated Grandfather to no end watching Hugo waste everything Grandfather worked so hard for."

"Ouch." Shane shook his head in sympathy. "It'd be karma except you're the one who really got the shaft."

Rory shrugged. "Grandfather's been giving me stock tips, so I'm doing okay. Maybe one day I'll have a fund like one of your Financial Wizards, and I can help all the District Monitors like you."

"Hold up." I jabbed my pointer finger into Rory's thigh. "What happened to the two guys you were seeing?"

He smiled and shook his head. "We were twenty. The relationship didn't survive my change in financial circumstances, plus I was always working or going to class." He hesitated. "Then I met Beth and Thom. I'd just graduated, and they were several years older than me. We dated seriously for almost a year." He sucked in a deep breath. "Beth wanted to have a baby. I decided if the three of us were going to start a family I should tell them about being a Medium."

"Uh oh." I gripped his leg again. "I'm guessing it didn't go well?"

He let out a harsh laugh. "You could say that. They were horrified, as if me being a Medium would mean they'd be constantly surrounded by ghosts." He rolled his eyes. "News flash: everyone's *always* surrounded by ghosts. But they couldn't be convinced, and they didn't want the baby to be exposed to ghosts, or, even worse, what if I ended up fathering the baby? Then they might end up with a child who was a Medium."

"Oh, Rory. I'm so sorry." I rubbed his arm.

"Those assholes!" I glanced back to see Shane glaring out the window, his arms crossed. "And them breaking up with you over that, on top of your Grandfather cutting you off? Shit, it's impressive you even talk to *us* about ghosts, and we're predisposed to believe you."

Rory grinned. "Now you know why Manny was pushing me to get together with you two. Not that I needed much of a push."

I couldn't suppress my smile. "I can't wait to be bonded to you. To both of you."

"Same." Shane rubbed his chest. "And not just so I can get rid of these extra connections."

"Soooo...." Rory rubbed his hand along his thigh. "Once we're bonded, it's like some sort of mind link?"

Oh, shit. Had we forgotten to tell Rory what bonding meant?

Shane dove in. "Partially. We'll be able to tell how each other are feeling, much more than we can do now. We'll also be able to talk to each other mind-to-mind."

I held up a finger. "And you'll get a power boost. Well, we all will. Our magics will combine and become stronger. So, like your grandfather and Shane's granny being visible? You'll probably be able to do more stuff like that. Shane and I will know where all the Wonders we're connected to are, and whether they're under stress or anxious."

Rory rubbed his thigh again. "Okay. That all sounds... okay."

I frowned. I wasn't getting anything through the connection. "What are you worried about?"

"I, uh...." He glanced at me and then back at Shane. "Sometimes I think about weird shit, and I don't want you to think I'm strange or regret being bonded to me."

I laughed. "Sorry, I'm not laughing at you, I promise. But we all think about weird shit. And all the bonded couples say you learn how to wall it off. So we'll have our privacy eventually."

His body lost its tension. "Okay. Good."

"I have an idea." Shane reached through the gap in the seats and patted Rory on the arm. "Let's tell each other some of the stupid crap we think about. Just get it out there."

I looked back and raised my eyebrows at him. "You can go first."

"Duh." He leaned back in his seat and drummed his fingers together. "Okay, like I've been imagining getting one of my old coworkers to discover a landscape design I *left behind*." He made air quotes. "Ricky would be all over it and sell it to the next client who came along. But it'll be made up of plants that'll change colors with the season and suddenly for a period of time there'll be a giant dick in the middle of their esplanade."

Rory and I laughed, but Shane sighed. "I know. It'd be hilarious, but I can't do that to the poor unsuspecting company. They're not the ones I'm mad at."

"Alright, I guess it's my turn." I tried to think of something "weird" to discuss, but all that was coming up was dirty thoughts I'd been having about Shane and Rory. I was slightly panicking when I remembered something. "Oh, I have one. I've been wondering what form Ms. Jackson will choose when they finally take on a human shape."

Rory stared at me a little too long and I had to point at the windshield to redirect his attention to the road. "Holy shit," he muttered.

"Y'all haven't thought about it?"

I glanced back at Shane, and he winced. "I thought about it, but I didn't want to, so I stopped."

I threw up my hands. "Okay, whatever. Rory, what weird thoughts should Shane and I brace ourselves for?"

He glanced at me, then he ran his hand over the stubble on his jaw. His beard was as blond as his hair, so when he didn't shave he got a sort of golden glow on the bottom half of his face.

Shane leaned forward. "You don't have to play this game if you don't want to."

I frowned, but then I noticed the unease coming through our connection from Rory. "Shit, man. This wasn't supposed to be some sort of test or anything. We were only playing around. No need to participate if it makes you uncomfortable."

Rory lifted one shoulder. "It's not that. It's just, I have more of a question for you guys, and I guess it's kind of awkward."

He had both of his hands on the steering wheel, so while I wanted to grab one of them, I settled for putting my hand on his knee. "We're about to be the equivalent of married without the possibility of divorce. We need to hear anything that's bothering you, and I promise we won't laugh."

He blew out a breath. "I guess you're right. Um, I'm curious about the bonding itself. I mean, I understand we'll have sex, but is that all there is to it? Is there—I don't know—a ritual or something?"

I grimaced, and when I glanced back, Shane had a similar expression. "I'm so sorry, Rory. We've been rushing this, and we didn't make sure you understood everything that was happening."

"Yeah, it's a good question." Shane lifted his phone. "There's a whole series of entries on bonding in *Cal's Campaign Compendium*. Why don't I read those to you, and then Ellis and I can answer any questions you have afterward?"

Rory nodded, seeming relieved. "Sounds good. How can I get access to that compendium for myself?"

I squeezed his knee. "First we have to get you on our Discord server. There's a link pinned there. We'll message Cal and ask him to send you an invite."

"Okay."

Shane read the entries to us, and I learned some things I hadn't known. I should probably read the entire compendium, but who had that kind of time? I still couldn't believe how quickly Cal had put the thing together. Didn't he have a full-time job?

Rory relaxed more and more as Shane read. I felt awful for how stressed he'd been about the bonding. We'd all have to do better at communicating with each other. But was Rory really okay with bonding so quickly? The three of us still barely knew each other.

And it wasn't only Rory being rushed. It was my fault Shane had ended up with the burden of all my connections on top of his own. Which were causing issues with his *health*.

All I could do was take them at their word that they were ready and try to make it up to them after we were bonded. Or, heh, *during* the bonding.

"What are you smirking about?" Rory's question snapped me out of my reverie.

"Oh, sorry. I was imagining our bonding, if you want to know the truth. I'm looking forward to finding out what y'all like to do in bed."

"Yeah?" Rory wiggled his eyebrows. "We've still got a while to drive. We could play a guessing game. Though you probably already know what Shane likes, right?"

I ran my hand over my hair. "Um, actually, we didn't really discuss preferences. It was more of a spur-of-the-moment thing. We just sort of pounced on each other." I glanced back and winked at Shane, who blew me a kiss.

"Oh? What kind of pouncing are we talking about?"

I felt more than heard Shane spread his legs apart in the back seat. A low hum of arousal came through our connection.

"Shit." Rory shifted in his own seat. "Maybe we shouldn't do this while I'm driving."

I looked around and the traffic was getting heavier as we approached Houston. We'd long since lost sight of Arch's SUV. "Yeah, you're right. Sorry."

He flashed me a toothy grin, and he reached back and squeezed Shane's leg. "Just save it for tonight."

After we all took a moment to get ourselves under control, Shane told us about a Wonder in Houston who had set up a school for Wonder children. We decided to go talk to her next week to see if it would be a good fit for Pia.

We were going against the worst of the traffic as we headed downtown, but it was still rush hour. We decided to make a detour for a quick dinner since Shane didn't have a lot of groceries at home. We probably should've stopped at the store, but none of us were that patient.

Shane directed us to a hole-in-the-wall Korean place that was quick and delicious. Then finally, *finally*, we got to Shane's house. Shit, our house. There wasn't anywhere to park on the street, so Rory pulled into the driveway behind my SUV and Shane's ancient sedan, which was under the carport.

Shane let out a heavy sigh. "I hate to mention it, but we're going to have to empty the car. This isn't a great neighborhood."

Rory frowned. "How bad is it? Do we need to be concerned about Pia's safety?"

I unbuckled my seatbelt, and Shane still hadn't answered by the time I was done. I turned to see him making a face. He looked out the window towards the house. His granny's house. Fuck.

"We don't have to decide tonight. We have plenty of time."

Still looking at the house, he smiled sadly. "If we can afford to move to a better neighborhood, we should do it for Pia. This isn't a place where I'd let her ride her bike down the street."

I met Rory's eyes. I could tell he regretted bringing up the topic. He said, "I don't think your grandmother would be upset if you moved. She seems... practical."

Shane seemed surprised at his own laughter. "She's always been that." He unlatched his own seat belt then slid over to the passenger side door. "Let's get the car unpacked."

"Between the three of us it'll go quickly." I didn't mention that I was exhausted. I should've napped in the car, but I hadn't wanted to miss out on spending time getting to know Shane and Rory better.

I did a couple of stretches when I got out of the car, hoping that would get the blood flowing. Rory opened the back hatch, and Shane palmed his keys before shouldering a duffel bag and hefting a box of my books in his arms. The man had some fine muscles, as I recalled. After we finished unloading and I got to sit down for a bit, I was looking forward to getting my hands on them again.

Shane headed for the front door, and Rory passed me the handle of a rolling suitcase and tucked the bottle of tequila in my other arm. "You doing okay?"

"I'm alright. Can you hand me that duffel, please?" I pointed at the one with my Yo-Yos and sex toys inside. Then I headed for the house, ignoring his narrowed eyes.

He followed behind with another box and the larger suitcase. The three of us emptied the car in two more trips. I was the last one inside, and after shutting the front door I dropped the bag of non-perishables on the kitchen counter before stumbling over to the couch and falling onto it.

Shane and Rory were in Shane's—our—bedroom, but I didn't have the energy to see what they were up to. I leaned my head back on the cushion and closed my eyes.

I just needed a minute, and then we'd get naked for the bonding.

CAL'S CAMPAIGN COMPENDIUM

MAGICAL CORE, A.K.A. MAGICAL WHEEL

Inside each Wonder or magic carrier is their personal source of magic. This magic source has been called many names, most frequently a "magical core" or a "magical wheel" due to the core's appearance as a spinning wheel of sparks.

Connections can be seen extending from the magical core, and if you focus on each one you will know who is at the other end of it.

During bonding, partners pool their magic together to create one larger core or wheel, and the connections of each individual will now be shared among the partners.

Depletion*: If a Wonder or magic carrier overuses their magic, their core can become depleted. The best way to refill a depleted magical core is to eat well, get enough sleep, and reduce stress. Over time the core will refill on its own.*

CHAPTER 20
RORY

"I DON'T WANT TO WAKE HIM UP, BUT HE CAN'T SLEEP THERE ALL night. He'll end up with a crick in his neck." Shane was barely whispering, trying not to disturb Ellis.

Except I doubted a freight train would disturb him at this point. He'd obviously sat down on the couch—and it was an extremely comfortable couch—and leaned his head back before closing his eyes. Now his head was lolled to one side, his mouth was gaping open, and he was snoring.

Something must've been wrong with me, because I found him adorable. I dearly wanted to hug him and curl up beside him to cuddle.

But we were supposed to be bonding. With sex. And we only had eleven hours until Manny's deadline of 10am tomorrow morning when he was bringing Pia back.

I sighed. Ellis was in no shape for sex right now, much less something as significant as bonding. "Will you be okay magic-wise if we wait until morning for the bonding? We can set an alarm."

"Yeah, that's fine." But Shane rubbed his chest. Before I could say anything, though, he turned to me and put his hand on my arm. The heat of his touch went right to my balls. "Why don't we get ready for bed and then we can just tuck Ellis under the covers with us?"

"Good plan." I followed him back into the bedroom. We'd put all of Ellis' clothes away, leaving only a duffel bag Ellis had placed on Shane's chest of drawers. It didn't feel like clothes, so we weren't sure if we should open it or not. Shane had also moved a bunch of sweaters and other items he didn't wear often into the attic so there'd be room for my stuff when I was ready. Given that we'd be almost literally joined at the hip starting tomorrow, I was sure I'd be ready sooner rather than later.

We undressed down to our boxers. I'd kind of planned to leave my t-shirt on, but Shane took his off, so I followed suit. Shane, for all that he was over a decade older than me, was in fantastic shape. The physical labor required by his job had given him some amazing muscles. His back was a work of art that I couldn't wait to map with my tongue.

I went to the gym fairly regularly, but my frame wasn't designed to carry much muscle. My brain automatically tried to feel self-conscious about my physique, but when Shane turned and blatantly eyeballed me, the lust came through our connection loud and clear.

Damn. I couldn't wait to experience that feeling during sex.

But that reminded me. "Shane. Last night when I was putting everyone's clothes away. Um, you were in the bathroom, and I got the feeling you were upset about something? It didn't seem like just Ellis getting kidnapped. I got distracted so I didn't get to ask you today, but are you okay?"

He turned ruddy under his tan. The blush went all the way down his neck to his sternum, creating a V between his pecs.

"It was nothing." He busied himself putting toothpaste on his toothbrush.

My eyebrows met my hairline. "Really? Because you looked like you'd been crying. I want to respect your privacy, but if all that stuff in the compendium about bonding is true, we'll be all up in each other's business whether we want to be or not. Do you want to tell me now, or should I just find out through the bond tomorrow?"

He glared at me in the mirror as he brushed his teeth. I leaned my hip on the counter and crossed my arms as I waited for him.

He spat and rinsed, then he dried his hands and face on a towel.

I waited.

His posture changed when he decided. He straightened his spine and threw back his shoulders before spinning around to face me. His expression was defiant. "I was going to do it for Ellis. Let him have a relationship with you at the same time he had one with me." My eyebrows flew back up. "Especially after he was... taken." His voice broke on that last word. "I knew he wanted you, and I wanted him to have whatever made him happy."

He crossed his arms and hunched his shoulders. "But then you were nesting. Putting Ellis' things away in the closet and making sure he was comfortable. It's something magic carriers only do with mates." He looked away. "I was jealous. I knew Ellis and I were mates, and the nesting meant you and he were mates. I'd been ready to just have a platonic relationship between you and me, but I... I wanted you to want me the same way you wanted Ellis. Like a mate."

I'd been trying not to touch Shane, not wanting to risk starting something that Ellis wouldn't be here to participate in, but I couldn't stand to see him in pain, even if the pain was only a memory. I closed the few steps between us and circled my arms around him.

He hugged me back. "And then you were asking me about ironing my shorts. Mine, not Ellis'. And I was so happy."

Fuck. I couldn't *not* kiss him after that. Ellis would feel the same way in my place.

I ducked down and caught Shane's lips in mine. He hesitated for half a second before responding, opening his mouth to take my tongue inside.

I couldn't see the connection between us, but I tried to push my feelings toward him—all the affection, admiration, fascination, and lust I'd been feeling since we'd met.

He gasped, and our kiss faltered before he pulled me closer with renewed hunger. I ran my hands over his back, which felt as incredible as it looked. His furry chest teased my nipples, so I brought my hand around and gently pulled on one of his nubs. He sucked in a breath, and a bolt of lust went from my own nipple down to my dick. Fuck, the compendium hadn't been kidding about that feedback loop.

Shane's rock-hard dick ground against mine, and I barely stifled my groan. Shit. We needed to stop before I blew.

I grasped Shane's upper arms and pushed against him, separating our mouths and our bodies enough so I could step back. Reluctantly—and I felt his reluctance *very* clearly through our connection—he moved away as well. We were both panting, and in the mirror above the sink I could see our matching lips, swollen and shiny with saliva, and our chins red with beard burn.

I wiped my mouth and stared ruefully down at the erection straining against the front of my briefs. "Probably a mistake to do that before getting into bed with both of you when I can't do anything about this."

Shane reached out a hand and hovered it over my sternum. "Our connection is even stronger, though. It'll make bonding that much easier."

"Oh, yeah? Shit, I can't wait til I can see connections."

"Maybe the bonding will help with that." He blew out a breath. "Let's go get Ellis off the couch."

———

I forgot to set the alarm.

In my defense, Ellis was almost completely out of it, and Shane and I had our hands full wrestling his shoes, shorts, and shirt off. We didn't bother making him brush his teeth.

By the time we had him stretched out under the covers, all Shane and I wanted to do was to join him in slumber.

"Guys?"

I blinked at the sunlight coming in the window. Oh, fuck.

Ellis had realized the same thing. "It's late, and we don't have much time if we're going to bond."

Shit. I whipped the sheet off and sat up. Ellis, also sitting, held up his phone. 8:47am. Fuck. On Ellis' other side, Shane cursed.

"Dammit, I'm sorry." I ran my hand over my face. "I was supposed to set an alarm."

"It's okay." Ellis patted my leg. "We can bond without sex. Cal and Greg did it, so we know how."

I... had questions, but they weren't important. "Fuck that. Give me five minutes and we're doing this." I didn't wait for an answer, just slid out of bed and rushed into the bathroom.

When I came out, Ellis was waiting for his turn. "Shane went to use the guest bathroom."

One day we might be comfortable enough with each other to share, but not today. I did delay him for ten seconds so I could steal a kiss. His neck looked better, the scars not as noticeable under my hand.

It was 8:58am when we all got back in bed, Ellis and I flanking Shane. We didn't bother with the top sheet.

"Uh, maybe we should be naked." Shane went red as he plucked at the waistband of his boxers.

"Shit, yes." I hurriedly peeled off my briefs and tossed them aside. My dick was mostly hard. Maybe it had started as morning wood, but my brain was beginning to understand what was about to happen. It wouldn't take much to get me there.

Ellis did the same with his boxer briefs. I took a second to mutter an admiring, "Nice," before turning to Shane. "You need help with those?"

He glanced at the nightstand, where our phones were laying, then he seemed to steel himself and tucked his thumbs under his waistband. I could feel the stress coming through our connection.

"Wait." I put my hand up. "No. Uh uh. What's the matter?"

He turned even redder. "It's nothing."

I raised my eyebrows at him. Ellis scooted closer and ran a hand down Shane's back. "It's something. Tell us."

He looked down at his hands. "I'm sorry. The time.... I'm just tense. I'm not... ready." He waved a hand in the direction of his crotch.

"You're not hard?" I slid my hand along his shoulders until I was giving him a half-hug.

He shook his head. "I just... It's too much pressure."

I squeezed his shoulders, but he wouldn't look up. Should I kiss him? I tried to keep my expression cheerful in case he saw it, but I was at a loss.

Ellis nudged my arm, then he said, "Well, whether or not we do anything right now, we do want to bond at some point. And to do that, Rory needs to be able to visualize his magic."

Where was he going with this?

Shane lifted his head. "Okay?"

Ellis beamed. "I was thinking it'd be fun if we had a hands-on lesson."

Oh. He was making me the focus to take the pressure off Shane. Smart. Very smart. And my dick was very interested. I held my breath until Shane agreed. "Okay."

"Great!" Ellis grinned like he'd won a carnival prize. "Rory, you stretch out on your back here in the middle, and Shane, you get on his other side."

We arranged ourselves to Ellis' satisfaction. I let my hands rest next to my thighs. I had two sexy men hovering over my naked body. Damn, I was fucking lucky.

But I needed to pretend to be interested in visualizing my magic or whatever we were supposed to be doing. "Okay, what now?" Hopefully Shane wouldn't notice the precum oozing out of my slit.

Ellis put his hand on the right side of my chest. "Close your eyes." Another hand, Shane's I was sure, rested on my left pec. If he moved it half an inch more, it would be on my nipple. I willed myself not to wiggle.

"Rory, can you feel our connections? We're touching you where they emerge from your magic wheel."

I scrunched up my face in faux concentration. "What kind of wheel? Do all of our wheels join together to make a tricycle?"

Ellis, I was absolutely certain, was silently cursing me.

But Shane chuckled. "He means your magical core. The well of magic inside you, but it spins and looks like a wheel for those of us who can see it."

"Ohh. Got it." My dick was rapidly losing interest in this conversation, but Shane wasn't tense anymore.

Shane's other hand landed on my thigh. Oh, hell, yeah! Now we were talking.

But I was supposed to be visualizing the magic. Right. I scrunched my forehead again so they'd know I was trying. "Okay. So if your hands are where the connections are coming out of my chest—hey, does it look like the creature from *Aliens*?" I lifted my hands and curled them into little alien heads.

"Rory!" Ellis sounded scandalized. "This is serious!" He grabbed my right hand and held it. Well, I was okay with that too.

"Fine." I let my left hand fall onto Shane's knee. He was sitting cross-legged facing me. "Your hands are on our connections, so the magic wheel is right beneath them?"

"Yes," Ellis gritted out. "Try to relax and let your mind follow the path from our hands into your body."

Shane patted my thigh. My dick twitched and I wished he would move his hand a little higher. "Think of it like an electrical connection. You've got the power source in your chest, and the electrical current is moving in and out through where our hands are."

"Huh." I wasn't sure electricity went in both directions, but the description itself sounded logical. I focused on how warm their hands were on my skin, then I followed that warmth down—"Holy fuck!" I grabbed Ellis and Shane's hands on my chest, and I pulled my knees up in an instinctive need to... protect the magic? Who knew.

It was beautiful. A spinning wheel of bright sparks. I might not be able to see the connections when they were outside my body, but I could damn sure see them here. I had several, including two super huge ones I knew were Shane and Ellis. I even knew which was which.

"Wow. This is amazing. Um, when we bond, then do the connections just get stronger? No, wait. The compendium said something about pooling our magic?" Even now my magic looked like it was trying to climb the connections to Shane and Ellis like Tarzan on a couple of vines. I guessed the consent part was taken care of.

I'd dislodged Shane's hand from my thigh when I'd curled my body up, but now he put it back on my knee. "Yes. We'll each see our magic wheels exactly where they are now, but they'll look bigger and brighter, with all of our connections shared among the three of us. We won't see the connections between the three of us anymore, because our magic is already combined."

"Got it." I straightened my legs. Shane let his hand slide back up to my thigh. Yes! Reluctantly—because I could've stared at my magic wheel for a couple more hours—I opened my eyes.

Shane and Ellis smiled down at me. I felt their affection—love? It was getting close—through our joined hands on my chest. Through our connections.

It wasn't enough. I wanted, needed to be bonded. To share our magic, our souls. I pushed my want/need/lust out toward their magical wheels.

I lifted their hands to my mouth, but I needed more. "Kiss me."

I had to let go of their hands so they could move, so I spread my arms out, waiting for Shane and Ellis to fill them.

Ellis pulled his glasses off and tossed them toward the nightstand. "Anytime." He leaned down and took my mouth. My eyes closed, but I reached out for Shane—we needed him too.

This time there was no hesitation. He slid down to lie beside me, pressing his body against mine. He was still wearing his boxers, but they were damp with precum and he was hard, so hard. I moaned and tore my mouth from Ellis' so I could see Shane's hot gaze.

But he was doing more than just looking. He'd put his hand on Ellis' back and was urging him to press into me. I gasped when Ellis' dick slid along mine.

"There you go." Shane stroked Ellis' flank and drew his fingers through his crease. Ellis shuddered against me, And I could swear I felt Shane's fingers on me. I was a big fan of this feedback loop.

Shane leaned away again and once more I had to break off from Ellis' kiss to see what he was doing. This time he was reaching over to open the drawer in the nightstand.

"I've been tested recently." I didn't want anything between us, and I didn't want to risk condoms impacting the success of our bonding.

Ellis smiled down at me. "Shane and I are good to go as well."

Shane tossed the bottle of lube next to my hip. I lifted my head toward him, hoping for a kiss, but he dodged me.

"Hold on, I need to do this first." He nudged Ellis slightly to the side and, gripping our cocks together in one hand, he bent down.

I wanted so, so badly to thrust into his grip and feel Ellis' cock moving against mine while being held by Shane. But instead all I did was watch, frozen in anticipation as Shane stretched out his tongue and licked our weeping slits with one long stroke.

"Shit!" Ellis wriggled in Shane's grip. Spikes of lust were arrowing through our connections, and they bounced back and forth so much I couldn't tell who was originating them.

My balls were swollen and aching. "Fuck, we need to get to the main event, or I won't last."

"Are you sure?" Shane opened his mouth wide and hovered over our dicks, trapped in his fist.

Holy shit. Three lightning strikes of arousal ricocheted through us. These were so strong and sharp, I could feel who'd sparked each of them. I half sat up to stop my orgasm.

Ellis sucked in a breath and pulled out of Shane's hold, clamping his fingers around his dick. Shane released me and rolled onto his side. He lifted his hand, soaked with our precum, and brought it to his mouth.

I squeezed my eyes shut. "Fuck, fuck, fuck." This was the hottest sex I'd ever had, and Shane was still wearing his boxers.

"Anybody object to a train?"

I opened my eyes to see Shane had picked up the bottle of lube. For someone who'd been so hesitant a few minutes ago, and who I was pretty sure had never had a three-way before, he was spectacularly confident.

"Ellis, you get Rory ready, and I'll prep you."

I couldn't help the jolt of lust I sent out to the others. "You are so fucking sexy."

Shane smiled shyly. I wanted to hug him and fuck him at the same time. "Yeah?"

"Oh, yeah." I pulled him down into a dirty kiss, tasting the tang of precum on his lips and tongue. "Fuck," I panted as he pulled away.

He rolled me onto my side and slapped my ass. "Stay there. Let Ellis play with you." I heard the cap on the lube bottle open as he gave Ellis a messy kiss of his own.

Fuck, I didn't know how I was going to last. "Not much prep," I told Ellis over my shoulder. "I can't take it."

"I gotchu." He grunted, which, based on the phantom fingers in my ass, meant Shane had already gotten to work.

I cried out when Shane hit Ellis' prostate. "No! Dammit, I'm right on the edge!"

Ellis panted hard as two of his shaking fingers pressed into my hole. I forced myself to relax, breathing out and bearing down. In front of me, all three of our phones lit up on the nightstand. I closed my eyes and hoped the others didn't see that.

I forgot the phones when Ellis added a third finger. He was... how was he doing that? "Ellis, Jesus, fuck." It was like his fingers were everywhere—everywhere—except on my prostate.

He snickered. "It's the Yo-Yo practice."

"The what? Fuck, never mind. Get your dick in me right now." I tried to squirm away to get his fingers out of me, but he clamped a hand on my hip to keep me still.

Through the connection I felt more than his fingers as he gasped out, "Just... as soon as Shane is in... me." He gave a grunt, and after a few seconds I felt Ellis' real cock replacing his fingers. Fucking finally.

I groaned as he pushed inside, gritting my teeth as he grazed my prostate. I didn't dare touch my dick. I looped my ankle around Ellis' leg to make sure I stayed on my side and didn't fall forward. One thrust of my dick against the sheet and I'd be a goner.

Oh, fuck. "Guys, we can't forget—*hnngh*—to bond." Ellis froze. "What are we supposed to be doing again?"

I reached back and found Shane's forearm. I remembered we all had to be touching.

"Fuck." Ellis panted in my ear. "Intent and consent. Visualize our magic combining."

Shit. Visualizing would be difficult right now. "Okay. I intend to bond with you, Shane and Ellis. And I consent to the bonding and combining our magic." As Ellis and Shane repeated what I'd said, I closed my eyes and looked for the magic wheel. The sparks were consuming the connections to Ellis and Shane.

I felt an odd pressure in my chest, and then I was coming, and I felt Ellis and Shane coming too. Wrapped around me, in my head and in my heart. The magic wheel threw off a shower of sparks, and then it was huge—much more than three times its original size. The filaments of hundreds of connections extended out, away from us. I could see Pia's, and Manny's, and Arch's, and all of the Wonders in Shane and Ellis' Districts.

Ellis gathered me close, and Shane's arm cradled both of us. I put my hand over theirs on my chest and closed my eyes, smiling.

This is so much better than last time.

"Fuck!" I scrambled to sit up, wincing as Ellis' dick was unpleasantly yanked from my hole.

Shane and Ellis wore identical chagrined expressions. Ellis chuckled. "I guess we forgot to ease you into being able to speak mind-to-mind after bonding."

CAL'S CAMPAIGN COMPENDIUM

BONDING, PART FOUR: AFTEREFFECTS

After the bond is created, you and/or your partner(s) may experience some new sensations and abilities. This section is intended to make you aware of these potential aftereffects so you are not surprised if you experience them.

Bonding aftereffects may include:

- *Limited distance apart (temporary): Most newly bonded partners are unable to be at a significant distance from each other for a period of time. This distance could start out as little as a few feet, so make plans to stay together for up to a couple of weeks after bonding. As the bond settles and gets stronger, you and your partner(s) will be able to get further away from each other without discomfort, though it may take months or more before you can spend an entire 24-hour period apart from each other.*
- *Constant mind-to-mind communication: You and your partner(s) may have experienced this ability as your connection became stronger and you were physically touching. Once you are bonded, you will be able to enter each others' minds at will. Most people learn to filter*

and/or block their partner(s) so as to not get overwhelmed with each other's thoughts and emotions.

- <u>*Physical intimacy feedback loop*</u>*: Bonded partners who are sexually active have reported being able to sense erotic pleasure from both their own perspective and from their partner(s)'s.*
- <u>*Self-healing*</u>*: Bonded partners may enjoy faster healing from injuries and slower aging. Individual experiences will vary.*

CHAPTER 21
SHANE

Rory glared at me. "I guess! Fuck."

I couldn't help the goofy smile that took over my face. We were bonded. Me, Ellis, and Rory.

Forever.

Rory had definitely been the piece missing when Ellis and I had tried before. This time the magic wheel was smooth, robustly spinning without a hitch.

I held my hand out to Rory. "I need a hug."

He huffed. "Fine." He crawled over to us. Ellis sat up, and we circled our arms around each other. One of them—Ellis—was thinking about our lovemaking.

I smiled. **Is it okay if I talk like this now? Rory, you should try.**

He scrunched up his face. Ellis chuckled and kissed his cheek. "Just relax. It'll happen."

Rory exhaled. **Can you hear me?**

I grinned. **Yes!**

Good, because I wanted to say, I thought I was bossy in bed, but damn, Shane! That was so fucking hot!

I laughed and tucked my face into his neck. I didn't know if I'd be able to conjure up that confidence again, but it had been fun.

Someone pounded on the front door. Before the three of us could do more than sit up, it opened, and Manny shouted, "I hope you're awake and dressed!"

Our horrified gazes went to the open bedroom door. I bolted off the bed, covering my junk with one hand in case Pia was in sight. Manny must've held her back, because I slammed it shut without seeing anyone.

I leaned against the door in relief as Manny laughed. "We'll be making brunch when you're ready!"

Ellis ran his hand over his face. "Fuck. I forgot Ms. Jackson can open locks."

I stood up, then stooped to gather the bedding on the floor. "I guess it's time to get cleaned up." Ellis sucked in a breath, and I felt surprise through the bond. "What is it?"

He pointed to the door. "That's twice as far as you and I could get from each other the first time we bonded."

Holy shit. I'd gotten at least ten feet from him and Rory without feeling a twinge. "Hang on. I'm going to go into the closet—no stupid jokes—and one of you go into the bathroom. That'll be about twenty-five feet."

We determined we had a range of about fifteen feet. And it was to both of the others, so we couldn't spread out too far. It wasn't ideal, but it was a damn sight better than the five feet Ellis and I had been restricted to.

We rotated through the shower as quickly as possible. Ellis went first so he could style his hair while Rory and I took our turns. I wished there was room to expand the shower stall so the three of us could all fit at once.

As I had that thought, I caught a brief glimmer of a thought Rory had in response, but he hid it away almost instantly.

I paused my toweling off. "How did you do that? Hide your thought, I mean." He grimaced, and I held my hand up. "I don't need to know what the thought was, you're entitled to think what you think. But I tried to hide my thoughts from Ellis the first time we were bonded. Uh, when I was jealous of his attraction to you. But I don't know how effective it was. How did you figure it out?"

He shrugged. "I just did it. I didn't want to hurt your feelings, and I kind of... tucked the thought behind a barrier?"

"Oh." I looking sadly around at the dated tile and ancient faucets. I could guess Rory's opinion about this house.

"Hey." He wrapped his arms around me. "It's home. It's where you are."

I leaned my head on his shoulder. "But the neighborhood isn't great, and there's Pia to think about."

Ellis walked in, hair on point and fully dressed, including shoes. Today's ensemble was maroon shorts with a yellow polka-dotted button-up. "Hey, no one invited me to the group hug!" He threw his arms around me and Rory. "Here's my two cents on the house. We like it, it's comfortable, and we have bigger things to focus on for the near term. Like convincing our first-ever client that we're a real company, and how we're going to rescue the Wonders at the auction tomorrow night."

I nodded, enjoying that both Rory and Ellis had used the same shampoo and body wash as I had, so we all smelled like we belonged together. "We're swamped."

Rory chuckled. "Exactly."

I kissed both of them. Ellis let go first, but Rory gasped. "Ellis! Your neck! Look!" He dragged Ellis over to the mirror. The scars were almost invisible.

I pulled Ellis' collar back, then I kissed his cheek. "We've been bonded for like, half an hour? This is some powerful magic."

Ellis rubbed his neck, unable to take his eyes off his reflection. "I thought I'd wear those scars for the rest of my life."

Well, shit. Rory leaned his forehead against Ellis'. "It wouldn't have mattered to us."

He gave us both a teary smile. "I know. It was just a nasty reminder." He turned around and headed into the bedroom. "Get dressed so I can rescue Arch from Manny."

Rory and I hurriedly put on our clothes while Ellis poked around in the duffel bag he'd put on the chest of drawers last night.

"What's in there? Sex toys?" I experimented with sending the feeling of a dirty leer through the bond.

Ellis cackled, so he must've felt it. "Well, some of it is." He pulled out a bottle of lube, a butt plug, and a large green dildo and dumped them on the bed.

Rory scooped them up and took them over to the nightstand. "Excellent. We can have some fun with these." He opened the drawer and put the items inside.

"Um." Ellis rubbed the back of his neck. "Before we go out and see everyone, the rest of the stuff in this bag...."

I turned to give him my full attention. "Whatever it is, you can tell us, Ellis." I projected my feelings for him through the bond, and he turned shocked eyes on me. I smiled and shrugged. "We're here for you."

Rory stepped up beside me. "No judgment here."

Ellis looked down into the bag and took a deep breath. Rory and I both tensed, and I hoped his trick with the privacy wall worked, because I was trying like hell to hide my worry that I wouldn't appreciate whatever Ellis was into.

He reached into the bag and pulled out a round red... Yo-Yo?

"You can Yo-Yo?" I blinked. I didn't know anyone who knew how.

"Show us," Rory urged.

Ellis glanced toward the door. "Real quick." He put his finger through the loop on the end of the string. "This is called Sleeping." He threw the Yo-Yo toward the floor, and it stayed there, spinning without reeling back up the string. "Then from here you can do lots of things, but the most well-known is Walk the Dog." He jerked his hand up, and the Yo-Yo retracted to his palm. Then he threw it toward the floor again, but this time instead of just letting it hang in the air, he let it touch the ground. The Yo-Yo rolled in a circle on the floor before Ellis pulled it up into his hand again.

He looked up at us with a slightly sheepish but proud smile. Rory and I clapped and hugged him.

"That's so impressive," I gushed. "How did you learn it?"

"I've had Yo-Yos since I was a little kid. It's relaxing and I enjoy it." He snorted. "I had to hide them from my father, of course."

"You have to show Pia!" Rory tugged Ellis toward the door, but he balked.

"No. Arch never understood why I liked it. I'll show her later."

Never understood being code for *made fun of*. Got it. I wanted to protest, to tell him Rory and I would tell Arch off if he tried to say anything derogatory, but it wasn't our battle to fight.

Instead I hugged him again. "Whenever you're ready." I'd expected him to put the Yo-Yo back in the duffel bag, but he stuck it in his pocket. Maybe he was considering bringing it out later. I'd support him either way.

At long last we emerged from the bedroom. Pia cheered when she saw us, leaping up from where she'd been watching what looked like a Thai BL drama with Ms. Jackson. She hugged us, one after the other. "Manny said you were bonded! Is it true?"

Rory picked her up briefly and put her on her feet again. "It's true! Now we can be together for ever and ever, and you'll be with us too."

"Yay! Can Ms. Jackson and Manny and Uncle Arch stay with us?"

"Uh...." Rory gazed around a little desperately.

I took that one. "They're welcome to stay as long as they want. But Ms. Jackson sometimes travels around." Okay, they'd traveled once. "And Manny and Arch have jobs and lives of their own."

Pia pouted a little, but I was glad to see a hint of brattiness coming out. She seemed to be bouncing back from her kidnapping, but I still wanted to get her in to see a therapist.

"Speaking of Manny...." Rory pitched his voice loud enough to be heard in the kitchen.

"Sí, mi amigo? Also, congratulations on your bonding!*"*

Rory put his hands on Pia's shoulders, and they led the way to the kitchen. Manny was wearing one of Granny's old aprons, which had "Your opinion wasn't in the recipe" on the front.

"Don't you have to go to work today?"

"I've got an overnight tonight, but I'm calling in sick tomorrow so I can help with the rescue." He opened the oven a crack and peeked at whatever was inside. He still had a magic aura, and it didn't seem to have faded much, if at all.

"Not happening." Arch scowled from his seat at the breakfast table next to Ms. Jackson, who was in their black panther form.

Manny rolled his eyes. "Not the boss of me."

"My Hunter team will be setting up a perimeter starting this afternoon. We'll be the ones to breach the building and arrest the perpetrators. You wouldn't have anything to do."

Ms. Jackson materialized their Ouija board. *W-H-A-T-A-B-O-U-T-T-H-E-V-I-C-T-I-M-S*

Arch shrugged. "We'll take them to TWIST and help them get back home or wherever they want to go."

I opened my mouth, but Manny was faster. "You mean you'll just load them on a bus or something? What if they need medical care?" He pointed at himself. "Nurse, remember?" Pia high-fived him on her way to the fridge.

Ms. Jackson sparkled out, *M-A-N-N-Y-A-N-D-I-W-I-L-L-G-O-V-I-C-T-I-M-S-W-I-L-L-N-E-E-D-U-S*

Arch appeared to be debating which argument would work against a being who could turn into a dragon.

"What about the ghosts?" Rory asked.

"Finally! I've been checking back every fifteen minutes. Really, Rory, couldn't you have done all that sex stuff last night?"

I clapped my hand over my heart as Carlyle appeared next to Rory. Manny slammed the oven door shut, and Pia screamed before huddling behind him.

Arch didn't get up, but his gun and knife were in his hands, both pointed at Carlyle.

"Arch!" Ellis stomped over to him. "Put those away. There's a child present. This is Carlyle Blackbourne, Rory's grandfather."

Arch blinked and made his weapons vanish. "You're the ghost we were speaking to yesterday in the car."

Carlyle looked down his nose at Arch. "The same." He turned to Ellis. "I take it he wasn't the bright one in the family?"

Ellis laughed, and I couldn't stop myself from walking over and putting my arm around him.

Manny hooted. "Good one, Grandpa!"

Carlyle ignored him. "Rory, I have an update from Mercy and Garfield, but first...." He jerked his head toward the kitchen.

Rory tilted his head and scrunched his forehead. "What?"

Carlyle huffed. "This was easier when no one else could hear me."

Suddenly he blinked out of sight.

Rory looked around at our shock and grinned. "I hoped that would work. Tell me now. Oh, hi." His gaze moved slightly to the left of where he'd presumably been looking at Carlyle. "Hey, do you want to talk to...." His smile dropped. "Right. Yes. You're welcome, and I promise." He walked to the kitchen. Manny had pulled a casserole out of the oven, and Pia was carefully slicing it into squares.

"Pia, you saw my grandfather a minute ago, right?"

She set the knife down and looked at him warily. "Yeah?"

"I now have the ability to allow other people to see certain ghosts, just like you saw my grandfather. Your mom would like to talk to you."

Pia's eyes went wide before her face crumpled. "Mama? Where is she?"

Rory pointed at the back door. "She's waiting for you in the back yard."

Pia dashed around him and raced out the back door. We all watched her hug a slightly translucent woman with long, leafy hair.

"Lorraine wanted to say goodbye. She's ready to cross over."

"Oh, shit. Poor Pia." I rubbed my chest where grief poured through our connection with her. She was sobbing in her mother's arms.

"Fuck. Shane, do you have any chocolate? Something sweet can't hurt." Manny was rummaging through the wrong cabinet, so I went to show him.

When I came back to the breakfast room, Pia was alone outside, and Rory and Ellis were fidgeting near the window.

"How long should we give her?" I looked around, but none

of us were parents. "Where's Carlyle? Does he know what to do?"

Rory snorted. "No way. My dad was raised by nannies." He looked to his right. "Hush. You know it's true."

"It's been one minute. That's enough." Ellis walked to the back door, and Rory and I followed him outside.

Pia was sitting on the edge of the hammock, still sobbing her heart out. Rory sat carefully on one side of her, and Ellis and I sat on the other side. Pia's feet came off the ground, but somehow we managed not to flip the hammock over.

Rory put his arms around her, and she fell into his chest. "We're here, honey."

Ellis and I did our best to wrap our arms around the two of them, but the hammock wasn't having it. Ellis cried out when we all fell into a pile in the middle, our legs hanging over one side while we swung back and forth.

Pia sniffled and then gave a slightly wet giggle.

"I'm so sorry about your mom, sweetie." I rubbed my hand down her arm, which was all I could reach since Ellis was in between us.

She shut her eyes tightly and nodded. "Thanks. I'm glad I got to see her one more time though. She said—she said now that you were bonded and my connections with you were strong, she wasn't worried about me being safe and happy."

Aww. That got her another hug pile.

We swung in silence for a few more minutes, but then Ellis' stomach growled, and we all chuckled.

I cleared my throat. "Manny said he was making brownies for dessert."

Pia opened her eyes. "With ice cream?"

We all smiled. She'd be alright.

———

Rory's grandfather was arguing with Arch when we went back inside. Manny appeared ready to whack both of them with the spatula he was holding.

Carlyle lit up when he saw us. "Rory! Tell this jackass he needs us ghosts for the takedown."

Rory's eyebrows flew up. "Pia, go wash your hands before you eat. Arch, why wouldn't you want help from what amount to invisible spies?"

He set his fork down on his plate and carefully wiped his mouth. "Because we'd need you to be there so we could see them, and right now, because of your bonding, that means all three of you. It's too risky."

Grandfather rolled his eyes. "It's not like we can't report back to Rory here, and he could be on the phone with one of you."

Arch tilted his head. "I'll speak to Dominic about it."

I went into the kitchen to wash my hands, squeezing Pia's shoulder as I passed her. I would've preferred to go to help with the victims, like Manny and Ms. Jackson would be doing, but I could understand Arch's concerns about having a bunch of civilians underfoot.

Ellis followed me into the kitchen, but he seemed focused on Pia rather than Arch.

I nudged him as I dried my hands. "She'll be okay."

He gave a half-hearted nod. **I know. I just remember what it**

was like losing my mom when I was only a little younger than she is.

Oh. Right. Fuck. I dropped the dish towel on the counter and wrapped my arms around him. **I'm sorry. I didn't think about the memories it would've brought up for you.**

He hugged me back. **I didn't think it would hit me so hard. But this helps. Are you feeling okay now that we're bonded?**

Yeah. And you? Not so tired anymore? His magic, amplified with mine and Rory's, certainly wasn't depleted any longer.

He pulled back. "No, I'm good. Thanks for the hug." He went up on his toes, so I met him halfway in a tender kiss. I made sure to send what I was feeling through our bond to Rory. In the breakfast room, someone's glass thunked loudly against the table.

"Sorry," Rory muttered.

Grinning, Ellis stepped back. "How do bonded partners keep from tormenting each other all day?"

I shrugged and led the way back to the table. "I'm not the best person to ask."

Luckily for me, Rory was flanked by Manny and Pia, so I didn't have to sit next to him and risk getting any physical payback. Carlyle had vanished, and Ms. Jackson had gone to the backyard and was climbing into the hammock. Ellis aimed for the chair next to Manny, so I sat between him and Arch.

Manny pointed at the casserole dish in the middle of the table. "Help yourself."

It smelled incredible. "Thanks, Manny. I appreciate you taking care of us."

He lifted one shoulder. "I like to keep busy."

Arch pushed back from the table. "Thanks for the food. I need to go meet my team. They'll be infiltrating the area over the course of the afternoon." He hesitated. "I'll let you know what Dominic says about the ghosts helping tomorrow."

"They helped Rory rescue me, Uncle Arch. I couldn't see them, but they killed the cameras and made sure we didn't run into any security guards."

Arch raised his eyebrows at Pia. "Really? They can take out cameras?"

Rory rolled his eyes, much like his grandfather had done earlier. "Yes. I would've told you if you'd asked how they could help. They can destroy any electronics. That's how we stopped the vampires' van to get Ellis back. The ghosts fried the electrical system."

I leaned into Ellis in case the reminder was unpleasant for him, but he just kept eating. I wasn't sure what all Manny had put into the casserole, but I was feeling more awake and energized by the minute.

"Huh." Arch picked up his plate and took it to the sink. "That'll help convince Dominic."

Nobody walked him to the front door.

We ate in silence for a few minutes, then, just as I felt him brace himself through the bond, Ellis said, "We should probably talk about a plan for our meeting with Mr. Yamamoto."

I waited for the panic to come, but it didn't. I took one more bite of the casserole—I really hoped Manny made it again one day—then swallowed and said, "I'm going to treat it like all the other site visits I've done in the past. Walk the area, take measurements, get a soil sample, and talk to the client about what he wants. Then we'll come home, research plants and delivery costs, and put a quote together." Now that I wasn't freaking out, I was surprised at how easy it'd be to do on my own. I'd have to hire laborers for the actual planting, but if Ellis and Rory would help with the office work, we should be able to make a profit.

Ellis pulled out his phone and started making notes. "Do you know the suppliers in the area?"

"Of course. I have good relationships with several."

We discussed the logistics for a few more minutes. Pia, obviously bored by our conversation, excused herself to go play video games.

Oh, shit. "Pia, will you be okay for a couple of hours if we leave you here with Ms. Jackson?" I glanced out the window to make sure there was still a tiger in my hammock. "Manny has to go to work, and we have a meeting."

"Duh." Her back was to us, so we didn't have to see the eye roll. She might as well be related to Rory and his grandfather.

The Akagi Inc. office complex sprawled over several acres. The owners, I knew from previous visits, preferred a park-like atmosphere between the buildings to give their employees a mental break from the stresses of their jobs.

As we drove in, I automatically checked on the landscaping Fredericks & Son had put in near the entrance and around the other buildings. The area Mr. Yamamoto had called about was toward the side of the property that faced the main road leading to the entrance. Right now the area was completely grass, but we had the opportunity to put in something eye-catching for the people in their cars to look at.

I'd made us stop at a Build Barn on the way to pick up some supplies, like a measuring wheel and a few soil test kits. Over my objections, Rory paid for everything, and Ellis tucked away the receipt.

Mr. Yamamoto was waiting for us in the parking lot next to the grassy area. He seemed delighted to meet Rory and Ellis, and he shook my hand with both of his. "I could not be more pleased to be working with you directly, particularly now I know the designs we already have are yours." He gestured at the rest of the complex.

"Oh, uh, thank you. We're excited about the opportunity to bid on this project. Um, what did you have in mind?"

Mr. Yamamoto had been thinking along the same lines I was. "Something that stands out. Native plants, if possible, like the rest of the grounds, but I'd like a lot of color so people will remember where we are when they drive by."

I walked over to the grass and knelt to see what the soil looked like underneath. "I'll have to research the plants, but I had an idea the other day.... What would you think about two species that appear similar during the summer, but one is evergreen and the other will flower but also have leaves that change color and die back in the winter. Then, the evergreen plants are in the shape of your logo, and the surrounding plants will change over time to set it off differently each season." Fortunately their logo was a circle with a few lines through it. Nothing difficult to create with plants.

Mr. Yamamoto smiled. "I love that idea."

"Great. I'll see what plants we'd need and make it one of the options we submit."

Rory helped me measure the area and take soil samples, and Ellis made notes. Then he took over ending the meeting, telling Mr. Yamamoto we'd get him the quotes next week along with a proposed schedule.

I was on cloud nine on the way back home. I could do this. I could make this happen.

Ellis was smiling as well. "I've run the numbers, and, depending on how many projects you think we can handle in a year, I think we have the makings of a viable business."

Rory *hmmmed*. "How do we let Fredericks & Son's other clients know you're available?"

We bounced ideas around all the way home, stopping only to pick up some pizzas. Pia and Ms. Jackson would be thrilled.

Oh, shit. "Guys? After dinner can you help me figure out how to make Granny's room into something Pia would like?"

Rory groaned. "I forgot Pia would be right next door to us. Dammit. I had plans for tonight. Dirty, dirty plans."

In the back seat Ellis raised his hand. "I vote for dirty, dirty, *quiet* plans."

CAL'S CAMPAIGN COMPENDIUM

MAGIC USE BY
MAGIC CARRIERS

Unlike some Wonders, human magic carriers are unable to use their magic in an overtly proactive way. Over the decades since the Elves gifted magic to certain humans, many magic carriers have attempted to use their magic to influence people, events, or objects without success. In addition, the casting of "spells" has also never been effective.

Other than innate abilities such as enhanced senses or superlative physical proficiencies, the magical skills of magic carriers are always receptive in nature. Examples include Seers receiving visions and District Monitors receiving stress signals from a Wonder.

__Warning__: Attempting to use magic in a proactive way has been shown to frequently result in severe magical depletion. Please do not attempt.

CHAPTER 22
ELLIS

REALLY, HOW HARD WAS IT TO HAVE QUIET SEX? MAYBE QUIET shower sex would be difficult because of the echoes, but the shower in the en suite for the main bedroom wasn't big enough for more than two of us at a time anyway. If Rory or Shane couldn't shut up, I was more than happy to visit the nearest adult toy store for some gags.

That thought led to some musings about the three of us visiting an adult toy store together, so I was pretty quiet the rest of the way home. Though from the way Shane and Rory kept glancing at each other and breathing a little heavily, I may have been letting some of my arousal leak through the bond. But they didn't say anything, so I didn't mention it.

When we walked through the front door, Shane's granny was sitting on the couch next to Pia. Ms. Jackson was laying on the floor by the TV in their tiger form, and *Supernatural* was paused on the screen.

"Granny? What are you doing here?" Shane handed Rory the pizzas he'd been carrying and hurried over to the couch to hug her insubstantial body.

"Pizza!" Pia cheered. "Did you get cheese for Ms. Jackson? Granny Dimi's been telling me stories about you as a kid, Shane. Did you really pee in the refrigerator vegetable drawer?"

Shane turned red. It was adorable. "I went through a sleep-walking phase in first grade!"

He glared at his grandmother, who smirked. "I remember it like yesterday."

Rory, who'd been walking toward the kitchen, stopped in his tracks. "Wait. Dimi, how were you even visible when I wasn't here? We were pretty far away today."

She scoffed and turned to Shane. "Have you taught this boy nothing? He doesn't know about his own powers!"

Shane seemed as bewildered as I felt. "Granny, I don't know anything about his powers either."

She *tsked*. "I can't believe I raised you, and this is how you turned out." She reached up and grabbed his cheek. "It's a good thing you're cute and lovable." Then she let go and slapped his cheek lightly.

"Granny!" Shane rubbed his cheek.

I took the pizzas from Rory and put them on the table while Dimi talked. Because Shane was on the couch, I couldn't go as far as the kitchen, so we'd have to set the table later.

She sighed. "Rory, you're bonded. Your powers are bigger now."

I came back out into the living room in time to see him looking between himself and me and Shane. "Really? Because I still can't see our connections. Or bond I guess now."

Dimi groaned. "Shane and Ellis explained to you how that particular ability comes with age. Keep up!"

I wondered if I could go sit at the breakfast table so I didn't get yelled at. Probably not. I'd just get yelled at for hiding.

Dimi put a ghostly hand on Pia's shoulder. "This one is yours now, Rory. Same as those two knuckleheads." She waved a hand at me and Shane. Okay. I could live with being a knucklehead.

"A Medium's family can see family. Ghosts, not ghosts, blood or no blood, it doesn't matter. Family is family, and family can see family."

I raised my hand like a kid in class. "But this morning Rory was talking to Carlyle and Lorraine in the kitchen, and we couldn't see them."

Rory snapped his fingers. "But I did that. I didn't want Pia to hear what Carlyle said, so I forced him to be invisible to you. It must've affected Lorraine as well."

Dimi threw up her hands. "See? You do have some smarts after all. You're still a Medium, and being family doesn't give us the ability to override your powers."

"Is Arch family to you, Rory?" I grimaced. "As much as I wouldn't wish that on you, if he can see your grandfather and Dimi when you're not around, they could talk directly to him during the raid tomorrow night."

Rory and Dimi exchanged wicked grins, and she popped out of sight. I tried to feel sorry for Arch, but I wished I could watch his reaction instead.

"Come on, let's eat before the pizza gets cold." Shane got up, so I went to wash my hands and set the table.

Pia trailed Rory and Shane into the kitchen. "Shane, your granny isn't very nice to you and Rory."

I raised an eyebrow at him as I dried my hands. She wasn't wrong.

He put his hands on his hips and stared at the ceiling for a moment. Then he looked at Pia. "You're right. She learned it from her mother. It's a kind of twisted way of showing affection. She won't do it to you, Pia, at least not until you're a little older. And if you—any of you—tell her it bothers you, she'll try to do better. But underneath all that bluster, she'd fight to the death for any of us. Once you're family, you're hers to protect."

Pia frowned doubtfully at him, but I could see it.

Ms. Jackson yawned as they sat on the floor next to the table.

"Not enough napping time in the hammock today?" I asked as I set a plate in front of them.

They manifested their Ouija board. *R-E-G-E-N-E-R-A-T-I-N-G-M-A-G-I-C-F-R-O-M-H-E-A-L-I-N-G-M-A-N-N-Y*

"Oh. Wow, I didn't think about that. Are you almost, er, back to full capacity?"

The *Yes* sparkled on their board. Pia put a couple of slices of cheese pizza on their plate.

"Pia." Shane sat down in the chair next to her. "My granny's old room is going to be your room now." He smiled wryly. "You probably already figured that out—it's the only other option."

She smiled around a mouthful of pizza and nodded.

"Right. Well, tomorrow or Saturday I thought we could go pick out some paint and maybe new sheets and a bedspread. We'll move the old desk out and get you something you can use for schoolwork."

Pia bounced in her chair as she swallowed. "Yes, please! Thank you, Shane!" She threw her arms around his neck. I thought my heart would burst at the happiness coming through our bond.

Next to me, Ms. Jackson purred, and I exchanged a wide-eyed look with Rory.

When Pia finally let go of Shane, I said, "Um, before we do that, tomorrow morning we should go shopping for some new clothes for you, Pia. I'm sure you'd rather have something designed for someone your age."

Her face lit up, but before she could respond, Dimi appeared on Ms. Jackson's other side and said, "I told Pia that very thing earlier." She *tsked* and shook her head. "Poor girl wearing an old woman's clothes. How do you expect her to make friends?"

Once we'd all recovered from being startled—except possibly Rory, he was probably used to ghosts popping in and out—Shane glared at his grandmother. "We haven't had a lot of time up til now. That's why we're going tomorrow."

Rory put his hand on Shane's arm. "Dimi, were you able to speak to Arch?"

Her face twisted into an evil smirk. "Caught him right in the middle of talking to his boss. He screamed like a little girl—not you, Pia. You're a badass."

Pia turned pink but seemed pleased with the compliment.

"They agreed to let us help. Dominic said there's no need to keep watching Randolph and Hugo since we know the plan now, so Garfield and Mercy are going to take a break tonight while Carlyle and I make sure the buildings are clear for the Hunters to set up their surveillance points. Then tomorrow night the four of us will help with the raid." She nodded in satisfaction.

"That's great, Dimi. Thanks." Rory looked around at the rest of us as if asking if we had any more questions, but none of us spoke up.

Dimi seemed to read the room. "Enjoy your dinner. One of us will let you know how things go tomorrow night."

We quickly finished eating, and then Ms. Jackson watched another episode of *Supernatural* while the rest of us debated paint colors and other décor decisions for Pia's new room.

After that I lent Pia my Butterfly Yo-Yo and showed her how to do a basic throw, then the Sleeper and Around the World. Rory and Shane watched but didn't seem interested in trying it out. I'd wear them down.

Before bedtime we let Pia watch one episode of *We Are*, her favorite Thai BL show. Ms. Jackson made grumbling noises but agreed to pause Sam, Dean, and Castiel to allow Pia to use the big screen.

"Do we need to get Ms. Jackson their own iPad?" I whispered to Rory and Shane as we cleaned up the kitchen.

Rory nodded. "Let's do it. We owe them way more than that anyway."

"Um, then the iPad would be the only thing Ms. Jackson owns. They don't have anything else, except maybe that tiara Pia put on their head." Shane gestured at the living room. "What else do they need?"

We stared blankly at each other.

———

Bedtime was a comedy of errors. Pia didn't have any nightclothes of her own, and it turned out Dimi had liked to sleep in, um, lacy garments that none of us wanted to show Pia. We finally got her set with one of Rory's t-shirts and a pair of basketball shorts with the waist rolled up. Then we discovered she didn't have a toothbrush. The dryads had given her one, but she'd left it behind. Luckily Shane had spares.

At long last, way after a thirteen-year-old should be going to bed, we all exchanged cheek kisses with Pia and said good-night. We left her door cracked open so she didn't feel locked in, but I know all of us were worrying about sound carrying down the hallway.

Ms. Jackson elected to sleep outside on the hammock. I was a little envious—I hadn't been able to hang out in the hammock by myself yet, and given that Rory and Shane were still on a fifteen-foot leash around me, it'd be a while.

I was the last one into the bedroom, and as soon as I shut—and locked—the door, Shane and Rory crowded me, moving me over to back against the wall. Shane leaned on his forearm next to my head. I could feel his breath on my face. "Ellis." He dragged a finger from my earlobe to the collar of my shirt.

"Y-yes?"

Rory pulled my shirttails out of my shorts. "You were being very naughty in the car earlier."

Oops. "I don't know what you mean. I didn't do anything." Hah.

"Shh. We have to be quiet." Shane pulled my shirt to the side and licked my collarbone before kissing his way up my neck.

I couldn't help but tilt my head to the side, but I did stifle my moan.

Rory worked on my buttons. "You were sitting in the car, looking all calm and collected in your preppy clothes. But you were thinking some dirty thoughts, Ellis. Shane and I could tell. We could feel them."

Shane helped Rory peel my shirt off.

I panted and licked my lips. "Um, I'm sorry?"

Shane chuckled into my ear. His hot breath made every nerve ending send a message to my dick. "Don't be sorry. We weren't. Just tell us what you were thinking about."

"You, uh, didn't get that through the bond?"

"Nope." He bent down and sucked my nipple. I went up on my toes, but I managed not to squeal.

Rory put a hand behind my head to prevent me from knocking it against the wall. "Careful. If you wake Pia, you'll have to be the one to explain the noises to her."

I hissed as Shane gently took my nipple between his teeth.

Rory used his free hand to open the button on my shorts. "Now tell us what had you all hot and bothered, Ellis."

Shane opened his mouth and blew, and I almost cried out as the cool air hit my dampened nub. Then he fucking went down on his knees. Holy shit. He looked up at me as he took over opening up my shorts. "Tell us." I wasn't sure I had the brain cells to talk right then. The arousal reverberating through our bond was almost enough to get me off all by itself.

Rory ran his palm over my other nipple. "El-lis. What were you thinking?"

"Um. Something about us visiting a sex toy store. Together. Um. I can't remember why." I panted as Shane pulled my shorts and boxers down to my knees. My dick was rock-hard.

"But I thought it would be hot if we walked down the aisles discussing all the options. In public. Where other people could hear us."

"Ooooh." Shane's breath was hot against my dick as he spoke. "Ellis has a little exhibitionist streak." He ran one hand up the inside of my thigh. I spread my legs apart as far as my shorts around my knees would allow, and he rewarded me by rolling my balls in his palm.

Fuck. "Shane." I could feel he and Rory were almost as close as I was. The sound of our breath and moans filled the room.

Rory's dick, slick with precum, pressed against my hip. When had he taken his clothes off? He twisted my nipple, so I put my arm around him and dug my fingers into his ass cheek.

I checked to see if Shane's clothes had magically vanished too. They hadn't, but he'd opened his fly and was working his dick as he mouthed mine.

"Shane, please." Please put my dick on your tongue. Please swallow me down. Please suck me.

As I imagined Shane performing each of those actions, he and Rory thrust their hips in time with my thoughts. Rory moved his hand from my nipple to Shane's head. He had his feet on either side of my leg, grinding into me.

Rory caught my lips in a kiss, invading my mouth with his tongue. I tried to engage with the kiss, but Shane nosed his way from my balls to my crown, then he finally took my dick in his hot, wet mouth. I lost it, my orgasm slamming through me as I tore away from Rory's kiss and bent over Shane's back, my mouth opened on a silent scream.

Shane swallowed as best he could, but my cum spilled out of his lips. He stiffened, his mouth and tongue going slack. Through the bond I felt his orgasm crash into me, into us.

Rory pulled me tighter, his release spurting hot onto my skin. Shane and I both shuddered as if Rory's orgasm were our own again.

We rested against each other, panting, for a good minute. My brain was fuzzy, but my feelings for Shane and Rory were bright and clear.

"I love you. Both of you."

The seconds of silence following my confession ticked by, and I cringed. Shit, I'd only met Rory on Monday, and Shane and I hardly had more history than that.

I straightened my glasses and reached down to pull up my shorts, though I didn't bother fastening them. "I'm gonna get a shower." I didn't look at either man as I edged to the side to disentangle myself.

"Wait." Rory clamped an arm across my chest, pinning me against the wall again. I kept my eyes on the floor.

Shane stood up. "You can't just drop that and run."

"Pretty sure I can." I tugged on Rory's arm, but he wouldn't let go.

Shane cupped my cheek. "You were brave enough to say that, but you didn't check the bond to see what our reactions were?"

I finally lifted my gaze. Shane's eyes were warm and caring, full of... love? Or that's what the bond was telling me. I jerked my head toward Rory, and he was sending the same emotions through the bond.

He leaned in and kissed me softly, not full of lust like before. This kiss was full of love. "I love you too. Both of you." He put his hand around the back of Shane's head and pulled him in for a three-way kiss. Even with the taste of my cum on

Shane's lips, this kiss was sweeter and a lot less clumsy than the last time we'd tried it.

Shane smiled. "I think you can feel it already, but I love both of you too."

I kissed him, just from me, before pulling Rory in for another three-way. We ended with the hug to end all hugs, our feelings bouncing between us through the bond. I'd never been so happy.

CAL'S CAMPAIGN COMPENDIUM
WONDER TRAFFICKING

Overview: Trafficking is the horrifying practice of kidnapping Wonders with the intent to sell them to humans for financial gain. Wolf shifters are the most frequently trafficked Wonders, but many species have been discovered to have been kidnapped and sold. It is estimated that between fifty and one hundred Wonders are kidnapped worldwide each year for the purpose of being trafficked.

History: While Wonders were regarded with fear and occasionally attacked by humans during the centuries the portal to the Elven dimension was open, it is believed that the capture of Wonders for purposes of sale and captivity did not begin until after the portal closed. The first documented instance of a full-scale auction occurred in 1983 in Saudi Arabia. Subsequent auctions have occurred in most countries where billionaires and multi-millionaires are found.

Perpetrators: Kidnappers and auctioneers are usually human, but Wonders have occasionally been involved. So far no magic carriers have been known to participate, and it is speculated that this is due to the magic gifts imbuing the carriers with protective instincts toward Wonders. Purchasers have so far been limited to the wealth-

iest humans, and communication surrounding Wonder trafficking is done mostly on the dark web.

Preventative Measures*: Fortunately Wonder trafficking, while it does occur, is still rare. But we are seeing more and more Hunters born among magic carriers. Most countries and states/territories have teams of Hunters who—among other duties—intervene when Wonders are discovered to have been captured and/or trafficked.*

If you find evidence or have suspicions of Wonder trafficking, please contact your District Monitor or the nearest Hunter team. You can also message @FightWonderTrafficking on Discord.

CHAPTER 23
RORY

WE WERE ABOUT TO EAT BREAKFAST WHEN MANNY SHOWED UP, having just gotten off shift, still in his cartoon character scrubs. Pia—via my phone—had texted him that we were going shopping this morning, and she wanted Manny along for fashion advice.

I couldn't blame her. Ellis at least had a sense of style, but I doubted his preppy aesthetic would appeal to a 13-year-old. If I wasn't wearing a suit for work, I was in jeans and sweaters or button-ups. And while I was sure Shane would clean up amazingly well, his wardrobe currently only consisted of jeans, cargo pants and shorts, and t-shirts.

Manny went around and hugged all of us, including Ms. Jackson. He sat down next to Pia and started quizzing her on what clothes she needed. I tuned them out and turned to Ms. Jackson, who was sitting next to me, tentatively chewing the tomato slice Shane had put on top of their cheese omelet.

"Do you like it?" They wrinkled their nose as they swallowed, and I laughed. "It's actually better if it's chopped up inside the omelet." We'd tried explaining that pizza sauce was made from tomatoes, but we hadn't been convincing enough. So far the only vegetables Ms. Jackson liked on their own were carrots, asparagus, and potatoes. "Anyway, what time do you need to leave to meet Arch and Dominic?"

They manifested their Ouija board and sparkled out, *2-P-M.*

"Got it. We'll come home for lunch and then when you leave, we'll take Pia shopping for stuff for her bedroom."

They nodded and ate another piece of omelet. After we'd had to watch Ms. Jackson eat a grilled cheese sandwich in one bite, we'd all learned to cut up their food before serving it.

E-L-L-I-S-M-U-S-T-B-R-I-N-G-H-I-S-Y-O-Y-O

I blinked. "What? Why?"

My tone must've been odd, because everyone at the table stopped talking.

N-O-T-S-U-R-E-J-U-S-T-K-N-O-W

"Okay. Um, Ellis, Ms. Jackson says you need to bring your Yo-Yo when we go furniture shopping this afternoon."

His eyebrows rose. "I can do that. Any particular one?"

The entire Ouija board sparkled. They didn't know.

"Whichever one goes with your outfit," Manny suggested.

Ellis' forehead creased, and his worry leaked through the bond.

I put my hand on his back. "Look at your Yo-Yos and go with your gut."

He nodded and relaxed slightly. I casually stroked his back to see if that would help. His muscles stayed tense, but he did lean into my hand a little.

Time for a topic change. "Ms. Jackson, do you want to come shopping with us this morning?"

In contrast to Pia's excited, "Yes!", Ms. Jackson was obviously not a fan of the idea. The nose wrinkle my question received was even worse than the one the tomato had gotten.

I chuckled. "Okay, no worries. Um, is there anything you need us to get for you? We were thinking you might want your own iPad."

They went absolutely still, their eyes wide and ears perked forward. The Ouija board sparkled out, R-E-A-L-L-Y-F-O-R-M-E.

I grinned. "Yes. Right now you have to share with Pia, and this way you can each watch something different. Or you can look stuff up, listen to music, or play a game. It'll be yours to do whatever you want with."

Ellis *hmmmed*. "Maybe you need a phone too. We already told Pia she's getting one. We'll pick one up for you as well. What if you wanted to tell Greg or Cal something? You could video call them and spell it out."

They cocked their head, then dropped their jaw open in what I assumed was a grin. I-W-O-U-L-D-L-O-V-E-A-P-H-O-N-E

"Done. I'll put you on my plan." I really needed to set up some sort of expense fund for District Monitors. Hell, with Grandfather's help, I could probably fund some stipends for them too.

Pia gasped. "Can we also get Ms. Jackson some toys?"

Ms. Jackson and I tilted our heads at her. "What kind of toys?"

She rolled her eyes. I couldn't wait until she was a full-on teenager. "Like toys a cat would play with, only bigger? Haven't you seen the videos of tigers playing with balls and boxes?"

Ms. Jackson stretched their head in front of Manny to get Pia's attention. He huffed and snatched his plate off the table as he sat back in his seat.

I-W-A-N-T-T-O-S-E-E-T-H-E-T-I-G-E-R-V-I-D-E-O-S

Pia gasped again. "You haven't *seen* them?" She scooted her chair back from the table.

"Pia!" Shane pointed at her, then at her plate. "After you've finished your breakfast."

Pia and Ms. Jackson both slumped in their chairs. "Fine." Pia picked up her fork and shoveled an over-large hunk of omelet into her mouth.

I grimaced and looked at Shane and Ellis so I didn't have to watch her chew. Maybe Pia and Ms. Jackson could get table manners lessons together. "Anything else we need to shop for today?"

Shane groaned. "I think the list is plenty long enough already."

Manny stood and began to clear plates. "You're forgetting about the fine art of impulse shopping." He winked at us before sashaying to the kitchen.

Shane rubbed his face then turned his head and cupped his hands to hide his mouth from Pia. "Can I bring a flask?"

———

Luckily, Manny was willing to take Pia shopping for clothes while the rest of us—being magically tethered together and all—bought Pia and Ms. Jackson's electronics. Both of them got sparkly phone cases, Pia's in pink and Ms. Jackson's in purple. I badly wanted to buy Shane a new phone as well since his was over four years old, but he didn't even look longingly at the current models. I'd wait and get Ellis to help me convince him he needed an update for the new business.

We tracked Pia and Manny down in some godawful teen store with blaring K-Pop and cheap fabrics. I'd never felt so much kinship with Grandfather.

I'd given Manny one of my credit cards earlier, so we didn't have to go inside. We stood opposite the store's entrance to wait. Manny spotted us and dashed out with an armload of bags from other stores.

Shane held out his hands to take them. "Shit, Manny, we owe you a lot more than lunch."

"Nah, man. We're good. This is fun for me, and Pia's actually trying to pick things that can be worn with multiple outfits. This is our last stop."

They were done about fifteen minutes later. We picked up lunch on the way home, letting Pia choose the next vegetables for Ms. Jackson to try. Since we were having Chinese food, she picked spicy eggplant and stir-fried green beans. I had my doubts, but the rest of us would eat anything Ms. Jackson didn't.

When we got home, the street was lined with cars again, so I pulled into the driveway behind Shane and Ellis' vehicles. Manny had been lucky to snag a spot in front of the neighbor to the east. I felt awful having the end of the car block the sidewalk, but hopefully I wouldn't get a ticket. As we got out I looked up and down the street. The cars parked along the curb were a mix of older-models that matched the houses they were in front of and huge SUVs with blacked-out windows.

Did it make me a bad person if I immediately worried about drug dealers? We had Pia to keep safe. I blocked my thoughts from Shane and Ellis as I pondered how to get Shane to let me buy us a house in a better neighborhood ASAP.

We unloaded the bags and took them inside. Ms. Jackson was ecstatic over their new iPad and phone, and Ellis and I promised to get both phones set up after lunch. I for one would feel better if Ms. Jackson had a phone with them during the raid. If they couldn't carry it magically, I was sure Shane's grandmother had left a crossbody purse behind.

Ms. Jackson, it turned out, liked both the eggplant and the green beans. Well, first they gave all of us a severely skeptical glance, but then they licked at the sauce and gave a little purr. Pia put some rice on their plate and served up a little of each dish. Ms. Jackson cleaned their plate in less than a minute. I didn't watch.

"*Rayas*, you need some table manners." Manny spoke what all of us had been thinking.

Ms. Jackson sparkled out, R-A-Y-A-S.

"Stripes. It's a nickname. Don't change the subject. You eat like a wild animal, not like a wicked cool shapeshifter from another dimension." Manny cocked his head. "That reminds me, has anyone shown you *The Rocky Horror Picture Show*?"

"Manny's got a point," I interrupted. I couldn't think of how to explain *Rocky Horror* to Pia, much less to Ms. Jackson. They'd have to experience it. "I didn't want to say anything, because you've had enough to deal with adapting to the human world, but some table manners would make it easier for you to meet new people. New friends. When you swallow everything at once, it can be... off-putting."

"It's gross." Pia put her hand on Ms. Jackson's back. "I'll help you though."

They nodded, looking abashed.

Shit. I didn't want them to feel self-conscious. "It's okay. You didn't know, and it wasn't important enough to bring up before now. You've been learning so much every day, we felt bad adding more."

Pia held out one of the serving spoons. "Can one of your forms hold this?"

Ms. Jackson reached out a paw and it changed to an orange, furry... hand. At the end of the tiger's foreleg. My scalp prickled and I suppressed a shiver of revulsion.

"Cooool," Pia breathed as she handed the spoon over. "Hold it like this." She demonstrated with her fork.

Shane added more rice and eggplant to Ms. Jackson's plate, and we all stared as they used their new hand to scoop up a spoonful of food.

"Now put it in your mouth and close your lips around the spoon before you pull it out and leave the food inside." Pia demonstrated with her own food.

I was a little concerned about their fangs, but Ms. Jackson maneuvered the spoon around them and closed their mouth. Their forehead wrinkled as they seemed to be using their tongue to get the food off the spoon, but they pulled it out completely clean.

We all cheered, and they seemed pleased. They finished the food on their plate with the spoon, and the process became faster as they got used to it. I wasn't sure I would get used to the freaky hand though. None of us complained when they licked the remaining sauce off the plate.

We moved to the living room to set up Pia and Ms. Jackson's new phones. Pia didn't need my help, so I set up Ms. Jackson's for them. They changed into their panda form and sat on their butt. I held the phone out to them, and they took it from me with two furry, five-fingered hands. I worried I might let on how much their hands creeped me out, but to my everlasting gratitude, Ellis came over and told me he'd show the apps to Ms. Jackson because Shane needed to ask me about Pia's bedroom furniture.

I found Shane in the hallway to the bedrooms, at the end of the distance from Ellis the bond would allow us to be.

He opened his arms. **You okay?**

I stepped into his hug. **No. I feel awful about it, but I can't stop staring at their hands.**

He chuckled silently. **I guess being around Wonders all our lives helps Ellis and me not react to stuff like that.**

We stayed in the hug for a few minutes until Pia shouted, "Manny and Ms. Jackson are leaving!"

I gave Shane a quick kiss. "Thank you. I love you."

His smile was brilliant. "Anytime, and I love you too." **Weird hand phobia and all.**

I smacked him in the chest as I left the room.

Ms. Jackson was back in their black panther form. Ellis pointed at them and said, "I put all of our numbers in their phone, along with Greg, Cal, Arch, and Dominic. Arch texted that Carlyle, Dimi, Mercy, and Garfield have checked in and are helping watch the building. Um, I haven't met Garfield yet, but Arch was complaining about him not having clothes? Anyway, everything's quiet so far."

I hugged Manny and patted Ms. Jackson on their back. "Be safe, you two. Um, where's your phone, Ms. Jackson?"

Manny laughed, and he gestured at them. "They just sort of put it in their pocket, without having any pockets."

I didn't think I wanted a demonstration. I looked at Ms. Jackson. "Call or text if you need anything. Um, did you try texting with your, uh, hands?"

They sat, curling their tail around their hind legs. Then they opened their mouth, and a raspy, grating voice said, "Yessss. Thankh hyou for the phhhone."

My eyes went wide, and I gaped at them.

Shane muttered, "Holy shit."

Pia squealed, "Ms. Jackson! You talked!" She ran forward and threw her arms around Ms. Jackson's neck.

The rest of us crowded forward and congratulated them as well. I couldn't stop remembering Ellis speculating about what Ms. Jackson's human form would look like.

Manny clapped his hands. "Hey! Ms. Jackson and I have to go. Now that they can speak, there's a lot of singing along to the radio they need to catch up on."

"Wait." Shane held up a hand. "If there are any victims you think would be better off coming back here, um, it'll be tight quarters, but we'd be glad to have them." He raised his eyebrows at me and Ellis, and we agreed.

Manny, sober now, nodded. "Will do."

We all followed them to the door. None of the neighbors were outside to notice the huge cat getting into the passenger seat of Manny's car.

I shut the door as they drove off. "Everybody ready? We have the list?" In addition to a new desk, we were replacing the entire bed in Pia's room, as the headboard was probably from the 1980s and the mattress was almost that old.

"Wait! I have to get my Yo-Yo!"

We all followed Ellis into the bedroom. He'd put his sex toys in the nightstand, but his Yo-Yos were still in his duffel on the chest of drawers. I made a mental note to look for a display case while we were out.

"I'm taking this one." He held up a silver and red aluminum Yo-Yo with a red skull on the other end of the string. "It's called a Metal Drifter, and it's got this cool counterweight so you can do tricks."

He held onto the skull and spun out the Yo-Yo. Then he put his free hand on the string in the middle, so the Yo-Yo spun in a circle. "This is called a Pinwheel." Then he casually threw the skull in the opposite direction and moved his hand rhythmically to keep both objects spinning. "This is a Butterfly."

Pia clapped her hands. "Will you teach me?"

He flashed her a smile. "Of course." Expertly he grabbed the skull and did some sort of sleight of hand to get the Yo-Yo to stop spinning and roll back up into his palm.

"That's impressive, Ellis." I sent my admiration through our bond, and I could feel Shane doing the same.

His cheeks darkened, and he kept his gaze down as he stuffed the Yo-Yo in the front pocket of his shorts. "Thanks. I know it's a dorky hobby, but I enjoy it."

I blocked my anger at his dad or Arch—or both—behind a mental wall and went over to hug him. "No hobbies are dorky. You love it and you're amazing at it, therefore it's cool."

He flashed me a smile. "Thanks, um, let's get going."

He walked swiftly out of the room and headed to the front door. We all followed, but Pia dashed over to the couch to get her phone, so Shane and I waited for her. Which meant we weren't with Ellis when he opened the door.

"Um, hi? Who are you?" Then he made an *eep* noise and, raising his hands in the air, backed into the living room.

Uncle Hugo, followed by Randolph Chamberlain and three guys holding automatic rifles, walked in.

Fuck. I spun around. Shane had already picked Pia up and was running for the back door. But he skidded to a stop when two armed men stepped onto the porch. We could see three more spread across the yard.

Uncle Hugo surveyed us with the air of a bad TV villain. "Phones on the coffee table. Hands on your head."

We all complied, though Shane kept his hands on Pia, who'd latched onto him with all of her arms and legs. Her phone wasn't on the coffee table.

Uncle Hugo smirked at me. "Hello, nephew. Long time no see. Or, at least, it's been a while since I've seen you in person. I'm sorry I didn't know you were stalking me until I saw the footage on Randolph's security camera."

He must've noticed my surprise, because he chuckled. "That's right. You missed one. Randolph saw you carrying out the little creature there." He inclined his head toward Pia. "It wasn't hard to wait outside your condo and follow you over here."

Randolph smiled at Pia like a creeper. "I've missed you. It's time for you to come back home."

Pia cringed into Shane.

"Put her down," Randolph ordered. "We're taking her with us."

"No!" Pia shrieked. She sobbed into Shane's neck, her arms and legs around his back.

I shouted in my head for Grandfather, but he didn't appear. My abilities had never worked that way, but maybe things would change since now I was bonded. I tried Dimi, then Garfield and Mercy. Nothing.

I can't reach the ghosts!

Fuck. This was bad. No way would they leave us alive when they took Pia. Shane couldn't hold on to her if they put a bullet in his head.

The mere thought of that nearly sent me into a tailspin of panic, but Shane interrupted my freakout. **Pia has her phone. She's texting Arch and Ms. Jackson behind my back.**

I didn't relax, but hope was suddenly an option. Ms. Jackson wouldn't let them take Pia. But we needed to give Manny time to drive back here.

Keep him talking. I frowned at Uncle Hugo. "Aren't you supposed to be at an illegal auction right now?" They were both certainly dressed for it in expensive black suits.

Randolph stepped forward. "There's no auction. The auctioneer had heard some chatter about you stealing the girl, so he told me he wouldn't sell to me again until I could prove I wasn't under surveillance." He thrust a pointer finger at me. "Fuck you. Hugo and I faked an auction to see if you'd bugged my phone. And when the auctioneer found out there was some rescue team converging on Houston for it, he banned me for life. Said I was a security risk."

I grinned. "Excellent." Though it sounded like the Hunter team had a leak.

He smirked. "You won't be so happy when my men kill all those so-called rescuers. Who'll rescue the rescuers, *hmmm*?"

I doubted Randolph's men could take out a team of Hunters,

but if Arch and Dominic's crew were tied up, they wouldn't be able to come help us anytime soon.

Randolph gestured at the goons. "Get her."

One of the men kept his gun pointed toward me and Ellis, and the other two went over to Shane and Pia. They were on the other side of the seating area, pretty much at the far end of the distance the bond would allow. Shane backed against the wall, but there was no escape. One guy put the muzzle of his gun directly against Shane's head, and the other one grabbed Pia's arm and yanked. "Come on, or your friend here dies."

Shane kissed Pia's head and gave her a quick squeeze. "Go on now. It'll be okay."

Slowly Pia unwrapped herself from Shane. She let the goon drag her over to Randolph, but when he reached for her, she popped out all of her thorns. The guy holding her jerked his hand back and swore. Pia turned to run back to Shane, but the first goon still had a gun to his head. She froze.

The goon with Shane was staring wide-eyed at Pia. "Uh, boss?"

"No questions! You've seen nothing!"

The man jerkily nodded. If there hadn't been two other guys with guns in the room, Shane could probably have gotten away from him. Dammit, there was nothing I could do.

Except stall.

"Uncle Hugo, do you really want to be involved in the trafficking of people? What would your high society friends say?"

He snorted. "People. This girl isn't people. You spent too much time with my do-gooder brother and his trashy wife. At least I made Father see the truth about you before he died."

I stifled my rage. It wouldn't help us get out of this. "Yeah, well, it's too bad after he died, Grandfather saw the truth about *you*."

Hugo sneered. "Are you still going on about seeing ghosts? Father and I never believed that bullshit from you or your slut of a mother."

I raised my eyebrows. "Ghosts are less believable than a girl with thorns coming out of her skin?"

Grandfather chose that moment to pop into the middle of the room. "Really, Rory, you forgot to invite me to a party?" Grandfather wasn't translucent for once. Even I couldn't see through him.

The goons all pointed their guns at him. Pia started slowly moving toward the kitchen, getting out of the line of fire. Shane, blocked from Pia by the gunmen, edged in Ellis and my direction, sliding behind the couch to reach us.

"Sorry, Grandfather. They stopped by unannounced."

Uncle Hugo's eyes were bugging out of his head. "F-father?"

Randolph pointed at Grandfather. "Where did he come from? Get him!"

While one of the goons kept their gun trained on him, another one clamped a hand on Grandfather's arm. He instantly stared at his hand. "Why's he so cold?"

I was impressed at Grandfather's solidity. This bonding stuff had some interesting side effects.

He allowed himself to be pulled toward Randolph and Hugo. "Hello, son. How unpleasant to see you here."

"Wh-what?"

Randolph rounded on Hugo. "I thought your father was dead."

Uncle Hugo pointed at Grandfather. "He is! He's supposed to be!"

I *tsked*. "I told you he wasn't happy with you, Hugo."

Out of the corner of my eye I saw Dimi appear behind Pia and wrap herself around the girl. They moved slowly toward the kitchen.

A muffled cry came from the back yard. Hugo didn't react—his attention was all on Grandfather—but Randolph pointed. "Check it out!"

The guy who'd had his gun on Shane earlier jogged over to the back door. "Uh, boss? I can't see any of the guys."

I sensed relief from Shane and Ellis. Ms. Jackson was here. Or maybe Arch and his crew. Either way, we had backup.

"Guard the door!"

The goon stayed in place. Shit. Ellis and Shane were now pressed up against me, but we couldn't get to the front door without Randolph and Uncle Hugo noticing. At least the goons were more worried about Grandfather than us. As long as Randolph didn't notice—

"Where's the girl? Find her!"

Fuck. Probably the only place Pia and Dimi could be was in the pantry.

The goon who wasn't holding onto Grandfather headed around the corner to the kitchen. We heard the pantry door open. "She's not here!" Cabinet doors slammed open, then a moment later he came back shaking his head. "There's only the kitchen and a pantry. She's not in either, and she's not in the cabinets, up or down."

Randolph's face turned purple. "She didn't just vanish. Search the bedrooms." We all looked toward the entrance to the bedroom hallway. No one mentioned that we would've seen Pia go that direction if she'd done so.

Had Dimi somehow hidden Pia?

The goon took off, and we heard more slamming doors and bathroom cabinets.

I put my arm around Ellis and Shane. Shane moved oddly, like he wanted me to scratch his back. **Get the phone! Pia put it in my waistband, and I'm worried it's going to fall.**

Ah. Ellis pressed closer to me to give me more maneuvering room. I slid my hand down Shane's back until I bumped into Pia's phone tucked into his waistband. Ellis shifted in front of me as I slipped it into the back pocket of my jeans.

We'd edged along the wall enough that we were in the corner of the room. The front door was about fifteen feet away from us along this wall, but if we ran for it, we'd be easy targets, especially for automatic weapons.

Hugo pulled a handgun from his pants pocket and pointed it at Grandfather. "Did you fake your death or something? Was this all some sort of con?"

Grandfather rolled his eyes. "Did you or did you not see me appear from thin air? I'm dead, Hugo. Shoot me if you want to; it won't make a difference."

Mercy and Garfield popped in next to Grandfather. Ellis and Shane jumped. Right. They hadn't met those two yet. Garfield was in his naked, hairy glory. The goons in the room shouted and pointed their weapons, and Randolph pulled out a gun of his own. "Who—what? You're dead! You're both dead! I buried you myself! How are you here?"

The third goon ran back in and hovered uncertainly near the hallway to the bedrooms, his gun pointing between Mercy and Garfield.

Mercy ignored Randolph and gave me a thumbs up. "The Hunters took out all the bad guys who were guarding the house. Ms. Jackson has Pia. Arch and Dominic said we could deal with this asshole." She pointed at Randolph. "And it's up to you about the other one."

Randolph was still sputtering. "How are you even here?"

Grandfather snorted. "Ghosts, you dumbfuck. Get with the program!"

Garfield held up his hand. "It's our turn, Carlyle." His voice became loud enough to be heard outside. "Randolph Chamberlain, the charges against you include trafficking, enslavement, and causing death by neglect. How do you plead?"

Randolph raised a shaking hand to point his gun at Garfield. "Plead? This isn't a court. You don't have any jurisdiction here."

Mercy intoned. "Randolph Chamberlain, you are sentenced to death. You will not be allowed any last words, because we don't give a fuck."

Garfield morphed into a huge gray wolf, and Mercy changed into an even larger polar bear. But instead of attacking Randolph, Garfield leapt toward the goon near the back door, and Mercy lunged toward the one near the hallway.

Both men fired a spray of bullets at the ghosts, but the ghosts vanished before they reached their targets.

Shane, Ellis, and I dropped to the floor when the guns went off. We looked up in time to see Randolph Chamberlain fall to the ground, riddled with bullets.

I could tell it wasn't visible to anyone else in the room, but I saw Randolph's ghost rise from his body. He barely had time to look around before the translucent wolf and polar bear, who'd been waiting nearby, tore him to shreds.

I gulped and focused on Hugo, who'd ducked behind Grandfather and the third goon. He was clutching one hand to his chest and shouting what looked like, "No! Randolph!" but I couldn't be sure because my ears were ringing from the gunfire.

The goon near the hallway raced to the back door, and he and the other one who'd shot Randolph ran into the night. They wouldn't get far.

Ellis, Shane, and I slowly stood up. The third goon let go of Grandfather's arm. He pointed his gun at Hugo and backed away, occasionally glancing toward me, Shane, and Ellis to make sure we weren't a threat.

Hugo didn't bother watching him go. He spun around and pointed his gun at me. I didn't have any trouble making out his words. "This is your fault!" His face was white, and he was sweating. He waved his free hand as if he was swatting a fly.

Shit. I held up my hands and walked a few steps along the wall away from Shane and Ellis.

Rory! Ellis was pissed.

Dammit, don't be a hero! Shane tried to grab at me, but Hugo swung his gun over, so he stopped and held his hands up like I was doing. Ellis shrank back into the corner.

I nodded to indicate I'd heard both of them but kept moving slowly toward the door. My hearing was coming back a little at a time, but I heard Grandfather.

"Hugo, don't make this worse. Did you know you're having a heart attack? You should sit down." Grandfather uttered this in the same tone he'd use to advise Hugo to take an umbrella because it might rain.

Hugo continued to advance toward me, gun first. "I'm going to kill Rory, Father. You always loved him more than me. Same with my unlamented sibling."

I kept my hands up high. "Uncle Hugo, we need to get you to the hospital."

His breathing was becoming labored. "I'll go after...." He waggled his gun at me. "After I kill you."

"No!" Grandfather roared. "If you harm Rory, you will never see the afterlife. I will rip your soul apart just like Mercy and Garfield did to your buddy Randolph."

Hugo was getting closer, about five feet away. His hand was shaking, but I wasn't sure if I could move fast enough to shove his arm up before he pulled the trigger. From the way he hovered next to Hugo, Grandfather seemed to be having the same debate with himself.

Out of the corner of my eye, I could see Shane clenching his fists and almost vibrating with the need to do something. I didn't dare look at him in case Hugo decided to shoot him or Ellis first.

Distraction incoming.

I felt more than saw Ellis lean over and swing his arm out. Then a rolling sound with a clatter following it ran along the wall behind the sofa.

Hugo whirled to face the noise, and Grandfather and I jumped at him, pushing his gun arm up. He pulled the trigger, but the bullet went into the ceiling.

Shane reached over Grandfather to yank the gun out of Hugo's hand. He tossed it toward the couch. He was saying something, but I couldn't make it out since my ears were ringing again from the gunshot.

The front and back doors burst open, and a swarm of Hunters ran into the house.

Hugo's legs went limp, and we lowered him to the floor. He clutched his left arm, and his breaths came fast. His eyes drifted shut. I could barely make out Grandfather yelling about Hugo needing to cross over damn fast because if Grandfather caught him, he'd never make it to the other side.

One of the Hunters patted Hugo down for more weapons. "I'm Dominic. Y'all okay?"

"Yeah. Yeah, we're fine." I looked around for Ellis and Shane, who were trying to get over to me but were held back by another Hunter. I left Hugo in Dominic's hands and ran to my men, wrapping them in my arms. **Thank fuck. Are you okay?**

They nodded. **Let's find Pia so she knows we're all right.**

Plus I was dying to know how Ms. Jackson and Dimi had gotten her out of the house.

We hadn't even taken a step toward the front door when Arch ran up and nearly tackled Ellis into a hug. Then he released him and scanned for injuries. "Are you hurt? Did you see a medic yet? Let's get you to a medic."

He began to drag Ellis toward the door, but Ellis dug in his heels and held onto Shane. "Arch! I'm fine. Stop it!"

Arch hesitated. "Are you sure? I'd feel better if you got checked out."

Shane and I exchanged an amused glance, since apparently we didn't rate the same level of care.

"I'm fine. I'd like my Yo-Yo back, but other than that I don't have a scratch on me."

I smacked a kiss on Ellis' cheek. "You were amazing." I turned to Arch. "Ellis distracted Hugo at exactly the right time."

Ellis shrugged, his cheeks darkening. "It was just Runaway Dog. It's a kid's Yo-Yo trick. Like Walk the Dog but the dog gets away."

Arch puffed up and he scowled. "What? Didn't the man have a gun? That was dangerous, Ellis. You should leave the heroics to people who've been trained."

I got between Arch and Ellis. "The *people who've been trained* weren't there. Ellis is a grown man, fully capable of evaluating risks and making decisions under pressure."

To my shock, Arch deflated. He ran his hand over his head and face. "You're right. I'm sorry. Ellis, I'm sorry. I shouldn't have talked to you like that. I was just scared for you."

I moved to the side so Ellis could respond, but all he said was, "Yeah? Well maybe next time have this conversation with yourself *before* you talk to me like I'm a child. And speaking of children, we need to go find Pia." He brushed past Arch and led the way out the door.

Shane and I mentally high-fived each other through the bond, and Ellis glanced back and made a face at us. But he was smiling.

Before we left the house I looked back at Hugo's body. A loose circle of Hunters still surrounded him, but they were chatting and not on their guard. He'd passed.

Grandfather smirked at me. "He was so scared he crossed over in a blink. Hugo won't trouble you again."

As soon as we walked out onto the porch, Pia shrieked, "There they are!" She dashed through the crowd of Hunters and threw herself into our arms.

I wasn't the only one of the three of us who got choked up as we held her.

"Are you okay, Pia?" Shane stepped back to scan her up and down, much like Arch had done to Ellis.

"Yep! Ms. Jackson came through the cracks in the window! And then they picked me up and we went back out the same way! It felt like we melted, and then we were solid again. It was *so* cooooool!"

"Uh, sounds like it." I was pretty sure my eyes were as big as Shane's and Ellis' right now.

I gave Pia another hug. "Did they tell you that you don't have to worry about Randolph Chamberlain anymore?" Shane had mentioned he knew a Wonder who was also a trained thera-pist. We'd been leaning toward taking Pia to see her before, but now it was imperative.

"Yep! We met Garfield and Mercy, and they told us he's dead and so is your uncle." Fuck, I hoped Garfield had manifested some clothes or appeared in his wolf form for that conversa-tion. "Are you sad about your uncle, Rory?"

I shook my head. "I'm sad he turned out to be the person he was. He seemed a lot nicer when I first met him after my parents died."

Manny walked up, trailed by Ms. Jackson in their black panther form. "*Hombres*, I need a vacation after this week. Who's with me?"

We laughed, and I gave Manny a hug. Then I got on my knees and threw my arms around Ms. Jackson. "Thank you," I said into their fur. "We owe you everything. Anything you need, just ask."

Their growly, raspy voice rumbled out. "You're welcome, but I did it for Pia."

I sat up and looked them in the eye. "All the more reason."

They made a weird snuffly snort sound and gave me a jerky nod.

Then Pia came over and wrapped her arms around my shoulders. "Can we have tacos for dinner?"

CAL'S CAMPAIGN COMPENDIUM
MEDIUM (UPDATED)

Type: Medium

Class: Magic Carrier

Overview: Mediums are able to see, speak to, and hear ghosts who have not crossed over to the other side. They are not able to compel ghosts to come to them, and if a ghost is not visible to them, they do not have the ability to contact or communicate with them.

Skills:

- _Can interact with ghosts who are visible to them at the current time_

Enhanced Skills When Bonded:

- _Can prevent ghosts from entering a room_
- _Can speak to ghosts mind-to-mind_
- _Can give ghosts the energy/magic to become visible and/or audible to non-Mediums in the same general area as the Medium_

- *Ghosts the Medium is in close regular contact with will become visible to the Medium's family (whether blood-related or not)*
- *(Allegedly, according to an older ghost) Can destroy ghosts by draining their energy or "tearing them apart"*

Childhood Aptitudes: Ghosts are visible to a Medium from birth.

EPILOGUE

SHANE

"This is it." Rory pointed out the window at the mansion. "What do you think?"

It was huge, and if I was being honest, beautiful. The fieldstone and stucco facade blended with the lush landscaping better than the surrounding houses did, that was for sure. I rolled down my window and listened to the quiet neighborhood. In the distance we could hear cars on Memorial Drive, but the closest sounds to us were someone mowing the lawn on the next street over.

The yard was enormous, and I itched to replace most of the grass with native plants. But that could come later. First, Pia would need an apple tree in the backyard, and I also wanted to plant a beech tree, which had been Pia's mother's favorite.

"It's pretty," Pia announced. She'd unbuckled her seat belt and was hanging out her window to look around. Hugo Blackbourne's estate was still in probate, but since he'd died without a will, in a few months this house would be Rory's.

And ours to live in.

It was funny, but if you'd have asked me a few months ago if I could ever see myself in a house like this, I would've laughed. No way would I have felt comfortable here, worthy of this house, this neighborhood, this life. But now I felt fucking worthy. I had the love of two men and a daughter, I co-owned a business, and I helped the Wonders in my District every day. I belonged wherever the fuck I wanted to.

For the past two months we'd been staying in Rory's condo. It wasn't ideal. We'd filled the place with potted plants, but we'd still had to take Pia to a local park almost every day. But even so, none of us wanted to live in my house again.

Well, except Manny. He'd taken it upon himself to clean up the blood and patch the bullet holes in the living room. When we'd told him we weren't moving back in, he'd asked if he could rent the place since his lease was almost up. I'd told him he could live there for the cost of the utilities and taking care of minor maintenance issues.

Frankly I was glad to have more concrete ties to Manny. He still sparkled with Ms. Jackson's magic, and I wanted to be close in case he manifested any talents.

Granny, along with Carlyle, Garfield, and Mercy, popped in every now and then to check up on us. They'd all decided to work with the Hunters to rescue Wonders, and the Hunters were helping Garfield trace where his other pack members had been taken. Arch, being the only Hunter who could see the ghosts, was their official point of contact. He'd reached out to Ellis a few times since that night, and they were slowly rebuilding their relationship.

Rory had big plans for Hugo's millions. He'd already decided to set up a fund to provide the District Monitors with a monthly stipend, and he was looking into other states where District Monitors didn't have any financial compensation. Not gonna lie, that money would make a big difference in my life. Ellis had found several clients for our new landscaping business, including Greg and Cal's contractor friend Ruben, but we'd barely started getting things off the ground. I didn't love relying on Rory to pay for everything, even though I knew he enjoyed providing for our family.

Pia had started school with other Wonder children a couple of weeks ago, and she loved it. Her therapist was very positive about how Pia was dealing with the loss of her mother and the trauma of her kidnapping and the home invasion. The four of us had even done family therapy a couple of times, and I think we all felt better afterward. We were figuring out how to operate as a unit. It was a work in progress, but we were all committed to doing our best.

Personally, I couldn't believe I got to live this life. Two men—two!—who loved me. Who were bonded to me. I couldn't be lonely, because we were tied together by the magic we shared.

Not that everything was roses, especially trying to get private time together in Rory's tiny condo. Pia was too old to have an early bedtime, so if the three of us wanted to get naked, we had to either stay up really late or be very, very quiet. It was fun for the first week, but now all of us—probably Pia especially—were looking forward to having more space in the new house.

Rory had gotten in touch with Randolph Chamberlain's former staff, the ones who'd helped him rescue Pia. A few would be working for us as soon as we took possession of Hugo's house. I'd also given several of them jobs doing landscaping. Digging in the dirt in the hot sun was harder than being indoors all day, but they all claimed to just be relieved to work for someone honest.

After we'd all looked our fill, we stopped to pick up burgers and fries at Beck's Prime in Memorial Park. Pia loved their milkshakes, and Ms. Jackson was partial to their veggie burger.

They hadn't been interested in checking out the new house, wanting instead to stay home and watch another episode of *Supernatural*. Pia had gotten them to watch a few other shows, like *Heartstopper* and *Buffy the Vampire Slayer*, but *Supernatural* was their favorite.

So it wasn't a surprise when we returned to the condo to find Misha Collins frozen mid-stride on the big TV in the living room.

But it *was* a surprise to see Misha Collins, complete with trench coat and necktie, standing in front of the TV.

We all stopped dead in the doorway.

"Ms. Jackson?" Pia whispered.

They looked over at us. "I need a ride."

MEANWHILE, 200 MILES AWAY...

SIMON

I CREPT THROUGH THE WOODS, OCCASIONALLY DOUBLE-CHECKING the app on my phone to make sure the tracking device hadn't moved. Man, I would've killed for this tech all those decades ago. Hell, if we'd had this back in the 1940's, the entire portal-closing probably could've been avoided, and I'd be back home right now.

I had to have been near the rear of the property by this point. I hadn't dared drive by the front for fear they'd spot me, even though my SUV had tinted windows. Instead I'd used Google Earth to figure out how to approach from the back. Once I could see what I was dealing with, I'd call in the Hunters from TWIST that Shane and Ellis had told me about.

Or, the little voice in my head suggested, I could go inside and kill all the vampires right now. There were only four left, after all. But there'd be several captives, which was more than I could handle on my own. I'd need help getting them medical attention and transporting them somewhere safe.

But being this close to my goal, this close to *him*, was making me antsy. I had to make sure I didn't get careless. After this many years, I could not fail.

Waiting a few more days was better than screwing up and having to start over. Or getting myself killed.

I ignored the old Seer's vision, the one that had shown me with my mate by my side during the final rescue. She must've been mistaken.

The trees thinned out, and I crouched down to stay hidden. There was the house, innocuous and run-down. You'd think it'd stink of the evil perpetrated within its walls.

The crunch of a boot on a twig was all the warning I had. I spun around and up, just managing to get inside Tormod's swing. I shoved my chest against his, blocking his knife thrust with my forearm. So much for waiting for backup to arrive.

I twisted under his arm and put some distance between us so I could draw my mek'leth. I couldn't use my gun without alerting the others.

"You won't die. You're like one of those Earth cockroaches, always showing up," Tormod spat.

I grinned at him. This crew always wasted time on idle chitchat. "You ever watch that show *The Boys*?"

"What?"

As his mouth opened to form the word, I executed a move I'd been practicing ever since I'd seen that iconic episode.

I transitioned to fog form, but instead of dispersing into an amorphous cloud as we'd been trained, I spiraled into a thin thread. I arrowed between Tormod's teeth, slamming into the back of his throat. I felt him bring his knife up as he fell back, but it was too late to save him. I retook my human form and focused on holding the mek'leth against his spine as I solidified. Fuck, that hurt.

Not only did his bones scrape against my skin as the ligaments and muscles tried to stay in place before they tore, but he'd been lucky with the placement of his knife. It ended up right in the middle of my gut. Dammit.

We fell to the ground with a nasty squelch, and I rolled over, hissing as Tormod's knife jostled, slicing more of my innards. Fuck. I was bleeding out. I wouldn't die from the wound, but if I couldn't heal myself fast enough, the other three would find me, alerted to Tormod's death through their connections, before I could get away.

And apparently I would *not* be performing a heroic single-handed rescue today.

I wiped the gore from my eyes and licked it off my hand. Tormod had fed recently, and I shuddered in revulsion. I knew where the magic on my tongue had come from, but I didn't think the original donors would begrudge me having it. Probably the opposite, considering I'd killed Tormod.

I couldn't heal myself without more blood, even if it was secondhand, but I couldn't get to his body without removing the knife. I braced myself for more pain.

I gripped the knife hilt, but the sound of footsteps through the grass and leaves made me pause. Shit, I was in no shape to fight off another of them.

My mek'leth had dropped somewhere close by, but it was useless if it wasn't in my hand. I'd have to pull Tormod's knife and kill the new arrival in one move. I turned my head to see which one of them it was.

He wasn't a vampire.

He had the most amazing pair of brown eyes I'd ever seen.

He scowled down at me. "That was fucking disgusting."

———

Thank you for reading *Medium*! Don't miss *Wonder*, the final book in the Wonderfall series!

ALSO BY BIX BARROW

BENT OAK, TEXAS

Holding On to a Hero (Will, Cole, and Jason's story)

Heart Me Up (Craig and Foster's story)

Head Over Feels (Felix and Malcolm's story)

What's Santa Got to Do with It (Steve and Baz's story)

We Don't Need Another Santa (Phillip and Lucas' story)

I Touch Hoses (Keson and Wesley's story) – Related novella

Last Mango in Palm Springs (Ford and Zachary's story) - Related novella

Voices Harry (Mitchell and Harry's story) – Free when you go to www.bixbarrow.com and sign up for my newsletter!

WONDERFALL

Seer (Cal and Greg's story)

Medium (Shane, Ellis, and Rory's story)

Wonder (Simon and Reno's story)

SINGULAR MAGICS

Unprecedented (Manny, Oz, and Arch's story)

LOVE IN MAPLEWOOD (MULTI-AUTHOR SHARED WORLD)

Can You Feel the Maple Tonight (Drake and Finn's story)

ABOUT BIX BARROW

When Bix Barrow got an idea for her first book, it ended up turning into her second — and thus the first two stories in the *Bent Oak, Texas* series emerged. An aspiring author for most of her life, it took a foray into the MM romance genre to spark the humor, suspense, and blazing banter Bix now weaves into her novels. Accompanying her on her writing exploits are her two dogs and multitude of cats (six at last count). An avid traveler, Bix has started to view her expeditions as interviews for her future home. Born and raised in Texas, she is eager to move somewhere with fewer politicians, hurricanes, and flooding.

Join Bix Barrow's Boom Boom Room on Facebook for sneak peeks and fun conversation!

Sign up for Bix's newsletter and get a free novella! www.bixbarrow.com

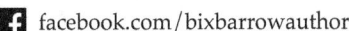 facebook.com/bixbarrowauthor

 instagram.com/bixbarrow

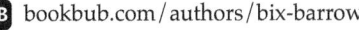 bookbub.com/authors/bix-barrow